PEWTER ANGELS

"PEWTER ANGELS"   H.R. RIPPLINGER/2009

THE ANGELIC LETTERS SERIES

Book One

—✳—

PEWTER ANGELS

1956-1957

THERESA

ENJOY!

[signature]

HENRY K. RIPPLINGER

Library and Archives Canada Cataloguing in Publication
Ripplinger, Henry
Pewter angels : 1956-1957 / Henry K. Ripplinger.

(The angelic letters series ; novel #1)
ISBN 978-0-9865424-1-1 (pbk.)
I. Title. II. Series: Angelic letters series ; novel #1

PS8585.I565P48 2010   C813'.6   C2010-901279-8

PIO-SEELOS BOOKS
Ph: (306) 731-3087, Fax: (306) 731-3852.
E-mail: henryripplinger@imagewireless.ca

Printed and bound in Canada by Friesens Printers
First printing March 2010
Second printing November 2010
Third printing September 2011
Fourth printing November 2011

I dedicate this book to my wife, Joan,
my first and only love.

ACKNOWLEDGMENTS

WRITING A SERIES OF NOVELS, I have learned, requires a lengthy commitment, a withdrawal from the usual routines of daily living, a time to be alone, to reflect, to write. My wife Joan has given me this gift of freedom to realize what was in my heart, to put down on paper what was only a dream for so many, many years. I thank my lovely wife for this time, her understanding and patience. For reading and re-reading the story at each stage of development, being a sounding board and her assistance in editing.

I also thank my family and friends for reading parts of the series and their input and support.

The goal for any author is to see their manuscript shape into the best it can be. I am very fortunate to have gathered together an editing team that have not only strengthened, tightened and clarified the language and the story, but for each bringing their own special skills and judicious input. To the editors: Darlene Oakley, Jody Ripplinger and Heather Nickel, my heartfelt thanks for realizing my goal and your commitment to this huge undertaking.

I am grateful to the numerous writers of books I have read

over the years that have shaped my life and thinking. The most influential and everlasting of course is the Bible. I thank the Lord for all the trials, joys and life's experiences that have helped me grasp some of the wisdom and truths of His Word and their application to my life and writing.

PREFACE

IT IS SAID THAT WITHIN EACH of us is a story to tell. For years, I must admit, it has been my heart's desire to write a novel. For the longest time I thought it was just wishful thinking, an illusion or fantasy I was nurturing. Over the years, I started several stories that never went anywhere except into my drawer and then fizzled away in the recesses of my mind. And yet, I have long known that if one has a dream, a burning passion in his heart, that someday it will come to pass. Never would I have envisioned, however, the wonderfully creative way it would come about. How, one day, an unbelievable occurrence would eventually transform a fantasy into reality.

The "occurrence" tugged away at me for days, months and then years, begging my attention. Seeking understanding, I spoke of it to family and friends but I was so focused on the event itself that I missed the underlying significance of it all. It wasn't until I found myself in the sunroom of our farmhouse one sleepless morning in June 2005, watching the sun near the edge of the earth, that the deeper meaning of the occurrence came to me. As the rising sun brightened the room in which I sat, it also seemed to illuminate my mind. Insight, previously obscured in the shadows of my psyche, bloomed and intensified as dawn spread out across the prairie sky. As I traced the occurrence back to its beginning, I finally realized how it was a testament to the enduring miracle of love. Immediately, an overwhelming, almost feverish rush to write my story welled up inside me, and I began.

Without any outline or any knowledge of how to write a novel, I picked up a pen and scribbler on the end table and simply began to write. For two weeks, I wrote almost non-stop until my wrist and hand gave out. Then I purchased a laptop computer—the best investment of my life—and continued to write as fast as my fingers could type. Corrections could be made in an instant. Paragraphs moved here and there with incredible ease. The thoughts began to flow. It was as if during all the years I had been thinking about the occurrence, ideas had been incubating in my mind, stored, packed, imprisoned inside, until the writing process released them like a gusher, exploding and spilling onto the pages.

Sentence followed after sentence almost effortlessly as the scenes unfolded in my mind's eye. I relied not so much on my intellect as I wrote but rather on my imagination, ablaze as it was with imagery and thoughts. I began to write an outline, a list of chapters that would take me from beginning to end. It was like going on a journey, and I was tracing out the map where I wanted and needed to go to reach my destination.

Characters came alive and I followed them and their lives; we talked and laughed and cried together. They took me in directions I never would have thought of on my own … they led and I followed. This resulted in more chapters. My map expanded as twists and turns in the road came from nowhere and everywhere and from deep within. As the weeks of writing progressed, the vision before me became clearer and richer. It was like watching a movie. All I had to do was write down what I saw before me on the screen of my mind.

Incredibly, three years to the date I started writing, when all was said and done, a huge book of over 1000 pages was in my hands. Once the editing process began, even more pages were added, strengthening the story and dividing it into five parts and timeframes. The result is a chronicle of love and adventure in the lives of two people, whose story shows us how angels and the heavens are intricately involved in our lives and that miracles happen when we follow our hearts.

As I look back on this experience, I am still amazed by the effortlessness with which the story emerged, as if the chapters, their order and all the key elements were guided, predetermined—or perhaps more accurately—inspired.

The writing of this book also answered another prayer long held in my heart. As a teacher and then a high school guidance counsellor, it was always my aspiration to write a self-development book. From an early age, insights and understanding of human behaviour came naturally to me, and my study of psychology and counselling in university further added to my empathetic abilities.

Writing this novel utilized those aptitudes. Through the lives of the characters, I could infuse values and principles to live by and show how the choices we make determine our happiness. I wanted to demonstrate the importance of living our lives in the now so as to carry out our life mission to love and serve our Lord and others. These teaching and counselling skills were indirectly at work while I also re-examined my own life and the direction I was going. Ultimately, I realized that lessons are more effectively absorbed intellectually and emotionally when revealed through a story; my novel had simultaneously become my self-development book.

The story begins in Regina, Saskatchewan in the 1950s—the place and time of my own coming of age—though I have taken liberties with the details of its places and events. But though this book is a work of fiction, the occurrence that motivated it was something I experienced personally. My initial intention was to simply write about the occurrence; what resulted was a work of fiction that took on a life of its own. As I'm sure must be the case for many writers, my own life experiences provided the ideal backdrop for the story and moulded the development of the main character to the extent that it was inextricably woven into the fictional narrative.

I firmly believe that God has a plan for each one of us. The desire to write was planted in my heart long before the Lord had me experience the occurrence. Fortunately, I finally listened to His calling to do so, to carry out His plan. I think the Lord knew that as I began to realize the underlying love associated with that event, the power of that love would draw me into the wonderful world of writing and give witness to love's beauty and ever-enduring wonder. And, just like the warm prairie summer sun eventually ripens a crop of golden wheat for the harvest, so too, as the seed of this story took root, warmed and nourished by the timeless love of two people, "The Angelic Letters" series grew and blossomed. You and I are its reapers.

Henry K. Ripplinger
December 2009

"He hath given his angels charge over thee; to keep thee in all thy ways . . . in their hands they shall bear thee up: lest thou dash thy foot against a stone."

PSALM 91:11-12

PROLOGUE

A THOUGHTFUL MAN ONCE SAID *that in between our thoughts or in between sounds there is a silence in which we can reach our Creator. I believe this to be true: often in my own mediations I have enjoyed moments of pure joy and love. I have also experienced this bliss and delight in everyday life, overwhelmed by the beauty of God's creation and the love that resides in the core of each one of us. You see, Heaven is right here—not only in the silence but in between the spaces of everything in the universe. The Kingdom is within us, in the flowers, the sky, the rocks and mountains ... it was all made by Him out of nothing, and so He is in all things seen and unseen.*

It is the unseen that has always intrigued me—I hope to spend eternity in the presence of my God. It is my final destination and I know that what I do in the time between when I was born until I leave this earth determines the heavenly mansion prepared by the Lord in which I shall reside.

The Lord desires me and all mankind to be close to Him. So, to help us on our journey to Him, He has, from the beginning, created a legion of angels. At the moment I was conceived, a guardian angel flew to my side. For nearly a hundred years he has watched over me, protected me, answered my prayers, and entreated the Lord to have mercy on me when I strode off on my own, fighting fervently to set my feet on the true path each time. I can say with love and conviction that my guardian angel is my closest friend and ally—my unseen link to God.

And I am grateful. I have been one of the fortunate few to know of my protector and thus cooperate with him. For many, this gift from God might as well be a secret, their angel so taken for granted they are oblivious to the tremendous help and support available to them in their daily lives. As a result they forfeit a thousand blessings and fall victim to a thousand misfortunes that might have otherwise been avoided.

Whenever I can, I speak of my protector and encourage others to do so as well.

"Have you never had a feeling you should visit someone, help another or lift in prayer a long lost friend?" I ask. "These are not just idle thoughts or whispers in our dreams, they are born of our celestial patron or the promptings of another angel seeking help for his charge."

Great indeed is our debt of gratitude to the angels for their tender care, protection and untiring solicitudes on our behalf. We owe our angels profound respect for their presence, their love and their power to watch over us daily, and humble thanks for the care they bestow upon us.

Not until we enter eternity shall we know the number of benefits our guardian angel has nurtured from the first moment of our existence. There are rare times, however, when just such a thing happens. Less than a year ago, I had cause to meet Zachariah, my personal protector. The medical community attributed my stint on the other side to "a near death experience," but I know it to have been a miracle—and there was purpose in my return.

For the one who has been granted a second chance in life, memory of their visit to the other side is often almost absent, or so foggy and distant that their retelling of the experience lacks coherence. For me, the memory is perfectly clear, as if it happened yesterday.

What I learned from my protector during those minutes when time stood still was more than three lifetimes of learning, the knowing of the ages absorbed in a single thought. Tears of gratitude flowed from my eyes as I saw how he had guided, protected and assisted me in every endeavour of my life to help keep me in harmony with God's will.

But perhaps Zachariah's greatest sharing was the involvement of the guardian angels assigned to lives close to my own. Now, there is a love story if there ever was one ....

When I returned to the land of the living, I knew what I should do. "Yes," I whispered to the unseen, "It is the perfect way for others to see, as I do, the presence of God's heavenly angels in their lives."

CHAPTER ONE

HENRY LUNGED FORWARD and pressed his nose against the storm door glass as the most beautiful girl he'd ever seen passed by. She captivated him and held him spellbound, his attention drawn to her like a straight pin to a magnet.

She must have felt his gaze on her; she stopped and looked towards his door. Her initial quizzical look relaxed and softened into an engaging smile before she turned and strolled away, her hips swaying gently under the warm summer sun.

Henry's nose slid along the windowpane as he followed her, a thin layer of fog forming on the glass from his breath. He pushed up on his tiptoes to rise above it. As he gazed at her, something powerful stirred deep inside him, turning the boredom he'd felt all morning into an unexplainable excitement.

He followed as far as he could until his head bumped into the door frame. When she was out of view, Henry lowered himself and took a few deep breaths to slow his racing heart before opening the front door and peeking out.

At that precise moment, she stopped and glanced back, her eyes meeting his. Henry gasped then jumped out of her sight behind the storm door. The momentary embarrassment was more than worth the peek at that winsome creature.

Still in a daze, he relived the thirty seconds or so it had taken her to pass his house. She had come and gone so quickly that he couldn't describe anything more specific than her wheat-coloured hair. He needed to know the shape of her lips, the colour of her eyes, the complexion of her skin. Did she have any dimples? How did her mouth curl when she spoke? He could only imagine she would be perfect in every way.

Henry closed his eyes, pressing his mind to recall more. Her maroon sweater had curved over small breasts and her black skirt hung just below her knees. Spotless white bobby socks sprung from black and white saddle shoes. And she had carried something in her hand. A piece of paper, perhaps a grocery list. If it was a list, she was probably headed for the corner grocery a little over a block away.

His plan to go for a bike ride to kill time while waiting for Timmy Linder to get out of summer school suddenly changed.

He just had to get a closer look at this intriguing girl.

Henry dashed out the door and scooted between his house and the neighbours'. His shiny red bike—a present for his fifteenth birthday two days before—waited for him. He knelt beside it, fumbling with the lock.

"Henry?" Mrs. Goronic called from her garden when she heard him unlock his bike. "Can you carry away the weeds for me?"

Oh, not now! Henry enjoyed helping his neighbour, but not even the promise of being paid a nickel for the job could distract him from his mission.

"Sorry, I have to go to the grocery store, Mrs. Goronic," he answered, desperate to be away. "I'll help you when I get back."

Henry flipped the bike around and pushed it to the street. He grabbed the handlebars, stepped on the left pedal and threw his leg over the seat. His right foot hit the other pedal—and slipped off; the bar of the metal bike frame slammed into his groin.

A fiery rocket of pain surged through his body as he fell, knocking the breath out of him. Henry crouched over, unable to straighten up. Embarrassed, he glanced around to see if anyone had witnessed his accident. Thankfully, it didn't appear so. But every moment he spent recovering was a moment that kept him from meeting her. Consciously he inhaled through his nose and out through his mouth to control his breathing, straightening as the pain subsided. He gingerly remounted the leather seat, planted his foot on the pedal and propelled himself down the street, weaving from side to side to ease the sting he felt each time his right leg rose on the pedal's upstroke. Hopefully, no one watching would think he was drunk.

As he made his way to the grocery (much more slowly than he would have liked), Henry marveled at his bold and impulsive behaviour: chasing after a girl! He'd had crushes on girls before, but until that morning he'd always lost his gumption when it came to matters of romance. It wasn't that Henry was particularly shy or uncouth—he had plenty of friends and was generally well-mannered and well-spoken—he just always seemed to lose his cool and ability to speak coherently around pretty girls. But today, something felt different. He didn't know what had gotten into him this morning, but Henry was not only smitten with his new neighbour, he was bound and determined to meet her as soon as possible. And, with that thought, despite his aching groin, Henry's feet began to pedal faster and faster, his bike propelling him forward through space so quickly it almost felt like he had wings.

Henry had hoped to beat her to the store and meet her at the front door—assuming that was where she was going. But a good ten minutes had elapsed since his little accident. By the time he arrived at Engelmann's Grocery, she was nowhere to be seen. Maybe she was already inside. Or maybe she had taken the trolley that had just pulled away. Or maybe she had gone to Victoria Pharmacy, two blocks down the other way.

Still, he was here now. Better check the grocery first.

He set his bike on the walk in front of the stairs, even though he knew Mr. Engelmann would holler at him for blocking the entrance. He wouldn't be long.

He pulled open the heavy wooden door and was greeted by

the pleasant odour of fresh ground coffee. Dust motes hung in the sunlit square of the doorway before it clapped shut behind him. Mr. Engelmann was at the counter serving a customer; over the years his regular place by the till had worn a slight groove into the wood. The store only had two aisles, so Henry walked over to the one nearest him and glanced down it. No one. The wooden floor boards squeaked and creaked as Henry stepped to the other side. It too was empty.

"Henry!"

He jumped.

"Are you looking for the young lady who came in here a few minutes ago?"

Henry's face burned. He swung around to face Mr. Engelmann and as he did so, his arm caught the edge of a huge pyramid of salmon tins, sending them rolling and skittering everywhere. Henry wanted to dive through one of the open knotholes in the floor to escape the tide of red surging up from his collar to the top of his head. It was bad enough to have an accident in Old Man Engelmann's store, but for the girl of his dreams to see his clumsiness was another thing entirely. He only hoped that she'd already left and hadn't witnessed his accident.

"Sorry, Mr. Engelmann," Henry said in a low voice. He knelt down and began gathering the tins. Crawling on all fours, he reached for one on the other side of the aisle and there she was, squatting in front of him.

She picked it up and handed it to him. "Here, can I help you?"

Henry looked up. *My God, she* is *beautiful*, he thought. The morning sunlight was beaming in the front window behind her, and its glow on her blond hair gave her a soft halo. It reminded Henry of the painting of the Virgin Mary hanging in his parents' bedroom.

Humiliated, he couldn't answer right away. He felt another flush of heat on his cheeks and ducked his head.

"Yes, yes, please help him," Mr. Engelmann called from across the store. "Looks like he could use another pair of hands."

That broke the tension and a wave of relief washed over Henry. Trying to be cool, he looked up at the girl again and this time he smiled. She did not avert her gaze and he was inordinately pleased. Her sky blue eyes looked on him with compassion and her lips curled just enough to let him know she was not laughing at him, though they conveyed a lightheartedness, nonetheless. She tucked a strand of hair behind her ear as she leaned towards him to pick up another tin and Henry smelled lilacs.

"Yeah, I could use the help," Henry finally replied with a semblance of composure. He took another can from her hand. "I'm a bit clumsy this morning."

Her smile broadened and she handed him more tins.

So far, so good, thought Henry. Although he had already made a complete fool out of himself, he had actually managed to smile and speak to a pretty girl. And she had smiled back! He certainly wasn't out of the woods yet, he could still easily blow it like he usually did. But for some reason, today felt different; Henry felt different. He was overcome with a sense of assurance that he was doing exactly what he was meant to do.

As they crouched, gathering up the tins in silence, Henry studied her covertly, hoping she wouldn't notice. The sunlight continued to dapple and tint her honey-coloured hair, and now he noticed that it fell just below her ears. As she reached for a wayward tin, her hair swung forward, hiding most of her facial features except for the tip of her slightly upturned nose. Her neck was long and slender, reminding Henry of Egyptian ladies he had seen in the encyclopedia.

Suddenly, she turned to Henry as if to speak, catching him off guard. He didn't have time to pretend he wasn't staring. He'd been caught. Their eyes met now for a second time and although he felt his face warming again with a blush, this time he couldn't turn away. Her gaze locked with his and his with hers. They rose from their knees simultaneously, as if lifted, and were at once standing, facing each other. Nothing existed except this moment and this place...

A charged, earthly attraction united their hearts while a spiritual energy traveled the length of the gaze they shared, drawing their souls from their bodies and joining them at the halfway point. The aura around them brightened, enclosing both in the surrounding glow of their celestial connection.

Time stood still...

Mr. Engelmann looked up. "How are you two doing over there?" The sound of his voice pierced the rapture of the moment.

Henry caught his breath. His soul slammed back into his chest. "O-okay," he answered, though he wasn't sure what the question had been. Heat returned to his cheeks. What in the world was he doing, staring at her like that? She would think he was a nut. He blinked several times as though something were in his eyes.

She tilted her head and moved back, then bent down to retrieve the remaining tin cans at their feet.

Henry looked at Mr. Engelmann, saw him nod in their direction and wink to the customer he was serving. The pink staining Henry's cheeks deepened to red, his composure crumbling. Whatever confidence he had felt a few moments ago was quickly diminishing. Looking away, Henry placed the last of the collected tins onto the stack.

"Guess I should watch where I'm going, huh?"

"We all have accidents." Her voice held a gentle humour, erasing his lingering embarrassment.

"Thanks for your help. Did you find what you came for?"

"No, not everything. I better go ask for help and get back home before they send a search party."

As the only other customer in the store gathered up his bag and left, she approached Mr. Engelmann.

"Hi. Could you please show me where the sugar is?"

Henry stole another look at her. She sure didn't need any sweetening.

"It's just down this aisle," Mr. Engelmann pointed, "at the end on the second shelf."

"And the baking soda? Where might that be?"

"Also with the baking supplies but on the first shelf."

Henry continued straightening the stack of tins, propelled by a yearning he could not suppress. He felt ridiculous. On the one hand, he just wanted to get out of there as quickly as possible, but on the other, he was rooted to the spot and seemed to have no control over his actions. It was obvious he was stalling now, but the girl seemed to be stalling, too—or so he hoped. By the time she'd found her items and paid for them, Henry's mountain of salmon tins was perfectly stacked. As she strolled towards the door, taking her time and looking at everything along the way, Henry sprinted to the front.

"Henry," Mr. Engelmann called. "What did you come in for? Were you supposed to pick something up?"

Henry froze. *Of course!* The girl was probably wondering the same thing! He didn't want to let on his real reason for being there. Silently, he begged the girl to wait for him. He turned and spotted several loaves of wrapped bread, lined up neatly on the paint-chipped shelf. He snatched one up.

"Please put it on our account," Henry said as he dashed to join the girl lingering by the door.

"Don't you want a bag?"

"No, no. This is fine. I'm really sorry for being so clumsy."

"It's okay, Henry." Mr. Engelmann leaned forward to rest his hands on the counter. "I think I stacked the tins out too far in the aisle. Not to worry."

Henry nodded towards Mr. Engelmann and at once turned back to the girl. She seemed to be holding back a chuckle, which then turned into a wide warm smile.

He dashed past her, opened the heavy door and held it for her. She cast him a furtive glance then looked down, her cheeks faintly tinged with pink.

Henry's heart skipped a beat. Together they walked down the two steps to the pavement. The bike Henry had dreamed of and hoped for and had been so happy to get only two days before blocked the path. Henry did the unthinkable. He stepped over his longed-for birthday gift as if it were a discarded candy wrapper and walked on, in step with the girl.

Just then, she turned to him, her crystal blue eyes sparkling, and made Henry's day. "By the way, I'm Jenny Sarsky. We just moved into the neighbourhood a few days ago."

Thrilled that she had freely offered her name and relieved that she didn't think he was a complete moron (he hoped), he blurted, "I know. I live just three doors down from you. I watched the movers unload your stuff." As soon as the words tumbled out, Henry wished he had them back. *Geez, there I go again.* Now she would know he'd been spying on her.

But Jenny didn't seem to notice, "This is our third move in four years. I hope we stay longer than the last time."

Henry silently echoed that sentiment.

"We were just settling into our house in Vancouver when someone got sick and they called my dad to move here to Regina to take his place. He said we had to go, it was such a great opportunity." Her eyes turned toward Henry and they stepped off the curb in unison. "So, here we are." After a brief pause, she added, "I'm sure you're not interested in this."

"Oh, yes," Henry responded. He would have been interested in hearing her recite the phone book. But Henry couldn't believe that this gorgeous girl could possibly be interested in *him*.

Just when his heart began filling with doubt and despair, Jenny jumped as a passing car honked its horn. Neither of them had been paying very close attention, and they had just about stepped directly onto Victoria Avenue without even noticing the traffic. Henry caught her eye and they shared a startled chuckle.

Crossing Victoria Avenue was always dangerous. Cars zipped by in a steady stream in both directions. As they waited for the opportunity to cross, Henry noted the sky was clear, not a cloud in sight. Somewhere between the zenith and the horizon was a shade of blue that matched the colour of Jenny's eyes. He smiled and stole another look at her. The wind gently lifted her hair, exposing the silver stud in her ear, the light glinting off the silver chain she wore around her neck.

Standing next to Jenny on that perfect summer morning, Henry quickly forgot the anguish he had felt just a moment ago and was suddenly flooded with hopeful anticipation.

Finally, a break in traffic allowed them to dart into the street.

"Quickly, hold my hand," Jenny blurted.

He didn't know if she'd asked because the traffic frightened her or if she just wanted to hold his hand. It didn't matter. He thrust his hand out and grabbed hers and ... all heaven broke loose. An electrifying thrill charged through him. Warm and soft, her hand fit perfectly into his. The sound of traffic faded into the distance; the sun shone like it never had before. The world marched on without them.

Oblivious to cars and traffic, Henry glided blindly across the avenue, unsure if his feet even touched the pavement. The curb arrived a second or two sooner than he expected. Henry stumbled, tearing their hands apart and snapping him out of his reverie. He struggled to regain his balance and composure.

"You really are having a rough time today," Jenny ribbed him good-naturedly.

"I was paying so much attention to the traffic I didn't see the curb," Henry grasped for a reasonable excuse.

"They should have traffic lights or a crosswalk at this corner." Jenny observed.

"Yeah, you're right."

As they walked towards home, Henry shifted the loaf of bread from the hand nearest hers to the other. He wanted to touch her again so badly, he brushed his free hand against hers. Inching his way towards her, his hand finally hit its mark; a warm sensation shot through him as their fingers met.

Jenny stepped away.

"Sorry," Henry lied as he moved over a bit to give her a little more space, pretending it was an accident.

They were nearing home and Henry wondered if he should walk her to her door or if that would be awkward. Without thinking but immediately wishing he hadn't, he blurted, "Do you want me to walk you home?"

"I think I can find the way," she laughed.

Henry loved her laugh. It was natural and easy, and the way

her eyes lit up ....

She glanced over at him, "I just wondered ... your name is Henry, right? I overheard the man at the grocery store call you that."

How could he have forgotten to introduce himself to the girl of his dreams? Realizing he had another opportunity to touch her hand, he quickly held his out for a handshake. "Yes, it's Henry Pederson. Pleased to meet you, Jenny."

She stared at him and his outstretched hand, then chuckled. Her hand came towards his. He could see it coming, soft and smooth-skinned. No rings, just a small, elegant hand coming closer and closer. He couldn't wait any longer. He thrust his hand into hers.

Jenny stepped back a bit, startled, but Henry wouldn't let go. That incredible warm feeling of her hand inside his blitzed through his body again and he wanted it to last forever.

"I really must get these baking supplies home," said Jenny, juggling the bag in her free arm. She looked at the hand that held hers captive, then at Henry's eyes. As she began to understand the underlying motive for the handshake, a rosy hue bloomed on her cheeks and she smiled as she gently tugged her hand free.

"Nice meeting you, Henry." She looked up at the house on the corner. "Is that where you live?"

"Yeah."

"Oh." Jenny's eyes widened in surprise. She blushed again.

Henry looked at her sheepishly, fearing that she now knew he was the one she'd seen spying on her earlier—and that he'd followed her to the store. Henry cringed inwardly. He had done one klutzy thing after another; would she ever want to see him again? But if Jenny had any reservations about Henry, she didn't let on.

"If you're not busy this afternoon," she said, her smile covering her words, "could you show me how to get to Balfour High School? I'll be registering there next week for the fall semester."

Trying to conceal his utter joy and keep the grin from splitting his face, Henry said, "Sure, Jenny! See ya later."

He lifted a hand in farewell and nearly floated into his yard and up the three stairs leading to the front door. Not even his buddy Timmy Linder getting out of summer school could keep him from being with Jenny. He glanced over to Jenny's place. She was just walking through her gate. He waited for a brief moment to make sure she wasn't looking, then jumped over the banister and slipped between the houses to where he usually kept his bike. He half jogged to the alley behind his house then burst into a run.

Mrs. Goronic was still weeding in her backyard and she called out to him as he darted by. He pretended not to hear her. He had to get his bike.

His bike. *Oh, man.* What if it had been stolen or Old Man Engelmann had taken a sledgehammer to it for cluttering the entryway? Henry's heart pounded as he ran faster and faster. Sweat trickled down his sides. The traffic on Victoria Avenue was as heavy as it had been earlier. Between cars, he glanced across the street to Engelmann's store. Was his bike still there? One big truck after another blocked his view. Finally, a break in traffic allowed him a peek. It was gone!

He waited for another break and looked again. It really was gone. He couldn't believe his eyes. His elation over meeting Jenny plummeted into his shoes along with his stomach. He heaved a sigh and his breathing eased a bit, but he ached from head to toe. The exhaustion of emotional overload hung heavy on his limbs and the pain from his earlier mishap on the bike made itself known again. Queasiness gnawed at his gut.

The traffic finally abated and Henry jogged across the street, the spring gone from his step.

Mr. Engelmann emerged from the store as Henry approached.

"Don't worry, I have your bike," he said. "Come on."

Henry didn't know whether to laugh or cry. The rollercoaster morning had taken a toll on his nerves.

"When I saw you walk away with that young lady I knew your mind wasn't on your bicycle, so I decided to look after it for you."

Henry stared at him, speechless. He'd fully expected a scolding from Mr. Engelmann for leaving the bike on the doorstep and obstructing the entry to the store. This was turning into the best and most unusual day of his life.

"You must be quite taken by that young lady, eh? Leaving your new bike behind just to walk her home. But sometimes other things in a man's life can become more important, no?" With a wink and twinkle in his eye, Mr. Engelmann added, "I was young once, too, Henry. I may be an old man now but I still understand such things."

Henry met the store owner's knowing gaze head on. "Thanks a lot, sir." And to show his appreciation—and attempt to act more mature than he felt—he put out his hand.

Mr. Engelmann studied him for a moment and his eyes seemed to get a little watery. "You're a good boy, Henry." He took Henry's hand and shook it. Where Jenny's had been warm and soft, Mr. Engelmann's hand was dry and coarse and marked with age, but that handshake sealed their friendship.

Mr. Engelmann took Henry around the back of the store. He opened the door to a large shed, and there among the many boxes was Henry's shiny red bike. Henry took hold of the handlebars and backed the bike out of the crowded storage shed.

"Thanks again, Mr. Engelmann," he said, then jumped on his bike, careful not to slip and re-injure himself.

Mr. Engelmann waved off his thanks.

Secure on the seat, Henry picked up speed and headed down the street as fast as his legs could pedal. The breeze felt so good. His T-shirt, which had stuck wetly to his back minutes ago, quickly dried as the wind surged beneath and through it. It swelled out behind him like a parachute as he raced down the road passing, 13th, 14th and 15th Avenues in a flash, taking the long way home.

Jenny filled his thoughts once more. How beautiful she was, and how wonderful it had been to hold her hand and look into her eyes. He just couldn't believe that despite his mishaps and complete lack of flair, she still seemed to like him. It wasn't just his imagination; they had clicked. Elation soared through him.

He felt like he was in a hot air balloon instead of on his bike, coasting over the streets and intersections, fueled by the torch in his heart. This must be what it felt like to be in love!

Gradually Henry's pent-up energy was expended. Relaxed, cooled off and coming to his senses, he slowed down. But as he neared his home his spirits shot up again. His breath caught. There she was on the front steps of her house, reading a book!

She looked up as his bike *kathumped* over the spaces in the wooden sidewalk, sunlight brightening her face.

An angel. She looked like an angel with her blond hair glistening gold in the bright sun and her smooth skin shimmering in the warm light.

Looking into the sun, she squinted to make out who was in front of her. A lone cloud sailing tranquilly in the vast expanse of the prairie summer sky cast a soothing shadow across Jenny's face, which relaxed into a welcoming grin.

"Oh, hi, Henry, I didn't expect to see you again so soon. Just out for a bike ride?"

"Yeah, something to do," he replied, trying to be casual. "Oh, yeah. When do you want me to show you where Balfour is?"

"Maybe after lunch, say around 1:30 or so. Is that okay?"

"Sure," Henry replied, his brain whirling for something else to say to keep the conversation going. "What are you reading?"

"*Catcher in the Rye.* My mom just finished it and said it's such a good book. So far it's kind of boring." Her eyes rested on the bike. "Say, isn't that the same red bike that was lying in front of Mr. Engelmann's grocery store this morning?"

Fire rolled up Henry's neck and consumed his face. Should he tell her the truth? Should he let her know he'd left his prized possession behind just so he could walk her home and be with her a little while longer? He swallowed hard.

"Yes," he croaked, offering no further explanation.

Jenny's eyes brightened and a knowing smile played on her lips.

His secret was out.

CHAPTER TWO

HENRY SAT AT THE KITCHEN TABLE, memories of his morning with Jenny keeping her with him as if she sat beside him. He could not stop thinking about her, seeing her in his mind's eye, or appease the aching desire to be near her and hold her hand. How could he feel so strongly about someone he'd just met and had been with for less than an hour?

"Is something wrong, Henry? You look flushed," his mother said, reaching to press her hand against his forehead.

The gesture lacked Jenny's electrifying warmth.

Satisfied her son did not have a fever, she removed her hand and said, "I made grilled hot dogs with fried potatoes and onions for lunch."

"You did?" Henry looked at his mom in surprise. Thoughts of Jenny had crowded out the heavenly aroma of fried onions and potatoes that normally would have had him salivating by now.

"Perhaps you should lie down for awhile," Henry's mom advised as she handed him a plate and watched him twirl the potatoes around with his fork instead of gulping them down as usual.

"Yeah, you're right, Mom. I'm just not hungry today, I guess.

Sorry."

"Well, we can always warm them up in the oven later."

Henry left the table and trudged to his room. Maybe he was suffering from the same thing his Uncle Ron had when he met Aunt Darlene. He recalled his mom saying that it had been love at first sight and that Ron had been lovesick for her.

Twelve forty-five. Still another forty-five minutes before he was to call on Jenny. How would he keep himself occupied until then? The suspense of waiting gnawed at him like the time he and his dad had planned their first fishing and camping trip. Henry walked over to his bed and lay down, and without realizing it, drifted into a deep sleep with visions of Sleeping Beauty occupying his dreams.

He was the charming prince racing through the woods on foot until he arrived at a clearing, and there in the middle of the wildflower-filled meadow lay Jenny, asleep on a bed of white daisies. Henry knew what he had to do to awaken her. Eagerly he ran to her, his lips puckering in anticipation of hers when an elderly man in a tan suit with a yellow flower in his lapel suddenly appeared where Jenny had lain. What was happening? Where was Jenny? He must get to her. Henry quickened his pace but as he drew near another figure, this one hidden in the black cavity of a hooded cloak, loomed in front of him. Cold swept through Henry as the faceless entity grabbed his arm, holding him back. Henry struggled to get free, he just had to get to Jenny, but the cloaked figure was bigger and stronger—

"Let go, let go!" Henry cried.

"Henry, Henry," his mom said, shaking him, "Wake up! You must be dreaming."

Henry roused, unsure where he was or what was happening until his gaze focused on his mom smiling down at him.

"You all right, son?" she asked.

He looked at her without answering; hot beads of perspiration rolled off his forehead even though the hard, rigid grip of the cloaked figure continued to send icy shivers up and down his spine.

"Are you okay?" she asked again, "You still look flushed and … did you have a bad dream?"

Henry shook his head. "Yeah, no … I'm fine."

"There's a pretty young girl at the door wanting to see you. She says you're going to show her where Balfour is."

"Geez, Mom, what time is it?"

"Oh, it's twenty minutes to two."

"Tell her I'll be right there." Henry jumped out of bed and ran to the bathroom. After washing his face, he rubbed a little Brylcreem into his hair and combed it, slicking one side back towards his right ear. He tucked his T-shirt into his jeans, took another look in the mirror, then headed down the hall to the front door. Jenny was just inside holding onto the screen door.

"Did you fall asleep?" she inquired.

"Yeah," Henry replied, a bit embarrassed.

"Boy, it sure smells good in here. Fried onions?"

"Yeah."

"I love them too, especially with hot dogs."

"That's what we had for lunch," Henry said, a surprised look on his face. *She even likes what I like!*

He knew his mom was standing in the background, watching and smiling. Not wanting to see if she had noticed the extra Brylcreem in his hair, Henry didn't turn around. Instead, he just looked at Jenny and motioned over his shoulder, "This is my mom."

"Yes, I know. We just met. Are you still able to take me to Balfour High School?"

"Yeah, for sure," Henry replied, trying to hide his excitement, and anxious to be with her and away from his mom's scrutiny. "Let's go."

"Nice meeting you, Mrs. Pederson," said Jenny as she pushed open the storm door and Henry followed her out.

"'Bye, Jenny. Nice meeting you," his mom called after them.

"Is it okay if we walk? My bicycle is still in storage. You can ride yours though, if you want."

"Oh no, I like walking," Henry lied.

"So, what grade are you in?" Jenny asked as they headed down Broder Street towards College Avenue.

"Just starting Grade 9, even though I'll be a year older than most of my classmates. I got pneumonia when I was eight and missed almost a whole year of school, so my parents held me back."

"That's funny, the exact same thing happened to me, except I had scarlet fever and missed most of Grade 4. Just as I got better, my dad got transferred to Vancouver and my parents decided to have me repeat fourth grade."

"So how old are you?" Henry asked.

"Fifteen."

"Me, too. I just turned fifteen a couple of days ago."

"So we're both fifteen and starting Grade 9 at the same high school? Henry, we already have so much in common!"

Just the way Jenny put it, his spirits shot up.

"I'm so excited about starting high school. In a way, I'm happy we moved when we did. Everyone is starting at the same time and I won't stand out so much as a newcomer. I'd feel a little shy and afraid that I wouldn't be accepted if I had to start at a new school after the school year had already begun."

"Oh, I'm certain everyone will like you," Henry assured her. "But I know what you mean. I remember when we moved into Regina from the farm and I started school late in the fall after harvest how everyone just stared at me for the first day or so." Actually, Henry didn't really remember it being such a big deal, but for Jenny's sake he wanted to agree with her.

As they approached College Avenue, Henry schemed for ways he could hold Jenny's hand again. If they turned right and headed west down College Avenue three blocks, they could cross at the crosswalk in front of the high school. If he suggested they cross College Avenue right away there might be a chance they could hold hands as they crossed the busy street.

"Balfour's on the other side of the street, Jenny. Maybe we better cross here—it might be busier further up."

Jenny nodded. "Okay."

As they waited for a break in the traffic, Henry wondered if he should just grab her hand or suggest that he hold it as a safety precaution. Jenny resolved his internal dilemma with a quick "Hold my hand" as they stepped off the curb.

Henry put his hand into hers and the wonderful feeling of that morning was instantly recaptured. He tried to recall every aspect of her touch and imprint it on his mind so he would never forget. They dashed across the street then slowed to a walk again. It took several steps and tuggings from Jenny before Henry realized he still held her hand in his.

"Oh, sorry," he said, his cheeks heating once more.

Elm trees lined this side of College Avenue, the blanket of shade adding a pleasant coolness to the breeze on their faces. Balfour lay a block or two ahead of them. At a clearing in the trees the football field came into view. A team spread across it in a scrimmage, preparing for the fall season.

"They have a football team?"

"Yeah, the Redmen. Guys who want to play in the fall are trying out this week. I was going to play this year but decided to wait and see," Henry said.

Jenny took in the high school and its setting. "This reminds me of the last school I was at, so well treed and lots of fields around it."

"Where were you last?"

"In a suburb of Vancouver."

"Oh, yeah?" Henry replied, even though he had no idea what she meant. She must have sensed his ignorance because she explained what a suburb was and how some cities grew so big that smaller cities developed around them.

"Vancouver must be pretty big then," Henry concluded.

"Yes, it is. It's a lovely place, but I still like smaller cities like the one I grew up in."

"Yeah? Where were you born?"

"Kelowna, British Columbia. It's a small city and very beautiful. We lived near the lake and did a lot of boating before Dad got so busy with work."

Less than a block away from the school, Jenny noticed the crosswalk where other kids were crossing College Avenue.

"There *is* a crosswalk."

"Oh, yeah, I guess so. I forgot all about that." Henry didn't meet her gaze.

Jenny slowed and raised an eyebrow at him. Henry knew she was wondering whether to believe him or not. When she shied away, smiling, he knew she realized what his real intent in avoiding the crosswalk had been.

She seemed not to mind too much though, because she fell into step with him again. A moment later she turned and looked up at the two-storey high school stretching over a city block. The brown brick structure boasted an impressively tall, pillared entrance smack in the centre of its otherwise standard design.

"Seems like a nice school. How many students go here?"

"I don't know, probably a hundred," Henry replied.

"Oh, is that all? It seems big for just a hundred."

Henry's face flushed again as he realized his estimate was likely in serious error. "Oh, did I say a hundred? I meant five hundred."

"That sounds about right for a school this size, but we can ask when we go in."

They started up the stairs leading to the front door. Other students, some alone and some accompanied by their parents, also entered and left the building. Henry slipped behind Jenny as they moved to the side to let those heading down the stairs go by, scooting in front of her to hold the door open for her as soon as there was a chance.

"Thank you, Henry."

Henry just smiled and motioned her inside with a bit of a flourish, following Jenny in as the huge oak door slowly swung closed behind them.

Trying to imagine how Jenny might see it, Henry took in the high ceiling and open hall. It was spacious and impressive and Henry felt a flutter of pride that this was his school. A few people milled around, one or two studied the trophy showcases.

Just beyond the trophy displays was the administration office.

Before Henry had a chance to mention it, Jenny spotted the office and marched ahead of him through the door.

An older lady behind the high counter looked up at them and smiled as they entered. Three other women worked at their desks behind her, two of them sorting through piles of forms, the other clacking away on a typewriter. The principal's office was to their left.

"May I help you?"

"Yes, hi! My name is Jenny Sarsky. I'll be attending Balfour in September. I came to pick up the registration forms."

"Certainly, I have the forms right here. Your mom phoned just a few moments ago to tell me to expect you." The woman flipped through an accordion file on her desk. "I got the forms started and put your name on one of them. Let me go through this again ... Sarsky, Jenny. Oh, here it is. You go by your second name rather than your first, do you?"

"Yes, I like Jenny better."

Henry wondered what her first name was but didn't want to interrupt.

"Well, here you go. You'll need to return them before the middle of August. That's the cutoff date for new student registrations."

"Okay. Oh! By the way, how many students go here?" Jenny asked.

"As of yesterday, we have 428 attending this fall, but we expect it to be higher than that, probably closer to 450."

Henry smiled, pleased with his off the cuff assessment.

Jenny turned to him. "You were pretty close, Henry."

Out in the hall, Henry was about to ask Jenny what her first name was when a group of football players trotted through the front entrance on their way to the gym and showers. Jenny was greeted with whistles and howls. "Hey, what are you doing tonight? Can you help me with my homework?" Another player boasted to a teammate that he'd get her phone number.

Henry felt sick. He thought for sure he was going to lose the girl of his dreams to some undeserving football player.

Jenny only said, "Let's go."

"Yeah, sure," he answered, his voice cracking. "There's a confectionary down the street where some of us hang out from time to time. It's on our way home, if you want to go."

Jenny nodded. Henry was glad to get out of there. Those darn football players had tried to steal his girl! Between the warm weather, the long walk and his storm of emotions, he needed a drink in the worst way.

They headed towards the front doors. Once again, Henry rushed ahead of Jenny to open the door for her. As happened often on the prairies, the beautiful summer sky was suddenly marred by dark grey clouds rolling towards them from the west. The wind had picked up even more since they had arrived, stirring the first few fallen leaves as they strolled down the walkway.

"So, where's this confectionary you mentioned?" Jenny asked. "Is it near here? Should we use the crosswalk ... or go down further and take our chances?"

She'd succeeded in surprising Henry. Was it possible Jenny felt the same way he did when they held hands? His heart juddered at the possibility. But it would be an even longer walk back if they went that way and Henry decided to go with his better judgment.

"Nah, we'd better cross here. The confectionary is only a block away and straight ahead."

Jenny nodded, but kept her eyes down and Henry sensed her disappointment. At least, he hoped she was disappointed.

They crossed College Avenue and headed down Toronto Street into an older part of the city that was well treed on both sides. Traffic was minimal in this area as most residents parked their cars behind their homes.

"The Golden Gate Confectionary is right up there," Henry finally said, breaking the silence. "You can just barely make out the sign."

"Oh, good, I'm really thirsty. I can hardly wait to have a drink." Jenny's eyes sparkled and Henry was glad to see it.

At the confectionary, Henry opened the door for her once more. It was bright, freshly painted and well-organized, nearly the opposite of Mr. Engelmann's grocery store.

The drink coolers lined the back wall from one end to the other. They walked to the back and peered through the glass doors. These coolers displayed the entire bottle, quite different from Mr. Engelmann's half cooler where the doors slid opened horizontally to reveal only the bottle caps on the top. Henry couldn't help but feel that unless Mr. Engelmann made some major changes to his store, he wouldn't be able to compete with the new ones opening up.

Henry grabbed a Dr. Pepper while Jenny opted for an Orange Crush. They took the drinks to the cashier, who asked if there was anything else they wanted. Henry had only enough to pay for his drink with a few cents left over. He couldn't even offer to buy Jenny's. Briefly he wished he'd thrown out Mrs. Goronic's weeds. He could've used that nickel now.

Jenny reached into her sweater pocket and pulled out a small change purse. "Do you want to share a chocolate bar? I think I have enough for one."

Henry hesitated for a moment, not wanting to sponge off the girl he was trying to impress, though he didn't want to insult her by turning down her offer either.

"Sure, that would be great. I still have eight cents left that I can give you."

Jenny reviewed all the bars in the display then said, "How about an Oh Henry?" She turned to him, giving him a teasing wink.

Henry chuckled and said, "It's my favourite, of course."

Jenny took the bar to the counter and paid for it along with her drink. As Jenny took the change from the cashier, put it in her purse and returned the purse to her pocket, Henry savoured the chance to watch her every action. Then, grasping each end of the bar she pulled it apart, tearing the wrapper and gauging the pieces before offering the larger portion to Henry.

"Thanks, Jenny," Henry said.

They unwrapped their pieces at the same time and almost simultaneously took a bite chewing slowly before gulping their drinks. As they finished, a sharp flash of lightning lit up the sky through the window, followed a few seconds later by a clap of thunder that shook the glass in its frame. Bottles rattled and shivered in the coolers.

"Should we make a dash for it to see if we can make it home?" Jenny wondered.

"We can try. If we don't, we might be stuck here for God knows how long."

They looked at each other and in a moment of reckless abandon said at the same time, "Let's go for it."

Without a further word they headed for the front door, the wind almost ripping the glass door from Jenny's hand as she opened it. They had to push together to close it.

"Quickly, hold my hand," Jenny shouted over the whipping wind. Henry caught her fingers in his, squeezing her hand and feeling a rush of joy when she squeezed back. They took off east towards home, knowing they would never make it before the rain started.

Papers and dust swirled in all directions. Low branches whipped across the sidewalk, barely missing them as they sped along, dust and little bits of gravel stinging their shins. Black clouds chased them, lightning flashed in rapid succession, thunder bellowed across the heavens. They ran closer and closer together, trying to protect each other and at the same time brace themselves against the intensifying turbulence around them.

A few drops of rain dampened Henry's hair and he knew it would only be a matter of moments before the clouds released their fury. For a split second Henry thought they should go back to the confectionary, but the thrill and excitement of the approaching storm overpowered his fear of the lightning and impending downpour. Jenny's hand in his gave him the strength to face anything.

A few more drops landed on his head and then—as if someone had turned on a heavenly faucet—the rain pelted down, drenching them instantly. Henry looked over at Jenny. Her mouth was open and she appeared to have lost her breath. Cold rain hammered down, gushing down the gutter beside them beneath the crashing thunder. Sheets of rain thick as fog clouded the objects ahead of them. Henry extended his arm, anticipating running into a fence or tree.

As they adjusted to the rain and cold, they ran with more ease and freedom, footfalls slapping in the cold wet wash of the sidewalk. Henry's sneakers had already begun to leak. Minutes later, they slowed to a walk, closed their eyes and turned their heads towards the sky, daring the clouds to loose more of their fury. They were young and free, their fears washed away by exhilaration. They had challenged nature, it had given its best and they hadn't backed down. They'd faced it straight on and were winning.

Jenny burst into laughter with the excitement of it all and swung their linked hands with abandon. There was victory in the motion and Henry joined in, raising their arms even higher on each upswing. It was difficult to believe that all these wonderful experiences could happen to him in a single day—one of the happiest of his life.

Gradually the rain abated and they slowed to a saunter. The wind also settled and visibility steadily improved. The rain stopped almost as quickly as it had begun, except for a few drops tumbling from the dripping trees.

"Gosh, that was fun," Jenny exclaimed through gasps.

Henry looked at her against the backdrop of the departing storm. Jenny's fine blond hair was plastered against her scalp. Her clothes drooped, her sweater stretched at least five inches below her waist. She must have sensed him studying her, because Jenny turned to him and burst out laughing. He laughed along with her as he suddenly realized how he must look too!

They stood there gazing at each other, only then becoming aware that they were still holding hands.

"Boy, are we ever wet," Jenny said, forcing her thoughts away from their joined hands. "I feel like taking my shoes off and just running. It would be like running through a sprinkler in our bare feet. Come on, Henry. Let's do it!"

Part of Henry wanted to, while a bigger part of him didn't want to let go of Jenny's hand, which he would have to do in order to take off his shoes and socks. But he couldn't resist Jenny's excitement. He wanted to please her and was willing to sacrifice just about anything to do so. He let go of her hand and crouched down to untie his shoes. Jenny did the same thing and their heads brushed together. Laughing like two little kids, they tugged off their shoes and socks. Henry held both of his shoes in one hand and was about to walk forward when Jenny surprised him again.

"Okay now, quickly, hold my hand." The instant his hand was once more secure in her grasp, she tugged him onto the wet front lawn of the nearest house. Henry squeezed more tightly, letting her know what he was sure she already knew, that he was crazy about her.

They ran in and out of one yard after the other, waving their arms as they dodged tree branches and fences, tricycles and wagons, rubber hoses and sprinklers. Henry couldn't remember having so much fun and savoured the feeling of complete freedom. It was as if he had only been half alive until today, seeing only half of what was around him and feeling only half of what was inside him. He felt more alive than he could ever remember feeling. To be out in a thunderstorm, then run through the wet grass in bare feet was something he would normally never do. Yet here he was, doing these crazy things and it felt normal and fun. It was Jenny. Her charm, playfulness, and spontaneity were contagious. Somehow she had opened Henry up to the fullness of life.

"Look at the beautiful colours in the grass and trees. It's amazing how rain seems to restore the colours," Henry said excitedly. Before Jenny could respond, he continued, "Did you notice how as the summer goes by the leaves turn darker and more olive, and as fall comes along, the colours change again into so many yellows, oranges and browns? See there." He pointed to a small tree in all the colours he'd just described.

"Henry," Jenny interrupted, "you sound like an artist." She said it with such excitement and awe that Henry considered the possibility.

They continued home and soon Henry saw the perfect ending to an amazing day. "Look, Jenny!"

The ominous clouds had dissipated, leaving behind a beautiful blue sky and a perfect rainbow. Its vibrant colours shimmered and arced, uniting one end of the horizon with the other, echoing the feeling in Henry's heart.

Awestruck, they didn't realize how tightly—and tenderly— their hands were joined.

"It's beautiful, Henry, just beautiful," Jenny said.

"I wish I could paint a scene like this," Henry's words were quiet and held the hint of a promise.

"Would you like to be an artist?"

"I do like drawing. I want to take art this fall, but my dad says it's too hard to make a living that way. Maybe I'll become a teacher or something."

"Sounds great. I think you would do well at either," Jenny replied. "Maybe you could even teach art."

"Yeah, I never thought of that. How about you? What do you want to do?"

"I just love reading and stories in general. I could sit and read all day long. I'd love to work in a library and be around books all the time."

"Sounds like you want to be a writer, Jenny," Henry said.

"Oh, I'd love to write a book! A romance novel. I love those kinds of stories." She stopped walking and looked at him. "You're the first person I've ever told that to."

Henry's heart nearly burst at her expression of trust.

Before they knew it, they were on Broder Street, a block and a half from home. They strolled down the sidewalk, holding hands, neither of them seeming to want to let go. Until Jenny stopped, released his hand and put both of hers up to her mouth in shock.

"Henry, I forgot my application forms at the confectionary."

"Oh, that's okay," he said. "I'll get my bike and go back and get them for you. It'll only take a few minutes."

"That would be great. Thanks, Henry," Jenny said, and the problem was solved as quickly as it had presented itself.

At the gate leading to Jenny's front door, they looked each other up and down, grimacing and laughing again at how soaked they were.

"I really enjoyed myself this afternoon," Jenny smiled.

"So did I." *More than you will ever know.* "I'll get the application forms for you as soon as I change into dry clothes."

"Thanks again, Henry."

Jenny turned and walked towards her front door, the subtle sway of her hips clearly outlined by the clothes that hung wet and limp on her body. Just before Jenny went inside, she turned and tilted her lips in a coy smile, her eyes sparkling. Henry almost melted right then and there.

As the screen door closed behind her, Henry heard Jenny's mother exclaim, "Jenny! What on earth happened to you?"

Henry couldn't hear the reply as he turned towards his house, fully expecting a similar reaction from his mom. Fortunately, she was in the kitchen preparing supper when he got there. Henry yelled that he was home then went straight to his room. After changing into dry clothes, he rushed to the front door.

"Where are you going now?"

"We stopped at the confectionary for a drink and Jenny forgot her application forms there, so I'm going to bike over and get them for her. I'll be back in a few minutes."

"Oh, that reminds me. Mr. Engelmann phoned and asked if it's okay with us if you work for him for the rest of the summer, and after school and on the weekends when school starts up again. We told him it would be okay. Maybe you could go and see him later on."

"Sure, Mom," Henry called over his shoulder as he headed back out the door and between the houses to retrieve his bike.

"Oh, there you are, Henry." Mrs. Goronic was outside in the

wet. A little rain didn't stop her, either. "See, you didn't take the weeds away this morning and now they are so wet."

"I promise I'll do it tomorrow, Mrs. Goronic." Before she could engage him in any further trivialities, he picked up his bike and headed for the street.

He arrived at the confectionary within minutes, jumped off his bike and ran inside. There on a shelf near the drink cooler were Jenny's forms.

Henry didn't speed home. He took his time, thinking about what had happened to him that day. Only hours earlier, Jenny had been a complete stranger. But since then his life had changed; things were undeniably different now, like the ever-changing prairie sky. He would never have predicted that the morning's clear sky would soon be covered by summer storm clouds and then the most amazing rainbow. He would never have known that today he would meet the girl of his dreams and, like the prairie sky, his life would never be the same.

At Jenny's house, he hopped off his bike and leaned it against her fence. He brushed his hair down and back and tucked in his shirt. He wanted to look as presentable as possible. It didn't occur to him that Jenny might be watching him through the screen door until he climbed the front steps. She smiled and winked at him as he handed her the envelope.

"Thank you so much for going back for those for me, Henry."

Jenny's mother came to the door behind her. "So this is your personal guide."

"Yes, this is Henry, Mom. He just lives down the street. Henry, this is my mother, Edith Sarsky."

"Nice to meet you, Mrs. Sarsky."

"You two certainly got caught in some downpour. You must've gotten as wet as Jenny," Mrs. Sarsky said.

"Yeah, that's for sure. It was fun, though."

"Are you and Jenny in the same grade?"

Henry nodded.

"Well, I'm glad she knows someone and won't start out the year as a complete stranger."

"Don't worry, Mrs. Sarsky. I'll introduce her to my other friends in the next few days."

"Oh, that sounds nice. We've moved around so many times in the last four years, I hope we're here for a long stay and can establish some roots."

"I hope so too, Mrs. Sarsky." Beginning to feel uncomfortable and not knowing what else to say, Henry added, "Well, I guess I better get home for supper."

"Maybe I'll see you tomorrow," Jenny said, a small question in her voice.

"I'm sure you will."

"Thanks again for taking me to the school. I had a lot of fun today."

"Me, too."

Henry turned, walked down the three front steps and out of the yard. He grabbed his bike and looked back at the front door. Jenny peered out at him with that playful sparkle still in her eyes. He smiled back and headed home. When he got there, his dad had already eaten and his mom had his plate of pork chops served.

"Well, I hope you're hungrier tonight than you were at lunch," she said. "And don't forget to thank the good Lord for the food you are about to eat."

"Yeah sure, Mom." Henry prayed over his meal, thanking Him for bringing Jenny into his life. In less than three minutes he'd devoured all the potatoes and two pork chops.

His mom stared in delight. "Want some more?"

"Yes, please. Are these pork chops ever good!"

His mother dished up another pork chop and the rest of the leftover potatoes and onions.

"Well, how did you make out with that young girl today?" she asked.

"Oh, you mean Jenny," he replied, trying not to show how strongly he felt about her.

"Mm-hmm," his mom nodded. "Did you show her to the school?"

"Yes, I did. Oh yeah, Mom, coming home from school, we got caught in the rain. I put all the wet clothes downstairs by the washing machine."

"It's so dangerous being outside when it gets that stormy. I'm always afraid someone might get struck by lightning, especially near trees."

"We were fine, Mom." She was such a worrier. "We just got a little wet and it was actually a lot of fun."

"It's not fun to be outside in a storm, Henry," she said as he left the kitchen. "Please don't do that again."

Unwilling to get into an argument or have her worry anymore, Henry opened the front door and called over his shoulder, "I'm just going outside to sit on the steps for a little while."

He had just settled himself on the steps and started to daydream about Jenny when Timmy Linder disrupted his reverie.

"Hey, Hank!"

Henry turned to see Timmy sauntering down the street. Timmy wore thick, dark-rimmed glasses, almost the colour of his dark brown hair. His lenses were thick because he was so nearsighted and his eyes appeared about the size of a dime.

"Geez, I was looking all over for you after class this morning. Where did you go? And, by the way, did you see that blond who moved in down the street? I just walked past her house, and man is she good-looking!"

"Yeah, I met her already. Her name is Jenny. I took her to Balfour this afternoon to pick up some registration forms."

"No kidding, you took that girl to school? You lucky dog, you. What's she like?"

Henry pushed himself off the step and walked over to his friend, who was leaning on the top rail of the fence.

"Take it easy, Timmy. You'll get to meet her soon enough. She's really nice. How was school today?"

"Boring as usual. I can't stand math, and I can't stand Mr. Morgan. He makes everyone feel like they're idiots."

"Well, just make sure you pass. You don't want to have him again next year."

Just then Mr. Linder called out from across the street, "Timmy! Get your ass home. You got work to do."

"Oh geez, he saw me. I was supposed to do my chores before supper. I'll come back after."

"Maybe I'll see you tomorrow, Timmy. I'm feeling pretty tired tonight. Think I'll go to bed early."

"Jenny take too much out of you?" Timmy teased, pushing his glasses back on his nose, not realizing how close he was to the truth.

"Yeah, sure," Henry tossed back.

"Okay, see you tomorrow, then, you dirty dog."

Instead of going back home like he was supposed to, Timmy purposely went down Jenny's side of the street and approached her house. Timmy turned to Henry and raised his arms, gesturing that she was no longer there on the steps. Henry could sense Timmy's disappointment.

It was only eight o'clock, but with the highs and lows of the day, Henry really was wiped out. He went inside and headed for his room.

"Going to bed already?" his mother inquired.

"Yeah, I'm kind of tired. G'night, Mom."

Henry went to the bathroom and studied himself in the mirror, thankful to see his usual boyish face maybe looked a bit more grown up and handsome. The Brylcreem made his dark brown hair seem almost black in the bathroom light. A soft sprinkling of fuzz was visible on his chin and upper lip. Henry wished he could shave already. In a way, his features reminded him of some of the football players they'd seen at the school.

Yeah, you're quite a hunk, Henry, athletic build, dark green eyes, a dashing smile, unruly hair—but who are you kidding? He knew some of the football players were better looking than he was. What chance did he have with Jenny compared to them? But, then, she had suggested that they leave. She hadn't even said anything to them. *Maybe....*

He turned out the bathroom light and crossed the hall to his room, promptly opening the window to flush out the heavy stifling air with a rain-soaked breeze. Before pulling down the blind, Henry gazed up at the full moon against a darkening background spattered with the first few sparkling stars. He wondered if Jenny was looking at the moon, too. A sleek silver cloud crossed in front of the moon, cutting it in half. It made him think of how he'd felt before he'd met Jenny.

What an incredible day, he thought as he turned from the window and began to undress. It had been so wonderful to hold Jenny's hand and run with her in the rain and over the wet lawns. He wished that she were beside him or they had a private phone or walkie-talkie so they could talk about the day and tell jokes to each other. He yearned for her in a way he hadn't for anyone else.

Just as he pulled back the sheets to lay down he remembered that he'd still forgotten to ask Jenny what her first name was. He should have looked on the registration form when he'd picked up the envelope at the confectionary. He'd have to ask her tomorrow.

But he never did ... and the oversight would come back to haunt him.

CHAPTER THREE

H ENRY STOOD ON THE FRONT STEPS of his home and drank in the cool, fresh morning air. Thoughts of what the day might bring swirled through his mind. Could it possibly hold the same amount of excitement, of joyous upheaval, as the day before? He couldn't imagine how anything could. He glanced over at Jenny's place and thought about her asleep in her bed, curled up under the covers. He wished he could be beside her, his arms around her, caressing her ...

"Henry!" His mother called, interrupting the pleasurable images in his mind, "don't forget to go see Mr. Engelmann this morning."

Working for Mr. Engelmann really didn't appeal to him. The neighbours all talked about how poorly the shelves were stocked and how they'd started shopping at the new Safeway instead. Mr. Engelmann was getting old, his wife was sick, and the store was rundown, dingy and musty. It was pretty much the last place Henry wanted to spend the summer, especially now that he had met Jenny—still, in spite of himself, Henry felt oddly compelled to go see Mr. Engelmann. Besides, he would never forget that Mr. Englemann's store was where he'd first spoken to the girl of his dreams! To decline Mr. Engelmann's job offer without even talking to him wouldn't be right. He figured he'd at least talk to the old man and help him out today if he needed it.

Henry rode his bike to Engelmann's Grocery and parked it on the west side of the building. Two men were putting up a sign in the empty yard right next to the store. The City of Regina was advertising a lot for sale. Was Mr. Engelmann selling the store?

When he entered, Mr. Engelmann was in his usual spot, leaning on his elbows on the counter. He was so absorbed by the letter he held in front of him, he didn't hear Henry enter.

"'Morning, Mr. Engelmann." When Mr. Engelmann didn't respond, Henry stepped closer and raised his voice a bit. "Good morning, Mr. Engelmann."

Startled and a bit confused, Mr. Engelmann looked up and turned his head side to side before settling on Henry.

"Ah, Henry," he said, taking off his glasses. "Good of you to come. Come over here. I want to talk to you."

It felt to Henry like Mr. Engelmann was examining him under a magnifying glass until after a long moment he finally said, "Henry, I said it yesterday and I'll say it again this morning: I believe you are a good boy with a good heart. I know I can trust you. I would like to hire you to work in my store for the rest of the summer, and after school and on Saturdays when school starts again. I hope you'll be willing."

Mr. Engelmann studied him thoughtfully and Henry steadfastly met the older man's gaze. They looked at each other, neither one wavering. With a start, Henry realized Mr. Engelmann was treating him like an adult and he straightened his shoulders imperceptibly. This was a man-to-man moment; what happened next would determine their relationship.

Mr. Engelmann needed his help, Henry knew. Looking after his ailing wife and trying to keep up with the demands of his business were taking a toll on him. He looked tired, yet his lined face was friendly and kind. Henry was drawn to the warmth of his clear hazel eyes. Despite his worries, Mr. Engelmann seemed … peaceful. A deep feeling of respect for the man who held his gaze filled Henry's chest. Maybe it wouldn't be so bad to work here. Maybe it would even be a good experience. Not only could he help the Engelmanns, but maybe there was something Henry could learn, too. The compulsion he'd felt earlier strengthened. He'd come here to turn down the job, but other words, ones Henry had rarely—if ever—said, came to his lips.

"It would be an honour and a privilege to work for you, Mr. Engelmann!" Henry was surprised by his reaction and could tell Mr. Engelmann was a bit too.

Mr. Engelmann held his gaze a moment longer, the rims of his eyes reddening a bit. After a silent moment, he finally shook Henry's hand and said, "Come, let me show you what I want you to do."

Henry's first responsibility was to keep the store shelves stocked. Mr. Engelmann showed him the back room where stacks of goods had been piled from floor to ceiling. Some boxes were empty, others contained only one or two items and still others had a variety of products in them. Detergents were stored with baking supplies; toothpaste and soups were mixed in with flour and sugar. He had to take down a stack to get at what was needed and then restack everything again. Henry couldn't believe how disorganized the storage room was. It took him almost the entire morning to reshuffle it all and by then he was exhausted from the lifting and sorting. Probably this was the least of Mr. Engelmann's concerns. Henry hoped this effort in organization would make his and Mr. Engelmann's job a lot easier.

After Henry had restocked most of the empty shelves, Mr. Engelmann asked him to watch the store for a few minutes while he checked on Mrs. Engelmann. While he was gone, an elderly lady entered the store. Henry recognized her, she lived next door to the Millers, but he couldn't remember her name. She looked surprised when she saw Henry in the aisle.

"Good morning. Is Mr. Engelmann in?"

"Yes," Henry said, "but he just stepped out for a few minutes." Henry put down the box of detergent he was holding, grabbed a wicker basket and handed it to her. "Here, you can use this if you want."

"Thank you," she said. She took the basket and walked down the first aisle. As Henry took Mr. Engelmann's place behind the counter he noticed the letter the store owner had been reading beside the cash register. He knew he shouldn't but felt compelled to read it, just as he had felt compelled to come and see Mr. Engelmann and accept his job offer. It was from the City of Regina Taxation Office and it was brief:

> *City of Regina*
> *Taxation Division*
>
> *June 1, 1956.*
>
> *Mr. David Engelmann:*
>
> *As per our letter dated March 1, 1956 you were granted 90 days to begin making payments to cover taxes assessed in arrears. Since no substantial payments have been received during this time, we regret to inform you that unless the amount owing on your properties is paid within 30 days, we will have to initiate foreclosure proceedings to cover taxes owed. The outstanding balance to date is $4,240.00.*
>
> *If we do not receive payment by July 6, 1956, action will be taken to sell the vacant lot adjacent to your store.*
>
> *We trust you will address this matter immediately.*
>
> *Yours truly,*
> *Mr. Alex Mahoney*
> *Assistant Director of Taxation*

Henry didn't know what all of it meant but he did understand that Mr. Engelmann owed the city a lot of money and, unless he paid it, he would lose his property. It also dawned on Henry that the sign being put up outside was the city taking action. Mr. Engelmann must not have paid them anything. Concern tugged at Henry.

He'd once overheard Timmy's dad tell his mom that Mr. and Mrs. Engelmann had both been teachers in Austria before they'd came to Canada during the war. Mr. Linder thought it was a shame they hadn't gotten their Canadian teaching certificates instead of running a grocery store. *If the store goes out of business, would Mr. Engelmann still be able to do that?* Henry wondered.

The wicker basket thudded on the counter, startling Henry. He looked up and set the letter aside, hoping the woman hadn't seen him reading it.

"Ah, uh, can I help you?" Henry asked.

"Yes, I want to buy these groceries."

Henry started taking the items out of the basket, hoping Mr. Engelmann would come back before he finished, but that did not happen. When the basket was empty, Henry set it on the floor beside him. Unsure how to operate the cash register, and leery of making a mistake he said, "Would you please wait just a minute while I get Mr. Engelmann?"

When she nodded, he rushed to the back of the store and headed towards the stairway that led up to the Engelmanns' living quarters. His foot had just touched the third step when Mr. Engelmann appeared at the top of the stairs.

"Henry, what is it?"

"There's a customer at the counter and I don't know what to do."

"Yes, yes, of course. I will come," Mr. Engelmann said, hurrying down the stairs. "Hello, Mrs. Tearhorst. How are you, today? So sorry to keep you waiting."

Mr. Engelmann calculated her purchases then packed them in a large brown bag. After she left, Mr. Engelmann showed Henry how to operate the cash register. Henry was so pleased by Mr. Engelmann's trust and confidence in him that he found it hard to concentrate on the explanation. Mr. Engelmann was patient, however, and reviewed everything until Henry knew what he was doing. Just as Henry rang in another practice sale, a tall man wearing a grey flannel suit and a black Stetson walked into the store. He wore rimless glasses and a serious, business like expression.

Mr. Engelmann let out a slow sigh. "Ah, Mr. Mahoney … good morning."

"Good morning, Mr. Engelmann. Have you noticed the sign in the lot next door?"

"No … just a moment Mr. Mahoney." Turning to his new hired hand he motioned to the back room. "Henry, you can continue stocking the shelves. I have some business to discuss with Mr. Mahoney."

"Sure Mr. Engelmann." Henry went to the far aisle and checked the shelves that needed stock. He couldn't help overhearing the discussion at the counter.

"… The director wanted to put both properties up for sale, but I talked him out of it, Mr. Engelmann. Hopefully the sale of the lot will help pay most of the arrears. If not …" he gestured at the store around him with a half shrug.

"That is kind of you to assist me. It has been a struggle these past two years keeping up with Mrs. Engelmann's medical expenses and maintaining the store … but that is not your concern, Mr. Mahoney. I know you are doing your job and I have to do mine. I hired a new employee this morning and perhaps together we can turn things around."

"You mean that young boy you were talking with when I came in?" Mr. Mahoney gave Mr. Engelmann a skeptical look and lowered his voice. "Perhaps someone older and more experienced might be of more value—"

Mr. Engelmann smiled at his creditor. "We shall see Mr. Mahoney."

"Well, I wish you the best, Mr. Engelmann. I don't know how much longer I can hold things off."

"Thank you, Mr. Mahoney, I know. You have already been most kind."

After the tax man left, only three more customers came in before lunch. Mr. Engelmann introduced Henry each time as his new assistant and let Henry ring in the sales.

"Well, it's almost lunchtime. You better go home and have something to eat. You did a good job this morning, Henry."

"Thank you," Henry said. "Do you want me to come back after lunch?"

"Yes, if you can. Mrs. Engelmann is not feeling well today and needs me for awhile. I may have to get the doctor."

Mr. Engelmann's furrowed brow of concern for his wife haunted Henry on the way home. And what was he going to do about the money he owed the city? Four thousand dollars was a lot and it was clear the store wasn't very busy. That Mr. Mahoney seemed to have doubts about his ability to help Mr. Engelmann, but Henry was determined to do as much as he could.

He purposefully biked past his house to see if Jenny was outside. She wasn't. The inside door was closed against the storm door, too, so it was likely no one was home. It bothered him that he didn't know her whereabouts. He had just turned his bike around and started home when Timmy Linder—on his way home from morning classes—shouted.

"Hey, Hank, wait up! What do you say we go hunt gophers out in the field this afternoon? I just bought some more BBs on Saturday." Timmy's glasses slid down his nose and he shoved them back into place.

"Can't, Timmy. I have to work."

"What do you mean?"

"Mr. Engelmann hired me to work for him at the grocery store and I promised I'd be back this afternoon to help him."

"Geez, Hank, you're not working for that old geezer are you?"

"Oh, he's not so bad once you get to know him ... and I think he needs my help."

"And just how are you gonna help Old Man Engelmann, huh? What do you know about running a store?"

Henry was insulted by his friend's lack of confidence. Timmy had a knack for pushing people's buttons. But instead of getting mad, Henry only shrugged, "Well, I'm learning awfully fast. I already know how to operate the cash register." Trying to change the subject, Henry quickly added, "Besides Tim, you don't have time to hunt gophers, you probably have lots of homework anyway. You don't want to have to take math again, right?"

"I'd sooner die," Timmy agreed, a disgusted look on his face. Still, disappointed that his buddy had taken a job, Timmy continued, "Well, when *are* you going to be home?"

"Maybe three or four. I'll call on you when I get back. Anyway Timmy, I gotta go. Better get home for lunch before I get heck. See ya later."

"Sure, Mr. Businessman. Later, 'gator," Timmy smirked.

Henry sped off home and parked his bike in its spot between the houses. Sure enough, old Mrs. Goronic heard him.

"Henry, when are you going to take my weeds away? If you don't do it soon they will rot and get stinky."

Geez, it had only been a day and already she was blowing things out of proportion. Unable to come up with any more excuses, Henry hopped the fence, went straight over to where she usually put the weeds and took them to the garbage cans in the back alley.

When he returned, she said, "Just wait a minute. I will go get you the five cents."

"Oh, it's okay. You can pay me next time. Mom's waiting for me to have lunch. If I don't get in soon, she'll be mad at me."

"Well, you better get going, then or she will be mad at me, too!"

The aroma of his mother's famous-to-him borscht soup and homemade bread greeted him as he opened the door. In between and during mouthfuls, he recounted what he had done at Mr. Engelmann's store with only a little embellishment.

"Sounds like you're enjoying working there."

Henry stopped eating and looked up. "Yeah … and I didn't think I would."

Later, when Henry returned to the store, he found Mr. Engelmann once again reading the letter. His spectacles hung on the tip of his round nose, threatening to fall off any second. White hair sprouted through the dark grey on the sides of his head and poked through what was left on the top, making him look quite distinguished. In all the years Henry could remember, Mr. Engelmann had worn a sweater vest in a red, blue and grey checkered pattern. Today was no exception. It was buttoned up all the way except for the last two around his mid-section. Henry studied him in the muted light from the store's grimy window: he looked kind of like a benevolent banker or accountant. Too bad he didn't have the money he needed now.

Mr. Engelmann smiled when he saw Henry, quickly folded the letter and slipped it under the cash register.

"What would you like me to do this afternoon?"

"Yes, yes, come. I'll show you."

They walked to the back of the store and through the door that led up to Mr. Engelmann's living quarters on the second level. Instead of going up, they detoured around that flight of stairs to another door. Mr. Engelmann opened it and flipped the light switch.

"Come," he said again.

The narrow stairs creaked under their footfalls as they descended the narrow steps. It took Henry's eyes a few moments to adjust to the dim light from the single bulb at the base of the stairs. On one wall were floor-to-ceiling shelves of goods that Mr. Engelmann used to replenish the stock upstairs. The floor itself was made up of patches of dirt and concrete. Behind the shelves on the east side of the basement was a huge old furnace that had been converted from coal to fuel oil. The odour of the oil mingled with the dank, musty smell of old basements everywhere. Beside the furnace stood an old wringer washer and next to that were several lines of sturdy string running from the wall to a support post for hanging clothes to dry.

In front of the north wall was a makeshift worktable that had not been used for a long time; dust had fallen on it so thickly the top was barely visible. Above the table a few tools hung under a veil of cobwebs. Beside the table was an alcove with two slanted doors midway up the wall to the ceiling. These opened up to the patch of yard behind the store. Sun streaming through the cracks in the doors revealed dancing dust particles and cast sharp bands of light on the rough floor.

Breaking the silence, Mr. Engelmann said, "I don't want to store too much down here anymore. It's getting too hard for me or Anna to carry things up and down. Try to make some room on the shelves upstairs and take up as much as you can."

"Sure, Mr. Engelmann."

As Mr. Engelmann trudged back up the creaky stairs, Henry began studying the goods to see where they might fit on the shelves in the store room upstairs. Everything was coated in dust. The labels on many of the cardboard boxes had yellowed and peeled off, and some showed signs of nibbling mice. Most of the boxes, though, contained canned goods that would still be usable. Henry hurried back upstairs and found a broom and a clean rag. He swept the dust and spider webs off the boxes then cleaned the products off with the rag. After carrying several boxes upstairs, he soon realized he would have to reorganize the upstairs shelves again to make room for all the additional items.

When Mr. Engelmann checked on Henry an hour and a half later, there were boxes everywhere. He stared at Henry and put both hands to his head. "*Ach, mein Gott*, what is going on here?"

Henry called him over to the end of the shelving and explained that he was storing the goods according to category and that each shelf now had similar or related supplies. It would give them more shelf space and make it easier to find things.

Mr. Engelmann looked at Henry quizzically. He then turned and began to study the shelves Henry had already reorganized. Gradually, Henry saw the concern fade from Mr. Engelmann's face and then he nodded.

"Maybe you have a good idea, Henry. Go ahead. Let's see what happens. But first of all, you take a break. Go to the cooler and take whatever drink you want—go out back and sit down a bit."

Henry pulled out a Dr. Pepper from the cooler, pulled off the cap with the cooler's front bottle opener and walked out the back of the store. The sun felt good and instantly thawed the chill he still felt from working downstairs. Just outside the back door were several large crates, the wood stained with age. Henry hopped onto one and folded his legs under him. He placed his drink on his bent legs, put his hands on top of the bottle and rested his chin on top of his hands.

He sipped his drink and took stock. The building sorely needed painting. Where the paint had already peeled away, the bare wood had turned a weathered grey. Over the years, signs advertising various kinds of soft drinks had been nailed over the entire back wall of the store. They were all different shapes and overlapped one another. Henry felt a sudden eagerness to make more improvements. He didn't know how just yet, but he began to get goosebumps thinking about the challenge of it all.

His thoughts turned from work to Jenny. He was surprised that he'd actually been able to think of something other than her. How could someone be so attracted to another person or fall in love so quickly? Henry only knew he wanted to be with her and gaze into her eyes forever. His body tensed as he tried to figure it all out. He raised both shoulders to his ears then deliberately allowed them to fall slack, releasing the pent-up stress.

He put the bottle, which had started to warm, to his lips and guzzled over half the contents in one long swallow, smacking his lips after it went down. When he'd finished, he jumped off the crate and headed back inside, eager to continue what he had started.

As Henry entered the store, he heard Mr. Engelmann talking with someone. *Jenny?* He rushed to the doorway and pushed aside the curtain that separated the stockroom from the store. It *was* Jenny! His heart bucked at the sight of her.

"Hi, Jenny," he said as nonchalantly as he could, trying to hide his surprise and excitement.

"Oh, there you are! Mr. Engelmann just told me you were working for him. That's great!" She rushed towards Henry, grabbing his hands. His face flushed. She dragged him toward the windows at the front. "Look, Henry. Mom and I went shopping for house supplies and things. We went by this wonderful shop and look what I got." Her sparkling eyes beamed as she raised her arms slightly and cocked her hip to one side.

What was she talking about? Oh! New clothes! Miss Universe was modeling in front of him. He scrambled to think of something to say, letting out a sigh of relief when Mr. Engelmann helped him out by saying, "You look beautiful, Jenny."

Henry nodded. She cast her eyes downwards, not waiting for any more compliments, and continued, "And look how shiny my new shoes are!"

Finally finding his tongue, Henry choked out, "Boy, you look great, Jenny." So that's why she hadn't been home at lunch. He was still stunned, but very pleased, that she had come here to show him her new outfit.

"So, when are you done?" she asked with a coy smile.

Henry looked at Mr. Engelmann.

"He needs to clear up what he started so we can walk in the back," the old man replied. "Perhaps, oh, one or two hours," he continued, looking more towards Jenny than to Henry.

"Well, call on me when you're finished, and maybe we can go for a walk or something," Jenny offered.

"Sure, Jenny, see you later, then."

"'Bye, Mr. Engelmann." She turned and danced out the door.

Mr. Engelmann and Henry watched as she left, savouring her youthful gait and playful manner.

"A very nice young lady," Mr. Engelmann commented, "reminds me a little of my Anna." There was a long pause and Henry sensed Mr. Engelmann was reliving some past experience. "I can see you are quite fond of this girl, Henry."

Henry's face reddened again. "Yes, I am." Had he said that out loud? He surprised himself by adding, "I sure am."

Mr. Engelmann raised his eyebrows and looked at Henry above smudged glasses. He nodded slightly and smiled.

Taking Mr. Engelmann's nod as both a sign that he understood and that their conversation was finished, Henry turned and headed back to the storeroom. Jenny's visit fuelled his enthusiasm to finish his work.

Henry stayed much longer than he had intended. In fact, over three hours had elapsed since Jenny left the store, but he got everything organized into categories. Much to his surprise, there were two empty shelves when he was finished, enough room to bring up the remainder of the stock from downstairs. He'd do that in the morning. He took all the empty boxes out back, broke them down and tossed them into the garbage. The back store room looked neat, tidy and organized. He was very proud of this evidence of his hard work.

As Henry headed to the front of the store to leave for the day, Mr. Engelmann came in. He stopped mid-step, his mouth and eyes wide open.

"Why, Henry, this looks beautiful. So clean and tidy."

He moved closer, studying the shelves, turning his head side to side and up and down, staring in disbelief, trailing arthritic fingers over the neat rows of cans and boxes, all facing front. For a moment, Henry thought Mr. Engelmann would tell him to put everything back where it had been. He'd made a lot of changes; it would probably take Mr. Engelmann months to get used to it

Finally, Mr. Engelmann spoke. "*Ach, mein lieber Gott.* My, my, Henry. In all the fourteen years I have owned this store, this storage room has never looked so good. I am very proud of you. Thank you for a job well done. I hope Anna is well enough to come down and look at what you have accomplished. It will make her very happy."

Mr. Engelmann smiled. He surveyed the shelves once more and when he looked back at Henry, Henry was surprised to see tears welling in the old man's eyes. Unaccustomed to seeing a grown man display such emotion, Henry quickly looked down. "Thank you, Henry," Mr. Engelmann stuck out his hand towards his new employee.

Henry met the watery gaze. "You're welcome, Mr. Engelmann." He shook the trembling hand, unbidden tears in his eyes too. "Well, I better get going. See you tomorrow." Henry turned and literally floated out of the store.

Since he wouldn't see Jenny until after supper now, he took his time biking home, his mind flip-flopping between Jenny and Mr. Engelmann and how amazing it was that he'd had two great experiences two days in a row. He felt like he'd known Jenny for a lifetime and he could hardly wait to share his success at Mr. Engelmann's store with her.

As his house came into view down the block, Henry remembered he had promised Timmy they could hang out together after work. Tim would go ape if he avoided him again. Until Jenny's arrival, Timmy had been one of his best friends. It would be wrong to simply abandon him now.

As Henry pulled up to his house, he was so deep in thought he didn't notice Jenny standing at her fence gate with Timmy Linder until the very last second. His heart lurched. Was Timmy making time with his girl? Henry sincerely hoped not. They turned towards him as he pulled up.

"Hey, Hank, come on over," Timmy shouted. "How's Mr. Businessman? How many old ladies did you coo and woo today? And how was the old geezer? You get a raise already?"

"Timmy, you're awful," Jenny scolded with a smile. "You're just awful," she said again, seeing that he had not taken any offense and rather enjoyed her reaction.

"Oh, never mind him, Jenny, that's just Timmy's way. How was school today, Tim?"

"Man, it's a drag and now I have to stay in tonight and study for a test tomorrow. The whole thing's stupid. I hate it, and I can't stand Mr. Morgan. I'll be so glad when this is all over." After a brief pause to shake off those ugly thoughts, he added, "By the way, Hank, my mom and dad want to go to the beach tomorrow as soon as my class is over. Wanna come along?"

Henry inwardly sighed with relief that Timmy had homework tonight and wouldn't be around the next day. It would leave him free to be with Jenny without Timmy tagging along.

"Nah, I can't," Henry said, feigning a sorrowful tone to hide his elation. "I promised Mr. Engelmann I would work tomorrow and Saturday at his store."

"Geez, Hank, you're not going to work for him again are you? This is summer holidays. Time to have fun and relax. What's wrong with you? You're spoiling everything."

"Well, Tim," Henry began, "Mr. Engelmann needs my help and—"

"Needs your help?" Timmy spluttered. "Who are you trying to kid? What can you do that's so important and helpful?"

"Well, I think it's wonderful, Henry," Jenny interjected.

"So, I see you two met," Henry said to Timmy, trying to change the subject.

"Yeah, I saw this beautiful blond sitting on the steps and I just knew she'd want to meet me." Henry knew Timmy was trying to be funny, but knew his friend well enough to realize that Timmy probably meant it, too. "So, I took it upon myself to come over and introduce her to the man of her dreams."

"Yes, it was very nice of Tim to come over and introduce himself like every good neighbour should. And I do appreciate—"

"Timmy! Tim!" came Timmy's mother's voice. "Time for dinner, and don't forget you have to study tonight and pack for the cottage."

"Yeah, yeah, I'm coming. Well, don't you two do anything I wouldn't do," he said with an exaggerated wink. Then, giving Henry a sharp poke on the shoulder, he said, "Don't work too hard, Mr. Businessman."

Henry was relieved to see Timmy go. As much as he liked Timmy, there were times, like now, when he wanted to haul off and give him a smack. Henry turned to Jenny. She was smiling at him.

"So, what are you doing after supper?" she asked.

Henry thought for a second. "I was hoping we could go for a walk. I want to tell you what happened today."

"I was hoping we could go for a walk, too. I'll wait for you on my front step after we've finished eating."

Henry smiled, feeling good again, free to concentrate on

Jenny and on how much he liked her. "See you soon." Henry turned his bike around and headed home.

As he opened the door, he saw his dad duck into the kitchen. It looked like one of those rare nights when his dad didn't have to work overtime at the plant and they could have a family supper together.

Without waiting for his mom to ask him how his day had gone, he said, "Boy, did I have a good day at the grocery store!"

His mom and dad stopped eating and looked up at him.

"Oh?" said his dad.

"Well, what happened?" his mom probed.

Henry told them about the storage room and the basement, his efforts to clean the downstairs and reorganize the shelves, and what Mr. Engelmann had said about never having seen the storage room look so neat and organized. Henry beamed at his parents, who beamed back at him.

"Well, you do have a knack for organizing and making things look nice," his mom said.

"You did a good thing today, son," his dad added.

Henry told his dad about the basement, how poorly lit it was and how he had tripped once or twice on the uneven floor. "I don't know how on earth Mrs. Engelmann can even find her way down there to wash clothes. They should have at least two more lights. And, Dad, the doors to the backyard where they sometimes bring down boxes are open and loose. The air just pours through all the cracks, and in the wintertime it must be freezing cold. Do you think you might have time to have a look at it?" Before his dad could answer, Henry excitedly continued, "I also noticed a couple of mice down there when I was moving boxes. Can I take the two mousetraps in the garage?"

His mom and dad exchanged glances before his dad turned to him. "Sure, and maybe mention to Mr. Engelmann that I have a door in the garage and some insulation that I don't need anymore. If he's interested, I can bring them over Saturday morning when I'm off work."

"That's nice, Bill," Henry's mom said, putting her hand on his dad's shoulder.

"He's a proud man, Henry, and may consider this to be charity. He may not accept our offering, so be careful how you put it to him. Make it sound as if he is doing us a favour taking these things off our hands."

Henry nodded. "I think you're right, Dad, and thanks for doing this." His dad smiled back, then turned to his mom. "By the way, Mary, Jim told me ... "

His father's words drifted away as Henry visualized where the door could go in Mr. Engelmann's basement and where the insulation would be best put to use. Still engrossed in his fix-it-up thoughts, Henry blurted out, "Where can I get some paint?"

His mom and dad glanced at him, somewhat startled and a little annoyed.

"What are you talking about, Henry?" his mom asked. "What paint?"

"Mr. Engelmann's basement needs to be painted and so does his storeroom. In fact, the whole store could use a coat. Everything's so old and dirty."

"Well, there's some paint downstairs that we won't be needing anymore," Bill replied. "And one of the fellows at work told me he'd bought brand new paint that had been mixed wrong for next to nothing at the paint store. You might want to phone Northern Paint and bike up there next week. It's only a few blocks down on Winnipeg Street. Just watch out for the traffic and don't haul any more than a gallon at a time. If there's a lot, tell me and I'll pick it up after work."

Henry's face lit up. "That's a great idea, Dad! I'll find the time to get over there tomorrow. He stood up, hardly able to contain his excitement. "Excuse me, I gotta go." He could hardly wait to share all this with Jenny.

His mother and father chuckled as he dashed from the table.

Henry rushed into the bathroom and washed his hands and face. He also splashed a little water on his hair and rubbed in just a little dab of Brylcreem. He combed his hair back instead of parting it to see if he looked more grown up that way. He thought he did, but it was too much change for one day. He quickly parted his hair the way he usually did and raced for the front door. As he passed the living room, his mom and dad looked up.

"Nice hair, son," his dad said before turning back to the paper.

"Off to see Jenny?" his mom dared ask.

"Yeah," Henry blurted as he bounded out of the house, letting the storm door slam shut behind him.

Jenny was sitting on her front steps. His pounding heart nearly burst from his chest at the sight of her; he was already anticipating her hand in his. Her face brightened when she saw him.

"Hi, Jenny," he called out when he arrived at the gate. "Have you had supper yet? I hope I'm not too early for our walk?"

"Oh, no, I was waiting for you. Dad had to work late again tonight so Mom and I ate early." She stood and walked towards him. "Which way should we go?"

"Doesn't matter to me. Anywhere, I guess. I have a lot I want to tell you."

"Okay, well then, let's just walk down to College Avenue. It's only a few blocks away and then we can circle back."

"Sounds good to me."

The sky for the most part was clear, except for a towering build-up of cumulonimbus clouds in the distant west. Some reached so high they hid the bright sun as it crept towards the horizon. Although it was already after seven, one of the best things about summer in the prairies was the long days; it would be at least another couple of hours before the sun finally set and darkness settled. There was just enough of a breeze to move Jenny's hair off to the side, exposing her ear and the tiny stud glistening on her earlobe. As they walked, Henry moved to the half of the sidewalk nearest the traffic.

"Why do you walk on the outside? I noticed you did that yesterday too."

"My dad always does that when he's walking with my mom. I asked him about it once and he said that it was to protect his girl from any harm that might come her way. It has do to with chivalry or something like that. I always thought it was kind of neat."

"Well, that's very thoughtful," Jenny said. "I must say that it does make me feel protected."

"Boy, did I have a good day at the grocery store."

"Yes, so you said when Timmy was over. What happened?"

The words bubbled out of him. He explained how he had organized the basement and the shelves upstairs, and how pleased Mr. Engelmann was, adding a few more embellishments to the story than he'd told his parents.

"That sounds great, Henry, and you seem so excited about what you accomplished. I'm thrilled for you!" Jenny's eyes were bright and happy. To know she understood how he felt—he thought he would burst any second. He moved closer to Jenny, wanting to touch her hand.

Their arms swung side by side and at times their hands brushed slightly. Henry began to purposely stick his little finger out a little bit more with each pass. Jenny responded by letting her little finger protrude a little more each time too, until finally their little fingers locked. Then without hesitation or changing the rhythm, they started swinging their arms. After several swings and steps forward in silence, Jenny, sensing that their little fingers couldn't hold on much longer like that, released her finger and purposely slid her warm hand into his, sending Henry instantly to cloud nine. Neither of them said a word for the longest time.

"What do you have planned tomorrow at the store?"

Henry explained his dad had offered to help and was willing to donate an old door and insulation, and that he himself planned to get some paint to spruce up the store.

They walked for about an hour and a half, stopping every now and then to comment on the colour and architecture of the houses. Jenny definitely liked blue; Henry liked it best of all, too. Their favourites were the houses with steep roofs and dormers.

"And I just love those lilacs," Jenny said, pointing out one house in particular with large green bushes in front of it. "It's too bad they're not blooming anymore—they must be gorgeous in the spring. Lilac is my favourite perfume," she added, by way of explanation.

Henry began to imagine he and Jenny married and owning a house like that someday, and what it would be like to give her a bouquet of lilacs from their own yard. A rush of excitement spread through him like wildfire at the very thought of it.

So he wasn't too surprised that Jenny's thoughts seemed to echo his.

"I can just picture my daughter in one of those bedrooms with the dormers," she said, "That would be Camilla's room."

"What do you mean? Camilla who?"

"Oh, last winter my parents and I went to Jamaica, and the maid who did up our room was called Camilla. It's so different. I just love that name. Don't you?"

"Sure. I've never heard it before, but yeah, I like it, too."

"Well, I told the maid right then and there that when I had my first daughter I was going to call her Camilla."

He squeezed Jenny's hand and she leaned into him. He could walk with her forever, they didn't even need words.

Cooler air swept in with the evening and the light dimmed under the shade of the huge elm trees. But even in the evening chill Henry felt warm inside. He wanted to kiss Jenny. Maybe just on the cheek. His hand tightened on hers. As they neared home, Jenny broke a long silence.

"I'm so glad you're here in this neighbourhood and that I met you. I just feel so comfortable and relaxed around you."

Henry wasn't sure how to respond. He was quiet for a moment, then mustered the courage to say, "I feel real good when I'm around you, too, Jenny."

As they reached their homes, Henry's heartbeat grew to a roar in his ears. Could he kiss her? Would she let him? But the roaring faded abruptly when they got to Jenny's gate and Timmy hollered out his window across the street, "Hey lovers, what's with the holding hands already!"

Henry was glad it was getting dark so Jenny couldn't see how bright his face had become. They let go of each other's hand and turned to face Timmy.

"Thought you were studying," Henry called back.

"Well, you can study and spy too, you know. Someone has to keep the neighbourhood informed."

"Timmy, get in here," his dad bellowed. "You should be studying. If you fail that test tomorrow you're not going to the cottage."

"Yeah, yeah, I'm coming," he said, and the window slammed shut with a bang.

"Well, Jenny, this has been a long day," Henry tried for casual but came off sounding more like his dad.

"Yeah, you had a very busy day … and it sounds like you're going to have another one tomorrow. But we forgot to pick up bread today while Mom and I were shopping, so I'll probably see you at Mr. Engelmann's store in the morning."

"Oh, good!"

The porch light came on above Jenny's front door.

"Hi, Henry," Mrs. Sarsky called out from behind the screen door. "Jenny said you're working at the grocery store over the summer."

"Yes, that's right," he raised his voice a bit so she could hear him.

"It's nice to see a hard-working young person. Well, Jenny, you better come in and get ready for bed. I think Dad will be along anytime now."

"I better go, too," Henry said, disappointed and a little relieved that the kiss wasn't about to happen now. "Good night, Jenny. Good night, Mrs. Sarsky."

"Good night, Henry," both said, almost in unison.

Henry turned and headed home. The evening was losing its last light and the sun had handed the sky over to a bright full moon. As the first star appeared, Henry made a wish.

This was the second night in a row he had noticed the moon. He hadn't really paid much attention to it up until now. As he gazed upward, he wondered what it would be like to watch the moonrise with Jenny, just the two of them holding hands all through the night.

His mom and dad were in the living room when he got in. His

dad was reading and his mom knitted while listening to the radio. Henry could hardly wait until they could afford a television.

"Have a nice walk?" his mom asked.

"Yeah."

Before Henry could add anything else, his dad said, "While you were gone, I checked down in the basement for paint. I brought up four gallons you can have them if you want. I left a tray, brush and roller at the back door for you as well."

"Gee, thanks a lot, Dad! That's great. What colours are they?"

"I think two are white, and the other two have numbers on them. I can't remember what colours they are."

Henry went out the back door to the landing. There was the paint his dad had found. Henry picked up one with numbers on it but didn't recognize the colour either. There was, however, a small trace of paint on the lip from the last time the tin had been opened. It looked like a shade of blue, but it was hard to tell. He set the can down and returned to the kitchen. He was anxious to get started. He wished it was morning already.

"G'night, Mom and Dad," Henry called out as he walked down the hall to his room. It was cool enough that he decided to put on his pajamas. Instead of reading, as he usually did, he turned off the lights and lay in bed thinking about what to say to Mr. Engelmann about the paint and the door and the insulation.

"Dad's right," he murmured. "Mr. Engelmann is a proud man." Henry considered it for a minute until he had an idea he thought might work.

That issue resolved, his thoughts turned again to Jenny. How they had held hands and what she had said about how he made her feel. Henry liked that, he liked that a lot. The name Camilla popped into his mind. It really was a nice name. *Our first daughter, Camilla.* A kind of restless anticipation flooded him and he chuckled at the very thought of it all. He sure would have liked to kiss Jenny, even if it had only been on the cheek. If it hadn't been for Timmy and then Mrs. Sarsky, he would have.

But it would feel so wonderful to put his lips on hers.

He could hardly wait.

CHAPTER FOUR

HENRY GULPED DOWN HIS BREAKFAST then took two gallons of paint and hung the handle of each can on his bicycle's handlebars.

"Be careful with all that," his mom cautioned as he swung his leg over the frame and pedalled off, wobbly at first and then straightening out as he picked up speed.

When he reached Victoria Avenue, he stopped and slid off the bike. Better to cross the street on foot. After a short wait, a break in the traffic appeared, and he steered his bike to the other side and onto Mr. Engelmann's front lawn. He again secured his bike to the fencepost with a chain and lock. He would need to talk to Mr. Engelmann about finding a safer spot for his bike; even with a lock on it he sure didn't want it to get stolen. With the wire handles of the full paint tins pressing deep grooves in his palms, he entered the store.

Mr. Engelmann was behind the counter, counting out the float for the day. He peered over his glasses as Henry entered.

"Good morning, Henry, you're early. What's that you're carrying?"

"Oh, this is just some old paint Dad was getting rid of and he said it was okay to take it. After you were so happy with the way the shelves looked, I thought maybe I could paint the basement a little. I hope you don't mind. I was so excited about making the basement look nice I could hardly sleep. That's why I'm early this morning."

Henry beamed at Mr. Engelmann and waited for him to say something. Mr. Engelmann was silent for a long time and didn't take his gaze from Henry.

"I don't wish to discourage you, Henry. Still … are you sure it's old paint? I don't want something for nothing, Henry."

"Yes, Mr. Engelmann. My dad was going to throw it out, and I thought it would be such a waste—especially since it could brighten up your basement."

"Well, it would help Anna to see things better down there. And last night after I told her what you did to the shelves, as sick as she was she made her way down to see for herself. I've never seen her look so surprised and happy in a long, long time."

Henry's heart soared. Working to improve this place was the right thing to do, he was sure—he felt it in his gut.

"What about a brush? Are you going to put the paint on with your hand?" Mr. Engelmann quipped.

Uh oh. He'd forgotten the other painting supplies.

"Uh, no. I've got some stuff to paint with. I'll go get it. Be back in a little bit." Henry was afraid if he told Mr. Engelmann it was still at home, he'd change his mind.

When Henry returned, Mr. Engelmann gave him a hard stare.

"Where were you? I went looking for you, but you were nowhere in sight. I was about to call your mom."

Henry was totally out of breath from the mad dash home and back. He inhaled and let the air out slowly. "I forgot something at home and went to get it. Sorry if I worried you, Mr. Engel-mann," he made for the storeroom, "I'll go directly downstairs and get painting right away."

"Not so fast, Henry. Does your dad know you have his brush and roller?"

"Oh yes, he even set them out for me last night. He said I was welcome to use his stuff."

"Do I need to call him?"

"Oh no, but wait …" Henry paused for a minute wondering if this was the right time to tell him about the door and insulation. *Well,* he thought, *if I don't do it now, I might chicken out later.*

"Yes, yes, what is it?"

"Well, there is one other thing. We were going through the garage last night, and there's this old door and half a bag of insulation that we don't need anymore either. I told my dad that you could use an extra door in front of those old ones in the cellar. That would help keep the cold out, especially in the wintertime."

Again, Mr. Engelmann stared at Henry in a sort of dumbfounded way. "What is going on here, Henry? No, no, I don't accept charity. No, no, I cannot take that."

"But you need it," Henry protested. "It's cold down there. The cellar doors have so many holes and cracks."

"For fourteen years it has been like that, and we have survived without anyone's help."

"Boy, my dad sure was right about you," Henry muttered.

"What was that, Henry?" Mr. Engelmann furrowed his brow.

"Dad said that even though we didn't need the door and wanted to get rid of it, you probably wouldn't take it. He figured you might buy it, though, and told me to tell you that he wouldn't sell it for more than a dollar. It would save him having to take it to the nuisance grounds."

Mr. Engelmann looked away as he considered. "That is a fair price, but I have no tools." He met Henry's gaze again.

"Dad said he'd be willing to come over on Saturday morning to put it up just to get rid of it. We really need to make more room in our garage."

After a brief pause, Mr. Engelmann agreed. "Okay, okay, you tell your father I will pay him a dollar for the door, and if he puts it up, I will give him three pounds of salami for this work. If he accepts that then it's a fair exchange."

"My dad will be so glad to clear out the garage, I'm sure you have yourself a deal," Henry said. "Now, I better get downstairs and start cleaning up so I can paint."

As Henry passed him on his way downstairs, he heard Mr. Engelmann mutter, "Yes, I think this is fair. I'm sure Anna will approve when I tell her."

That made Henry think of something else. "Oh, by the way, Mr. Engelmann, do you have a 100-watt bulb? The one downstairs is only a 60-watt. It will give me more light when I paint."

"Yes, yes, of course. I'll get you one right away." Mr. Engelmann muttered some more as he moved things around. "Ah, there it is." A moment later, Mr. Engelmann held not only a bulb but also a flashlight. "Here you go. That should help with the light down there." He hesitated and then asked, "Do you know how to paint? Do you need help?"

"Nah, I'll be okay. I painted a lot last summer—my dad showed me how to use the roller and fill the brush when we painted the fence. I got so good at it, Mrs. Goronic next door gave me a dollar to paint hers too. So I have lots of experience."

"What do you mean, 'fill the brush'? I've never heard of such a thing. Is it a special brush?"

"Oh no," Henry replied, pulling out the brush tucked into his back pocket.

"But that is an ordinary brush. How do you fill it?"

Henry held the brush in front of him and explained how all brushes have a hollow inside the surrounding bristles. "When you paint, most people simply dip the brush into the paint can, and then wipe off the excess on the side off the can or tray. My dad said when you do that, you're removing most of the paint except for a little at the tip that usually drips as you carry the brush from the can to what you are painting. And that little bit of paint doesn't go very far."

"Yes, that is true."

"Well, he taught me to pour the paint into a tray and dip the brush into the paint in the tray."

"And so?"

"Well, after I dip the brush into the paint, I tap it against the upper part of the tray, up and down vertically like this." Henry demonstrated the movement using the dry brush against the palm of his hand. "When you tap straight down, the bristles spread apart, exposing the hollow inside. When you pull up, as the bristles come back together, they suck up the paint into the hollow of the brush, loading it. When you do it that way your brush holds a lot more paint and because the paint gets sucked up into the hollow, the brush doesn't drip. That way you can paint more with each brushstroke and get the job done faster and easier."

"Wonderful, that is wonderful, Henry. It makes such good sense. In all my years of painting I have never thought of doing such a thing." Mr. Engelmann looked at the brush in Henry's hand and then at him and just shook his head. "I don't think you need my help," he said sheepishly. He turned back to the cash register. The last thing Henry heard before he went downstairs was, "It is hard to believe. He's such a young boy."

Downstairs, Henry retrieved a crate from the corner and set it down just under the light. He turned the flashlight on, stepped on the crate and changed the lightbulb. It was a big improvement, but the basement still could have used more light, especially near the washing machine. He stepped off the crate and headed there.

In the beam of the flashlight, Henry discovered another light fixture just in front of the workbench. There was no bulb. Dragging the crate over, he twisted the 60-watt bulb into it. The rusted socket gave him a little trouble, but as soon as the bulb started to turn it sprang to life, heating his fingers. Just those two simple things changed the whole atmosphere down there. After lunch he would exchange the 60-watt for another 100-watt, which would add even more light.

Henry went over to the cellar doors. The padlock only appeared to be locked and he took it off the hasp. Mr. Engelmann must've lost the key but still wanted the basement to look secure. That explained why Mr. Engelmann locked the door leading to the basement at the end of the day. Henry pushed open the cellar doors, flooding the room with sunlight. Fresh air and sunlight flowed into the basement, invigorating the atmosphere but clearly revealing all the work yet to be done. Henry figured he should sweep, take out all the garbage and set the mousetraps before he started painting.

He took the two mousetraps from his pocket and placed them behind the box where he had seen at least one mouse scurry the previous afternoon, then turned his attention to the rest of the space. He filled three garbage cans with old boards, tin cans, bags, papers, wire, old rope and other bits and pieces, carrying it all out through the cellar doors. Just as he lugged out the last load, a mousetrap went off. He set down the garbage can and checked the traps. He had caught one. He deposited the mouse in the garbage can, returned the trap to its spot along the wall, and reset it. By the time he went to pick up the garbage can, he heard the trap snap again. As he swept the basement and moved boxes around, he caught four more mice.

Around ten o'clock, Mr. Engelmann called his name. "Henry, come up and get a drink from the cooler and sit down a minute."

Henry brushed the dust from his clothes and headed upstairs.

When Mr. Engelmann saw him, his eyes opened wide above his glasses, "*Mein Gott*, Henry, you look like a ghost. You better go wash up a little. Go, you will see what I mean," he said, shooing Henry to the bathroom.

One look in the bathroom mirror confirmed Mr. Engelmann's assessment. He did look like a ghost. Henry went outside to brush himself off out back so it wouldn't all turn to mud when he started washing. Satisfied he'd swept off as much as he could, he returned to the sink, emerging fresh and clean a moment later. He opened the cooler and snagged an Orange Crush, Jenny's favourite, before heading back to the storeroom where Mr. Engelmann was getting down supplies to restock the shelves.

"I caught six mice this morning."

Mr. Engelmann turned and looked down at Henry from the ladder. "How could you catch mice without traps?"

"Oh, I brought a couple along with me this morning and set them here before I started to clean up."

"There were that many?"

"Well, there's a lot of food down there, Mr. Engelmann. Now that everything is getting sorted out downstairs, they'll come up here if we don't catch them."

"Yes, yes, of course, we must catch them. I didn't even think we had any, though Anna did tell me she sometimes hears something while she washes clothes. I thought it was just her imagination. After your break, I will give you some cheese so you can catch some more."

"Actually, Mr. Engelmann, I don't think I need any."

"But Henry, it attracts the mice to the trap."

"That may be," Henry replied, "but I caught six already this morning without anything."

"But how did you attract them?"

"My dad told me all you have to do to catch a mouse is to put the trap against a wall. A mouse will always run with its shoulder brushing against the side of a wall because it has poor eyesight and that gives it a sense of security. My dad said they used to have a real mouse problem where he works and the exterminators told him that was the way to do it. Besides, if you put cheese or peanut butter on the trap, it makes a mess and dries up after while, which makes it harder to set the trap."

Mr. Engelmann shook his head from side to side. "It's hard to believe that you know so much."

Mrs. Engelmann appeared at the top of the stairs. She was thin and frail. She seemed taller than Mr. Engelmann, but perhaps her slight figure only made it appear so. She had a kindly face, and her lips had a curl to them as if they were ready to smile. She looked pale, however, and her dark-circled eyes hinted at weariness. Her hair was grey, much like Mr. Engelmann's, but she wore it in a sleek knot at the back of her head. A full-length wool bathrobe, maroon in colour, brightened her pale complexion. Well-used slippers hugged tiny feet.

Henry watched her negotiate the stairs, uncertain whether

or not to offer help.

When she reached the bottom and didn't have to concentrate on the steps anymore, she looked up at Henry and smiled, showing surprisingly white teeth. Her face lit up as she spoke.

"I had to come down and meet you, Henry. All night long David kept talking about you and how well you organized the shelves. Well, I had to come down and look for myself and I, too, am amazed at what you have done in such a short time."

Henry couldn't help but smile at her warmth and charm. Her words were sincere and he was touched.

"Thank you, Mrs. Engelmann," he half-mumbled, suddenly shy.

Mrs. Engelmann shuffled towards him. It was easy to see she had once been a very attractive lady, and even in a bathrobe she had a sophisticated look about her. When she reached him, she took his hand. "Thank you for your help. We will pay you what we can."

The look in her eyes and the tenderness of her touch was payment enough, Henry thought.

"You're welcome, Mrs. Engelmann," Henry said, again, more firmly this time. He had never received such heartfelt thanks from anyone before, and he knew right then and there that he would do all he could to help them. "Nice meeting you, Mrs. Engelmann," he looked down at the pop bottle, unable to absorb the gratefulness in her eyes anymore. Such thanks was humbling. "Guess I'll go out back and have my drink."

"Yes, yes," she said, sounding like her husband.

Once outside, Henry sat on the crate with his legs folded under him and thought about the morning. How much would they be able to pay him? He knew they would insist. Until Mrs. Engelmann brought it up, he hadn't given it much thought. It didn't even matter because what he was doing made him feel so good inside. But what surprised him most of all was that he hadn't even wanted to talk to Mr. Engelmann in the first place, let alone work for him. He couldn't imagine Timmy working here. A bright sheen glazed his eyes as he told himself for the very first time in his life, *I'm glad I'm me.*

After putting the empty pop bottle in the trash, Henry went downstairs, refreshed and bubbling with enthusiasm to get back to work. He checked the mousetraps and found two more mice. After throwing them out and resetting the traps once more, he opened the first gallon of paint and stirred it thoroughly the way his dad had drilled into him the previous summer. By lunchtime, one whole wall and a bit of another had a coat of white paint, and three more mice had met their doom. Before heading upstairs for home, he surveyed his work. It was really starting to take shape. Thanks to the new lightbulbs and white paint, the basement looked much cleaner and brighter.

Upstairs, Mr. Engelmann was finishing with a customer and packing her purchases into a shopping bag.

"Thank you, Mrs. Thomas. Please come again and say hello to Mr. Thomas for me." It seemed like Mr. Engelmann knew everyone by name and could even remember special occasions like birthdays and anniversaries.

"Well, I'm going home for lunch, Mr. Engelmann. See you in about an hour."

"Yes, yes, but before you go, could you watch the store for a few minutes. I heard Anna call while I was waiting on Mrs. Thomas."

"Sure, Mr. Engelmann."

Just as Mr. Engelmann left, the front door swung open with a sudden thrust and Eddy Zeigler walked in. Henry knew of him and his east-end gang. A cold shiver ran down Henry's spine as Eddy made his way to the counter. He remembered only too well Halloween night in fifth grade when Eddy and his gang had pounced on Henry and his friend, Gary. They were heading home after a night of trick-or-treating with pillowcases full of treats when Eddy and his hooligans came along and demanded they hand over the candy. When the boys surrounded them, there was nothing Henry and Gary could do but surrender their loot. Henry could still recall how helpless he'd felt, holding back tears as Eddy and his gang, sneering and laughing, walked off with all their Halloween treats. Henry hadn't run into Eddy since, but he'd often heard of the trouble Eddy got into.

Eddy stood a yard or so in front of the counter and stared hard at Henry, maybe lost in memory as well. Eddy was short and slim, and the same age as Henry, yet his tough guy attitude sent shivers of fear through just about everyone—even guys twice his size. He wore his hair brushed up from his forehead into a high single wave. Secretly, he probably hoped it made him look taller, but it didn't do much to disguise his narrow face.

Eddy shoved his hands into his pockets and fumbled for some change. Just the way he stood there made Henry realize what looked so funny. Eddy's oversized shirt hung out over baggy zootsuit-type pants that tapered in to hug his ankles, making his already long feet seem twice as big. He looked like a clown.

The thought squelched some of the intimidation Henry felt.

Eddy brought out two quarters and tossed them onto the marble counter with a clang. One rolled for a second before it stopped at Henry's hand. "Gimme a pack of Black Cat smokes."

Henry knew Eddy smoked but wasn't sure if he should sell them to him or not. *Geez, guess I better though, otherwise there might be a ruckus and I don't want to get Old Man Engelmann all upset.*

Henry turned, grabbed a pack of smokes and tossed them on the counter in an attempt to show Eddy that he wasn't completely cowed. He took the quarters, rang in the cigarettes and laid the change in front of Eddy.

Eddy took the smokes, unwrapped the cellophane wrapper, opened the package, pulled off the aluminum foil, crumpled it along with the cellophane and let both fall on the floor. He pulled out a smoke and put it into the side of his mouth, closed the pack and slipped it into his front shirt pocket in exchange for a pack of matches. He struck a match with a quick swipe, lit the cigarette and let the match fall as well. He took a deep drag, squinted his left eye and stared right into Henry's. Trailing smoke covered his words, "Keep the change, kid."

Eddy took another deep drag, took hold of the cigarette with his thumb and second finger, held it in mid-air and jabbed his straight forefinger at Henry, turned and walked out.

Sweat rolled down Henry's sides beneath his armpits and anger burned in his chest. He shouldn't have allowed himself to be intimidated by that puny punk. Shaking off the feeling, Henry scraped the change towards him and put it in his pocket.

"Okay, Henry, you can go now," puffed Mr. Engelmann as he hurried down the stairs.

"See you after lunch."

"Yes, yes, an hour is just fine. Watch the busy street."

"I will."

Henry skirted around the counter, picked up Eddy's garbage and tossed it in the trash then ran out of the store.

His mom had lunch ready as usual. She liked to add spices or onions to a meal, creating an appetite-whetting aroma, and today was no exception. *Mmm. Chili.* Henry told his mom about his morning and all the mice he had caught. She told Henry not to mention the mice thing to anyone for fear that it might discourage customers from shopping at Mr. Engelmann's store. And while she cautioned him not to take on too much responsibility, she did say she was proud of him for having such a good attitude.

Henry knocked on Jenny's door before heading back to the store after lunch. A moment later, Jenny's mom appeared.

"Hi, Henry."

"Hi, Mrs. Sarsky. Is Jenny in?"

"Actually, she went down to Engelmann's to pick up some bread. You must have just missed her."

"Oh. I was home for lunch. Well, maybe I'll run into her on the way. Thanks, Mrs. Sarsky."

As he turned to go down the stairs, Mrs. Sarsky said, "Oh, by the way, Henry, we'll be out for dinner tonight and Jenny is coming along, so she won't be home."

"Okay, thanks for telling me." Henry hustled to his bike as fast as he could, ignoring Mrs. Goronic's summons as he flew down the street towards the store.

But Jenny was nowhere in sight.

Victoria Avenue was exceptionally busy. His heart galloped as he waited for the traffic to slow down. By the time the flow of cars had finally subsided enough for him to cross, he was sure he had missed his only opportunity to see her that day.

Mr. Engelmann was behind the counter and the store appeared empty. Mr. Engelmann looked up at him, smiled and, with a twinkle in his eyes, cast a look towards the back of the store. Henry followed his gaze to see black and white saddle shoes sticking out into the aisle. So she was hiding on him, was she? He decided to play along.

"Hi, Mr. Engelmann. Boy, I sure am unhappy. I went over to Jenny's after lunch and she wasn't home. Guess I'll have to call on another girl I know."

"Oh no, you don't!" Jenny blurted, jumping out from behind the centre aisle with a broad smile. When she reached Henry, she gave him a shove. "Gone for a few hours and you're all ready to abandon me for another girl, you traitor."

Henry laughed and was surprised to see Mr. Engelmann chuckling too.

"I had to see you, Henry," Jenny went on, "We're going to see my dad's business friend tonight so I won't be home later."

"Yeah, your mom told me. And thank you for telling me, too. By the way, I forgot to mention it to you last night, but there's a new movie starting at the Broadway Theatre—a comedy starring Bing Crosby that's supposed to be pretty good. Would you like to go?"

"I'd love to," Jenny replied, "I'll have to check with my parents but I'm sure it'll be all right. What time?"

"There are two shows tomorrow night. One starts at six-thirty and the second at nine. I was thinking we could maybe go to the early one." Out of the corner of his eye, Henry caught Mr. Engelmann's nod of approval.

"Sounds great, Henry. I'll let you know as soon I check with Mom and Dad."

Once again, Mr. Engelmann nodded in approval. Jenny and Henry tried to hide shy grins. Though Mr. Engelmann had said nothing, talking with each other was a bit awkward in front of an audience.

"Well, I better get home."

"And I better get back to work or Mr. Engelmann is going to fire me," Henry countered.

"Oh no, Henry," Mr. Engelmann said now, shaking his head. "You have a job here for as long as you want."

Jenny beamed, gave them both a wink, picked up her bread and bounded out of the store, leaving a trail of sunshine behind. Gravity itself could not hold down her buoyant spirit.

"Ah, Proverbs 13:15," muttered Mr. Engelmann as Jenny disappeared from sight.

"Sorry, what was that, Mr. Engelmann?"

"Oh, I was just thinking how that young lady is an example of what the Lord was trying to tell me in the passage I read this morning."

"And what was that?"

"A happy heart makes a cheerful face."

CHAPTER FIVE

FTER JENNY LEFT, Henry walked over to the front door and peered out the window, watching her as she strolled to the corner and stopped to wait to cross the busy street. When he first started school his mom had always watched him as he left the house and crossed the street, unable to do any housework or chore until she knew he was safely on the other side. Seeing Jenny scurry across the busy road, Henry felt the same way, his mind and heart sending out a shield of love to surround and protect her.

Halfway across Victoria Avenue was the boulevard where the trolley ran. Jenny made it to the boulevard and looked down the street. A huge delivery van was in the lane next to the boulevard, followed closely by a blue Chev. There was no other oncoming traffic for at least a block or so.

The van started to slow down for Jenny and she darted out onto the road. Henry caught his breath as the driver in the blue Chev swerved sharply into the other lane and accelerated to pass.

Henry's heart stopped. *Jenny.*

He grabbed for the door handle, seconds unfolding like hours though he knew there was no time for a warning.

The van honked its horn in one loud blast and the startled driver of the Chev turned and finally saw the girl, his car lurching forward as he hit the brakes. But it was too late. Tires screeched and skidded as Jenny turned and looked in horror at the blue car hurtling towards her.

And then something happened that Henry would remember for the rest of his life.

Just as the car was about to mow Jenny down, she raised her arm and opened her hand as if someone was reaching out to take hold of it. *"Quickly, hold my hand"* flashed through Henry's mind. And in that instant, it seemed that Jenny was half-pulled, half-lifted a few feet down the street and left standing unhurt on the curb just inches away from where the Chev finally came to a halt.

Mr. Engelmann had joined Henry at the door and lay his hand on Henry's shoulder. Perspiration beaded on Henry's forehead and his sweaty fingers clung to the doorknob as he stood frozen. But only for a moment. Panicked, he rushed outside.

"Jenny! Jenny! Are you okay?"

Across the street, Jenny raised her head and nodded. She waved, gesturing that she was fine and not to worry. She didn't even seem to be shaken. It didn't look like the bread was crushed, even.

Seeing that she was all right, the drivers of both van and Chev moved on, the Chev driver shaking his head and swearing to himself to pay closer attention. It was a good thing that girl had gotten out of the way so quickly.

Mr. Engelmann came out of the store and stood beside Henry as Jenny waved once more before resuming her walk home, swinging the loaf of bread. Once again he put his hand on Henry's shoulder. "It's okay, Henry, she's got a guardian angel."

Henry stood there, transfixed and baffled, replaying the scene over and over in his mind. Jenny should have been hit by that car and thrown like a rag doll. And, yet, at the last moment, she'd been pulled out of harm's way. By a guardian angel? It was the only conclusion he could reach. His goosebumps dissolved and faded away as a peace settled over him.

Mr. Engelmann patted Henry's shoulder. "Come, let us get back to work."

And that's another thing Henry wondered about as he turned to follow his employer. How had Mr. Engelmann suddenly appeared at his side to comfort him. He hadn't seen what was happening. Henry was certain Mr. Engelmann had still been behind the counter when he went to the front door to watch Jenny, and yet here he was with his hand on Henry's shoulder.

Mr. Engelmann had resumed writing up an invoice when Henry re-entered the store. Henry stared at Mr. Engelmann for a moment and then headed back downstairs, shaking his head. Mechanically, he picked up the brush and began painting again. Jenny was safe and sound, and that was all that mattered. Soon the brush moved with more vigour, covering both the unsightly wall and the awful memory of Jenny's near accident.

By the end of the day, Henry had caught a total of twenty-six mice and had completely painted the basement. The basement looked so bright and clean he couldn't wait for Mr. Engelmann to see it. He ran upstairs to get him, but Mr. Engelmann was unusually busy. There were at least ten customers in the store, most of them picking up supplies for the weekend.

Henry went to the bathroom and cleaned the paint off himself as best he could, rushing back into the store to help. He found a spot beside Mr. Engelmann and packed the items into bags as they were rung through. After Mr. Engelmann handed the customers their bills and thanked each one for shopping at his store (*He knows everyone,* Henry thought again), Henry handed them their bags and thanked them by name, too. The first time Henry did it, both Mr. Engelmann and the customer looked at him and smiled. Mr. Engelmann nodded once in approval and introduced him, "This is my new assistant, Henry."

It was six o'clock before the store emptied.

"Thank you for staying. You are a big help, Henry. Did you

close the cellar doors?"

"Yes."

"Did you lock the upstairs basement door?"

"No, not yet, I was hoping you'd come down and have a look."

"I know you want to show me and I cannot wait to see it, but is it all right if we leave it for tomorrow? It's already suppertime and I am worried about Anna. I heard her call just before you came up and I haven't had time to check on her yet. We will go down together tomorrow morning."

"Yeah, you're right. I better get home too."

Henry locked the upstairs basement door and said good night to his boss. After he left the store, Henry unlocked his bike and wheeled it over to the corner where he stood for a long moment, reliving the incredible scene. He was still awed that Jenny had escaped the impact. Traffic was light now: most people had already arrived home from work and were eating supper.

"There should be traffic lights here," Henry mused.

He walked his bike to the other side of Victoria Avenue and stood where Jenny had. *Thank you,* he thought, although he didn't really know to whom his thanks were directed. Prayer was part of his life, yet he had doubts. He questioned who people prayed to, why they couldn't see Him, how He could listen to everyone at the same time, and so on.

"Just accept it on faith," his mom had told him. "Don't complicate it, Henry. Someday it will make more sense."

Henry took a deep breath and slowly let it out, trying to release some of the tension he still felt. He swung his leg over the seat, pushed down hard on the pedal and biked home. It was too bad Jenny wasn't home tonight to talk to. He wanted to know exactly what had happened.

His mom and dad were already eating when he walked in. Henry washed his hands then sat down at the table and told them what he had done at the store. He wasn't as excited as he would have been, considering the incident with Jenny, but for reasons he couldn't quite work out, he'd decided not to tell them about it. Besides, it'd make his mom worry even more .

With nothing else to do, Henry went into the living room where his dad was reading the paper and told him about the deal he'd reached with Mr. Engelmann. His dad smiled, but his eyes never left the newsprint. Henry told him he figured they could bring all the supplies they'd need the next day through the cellar doors rather than going through the store. His dad nodded again and gave a noncommittal grunt. Finally taking the hint, Henry decided to take a shower and go to his room.

It was only seven-thirty, but somehow it felt later. Henry's muscles were sore and weariness mingled with pride and confusion. As he lay back on his pillow, the tension of the last few hours finally began to lift. He took a deep breath and let it go, relaxing even more.

He thought of Jenny and how close he'd come to losing her. Did she really have a guardian angel? In Grade 2, Sister Monica had taught them a prayer about guardian angels. How had it gone? He tried to remember.

Just before he drifted away, the words came to him:

Angel of God, my guardian dear,
to whom His love commits me here,
ever this day be at my side
to light and guard, to rule and guide
my life ... and Jenny's ...
forever and ever.
Amen.

CHAPTER SIX

THE CLOCK ON HENRY'S bedside table read six-fifteen. The sun was up but just barely. He rose, too, and went to the window to look outside. The sky was overcast and rain threatened. He was glad. If it was a nice day his dad would probably be wishing he was golfing or working in the yard rather than framing an old door.

When Henry entered the kitchen, he was surprised to see his dad already at the table, sipping coffee and gazing off into space. He had seemed kind of quiet lately, not really himself. It bothered Henry to see him that way. He much preferred when his dad was more talkative and joked around with them. Henry hoped nothing was wrong.

"'Morning, Dad."

"'Morning, son. Ready to get right at it, are you?"

"Yeah, I went to bed so early last night, I couldn't sleep any longer. Are you still game to help Mr. Engelmann today?"

"You bet. A man is only as good as his word, remember that."

"Yeah, for sure, Dad."

"I thought I would start carrying things over before the traffic gets too heavy," his dad said. "What time do customers usually start coming in?"

"I'm not really sure. Ive been working downstairs the last few days. Why do you ask?"

"Well, to build and frame a wall requires a lot of hammering and sawing and it'll make some noise."

"Oh, that's okay. I'm sure Mr. Engelmann and his customers won't mind. I think they're just happy to see things improve."

"Well, let's get started then. Maybe you can carry the tools and nails and I'll carry the two-by-fours and the insulation. I'll come back to get the sheeting and anything else I might need once I see what all needs to be done."

"I sure appreciate your help, Dad, and I know Mr. Engelmann will too."

They arrived at the store just after seven. Henry noticed a light on inside and tapped on the front window. Moments later, Mr. Engelmann appeared at the door, looking surprised. "What are you doing here so early?"

"My dad brought the door and insulation over. Can I get downstairs to open up the cellar doors for him?"

"Yes, yes, of course, come in. Quickly, go open the doors so he doesn't have to wait too long."

Henry brushed past Mr. Engelmann and galloped down the steps to the cellar doors, swinging them wide.

His dad stepped down carefully and surveyed the basement.

"Looks like you've made a good start. You're doing a good job, son." He walked over to the washing machine still in partial darkness. "Could use another light over here. How on earth does Mrs. Engelmann see to do the wash?"

"Dad, two days ago you couldn't see a thing."

His dad studied the situation for a moment. "I have an extension cord at home. We can plug a light cord into it and hang it over the wash area with a pull string on it so Mrs. Engelmann can turn it on."

"That would be great."

"So, what's with these doors?" his dad asked, crossing the room. He closed the cellar doors, noting the cracks and the open space between them. "Hmm. If we build a wall with a door in front of the alcove leading to the old cellar doors, we can block out most of the draft and cold—and keep the field mice out."

After sizing up the job, Henry's dad decided he needed more materials and supplies from home. "If you want, you can start stuffing insulation between the floor joists and the outside walls. Keep the insulation loose. It's more efficient when it's not packed tightly."

"Okay," Henry replied, then went to get the crate to stand on while his dad climbed the stairs back outside.

Before putting up the insulation, Henry checked the traps for more mice. One had a mouse; the other didn't. That was a good sign. They must be almost gone. After he discarded the mouse and reset the trap, he took out the insulation and began to work.

A few minutes later, Mr. Engelmann came down the stairs. At the bottom, he held his hand over his eyes to shield them from the brightness. He spun around in an astonished pirouette.

"Henry, this is amazing! It looks so bright and clean. Anna will not believe this." Mr. Engelmann drew near, sputtering words of gratitude before finally giving up altogether and hugging Henry instead. Straightening, he tugged on his sweater vest and attempted to regain his composure. "In the fourteen years I have owned this store, I have never seen this basement look so nice. From the bottom of my heart, thank you, Henry."

There was a call from outside. "Henry, can you come and get this? I'll hand it down to you." His dad was back.

Henry ran over to the cellar doors. Mr. Engelmann followed.

"Oh, hello, Mr. Engelmann."

"Hello, Bill. Nice to see you. Thank you for your help with all this. First your son comes, and now you come on your day off. This is very kind of you."

"Glad I can help."

"This is quite the boy you have," Mr. Engelmann said, patting Henry on the back as he reached for the things his dad was handing down to him. "He works so hard and he knows so much. You have taught him well."

"Yeah, we're very pleased with Henry."

"He's a good boy. A good man," Mr. Engelmann corrected.

"Yes, he's growing into that for sure."

"And don't forget I will pay you for that door and the insulation and whatever else you need."

"I'll keep an accurate record, Mr. Engelmann. Don't worry."

"And, remember too, for your labour I'll give you three pounds of my best salami."

"That's very kind of you."

"Okay, I will go back upstairs and get ready to open the store. If you need any help, call me."

"We will."

By noon, Henry's dad had built the wall and framed and hung the door. Satisfied that it opened and closed properly, he glued thin boards over the cracks in the cellar doors.

"Well, son, that about does it. I think I have the key for that door at home in the garage. You can bring it back with you later."

"Thanks a lot, Dad, that was really nice of you. Are you going up to see Mr. Engelmann?"

"Yes, I better go square things up or it will bother him until I do."

Henry wanted to see how they would negotiate their settlement but decided it would be better if he kept out of it. He didn't want Mr. Engelmann to feel pressured at all. He looked at his dad's repair job and decided he'd paint the old door, too, but he would need more paint.

It was near lunchtime when Henry scrambled upstairs.

"See you after lunch, Mr. Engelmann," he called.

"Yes, yes. When you come back we will discuss your wages."

"Sure, that's fine."

There wasn't much traffic and Henry didn't even have to stop as he ran across the road and toward his house.

"Hi, Mom," he called as he entered.

"I'm in the kitchen. We're having salami sandwiches today."

No doubt part of Mr. Engelmann's payment.

As Henry sat down, his father came in from the garage and presented him with the key for the door.

"Thanks, Dad. How much did he pay you, anyway?"

"Oh, that's between him and me, son. It was enough and I'm happy I could help out."

His mom joined them at the table.

"Jenny was over this morning. She said to tell you that she can go to the movie with you tonight but she has to be home by nine-thirty."

"Oh, that's good," he replied, trying to sound nonchalant. He continued eating, finding it very difficult to chew his sandwich and contain the excitement welling up inside him. Thankfully, his mother didn't pursue it.

When Henry returned to the store, Mr. Engelmann was telling a customer where she could find the Ajax cleaner. After she went to get it, Henry asked, "Is there anything I should do?"

"Yes, yes. Can you watch the store? Anna needs me upstairs for awhile. Do you still remember how to operate the cash register?"

"I think so. If I have a problem, I'll call you."

"Here is a cloth, too. You can dust the shelves."

"Sure, Mr. Engelmann." Henry took the cloth over to the far aisle and started dusting.

Mr. Engelmann nodded, then disappeared into the back room. Henry served eight customers in the two hours he was gone. It was almost four o'clock when Mr. Engelmann appeared again.

"How is Mrs. Engelmann?"

"Not well. She's sleeping now. She was so excited when I told her about the basement and what your dad did. She said to make sure I thank you for her."

"You can tell her she's welcome." Henry related his movie plans with Jenny and asked if he could leave early.

"Yes, yes, of course. And you need spending money." Mr. Engelmann opened the till, took out a ten dollar bill and handed it to Henry.

"Oh, this is too much," Henry protested.

"No, no, you earned it and more. Now off with you and have a good time. That Jenny is a very nice girl."

"Thank you very much, Mr. Engelmann." It was the first ten dollars Henry had earned in his life so he just stared at it for a moment. Ten dollars wasn't very much for three days' work, but he knew it was probably more than Mr. Engelmann could afford.

Henry arrived home less than five minutes later and went directly to his room. He undressed, except for his shorts, then peeked out into the hallway to make sure no one was there before dashing for the bathroom. As he turned the knob to open the door, his dad swung it open from the inside.

"Is that how you're going to take Jenny to the movie?"

"Geez, Dad, just get out of the way so I can take a shower."

As Henry darted past, his dad swatted him on the behind, adding insult to his embarrassment. Henry was in and out of the shower in two minutes and ready for the mad dash back. He opened the door. The coast was clear so he ran to his bedroom, only to collide with his mom, who was coming out of it. He almost knocked her over.

"Mom! What are you doing in my room?"

"I just laid out some clean clothes for you. You're going to want to wear *some*thing, aren't you?"

Henry didn't know how to respond to that. "Yeah. Thanks, Mom. Sorry."

"Honestly, I'm not looking," she said, moving past as if to leave then at the last second catching the end of the towel Henry had wrapped around himself. She tugged once, sharply, leaving him standing there in the nude while she laughed all the way to the kitchen, waving the towel behind her like a cape.

Geez! He ducked into his room and slammed the door. A clean, pressed pair of trousers and his favourite blue shirt waited on the bed. He dressed quickly then returned to the bathroom to rub a dab of Brylcreem into his hair. He combed it into three different styles before settling on the way he usually did it. Satisfied, he left the bathroom and headed for the front door.

"Not so fast, young man," his dad said, blocking Henry's exit.

"What is it, Dad?"

"Here." He handed Henry a dollar, probably the one Mr. Engelmann had given him for the old door. "Now that you're working for a living, your allowance will be cut. Consider this a bonus. Treat yourself and Jenny tonight."

His mother stood in the hallway, smiling. "You look nice, Henry."

"Thanks, Mom, Dad." Henry smiled and lifted the dollar in a kind of salute before tucking it into his pocket and walking out the front door. To his annoyance, the wind mussed his neatly combed hair. After several unsuccessful attempts to slick it back, he gave up. It was a battle lost by many hairdos on the prairies.

Jenny waved at him from her perch on the porch as he came up her front walk. He hadn't seen her for over a day and was again overwhelmed by her smile. Her eyes held a special twinkle of excitement for their first date. She was wearing the new outfit she had modelled for him two days ago and the breeze carried a hint of her lilac perfume. Her necklace caught the sunlight in a series of silver sparks.

"You sure look nice, Jenny," he said.

"You do, too. I love the colour of your shirt."

Mrs. Sarsky stepped into the doorway. "Going to see *High Society*, are you?"

"Yes," he answered.

"Mr. Sarsky and I will have to see it sometime, too. I just love that Grace Kelly."

Henry nodded, anxious to get going. "Well, we better go, Jenny. We have fifteen minutes to catch the trolley."

"Have a good time, and remember what your dad said. Be home by nine-thirty."

"We will, I promise," Jenny called over her shoulder as Henry closed the gate behind them.

As they walked past Henry's house, he noticed a slight movement of the curtain in the front window. He glanced quickly, but didn't see his mom, only the wide prairie sky reflected on the glass.

CHAPTER SEVEN

THEY ARRIVED JUST AS the trolley pulled into the stop. "Quickly, hold my hand," Henry said as they ran across the avenue. Jenny playfully smacked him for stealing her line but took his hand just the same.

On board, Henry paid for both of them. No sooner had they sat down than the trolley jerked forward, throwing their heads back sharply. Instinctively, Henry sought Jenny's hand once more. Jenny only stared ahead and smiled as she curled her fingers around his. Fifteen minutes later, they were on Broad Street. The Broadway Theatre beckoned from half a block away.

"Oh my, look at the line up!" exclaimed Jenny as the trolley rolled closer.

Henry couldn't believe his eyes. The line up was almost half a block long. As soon as the trolley stopped, they hurried to join the throng.

"I hope we get in on time."

"So do I."

By the time they reached the wicket, it was almost showtime. As they paid for their tickets, the theatre manager came out and announced to the people behind them that the theatre was full and they would have to come back for the second screening.

"Whew," Jenny remarked, "that was close."

Henry nodded and asked if she wanted something to eat.

"I'm not really hungry—we just finished dinner before you came. But we could share something if you like."

"Okay," Henry replied. He got them a bag of popcorn and a drink.

The movie was starting as they entered the theatre and there were very few seats to be found.

"Over there!" Jenny whispered, pointing. "There are two seats, but a man is sitting between them."

The man was enormous. His body flooded the entire seat, hiding any evidence of a second vacant chair. Henry politely asked if he would move down one so he and Jenny could sit together.

The man glared at him. "What! What are you saying? Just sit down, kid."

"Would you mind moving one seat over?" Henry repeated.

"Look, shut up and sit down or find somewhere else to sit!"

Unsure what to do, Henry shot an apologetic glance at Jenny, who stepped in front of him. "It's okay, Henry," she murmured as she leaned in to talk to the man herself. "Excuse me, I want to sit in that empty chair." He growled at her but pulled in his legs as much as he could, which really wasn't very much. Jenny slid by and collapsed into the empty seat.

Henry took the spot on the other side of the fat man, fuming; he could've killed him for being so rude and stubborn. Now he regretted not sending away for the Charles Atlas muscle building course advertised on the back of his comic books. *This might have been an entirely different story,* Henry thought.

They'd missed the first few minutes but settled in to watch the rest. Henry had seen Bing Crosby in movies before and really liked him. After eating half the bag of popcorn, he leaned forward to see that Jenny was absorbed in the movie. How would he get the popcorn to her? The back of the chair was too high for him to reach around. He leaned forward instead and tried passing the bag to Jenny over the huge man's knees.

"Hey, what do you think you're doing? You're not getting fresh with me are you?"

"No, no," Henry gabbled, flustered. "I'm just trying to pass the popcorn to my girlfriend."

The man grabbed the bag, spilling some of the popcorn and thrust it into Jenny's hands. Turning back to Henry, he snarled, "Now just watch the movie and shut up!"

A while later, Henry was worried Jenny would be thirsty from the popcorn. He decided to risk passing the drink. Halfway across, the bottom of the cup brushed against the fat man's knees. He swatted the drink from Henry's hands, spraying pop down the neck of the person sitting in the seat in front of him.

The guy jumped up and danced around, trying to rid himself of the cold wet slither down his back that soaked his shirt and jacket, drawing the attention of those around him. The guy turned around and leaned over the back of his chair, towering over the fat guy, who cowered into his seat.

"What the hell do you think you're doing?" the wet man hissed. Before the fat man had a chance to explain what happened and pin the accident on Henry, the wet guy demanded two dollars to dry clean his clothes.

Sighing, the fat man reached into his pocket with great effort and managed to pull out some coins. "This is all I have."

"Gimme it." The wet man took the money and, pointing his finger at the fat man, warned him not to do anything so stupid again. He turned and sat down. It took several moments for him to find a comfortable position.

The fat man glared at Henry and spat, "Now see what you've done! Get bent, kid."

The man in front motioned as if to turn around again, raising a fisted hand and the fat guy shut up.

Henry tried to concentrate on the movie but couldn't. This was not cool at all. He'd wanted to put his arm over Jenny's shoulder and hold her hand—maybe even kiss her cheek—but that sure wasn't about to happen *now*. He couldn't even see her over the big oaf beside him.

When the movie ended, Henry stood and waited in the aisle for Jenny. She was waiting for the fat person to move, but he didn't budge, seemingly intent on watching the credits in their entirety, though Henry suspected he was doing it deliberately. The crowd streamed around Henry, pushing him along the aisle towards the exit.

In the lobby he waited again, but Jenny was nowhere to be seen. Finally the fat guy came out, but Jenny was not behind him. Reluctantly Henry approached him and asked where the girl beside him had gone.

"Oh, she went out down the other side. Hey, aren't you the kid with the drink?"

Uh oh. "No, no," Henry replied, backing away.

"You owe me 45 cents!" the fat guy bellowed as Henry dashed outside.

People swarmed around the entrance. Henry looked everywhere for Jenny, but she was gone, vanished. He rushed to the trolley stop on 11th Avenue but before he got there the trolley they needed pulled away.

"She must be on it," he muttered under his breath. "She knows we have to be home by nine-thirty." He stood there, helpless and sweating, trying to think of what to tell her parents. "She came with me but somehow got lost." Yeah, *that'd* fly. My God, what was he going to do? His eyes followed the trolley as it trundled out of sight down 11th Avenue.

He turned back towards the trolley stop, totally dejected—and there was Jenny on the bench, elbows on knees, heart-shaped face resting on her palms, a slow smile blooming on her lips. She was as pretty as Grace Kelly, the actress they'd just watched, and Henry's heart skipped a beat. He ran across the street.

When he got close enough to hear her, she said, "I knew you wouldn't leave me behind, so I wasn't about to leave *you* behind."

He plunked down beside her with a sigh of relief and slung an arm around her shoulder. "I'm sorry, Jenny. I got swept away with the crowd and couldn't fight my way back."

"That's okay," she said, patting his knee. "Well, now what do we do?"

He looked at his watch. "It's ten past nine and we've missed the trolley. Guess we'll have to walk home. I've done it before; it takes about half an hour."

"Let's get going, then." She jumped up. "Which way do we head, oh great leader?"

"Straight ahead that way," Henry pointed east.

The sun set behind them as they walked along, humming bits of "True Love," the song Bing Crosby and Grace Kelly had sung in the movie. The clouds spilled fiery shades of deep orange and red across the evening sky.

"The skies here are sure beautiful," Jenny observed.

"Yes, they are. It would be one of the things I'd miss most if I ever move."

"In B.C, you're so surrounded by the mountains you really don't get to see these kinds of sunsets unless you're by the ocean."

They strolled along 11th Avenue, talking and laughing about the fat guy and the movie. Henry was just thinking that the lyrics they'd been singing described exactly the way he felt when a car crawled up behind them. Henry caught sight of the souped-up vehicle out of the corner of his eye and guided Jenny away from it, taking her place at the edge of the sidewalk. As it neared, he heard a bunch of guys yelling and snickering, out cruisin' for trouble.

"Hey, is that Pederson with that babe?"

The car pulled up beside them, trolling the curb. Jenny glared at them.

"Wow, that's a real cute dolly you got there, Pederson. How'd you manage that? Look! They're even holding hands, all lovey-dovey. Can we hold hands, too? Hey, John, pull over and lemme out, I want some of that action."

Man, Henry thought, *here it comes.* He didn't want to fight these guys, but there was no question he'd do so for Jenny.

As it turned out, he didn't have to. A patrol car crept up behind the car and honked.

"Geez, it's the cops! Haul ass, John!"

The car roared off.

The patrol car pulled up beside Henry. "Everything all right?"

"Yes sir," Henry replied. *It is now.*

"Have a nice night, then."

"Yeah, thanks," Henry half-lifted his hand in farewell before reaching for Jenny's again.

"Whew, that was close. I was ready to take my shoe off and throw it at that nincompoop," she said.

Henry laughed, relieved those punks were gone. He prayed they wouldn't see them again before they got home. As they neared the end of 11th Avenue, they passed a clothing store with bare mannequins. Clothes and an assortment of wigs were laid out on the floor of the showcase.

Jenny ran up to the large display window and pretended to be one of the mannequins, standing with her legs slightly apart and raising one arm to hang in midair. She raised the other arm, bent her elbow, and with a sharp movement, twisted her wrist and opened her hand, extending her fingers into the air. She held that position for a long moment.

Henry stood there mesmerized as she mimed a mannequin springing to life. First, she moved her head, then her hands and arms one at a time, then all together. She shaped her face in a variety of expressions. Henry was amazed by how she suggested action, character and emotion using only gesture, expression and movement. Her movements grew more and more exaggerated until finally she was miming the altercation between the irate man and the fat guy from the movie theatre. Already chuckling, Henry now laughed so hard he couldn't stop. This only encouraged her, but Henry couldn't help it; it was far more entertaining than the movie they'd just seen.

Henry couldn't believe he was with such a wonderful girl, so spontaneous and full of life. He couldn't imagine ever being without her. Jenny was beautiful, one of those people who could probably wear rags and still look lovely. She could be completely bald like the mannequin she had mimicked and still steal his heart. He wanted to be with Jenny forever. He would lay down his life for her.

The streetlight beside them flickered on and Henry started. "Jenny, I could watch you for hours—you're great!—but we'd really better get going."

She pulled a face like a stubborn little kid and stomped her foot, then laughed out loud and returned to real life.

"Oh, that was fun," she said, grabbing Henry's fingers, swinging their joined hands in the air the way she liked to as they walked.

At Winnipeg Street they turned south, the sound of their footsteps coming faster as they hurried a bit more.

"Oh, look," Henry gestured, "there's Northern Paint. I've got to pick up a couple more gallons on Monday to finish at Mr. Engelmann's store. I want to make it just as nice as—or maybe even better than—the confectionary we were in the other day."

"Yes, that *was* a nice place. It was clean, bright and well organized. And I loved how things were displayed, especially all the drinks in the glass coolers. Wow, if you could get Mr. Engelmann's store looking like that, it would be quite an accomplishment."

"Yeah, it sure would be nice to get new coolers. I'll have to ask the guy who delivers the pop how much they cost."

Henry had spent so much time thinking about how to improve the little grocery store and working to make it happen, he wasn't surprised to find he had started to feel a little like it was his, too. And there was a whole list of things they could do.

"What are you thinking about, Henry?"

"Oh, nothing really. Just Mr. Engelmann's store and what needs to be done."

After a long pause, Jenny said, "You sure are an enterprising person, Henry. You're going to be a really good businessman someday, and maybe an artist, too."

Henry squeezed her hand. Jenny always managed to confirm his feelings without him saying a word.

As they approached Victoria Avenue, Henry slowed down. Dead ahead was a parked car, the same one that had approached them earlier. It was stopped in front of Eddy Zeigler's place. Odds were Eddy was one of the guys in the car.

"What's wrong, Henry?" Jenny asked, curious and alarmed by the expression on his face.

"I ... I think that's the car with those guys in it."

Jenny stared ahead intently and they both held their breath as they neared. Raucous laughter and wild insults peppered the air around the car; its windows were rolled down and they could see several dark figures inside. Henry's heart thudded against his ribs. Winnipeg Street was not as brightly lit as 11th Avenue had been and wasn't as busy. Cautiously he took another step forward. Jenny looked at him and he could see she was scared.

"Let's cross the street, Henry."

Henry didn't want her to think he was afraid but he welcomed the suggestion. It had occurred to him too. "Yeah, maybe we should."

Just as they did, one of the guys stepped out of the car.

Eddy Zeigler.

"Hey, guys," he knocked on the hood, "look who's here."

Henry was taller than Eddy and had been hauling heavy boxes and crates around for the last few days. He could maybe take the short little punk if he had to. There was a scratch and a flare. The end of the cigarette dangling from Eddy's mouth began to glow, one of his eyes half-shut against the rising smoke. He swaggered towards Henry and Jenny with a smirk. Eddy thought he was so cool, but Henry thought he just looked goofy.

Who does he think he is, Marlon Brando? Not a chance.

"Let's go, Jenny." He hoped with all his might that his bravado would blow them off. Henry moved forward. Jenny squeezed his hand, sidled closer to him and followed in his shadow. His heart pounded as they inched past Eddy and the car, never turning their backs on them.

One of the guys hollered out the window, "Geez, just leave them alone already. This is a drag."

"You kidding?" chided another voice. "Let's have some action." And with that, the driver got out. He was big. In the flash that was his life's story, Henry recalled that the brute's name was John. He had to be a football player.

Henry was in for a pounding.

There was a tug on his hand and a fierce whisper in his ear. "Come on, Henry, let's cross the street and run. We can still get away."

Sweat trickled down the back of his neck. They were in the middle of the block and it was getting darker. The immediate future looked just about as dim. Where was that police car now?

"Well, isn't that romantic," Eddy taunted.

"Come on, John. I wanna hold the blond's hand, too!"

The passenger door opened to reveal another guy, this one even bigger than John. Though Henry thought he could handle Eddy, these other two were bad news. He pushed Jenny firmly behind him, blocking her from view.

"Look at the big man protecting his girl," Eddy jeered. He tightened thin lips around the cigarette, squinting in what he thought was a manly way and took a deep drag, pulling it out of his mouth with menacing thoughtfulness before flipping the stub away. A long trail of smoke spewed from Eddy's cocky grin.

"Look, Eddy," Henry tried to reason, "I know you. Just let us go home. We don't want any trouble."

"Yeah," encouraged the guy from the back seat. "Come on, John. Pete. Let's go. Leave 'em alone. They're not worth it."

Well, at least one guy has some sense. Henry and Jenny were still only an arm's length away when Eddy suddenly moved, stepping in front of them to block their path. The other two guys followed and closed in behind them.

Blood rushed to Henry's head; he felt faint, frightened and furious all at once. Eddy made a swipe at Jenny, but she moved out of the way and Henry shifted his stance to keep between her and the little thug. But Big John reached out and easily grabbed

Jenny's arm from the other side.

"Come on, baby," he cooed, "we just want to have some fun." He pulled Jenny towards him despite her desperate movements to get away.

Henry lunged for her, but Eddy blocked him again, pushing him back. When Henry tried to reach for Jenny again, Pete, now out of the car, swung at him with a beer bottle. Henry ducked, but it grazed him on the side of the head. He staggered back and fell to the sidewalk, barely able to see the guys surrounding Jenny, making kissing noises and laughing at her protests.

"No, please don't …!" Jenny pleaded, shaking her head from side to side, trying to dodge John's and Eddy's puckered lips.

Henry struggled to stand, shouting, "Leave her alone!"

They just laughed at him.

"Hey, Pederson's sauced! Look at him staggering around."

They laughed some more.

Henry could tell Jenny was crying and he felt so weak and helpless.

"Hey, Bud, open the door and move over," John said to the guy still in the back seat. "Let's take her to the park."

They pulled and pushed a struggling Jenny towards the car. At the moment Bud opened the back door, an uncontrollable rage surged through Henry. He ran at them, flinging his arms in all directions. He yelled, a bark of sound that was half fear, half battle cry, as he kicked and swung. His foot connected with someone, as did his swinging fists.

"Geez, the guy's flipped. Take it easy, Pederson."

Jenny scurried back as they let go of her, and then two of them charged him, Eddy circling around to grab Henry from behind. The other two surged forward and punched him in the stomach and face.

Jenny screamed and, with a running start, pounded one of the guys on the back. "Let him go, let him go!"

John turned and swung an arm at Jenny, pushing her away. Her screams grew louder.

Bud shouted over her from inside the car. "Guys! I said leave them alone. Come on, let's *go*!" He jumped out of the car and began pulling one of the guys away from Henry. "Come on, man. He didn't do anything. Let's split."

"No way! He kicked me and I'm gonna give him a knuckle sandwich he'll never forget."

Just then a car appeared, slowed and stopped.

"It's the police. They're back!" yelled Jenny, wild with relief. "They're going to arrest all of you!"

The guys looked up.

"That's no police car," one of them shouted.

The car honked at them several times.

This time Bud yelled out, "Geez, you morons, either you're coming or I'm getting the hell out of here. If you want to get into trouble, go ahead."

A bright light inside Eddy's glass-enclosed front porch flicked on, and a man emerged from the living room in his undershirt. One suspender hung at his side, leaving the job of holding up his loose trousers to the other. He held a bottle of wine that wavered in his fist as he wobbled over to the porch's screen door. He put his free hand against the screen, cupping it around his eyes to peer out.

"What's all the ruckus?" When he recognized Eddy, his expression turned to anger. He stepped back and swung the door open. "Eddy, what the hell's going on out there? Get in here, now!"

Eddy let go of Henry's jacket and walked up to the house, turning his back on his father for a moment to mouth obscenities at Henry and make a quick hand gesture. John rounded the car and slid into the driver's seat. The moment Bud and Pete jumped into the car it sped off.

Behind them, Eddy hollered in pain. Jenny and Henry whirled to see Mr. Zeigler's fist around Eddy's ear, yanking him up the steps. Eddy smacked his dad's hand away and ran to the door, his dad following, bottle raised. Eddy easily dodged the aimless swing and ran into the house. Mr. Zeigler slowly followed and the porch light went out. Unseen voices from within filled the darkness with argument then faded away.

Henry turned and Jenny ran towards him.

"Are you okay, Henry?" she asked, tears staining her cheeks as she fell into his arms. Together they turned to the car that had stopped beside them.

"Do you want a ride home?" the woman in the passenger seat asked.

"No, I—," he hesitated, "I think we're okay."

Jenny nodded, tears glinting in the lamplight as she dashed them away with a tremulous smile.

"Well, if you're sure." The lady kept looking over her shoulder at the two of them as the car pulled away.

Jenny straightened her skirt then looked up into his eyes, "Oh, Henry, I was so frightened. Did they hurt you?"

"Nah, I'm fine, just a little bruised," he said wearily, ignoring the clench in his gut as he reached up to finger the swelling on his head. "How about you?"

"Just so scared," Jenny answered, her voice quavering. "Oh, your head is bleeding, and so is your nose!"

Henry wiped his nose with the back of his hand and cleaned the trickle of blood off on his pants. Jenny reached into her pocket and pulled out a tissue, dabbing the blood from his lip and gently patting the side of his head. Holding her close, the two of them started again for home. Although his anger had ebbed, Henry felt the stain of bitterness. *One day I'll teach that Eddy a lesson.* Jenny trembled in his arms. He hoped it hid the shaking he, too, still felt inside.

By the time they got to Victoria Avenue, a sense of calm had descended. A few more blocks and they would be home.

Jenny's voice was quiet in the dark. "You were so brave, Henry. The way you hit those guys."

Henry didn't know how to answer. Bravery had been the furthest thing from his mind. He couldn't remember ever being so afraid. Finally he said, "We're pretty late, Jenny. I hope your parents aren't too worried or upset."

"I'm sure they'll understand when I tell them what happened."

Then, thinking it through, she added quickly, "But maybe they won't let us out again."

Henry thought about it. "Yeah, you might be right. Maybe we should just keep it to ourselves for now. I have a good mind to report that Eddy. Oh well. At least you weren't hurt by all that. Maybe it's best to leave well enough alone."

As they passed the drugstore, headlights blinded them.

Then, "Hey, Pederson, you and blondie there want a ride?"

Unbelievable. Henry really wished they had taken the lady up on her offer of a ride home, but it was too late now.

The boys' car pulled over to the curb and stopped.

"Come on, John," Pete slurred, "I'd like to get my hands on that blond."

The blood drained from Henry's face and the world swirled around him. Jenny screamed as both John and Pete scrambled out of the car towards them.

"Run, Jenny! Run!"

But Jenny was too scared to move. The boys stood in front of them, their eyes wild and unfocused. John grabbed Jenny's arm. Henry tried to shove him away, but Pete pushed Henry against the window of the drugstore hard enough to make his head rebound off against the glass and he slid to the ground. It happened so fast, it was all a blur.

"I got her, man. Let's go."

Henry's legs wouldn't move. Through his daze, he heard Jenny scream as the boys jammed her into the back seat. Henry pushed himself to his feet, reaching unsteadily for the car but catching only air as it sped away. He stumbled into the empty gutter.

Henry heard honking and someone yelling. The couple who had stopped earlier were on the other side of the avenue.

"Do you need help?" the man called.

The words wouldn't come; his fear for Jenny was too great to speak, but Henry waved his arm frantically, motioning for him to come. The man quickly made a U- turn and lurched to a stop in front of Henry.

"We're glad we came back to check on you. Where's your girl-friend?" the lady asked, looking over her shoulder for Jenny.

"They've got her!" Henry finally gasped out.

"I'll take you to the police!" said the man.

"No! There isn't time. I think they're taking her to the park. Please, please take me there before it's too late."

The man looked at his wife. "Maybe he's right." The man nodded, a bit hesitant at first, then nodded again more firmly.

"Right," he said.

Henry got into the back seat and the car skidded away.

"They headed toward Albert Street. They're probably going to the lakeshore."

"Are you okay?" asked the woman, her brief glance assessing.

Henry just shook his head, tears stinging his eyes. *Please God, please don't let them hurt Jenny. Send an angel to protect her.*

Henry wished the man would go faster, even though he knew they were already speeding. The traffic lights turned red as they approached the intersection at the entrance to the park. The man brought the car to an untimely stop and Henry cursed the light under his breath. He sat on the edge of his seat, search-ing the darkness. The thought of not finding Jenny sent a sharp shiver through him. Henry's head jerked back as the man hit the gas when the light turned green.

They turned into the park area and slowed down.

"They could be anywhere," the man said. "Maybe we should go to the police."

"No, no, please just drive down the park lane. Turn left at that corner," Henry pleaded.

Reluctantly, the man did as Henry directed, and headed for the roadway that hugged the lakeshore. Water shimmered in the moonlight. Frantically, Henry scanned the shadows beneath the trees. The man turned on the highbeams. It seemed to help.

Henry rolled down his window and shouted Jenny's name.

CHAPTER EIGHT

Jenny was only semi-conscious when Pete dragged her from the back seat. She'd fought and scratched and he'd had to ... subdue her a bit. John got out of the car and came over to help him. Bud stayed inside and turned his face away. As soon as they reached a secluded area beneath the trees, John forced her to the ground. Jenny, dazed and now overcome with fear, went limp.

"Oh, guardian angel, guardian dear, please help me ..." she moaned. The guys snickered and exchanged a few heated insults, but Jenny registered none of it. Her body and mind shut down as she passed out completely.

John shoved him and Pete got down on his knees, pushing Jenny's legs apart as he half fell on top of her. God, she smelled good. Something flowery and feminine. He could hardly wait. He fumbled with his zipper, then with her skirt.

"Damn, she still has her underwear on," Pete panted. He pulled aside the scrap of fabric and did his best to shove himself into her. He was so ready; he'd been wanting this since they'd first seen her and her futile struggles in the car had only fueled his desire.

"Hurry up, man, I want some of that, too," John whined.

From the distance came a voice calling Jenny's name.

"Holy shit! Let's go!" John crouched down to avoid the head-lights of the oncoming car. Hoisting him by the back of his shirt, John yanked Pete off Jenny.

Pete hastily pulled his pants up and grabbed hold of Jenny's arm, dragging her over the grass towards their car, making her skirt slide back down over her knees. Pete struggled with her dead weight.

"Leave her! We gotta get outta here!" Bud's voice was frantic in the chill air. Reluctantly Pete dropped Jenny's arm and dove into the car.

"There they are!" Henry shouted.

The man braked and Henry jumped out.

"Be careful, young man!" the woman called after him as she and her husband stepped out of the car to follow.

Henry ran towards the other car, but was only in time to watch it screech away, leaving him in a cloud of exhaust fumes and burnt rubber. A knot of dread twisted his guts. Where was Jenny? Did they still have her? He called her name again, his voice hoarse with worry.

Something stirred. Then Jenny sat up on the grass, holding her arms around her stomach. Henry rushed to her side, kneel-ing down to put his arm around her.

"Jenny! Jenny, are you all right?"

She looked up at him in confusion, trying to take stock. Frightened as she'd been, she wasn't entirely sure she knew what all had happened after she'd been shoved into the boys' car.

The man and woman who'd driven Henry to the park appeared at their side.

"Are you okay?" the lady asked, leaning over to study Jenny.

"I—I ... think so."

"Did they hurt you?" she wanted to know.

"I'll kill 'em if they did," Henry muttered.

Some of the colour returned to Jenny's face and Henry realized how ghostly pale she'd been at first.

"I think I'm all right. This arm is a little sore," Jenny stretched her shoulder, testing it, then brought her arm down to cradle her mid-section again, "and my stomach kind of hurts. That one guy was sure drunk, though. I can still smell his awful breath." Jenny was now more aware, regaining her composure with each passing moment. More colour returned to her face.

"No, I'm fine," she said again, slowly getting to her feet. Her legs were a bit rubbery beneath her. "I just want to go home."

The man looked skeptical, "Are you certain you're all right? I can drive you to the hospital."

Jenny shook her head, vehement—the last thing she wanted was a hospital trip; she just wanted to go home. Jenny looked over at Henry. "I'm fine. I've really got to get home, though. My parents are probably beside themselves."

"Oh, geez, it must really be late. What time is it?" Henry asked the man.

He tilted a wrist, trying to catch some light. "It's ten to eleven. You know, we should report this to the police. Those boys need to be reprimanded."

"Oh, no," Jenny said, urgently. "I'm fine." She'd promised they would be home on time and her mom would be furious. Besides, she really wanted to lie down and sleep and just forget about all of this.

"Are you sure, Jenny?" Henry asked. "Those guys should be sent to jail."

Jenny put her hand on Henry's. "Really, I'm okay, Henry. They were just drunk. We've got to get home."

The woman seemed as uncertain as Henry. She looked Jenny up and down, scanning for bruises. But seeing nothing more than a few grass stains, and understanding the girl's anxiousness to placate worried parents, she only said, "Well, if you're sure...?"

Henry held onto her as they led Jenny back towards the car.

"Yes, I'm okay. Just a little shaken up, that's all." Her next words were quiet. "Thank you for coming to get me. I sure was glad to see you." Jenny smiled into Henry's eyes as he tucked her into the back seat and he was gratified that something of her sparkle had returned.

Henry directed the man where to go. When they got to Mr. Engelmann's grocery store, he asked him to stop.

"We live just up the street," he said, motioning. "Thank you so much for the ride and for helping us. Not everyone would have come back to see that we were okay."

"Well, we're just glad we were there. My name is Jed Thomas, and this is my wife, Edna, by the way. If you decide to report this, let me know." He reached into his pocket, took out a business card and handed it to Henry.

"Thank you very much, Mr. Thomas. I'm glad you were there, too. God knows what might have happened if you hadn't been."

Jenny and Henry got out of the car, thanked them once more, then waved as they drove off.

Henry turned to Jenny and studied her for a long moment. "Are you sure you'll be all right?"

Jenny gave him a watery smile, tears brightening her eyes now that they were finally so close to home. "I'm certain." She squeezed his hand, "I just really want to get back home."

The sight of her tears sent a wave of fury through him. "I'm going to kill that Eddy when I see him. I'll find out who those guys are and get even with all of them."

Jenny blinked the tears back and put a hand on his arm, stopping him. "Henry, what they did was bad, but I just want to forget about it. Nothing happened except me being scared half to death. I don't want to start a fuss at school ... or at home."

"Are you going to tell your parents?"

Jenny thought about it for a moment, fear of her parents' re-actions rising like a sudden tide. "No, please, let's just keep it to ourselves, okay? God knows what my parents might do. I'd hate for either of us to have to deal with the police and I really don't want any trouble when school starts. Besides, I'm sure those guys wouldn't have done anything if they hadn't been drunk."

"Oh, Jenny, I was so scared they would hurt you." Henry let go of her hand to put an arm around her and pull her close. She put her head on his shoulder as they walked. "You know, this is the second time you almost got hurt. I almost died when I watched you cross the street yesterday and nearly get hit by that car, but you jumped out of the way in that last split second. I meant to ask you, what happened there, anyway?"

Jenny thought for another long moment, and then softly she said, "All I really remember is lifting my hand, and then it was like I floated for a second, you know? It was the strangest feeling. In the blink of an eye I was out of harm's way. And somehow I knew the car wouldn't hurt me. I can't explain it, but whatever happened, I'm glad it did."

"Mr. Engelmann said you must have a guardian angel."

"Oh, Henry, I think so, too!" she exclaimed, turning to him. "I didn't want to say anything in case you thought I was crazy, but all the way home after that I just kept thanking God for protecting me. I think we all have a guardian angel who watches over us." Almost under her breath, she added, "Angel of God, my guardian dear, to whom His love…."

Henry looked at Jenny, stunned. "You know that prayer too?"

"Oh, yes, I learned it when I was little. I hadn't thought about it for a long time, but last night when I lay in bed it came to me and I said it over and over until I fell asleep."

Henry could hardly believe it. "That's exactly what happened to me, too! Saying that prayer was the last thing I remember before falling asleep." They held each other's gaze for a moment then, without another word, linked hands and continued home.

At Jenny's place, Henry followed her up the steps to the front door. He was glad the stoop wasn't very large so he could stand closer to her.

Jenny looked up at him. "Oh my, Henry, your shirt sleeve is torn and there are a couple of buttons missing."

"My mom will sew it up, don't worry." Henry gazed at her, happy to see that the frightened look she'd had earlier had been replaced by her usual radiant smile.

"You know, even though those guys tried to ruin it, I sure had fun with you tonight."

"So did I. I'm just glad you're all right," Henry said. "Will I see you tomorrow?"

"We're going to church in the morning, and after that I'm not sure if my parents have anything planned."

They fell into silence. Henry ached to hold her. He so wanted to kiss her and inched a bit closer. Jenny sort of leaned into him, tilting her head slightly and Henry automatically lifted his arms to hold her, pulling her closer—so close he could feel the warmth of her breath on his mouth.

Then the door creaked and Jenny's mom appeared behind it. Henry stepped back, almost falling down the stairs.

"Jenny! It's about time you got home. We were getting very worried about you. Your dad was just about to call the police!" Mrs. Sarsky said, eyeballing the two of them, but saving a particular glare for Henry.

"I'm so sorry, Mom," Jenny apologized. "After the movie, it was so crowded that we got separated and then we missed the bus. We decided to walk home—the next trolley would only be coming about now anyway and that would have made us even later!"

Mrs. Sarsky's words were stern, "Well, I'm just glad you're home. Better come in and get to bed. I'm sure your father will want to have a word with you." She turned to Henry. "Good night, Henry." Her tone was curt.

"Good night, Mrs. Sarsky, I'm very sorry we were late. It'll never happen again," he promised. Mrs. Sarsky nodded briskly and backed into the house, followed by Jenny. She gave a brief half-wave and quickly closed the door behind her.

Henry stood there for a second, hugely disappointed with the way the evening had ended. The chill in the air threw an even bigger damper on the warmth of his tender feelings. But at least Jenny was home now. And safe. He turned and headed for home himself.

His dad had already gone to bed, but his mom was waiting up. "Hi, Henry, you got Jenny home okay? Her mother called here about fifteen minutes ago and seemed quite concerned her daughter wasn't home yet."

"Yeah, we missed the trolley and had to walk back."

"How was the movie?"

"Oh, it was okay." He wanted to tell her about the guys who'd grabbed Jenny and how he'd found her and her near-miss with the car the day before and whether or not there were guardian angels, and, most of all, how he felt about her—but he'd promised not to say anything. His mom would only tell Jenny's anyway, and then she'd really be in trouble. Still, he wished he had someone to share it with, someone to help him sort it all out.

He'd just opened his mouth when his mom spoke again, "Well, I'm headed to bed. I worked out in the yard most of the day and helped Mrs. Goronic with her weeding. She misses you now that you're working for Mr. Engelmann. Anyway, I'm bushed."

She stood to kiss Henry's forehead. "Is that blood in your hair?" His mom took a closer look and noticed that his sleeve was torn and buttons were missing. She stepped back and looked Henry over like a seasoned detective picking up clues.

"What on earth happened, Henry?"

"Oh," he hesitated only slightly, "Jenny and I were running and I fell."

"Well, put the shirt in the hamper. I'll wash it and see if I can mend it." She stepped closer again, assessing the bump on the side of his head. "That's quite a bruise you have there. Better put some ice on it before you go to bed."

"Yeah sure, Mom."

She patted him on the shoulder and smiled. "Good night, Henry."

Henry sat for a little while, debating what else he could have done, then got up and went to the bathroom. The swollen knot on his head was sore and he dampened a washcloth with warm water and dabbed at the bruises a few times like his mom used to do when he was little.

He crawled into bed and lay there, enveloped by the darkness, listening to the ticking of the clock on his end table. His dad's snoring wafted in from the next room. His feelings for

Jenny were so strong he felt he would burst if he didn't share them with someone. Timmy? Nah. Maybe Gary Franklin. He'd be back from holidays near the end of the summer. But neither of his friends had ever even had a girlfriend. Besides, they'd probably just tease him mercilessly if he starting spouting feelings about girls and angels.

Then Henry thought about Mr. Engelmann. Sure he was old, but he was experienced, mature and insightful. It was obvious he really loved his wife, too, so maybe he would understand how Henry felt.

And Henry had a feeling that Mr. Engelmann wouldn't laugh at him for wondering about guardian angels. All the stress of the evening lingering in his shoulders melted and dissolved into the mattress. *Yeah, Mr. Engelmann ....*

A deep peace settled within and he closed his eyes and slept.

CHAPTER NINE

HENRY TOLD MR. ENGELMANN about the movie and the date. Mr. Engelmann laughed when he described the episode with the fat man, but his cheerful expression turned to one of deep concern when Henry told him how Eddy and his friends had threatened them and taken Jenny to the park.

"Was Jenny ... harmed in any way?"

"No, she said she was fine, just frightened by it all. It was a good thing those people in the car came by, though. God knows what might have happened."

"Yes, yes, thank the good Lord you found her right away." Shaking his head, he said, "My, my, what can happen when people drink!" Mr. Engelmann pulled off his glasses and gave Henry a direct look, "Those boys should be reported to the police."

"Yeah, we were going to, but Jenny didn't want to cause any trouble being new here and all that. I think she's worried reporting them might cause problems at school. She just wanted to get home. But I *hate* Eddy and his cronies for scaring her so badly. Someday, I'm gonna pay them back."

Mr. Engelmann put his hand on Henry's shoulder. "I understand, Henry. What those boys did was wrong and very upsetting. Eddy, hmm? Mr. Zeigler's boy?"

"Yeah, that's him. Eddy Zeigler, short and cocky. He needs his face pushed in." Bitterness choked him and he clenched his fists.

Mr. Engelmann looked away. His next words were quiet.

"That young Eddy needs a lot of help."

"Yeah, I'll help him all right—to a swift kick in the rear end."

"And what good would that do?"

"It would smarten him up in a hurry, that's what!"

"Perhaps for a while, until he does it again, or something even more serious."

"So what would you have me do? Give him a hug?"

"You're too upset, right now, to …" Mr. Engelmann looked at Henry compassionately and said, "What they did was wrong and they should be punished. But you must let the injury go or suffer further injury, trapped by your own anger. Always remember, Henry, the Lord says that the blind cannot lead the blind or else both will fall in the ditch."

Mr. Engelmann held Henry's eyes for a long moment. Henry wasn't sure what to think. Mr. Engelmann had agreed that what those guys had done was bad, but it sounded like he wanted Henry to forgive them and maybe even try to help them. It sort of took the steam out of Henry's anger. Mr. Engelmann took a breath to add something else when customers entered the store.

The opportunity to talk further never presented itself. Henry's day was filled with serving customers, restocking shelves and managing the store when Mr. Engelmann was tending to Anna.

The next few days convinced Henry that he could confide in Mr. Engelmann. He treated his customers with caring and sincerity. He understood their problems and their feelings. Perhaps what impressed Henry most was the way Mr. Engelmann accepted everyone and never criticized. People were relaxed when they talked to him, never defensive. If he disagreed, he would remain silent and listen. He would reflect their feelings and concerns to show he understood, then sometimes offer a different path or a new thought for their consideration, trusting them to work it out for themselves. It was a side of Mr. Engelmann that Henry hadn't seen, and probably would never have known if he hadn't started working there.

AFTER TWO WEEKS OF WORK, Henry had noticed many of the customers were elderly and obviously had trouble walking to the store. Those who lived closer to Safeway would often go there instead so as not to have to carry their purchases so far.

"You know, Mr. Engelmann," Henry said one day, "I think we can increase our sales and help the customers who can't carry their groceries very far."

"Hmm.Yes, my heart goes out to our older customers who have trouble walking here, but what can we do?"

"Well, I could deliver groceries on my bike as a free service."

Mr. Engelmann raised an eyebrow, eyes widening. "Yes, yes, our seniors would find that such a blessing. That is a wonderful idea, Henry. I will buy a carrier for your bike."

"That'd be great! Then I could make several deliveries at once."

They smiled at each other. The weary look in Mr. Engelmann's eyes brightened into a joyful twinkle. The phone rang, startling them both. Henry answered.

"Good morning, Engelmann's Grocery. Good morning, Mrs. Feisel." Henry picked up a pencil and jotted down the items she wanted, then added, "By the way, Mrs. Feisel, you don't need to have your son pick up your groceries after work today. We just started a delivery service. I can bring them to you later this morning. No, it's no trouble, at all. We are happy to help you out .... Certainly, I'll add those items to your list .... Glad we could help. No, you don't have to pay for it. You're welcome. 'Bye."

Mr. Engelmann stared at his young employee. He shook his head and let his gasp of amazement turn into a chuckle.

Sales increased almost immediately. The older customers couldn't thank Mr. Engelmann and Henry enough. And Henry was thrilled when some customers started tipping him.

But Henry was even more personally rewarded by the exchange he overheard between Mr. Engelmann and Mr. Mahoney when the tax man walked into the store in the third week of July.

"Ah, good morning Mr. Mahoney." The cheerful, lively tone in Mr. Engelmann's voice caught the tax man by surprise. It was unusual for him to be greeted in such a manner, especially by someone who owed the city such a large sum of money.

"'Morning, Mr. Engelmann. I was in the area and thought I'd stop in to see how you're doing. An offer for the lot was tendered two days ago but it was so low, I flatly refused. It's hard to understand how people will try to take advantage of another's difficulties."

"I appreciate that, Mr. Mahoney. We're doing our best to make the payments you need."

"Well, just keep in mind that another offer may not be so easily turned down. The director is anxious to have this account cleared up—it's not good to have a business unable to meet its obligations like every one else."

"I fully understand, Mr. Mahoney, however, I believe we are getting back on track."

Mr. Mahoney turned and looked at Henry stocking the shelves. "I see you still have that young boy employed."

"Yes, yes, Henry is proving to be a huge help. A very fine, capable young man. The shelves are always stocked now, I am free to tend to my wife and look," Mr. Engelmann pointed to the back wall behind the meat deli, "he has painted the downstairs and now is starting up here ... see?"

Mr. Mahoney looked at the fresh coat of white paint on the back east walls where the painting had stopped. "I see. There is quite a difference."

"And we have started a delivery service, which is helping our sales as well." Mr. Engelmann beamed as he spoke. He hadn't had much cause to smile during the tax man's previous visits.

"Well, I hope these improvements translate into an ability to deal with the amount in arrears."

"That's just the thing, Mr. Mahoney—it already has."

Mr. Mahoney stared at the proprietor as he opened the till, lifted the cash drawer and pulled out a cheque.

"Just last evening after doing the books, I told Anna that we could make a payment to the city. Here, you can have this now and I won't have to mail it."

Mr. Mahoney took the cheque, fully expecting to see the usual $50 payment. His eyes widened, raising his thin brows as he silently mouthed the amount. *Three hundred dollars.* He slowly raised his eyes. "This is a more substantial payment, Mr. Engelmann, and before the end of the month, too."

Mr. Mahoney turned to where Henry stood behind the second aisle. He ducked just in time to keep Mr. Mahoney from seeing the huge grin overtaking his face.

"Well, thank you, Mr. Engelmann. I will visit you again in a few weeks." He looked Henry's way again, turned back to Mr. Engelmann, nodded and left the store.

AS THE SUMMER PASSED, Jenny and Henry became inseparable. They saw each other every day without fail. Whenever Jenny had to come to the grocery store for something, she timed her trip to coincide with Henry's break. They would go out back, sit together on the crate, hold hands and share a soda. Henry worked twice as hard when Jenny came by to lessen any concern Mr. Engelmann might have that her presence was a distraction.

Ever since Henry had brought Jenny home late from the movie, though, Mrs. Sarsky seemed distant towards him. Each time he called on her, Mrs. Sarsky's response was colder and more abrupt. Something was wrong, but he wasn't sure what to do about it. He talked to Jenny, but she only said not to worry, that it was just his imagination. Henry knew better. This was the first time he'd ever felt rejected and, despite Jenny's assurances, it bothered him.

Although Mr. Engelmann liked Jenny and always beamed whenever she came into the store, he expressed concern over how much they saw of each other.

"Henry," he jested one day, "Jenny is here so often, I think my sales of Orange Crush have tripled."

Henry just smiled at him.

"Do you still see your other friends?"

"Oh, sometimes, but not as much as I used to."

"Well, it's good to have a balance among your friends, to keep in touch and spend time with all of them."

"Oh, for sure, Mr. Engelmann, it's just that I like Jenny so much and—" A customer walked into the store then, ending their conversation, and Henry got back to work.

ONE EVENING IN EARLY AUGUST, Henry went outside to sit on the front steps after supper. He looked over towards Jenny's house, but didn't see her. After a few minutes, though, the screen door opened and Jenny bounded out. His spirits shot up as they always did when he saw her.

She waved at him as she skipped down her front steps and walked towards his house. He was glad she was coming his way—he was becoming more and more anxious about calling on her.

They met at his gate and headed north. As soon as they crossed the street, their hands found each other. They walked in silence, desiring only to be together for every minute possible, yet both had sensed growing concern from their parents—especially Jenny's—about the amount of time they spent together and the fact that they'd grown so close so quickly. Henry had kissed Jenny for the first time two weeks ago. A wonderful sensation had swept through his body as her full lips touched his. He'd been overwhelmed, only wanting to feel that way again. And Jenny felt the same way, he knew; they'd kissed twelve times since then, every one fanning the flames of their desire to be together. Henry wanted Jenny more than anything he ever wanted in his life.

But there was such turmoil and frustration too. Henry wondered if Jenny felt it too. He stopped and turned towards her.

"Jenny, what are we going to do? I want to be with you so much. I don't think I can bear it, not seeing you every day. I just want to—"

Jenny put a finger on his lips to silence him. She looked at him tenderly, love glowing in her clear blue eyes.

"I want to see you all the time, too, but perhaps our parents are right. Maybe we do need to slow down a bit—"

"But, Jenny," he argued, moving her finger away and holding her hand to his chest, "I can't live without you! You're all I think about!"

"I know. Me too. But if we keep seeing each other all the time, they might tell us to stop seeing each other altogether."

"They can't do that!" Henry was outraged, fearful. "That would be awful!"

"I know," said Jenny, the sparkle in her eyes fading a bit. "That's why I think it's important to lessen everyone's concern a little. What if ... what if we saw each other every other day? And maybe then you'd like me all the more!" she quipped with a wink.

Before Henry could form a protest, she stood on her tiptoes and brought her soft, warm lips to his. Then nothing mattered. The heaviness Henry had felt only a moment earlier vanished as he was instantly transported into a state of sheer ecstasy, a complete oneness with Jenny.

Reluctantly, they released their embrace and resumed their walk. As they did, Henry saw Mr. and Mrs. Tearhorst sitting on their front steps. They had been watching them the whole time.

"Good evening, Henry. Nice night," Mrs. Tearhorst said with a smirk.

Henry went bright red but Jenny just smiled and looked down. "Good evening, Mr. Tearhorst, Mrs. Tearhorst," Henry mumbled as he and Jenny walked a little faster to get out of their sight.

As the Tearhorsts faded behind him, Henry found himself wishing he had met Jenny four years from now, when he'd finished with school and had a job. He'd marry her in a flash. He would work two jobs—even three if he had to—to support her. It all seemed so distant, so far into the future. He wished they could be together now, but he knew Jenny was right. They were seeing a lot of each other, and his wanting wasn't just to hold and kiss her but to have her totally. His yearning was a physical ache. He squeezed Jenny's hand all the tighter, thinking about it.

"You're so quiet, Henry. What are you thinking about?"

He sighed. "Maybe you're right. Maybe we should slow down a little. But I don't know if I can."

"We'll make it, Henry," Jenny said. "It's just one day. I need to sort things out in my closet and straighten out my room. Maybe I can do that tomorrow night, and spend a little time with Mom and Dad. You know? Show them they don't need to be so concerned about us. And maybe you can spend some time with Timmy or … what's the name of your other friend?"

"Oh, you mean Gary Franklin?"

"That's him."

"Yeah, he's not back from holidays yet." *I would rather see you.*

As the two continued their stroll down the tree-lined street in silence, Jenny noticed that someone had carved initials and a lopsided heart into one of the tree trunks. That gave her an idea. "If you were a tree Henry, I would carve my heart into your bark."

Henry squeezed her hand. They passed Mr. Miller's front yard and Henry noticed a beautiful array of flowers in a rock garden. "And, if you were a flower, Jenny, you'd be the one I'd pick."

"Aww," she replied, leaning towards him to lay her head on his shoulder. "That's really sweet. If you were a book, I'd not only read and caress every page, but also never close the cover."

Henry squeezed Jenny's hand again. "If you were the sun, I'd want to feel your warmth all the time. I would never want darkness to ever come again."

"And if you were the ocean, I'd want to be a fish and swim in you all the time."

"Oh, Jenny, if you were the stars I'd be the sky that held you for eternity."

She smiled up at him.

"Oh, Henry, I think you've got me there. I can't top that one."
As they turned toward home, Jenny leaned into him again,
welling up with love for Henry, and feeling as though she might
burst with happiness.

THE NEXT DAY, the store was very busy, so there wasn't time for
Henry to do much but work. He couldn't stop thinking about
Jenny, though, and had trouble keeping his mind on the job.

"Is everything all right, Henry?"

Henry wanted to tell Mr. Engelmann about their decision to
see each other only every other day, but there were several customers in the store. "Yes, I'm fine."

His boss studied him for a moment, and Henry got the feeling that Mr. Engelmann knew he wasn't being truthful.

By the end of the day, Henry was exhausted. Trying to do
his work with no hope of seeing Jenny that evening drained him.

"Good night, Mr. Engelmann."

"Good night, Henry, and say hello to—"

Henry waited at the door, but Mr. Engelmann didn't say
anything else.

"ARE YOU FEELING OKAY, Henry?" his mother asked when he
pushed his plate away, his cabbage rolls only half eaten.

"Just a little tired tonight," Henry replied and then excused
himself to avoid any further conversation. He went outside and
stared at Jenny's house. He had hoped that she would be out,
but she wasn't. He sat down on the steps, nothing in him but
loneliness. He'd just decided to head back in when Jenny's
screen door opened and she came out with a white piece of
paper in her hand. He brightened at the sight of her and lifted
a hand in greeting.

She skipped down the front steps and didn't stop until she
reached the gate at the end of her front walk. She fumbled
around the post that held the gate. After a few moments she
pointed to the top of the post and mimed that there was something there for him and that it came from her heart. She then

turned and danced back towards her front door, blowing a kiss at him before disappearing back into the house.

Wondering what she'd done, he got up and walked nonchalantly to Jenny's gate. An elastic around the post held a folded piece of paper. He retrieved the note and beat a hasty retreat home, keeping an eye out for Mrs. Sarsky.

Safe in his room, he eagerly unfolded the note and read:

> *If you were a bed, I would be your blanket and cuddle up all around you throughout the night. I can't wait to see you tomorrow after dinner when we can go for a walk.*

Henry brought the note to his lips. He kissed it and inhaled the scent of the ink, knowing that Jenny had just touched it, trying to feel any of the warmth that might still linger from her hand. He laughed to himself as he read and reread her words.

In a flash, he opened the desk drawer and selected a sheet of blue-coloured paper, tearing off a small piece. *Now, what to write?* He tapped his pen against the desk then put it to the page a heartbeat later.

> *If you were a chocolate bar, you'd be the sweetest ever made!*
>
> *Oh Henry*

He folded the note, rose from his desk and walked to the front door.

"Are you going out?" his mom asked from the living room.

"Yeah, for a minute. I won't be long."

A minute or two later, Henry was back in his room, reading and re-reading Jenny's note, hoping it would sustain him until the next time he could see her.

THE WORKDAY SEEMED to drag on forever, but Henry's mood improved as the day went on. He'd see Jenny after supper. He could hardly wait. At three o'clock, he made three deliveries and was gone for over half an hour.

When he returned, Mr. Engelmann, busy at the till, called out, "You just missed Jenny. She told me to tell you she has to go out to dinner again with her mom and dad and that she will see you tomorrow. Oh yes, she also said for you to look at the fencepost, and that you would know what that meant."

Henry shuffled away to restock the shelves, disappointment written all over him.

They were busy until almost closing time. As soon as the last customer left the store, he bade farewell to Mr. Engelmann, anxious to read whatever Jenny had left for him. As he passed by Jenny's house, he detached the folded piece of paper from the fencepost.

His mom and dad were already at the supper table when he got in. "Hi, Henry, please wash and come quickly," his mom called out to him. "Supper's getting cold."

"Be right there."

He left the note on his desk—he wasn't about to read it in front of his parents—then dashed into the bathroom to clean up before hurrying out to the kitchen. He crossed himself, said a private grace and began to eat.

He was so preoccupied with Jenny's note he hardly noticed the meal his mom had prepared. He just kept eating, finishing even before his parents. When he looked up from his plate, they were both staring at him.

"What?"

"Have you got something important on for tonight?" his dad asked.

"Oh, no, not really. I just have something I want to do. May I be excused, please?"

His mother looked at him, puzzled. "Sure, Henry."

Henry ran back to his room. Taking a deep breath, he sat at his desk and opened the note:

Dear "Oh Henry,"

Dad phoned home after lunch—a work friend of his had invited us out for dinner a week ago and Dad forgot to tell us. I am so sorry I won't be able to keep our date for tonight.

Thank you for your note, I loved it! And if you were a pie, I would want to be the sugar and the spice.

Jenny

"You *are* my sugar and spice … you're my whole life," Henry whispered. He took out the blue sheet of paper, tore off another piece, and started to write. He wanted to say how much he missed her and wanted to be with her, but worried that her parents might find the note. Instead, he simply wrote:

Dear Sugar & Spice,

Thanks for letting me know. I'll count the minutes until tomorrow night when I can see you again. And if you were a watch, I'd keep you in my breast pocket next to my heart so I could feel you tick all night long.

Henry

He went over to Jenny's place and tucked his note securely behind the elastic on the fencepost.

In the days that followed, they continued their game, each trying to outdo the other. But their efforts to see less of each other didn't seem to appease Jenny's mom. Each time Henry called on Jenny, Mrs. Sarsky was very abrupt with him. He tried everything to be friendly, but to no avail. It wouldn't have mattered if she wasn't the mother of the girl he loved.

HENRY WAS AMAZED by how quickly the summer was flying by. With Jenny in his life and work at the store, there was never a dull moment. Mr. Mahoney dropped in during the third week of August like clockwork. Once again Henry was very happy to see his employer hand over another cheque to the tax man. Judging by the expression on Mr. Mahoney's face, the amount must have been larger than the last time. Even though Mr. Mahoney didn't seem to have confidence in his ability to help Mr. Engelmann, it just made Henry all the more determined to prove the tax man wrong.

Henry's help at the store over the summer had also freed up Mr. Engelmann to spend more time caring for his wife. Anna's health slowly improved, and she began to spend more time in the store. Henry just loved it when she was there. She was caring and kind and brought a special elegance to the business. It was surprising to Henry how many ladies came in just to talk to Mrs. Engelmann about their concerns, just like Mr. Engelmann and Henry did. Mrs. Engelmann would often escort troubled ladies back into the little store room to sit on boxes and have heart to heart discussions. Many times the woman in question would leave with joyful tears in her eyes. It was becoming clear to Henry that the Engelmanns had a mission beyond just selling groceries.

With Mrs. Engelmann's increased time in the store came more chances for Mr. Engelmann to steal away from the business and go out back with Henry for a break. Henry looked forward to those times and the moment he would finally be able to talk to Mr. Engelmann about Jenny and his overwhelming feelings for her.

CHAPTER TEN

"WOULD YOU LIKE to sleep with her?" Mr. Engelmann asked as they sat in the morning sun on the old grey crate.

Henry was startled by the bold question. They had been talking about his relationship with Jenny, and then *boom*, Mr. Engelmann zeroed in on what was really bothering him.

Despite his liking and respect for Mr. Engelmann, and how much he'd wanted to talk about his deepest feelings, Henry now found himself shy.

"What do you mean, sleep with her?"

"You know what I mean, Henry," Mr. Engelmann pressed. "Would you like to have sex with her?"

I guess Mr. Engelmann knows these things. But does he even have sex anymore at his age, and with Mrs. Engelmann being sick and all? Henry tried to think of something else to talk about. And yet there was something about Mr. Engelmann Henry trusted. He'd heard a couple of guys boasting about "rounding third" and "hitting a home run" while he himself was pretty clueless about the whole thing. Oh, he knew the mechanics of it all—he'd grown up on a farm, after all—but he had no idea what to do with his feelings.

And he did want to talk to someone—Lord knew he wasn't about to talk to either of his parents about it, he'd be grounded for months! All this ran through his head as he thought about Mr. Engelmann's question. If he told the truth, would Mr. Engelmann get mad at him?

"Yeah, I-I guess so. Actually, I want to more than pretty much anything," he finally blurted out, surprising himself.

Mr. Engelmann did not look at him and Henry was glad. His boss only nodded, smiling slightly.

"Thank you for your honesty, Henry. That was a good answer and came from the heart, no?"

"Yes." Henry felt heat on his cheeks and looked down to where the heels of his sneakers drummed a soft, hollow beat on the crate. *Geez, this is going to be hard to talk about, even with Mr. Engelmann!*

"You know, Henry, the feelings and desires you have are not new. All humanity has gone through what you are feeling, me included. When you look at me, you may see an old man, but I too was once young with the same wishes and urges you feel now. When I met Anna, I was a little older than you—eighteen, I think. Anna was a year younger.

"I lived in the country and Anna lived in town. Her father was a baker, the best in the village. Everyone respected his skill in making a fine bread that no one in all the territory could match. I can almost smell the bread baking." Mr. Engelmann paused for a moment, as he relived a special time in his past.

Then he went on. "Maybe, I too, am hesitant to talk about this. I am not sure I know the right way to answer the questions you might have ... so, perhaps, we will just continue to talk, no? And eventually it will all come out."

Henry hoped whatever Mr. Engelmann had to say would be expressed soon; he didn't know how much embarrassment he could stand.

"Anyway, Henry, Anna and I wanted to be together in every way possible, including the physical. We loved each other very much and that alone was justification enough. We planned to marry and live together even though we knew that was impossible at the time. What on earth could we live on? Sex? No. Love? No. These are very important elements in a marriage, but without trust and respect, without the security of a home and a job, it cannot last." Mr. Engelmann turned away and took a deep breath, giving them both time to reflect. "Just think about it, Henry. Could your parents have brought you into the world and cared for you without some secure base, without each trusting that the other had their best interests at heart, without being partners in life?"

"No-o," Henry said slowly, never having thought about it that way before.

"Would it be right for you to marry Jenny without learning about each other so there can be respect and trust between you? Would it be right to marry her without being able to support her?"

"No," Henry said again, this time with more certainty. "I would feel terrible."

"Well, then, what if, right now, you suddenly found out she was expecting your child?"

The thought hit Henry like a ton of bricks. "That would be devastating!"

They were both quiet for a long time. At least a half-hour had passed since the start of their break, but Mr. Engelmann didn't move to go in so Henry didn't either. He wondered what Mr. Engelmann wanted to tell him. Mr. Engelmann opened his mouth as if to speak and then closed it again.

Finally, he went on, "When I was teaching in the old country, I read the works of a Russian scientist named Pavlov." Mr. Engelmann paused and scratched his head as if that would help him to recall better. "He was doing experiments with dogs and learned he could change the dogs' behaviour by conditioning them."

"So? I don't understand."

"Just bear with me for a moment, Henry."

Henry looked down at his feet again, wondering if talking

to Mr. Engelmann had been a good idea.

Mr. Engelmann squinted as he turned his head up towards the sun, as if the warm rays would illuminate memories of the past. "If I remember correctly, Mr. Pavlov learned he could condition the dogs, creating a specific response to the various stimuli presented to them."

"What does that mean?" Henry asked, growing impatient.

"Well, let me explain and I think you will understand. Pavlov kept the dogs in a cage and would show them food behind a screen. As soon as the dogs got worked up and began to salivate at the sight of the food, he would ring a bell while opening the cage door to feed them. After many such trials, Henry, all Pavlov needed to do to make the dogs salivate was ring the bell, even if there was no food in the cage. He conditioned the dogs to respond to a new stimulus: the sound of a bell."

"That's interesting, Mr. Engelmann, but what's it got to do with me and Jenny?"

Mr. Engelmann looked at him over his glasses. "I know you want to know everything right away and have your problems solved immediately, but life's challenges take time. I will try to come more directly to the point."

Henry shifted his legs so his feet wouldn't fall asleep and waited. Following Henry's lead, Mr. Engelmann too shifted from side to side, settling more deeply into the cracks and spaces between the slats of the old crate, reflecting for a moment before speaking again.

"When Anna and I were dating, we decided not to be intimate until we were married for the reasons I have already explained to you, but there is more to consider. If Anna and I had had sex then, or if you and Jenny start to have sex now, it will be all you think about and want to do. Each time you think about it, you will begin to salivate just like the dogs in Pavlov's experiment, and each time you are rewarded by giving in to your desire, that desire will grow stronger until it becomes a total preoccupation. Your time together will not be for conversation or visits with other friends, but for sex. You will be thinking and scheming where and how you can be alone and away from everyone so you can indulge in that moment of pleasure and get your reward."

Henry was beginning to understand what Mr. Engelmann was getting at. *It's true,* Henry thought. He always regretted when Timmy Linder came between him and Jenny and how—

"When I was a young child I once stole a penny from my mother's purse, and the next day I went to the store and bought a candy. Every few days I would take another penny, rewarded each time with candy just like a dog in Pavlov's experiment. Since I was not caught, I kept stealing until one day the storekeeper told my mother. The stealing abruptly stopped, and my behind very quickly learned a new stimulus! That is why I watch so carefully when young people come into my store. I know some want to steal. I don't want them to get away with it and be rewarded." Mr. Engelmann looked at Henry again, sunlight glinting off the lenses of his glasses. "Now do you understand?"

"Yeah, it sort of makes sense."

"Let me go on," said Mr. Engelmann. "When God made the world, Henry, He instilled in every animal and human a sexual drive, a very strong urge, one with very pleasurable results. In men, this drive can be almost instant."

Henry nodded. The guys in gym talked about sex all the time.

"Women feel desire, too, but it takes a little longer for them. The main reason for this urge is so every creature will reproduce itself. If God had not put this drive in us, we would have no desire to procreate and the Earth would soon have no people. Do you understand, Henry?"

"Sure, but I still don't get the point."

"The point is this: all creatures, humans as well as animals, want to have sex—are, in fact, driven to do so—but there is a big difference between humans and animals. With animals there is no right and wrong, no moral code of conduct, but with humans there is. God gave man a brain, a mind to think, as well as free will to choose to do right or wrong."

Henry met Mr. Engelmann's gaze and nodded his understanding.

"The trouble with us, Henry, is that we want our desires to be met *now*. We can't wait. Many times we are like animals, acting on instinct and impulse without thought to the consequences of our actions. Sure we have desires. Sure we want to have sex. But when is the best time to engage in it?" Mr. Engelmann turned towards Henry and paused. Henry knew he was giving him a moment to consider the question.

"Henry, ask yourself: 'Should I wait until I can provide for Jenny and support her and the possibility of a child, or simply do what feels good and use her for my own sexual gratification?'"

Mr. Engelmann paused again. This time, Henry knew he was waiting for an answer. Knowing it was best to wait battled his need to be with Jenny in every way he could. It wasn't simply mind over matter; his desire for Jenny felt right, too.

He didn't know what to say.

"It's all about choices," Mr. Engelmann continued. "But even more important is why we make the choices we make. What is it that we really believe in, in our hearts and souls? What is it that tells us this is right and this is wrong? What is at the very core of who we are, Henry?"

Henry's eyes widened. "Tell me." For the first time since the start of their discussion, Mr. Engelmann had Henry's full attention.

"Henry, this is what makes us different from Pavlov's dogs: we have a set of beliefs that we learn to live by as we grow. We already talked about it a little this morning. If you believe in the sanctity of marriage, then you choose not to engage in premarital sex. If you believe in honesty, then you choose not to steal. If you believe you should be truthful, then you choose not to lie, and so on. These are *values*, Henry. Values are very important in life. And the choices we make as we live each day are based on the values and principles we believe in our hearts."

Mr. Engelmann paused, "I learn how I should live from the Bible. I try to live the way Jesus did, and make my choices based on what He said and did. He was the perfect example of how to live. The values He lived by are in the Bible. It is His legacy, His teachings to all the world, to help us live a good and happy life."

Mr. Engelmann eyed him again. "With what we've talked about this morning, Henry, how have you decided to be with Jenny? Like an animal—or like a man with reason who believes in values that are sound and right?"

Henry thought about it. Though Mr. Engelmann was maybe simplifying things a bit, Henry understood what he was getting at. Did he want to be like a dog and just seek gratification, or was he a man who would rise above his animal instincts and consider consequences and values? Thoughts of pregnancy, marriage and responsibility flashed through Henry's mind. There was so much more to sex than just sex.

He nodded slowly. Mr. Engelmann was painting the big picture, trying to get him to understand the whole issue, not just part of it. And, Henry had to admit, his arguments were persuasive.

"Your time together now, Henry, is to learn to love and understand each other, to have fun and enjoy your youth. If you choose to have sex, it's all you will condition yourself to seek, and eventually it may destroy you or Jenny. Many people have chosen this path. For some it has led to abortion, for others, adoption. Just imagine having to give your child away and the heartbreak it would cause. Sometimes the boy just leaves, making the girl feel used, wanted only for sex and not for herself."

Although the sun was getting warmer as it climbed in the morning sky, goosebumps prickled Henry's arms as Mr. Engelmann spoke. He'd never given these things any thought before. But he knew he'd never abandon Jenny, no matter how hard things got. He'd do whatever he had to and they'd be happy.

As if reading his mind, Mr. Engelmann said, "Sure, there are many, many relationships where couples really love each other and eventually get married and live together. But they may find that they have cheated themselves out of the joys, pleasures and fresh discoveries of sexual love. And if they marry early because of a child, they may sacrifice their educations and careers, and as the satisfaction of sex wears off, there may be anger, resentment and even blame. If you play with fire, you can get burned, as the saying goes."

It seemed that Mr. Engelmann had an answer for everything.

"It might sound like I am preaching to you, Henry, but avoid temptation. Keep your mind on the reasons why you choose to do the right thing. Think things through carefully and have a plan, especially for those times when you know you can fall. Be prepared, know the consequences of your actions. Most people succumb to temptation because they are guided by their feelings of the moment, without consideration of the consequences until it is too late."

Henry began to feel the weight of their conversation settle over him. It was his life they were talking about.

"Always remember the big picture," Mr. Engelmann hammered away, jarring Henry's wavering thoughts. "God created marriage in which two people are united into one flesh, and it is there that sexual intimacy becomes whole and valid and secure. Couples give each other the gift of themselves without shame, fear or worry. Its purpose is realized and validated in the sanctity of marriage. God gave us the desire to procreate, but He also gave us the ability, power and will to harness those desires. Every time you say no to temptation—say no to something you know is wrong—you strengthen your will and your belief about what is right and what is wrong.

"Build your house on a rock so that when temptation comes knocking on your door, it will not be washed away like a house built on sand. So, think carefully, my son," Mr. Engelmann said.

The pastor had spoken about the houses built on rock and sand in a sermon a few Sundays before. Now Henry understood what the scripture meant.

"As I already said, Henry, just like you and Jenny, Anna and I cared for each other very much. We decided not to have sex because the risk was too great. So we avoided situations or places that might tempt us and kept our minds always on other things. Think on it this way. If a woman wants to lose weight, she doesn't think about chocolate cake all day or set a piece in front of her to be tempted. No, she avoids sweets. She keeps them out of the house. She pushes it out of her mind and dwells on other things: how good she is going to look, and how much better she is going to feel physically and about herself.

"Remember, Henry, the thoughts we entertain lead to feelings of arousal or hunger or whatever, and eventually our feelings, driven by our thoughts, lead us to act—either like an intelligent person in control and guided by his beliefs or like an animal driven by instinct."

As if to drive home Mr. Engelmann's point, a dog started sniffing around the garbage cans in the back lane. There couldn't have been a better visual reinforcement of what Mr. Engelmann had said.

Henry thought the discussion was over, until Mr. Engelmann muttered "Temptation" under his breath. Henry glanced up at Mr. Engelmann as he continued, "Yes, temptation can be very strong, especially in the area of sex. That's why we refuse to carry a certain kind of magazine in our store. We could make more money by selling them, but we would be adding to the misery that already exists in the world. Those magazines exploit the sex drive within us. They take the act of loving one another out from under the umbrella of marriage where it belongs. Rather than picturing women as the wholesome, beautiful creatures they are, they become objects in those magazines, things used for pleasure. Their bodies are degraded, used and exploited."

Henry and his friends had once snuck a peek at one of those magazines in the drugstore. He hoped Mr. Engelmann couldn't tell that he had. He turned away from the sun, pretending to escape the hot rays in order to hide from Mr. Engelmann's perceptive gaze.

"I remember once when a salesman came into the store wanting us to sell those magazines. As soon as Anna saw them, she got angry. My Anna is such a quiet, peaceful woman, she would never harm anyone or any of God's creation—but when someone does or says something that goes against her beliefs or her sense of what is right, you better get out of the way! I will never forget how she picked up the broom and chased him out. That is one salesman who has never returned!"

Henry chuckled as he pictured frail Mrs. Engelmann chasing the salesman out of the store.

"Man has even devised a way to have sex and eliminate the fear of pregnancy," Mr. Engelmann mused. "It's called a condom. And I've even heard talk of a drug that might prevent pregnancy. These are just others ways of allowing ourselves to indulge in something that was meant for marriage."

"But isn't it better to prevent pregnancy?" Henry asked, finally thinking he'd found a flaw in Mr. Engelmann's thinking.

"Yes, but it's nothing more than a way to justify and cover up our weaknesses. If we have accepted our sinful nature and given in to temptation, there is no use even trying to avoid sex before marriage. I overheard one of our customers say she planned to give her son condoms to prevent him from getting his girlfriend in trouble. My, my, what is the world coming to?"

Mr. Engelmann's voice rose as he sternly added, "Rather than instill proper values, the gift of virginity at marriage, respect for women and their bodies and the sanctity of marriage, we allow permissiveness and even encourage it!"

Mr. Engelmann let out a long sigh, "No, Henry, it is our responsibility to teach discipline, sound values and principles to live by, to teach the reasons for living a chaste life before marriage. We must do the right thing, not the easy thing that only encourages our self-indulgence and whims. God did not make us helpless creatures. Many, many people have chosen to live righteous lives!"

Henry had never heard Mr. Engelmann talk for so long on one subject: he was on a roll. Clearly it was very important to him and Henry silently agreed with most of the things he'd said.

Just then, the little girl from next door wandered into the backyard.

"Look at this young child, Henry. Would you be prepared to

raise this girl, to provide for her?"

He was maybe only ten years older than she was, Henry suddenly realized. He was not ready to be a father. Seeing that young child made him realize his total lack of preparedness and maturity. A sense of righteous conviction stirred and he sat up straighter.

"Look how her mother is looking for her, so concerned, Henry," Mr. Engelmann said, then called out, "She is over here, Mrs. Robinson!"

"Oh my gosh!" Mrs. Robinson exclaimed as she rushed over, "How quickly she got out of the yard! I hope she hasn't been a bother to you."

"No, no, in fact she has been a help," Mr. Engelmann said, shading his face with his hand.

Mrs. Robinson frowned, a puzzled look on her face.

"Oh, not to worry. It's just something Henry and I were just discussing."

Mrs. Robinson looked at Henry, who just smiled, trying to hide his embarrassment and fervently hoping Mrs. Robinson wouldn't guess what they had been talking about.

Mr. Engelmann and Henry watched Mrs. Robinson take her little girl's hand and walk away. The little girl turned and waved goodbye and Mr. Engelmann waved back. Henry couldn't imagine himself as the father of that young child.

"I cannot stress this enough, Henry. Only in marriage, only in an atmosphere of love and caring and respect for each other in which the man and the women become one, is lovemaking a blessed and sacred thing."

And then he said something Henry would never forget.

"When we remove lovemaking from a marital setting, it is like inviting someone to a fine dinner and then giving them only dessert without the main course. It becomes a hollow act that only the sanctity of marriage can fill." He paused, before continuing with excitement. "Henry, this world so desperately needs people who have thought things through and don't go through life like a leaf tossed by the wind. We need, more than ever, strong people whom others will want to emulate because of the wholesome way they live.

"I have seen the way you and Jenny look at each other and want to help you to understand this whole matter, but I know from my own experience knowledge is not enough. Many times our problems are so big, or the temptation so great, that we need another form of help."

Henry moved closer to the edge of the old grey crate, his mind totally fixed on what Mr. Engelmann would say next. Henry knew he needed help beyond Mr. Engelmann's logic and reasoning. When the moment came, he doubted he would be strong enough to rise above his weakness like Mr. Engelmann was encouraging him to do.

"Henry, when trouble comes our way, or our loved ones get sick or die, who do we turn to?"

Henry knew the answer. He looked over to Mr. Engelmann. "We turn to God."

Mr. Engelmann looked into Henry's eyes. "Yes, that is what we do. When things are going fine, we have no need for God. But when trouble comes and overtakes us, all the knowledge or reasoning in the world just doesn't seem to help us deal with the situation. To God—that is where most, if not all, of us eventually turn. God gave us free will so that we can direct our own affairs. But because we are weak, we are not perfect and are sinful in nature. We need to be dependent upon Him and His strength to do what is right."

If Mr. Engelmann had said that right at the start, Henry was certain he would have tuned him out long ago, but now he knew the old man was right. In spite of all the knowledge and wisdom Mr. Engelmann had shared with him, Henry admitted to himself that he needed God's help. His feelings for Jenny were just so overwhelming.

Mr. Engelmann squinted and looked up at the sky, his pose prayerful, then glanced at Henry once more. "That is why I start each day by praying and meditating and reading the Bible. I offer up the day to Him and ask for help to do His will and not mine. He knows what is good for me."

Mr. Engelmann straightened his back. "Oh, I still sin—"

"But, how could you possibly?" Henry blurted. "You know so much and—"

"Yes, yes, Henry," said Mr. Engelmann. "That's the point. As you get older, you know more and so more is expected of you. You realize daily how you still fall short of being a godly person. While we are not expected to be perfect, we are expected to do what is right—and if we fail, we ask for forgiveness and try again. God understands our weakness. He looks more at our hearts than at what we do. You will soon understand this. It is just food for thought. Which reminds me, I think we both need to eat."

Henry nodded.

But instead of getting up and going back inside, they continued to sit in silence. It seemed to Henry that Mr. Engelmann did this on purpose so he could think about what had just been said.

Henry had to agree that he was tempted all the time, but had never really thought to pray unless he was facing a big problem or some huge calamity. Suddenly it didn't seem right that he should only turn to God and acknowledge Him only in times of trouble. He should do it all the time. Perhaps if he prayed more and his mind was on better things, maybe he wouldn't be so tempted all the time. And when he was faced with wrong choices, maybe he could deal with them better.

Anna surprised them both by appearing at the back door.

"Good Lord, what is it with you two men? It's almost noon and here you are, still talking. I was getting worried about you!"

"Not to worry," said Mr. Engelmann. "Just a little man-to-man talk."

Anna smiled, eyes brightening as she gazed at them. "Well, don't be too much longer. You both need your lunch." She held her smile as she turned back into the store.

Mr. Engelmann pushed his hands against the crate, trying to stand and straighten out. "*Ach mein Gott*, help me up."

Henry, too, was stiff from sitting for so long but he hurriedly stood and took hold of Mr. Engelmann's arm.

"Thank you for talking to me, Mr. Engelmann," Henry said as the older man stretched his back. "What you said about choices and what we believe in helps a lot."

"*Ach*, Henry, that's the heart of the matter. Making sound choices in life based upon values and principles is a most important lesson. You are and become what you believe in. But we have talked quite enough for today."

As Henry moved to follow his employer back into the store, Mr. Engelmann spoke again. "What I am saying may not be popular, but I believe it is the right thing to do, Henry. In any case, just like the Lord, I am not here to take your free will away. I've told you some of what I know. Take from it what you wish. In the end it's always up to you."

Henry held the door open for Mr. Engelmann, feeling the midday sun heat his skull and shoulders, hoping the hot rays would burn this morning's conversation deep into his mind. A final thought struck him before he went in. Something about what Mr. Engelmann said about getting older and knowing more and having more expected of you had created an awareness of responsibility that Henry hadn't felt or acknowledged before.

He'd have to think about all of this some more.

Both Mr. and Mrs. Engelmann were standing behind the till when Henry entered the main part of the store. Henry sure hoped that Mr. Engelmann wouldn't share their conversation with his wife—even the thought was too embarrassing to contemplate.

He addressed her politely, "Thank you, Mrs. Engelmann, for letting me and Mr. Engelmann have such a long talk."

"*Tcha*. Not to worry, Henry. It was my pleasure."

"I'll go for lunch, now, and I promise to work hard this afternoon to make up for the morning."

"Go, go on," said Mr. Engelmann, "get something to eat. A strong man like you needs a good lunch."

Henry smiled and darted out.

"YOU SPENT A LONG TIME talking to Henry."

"He needed me, Anna, and I could tell what he needed to hear. I was young once, too."

"I know only too well," Anna said with a wink.

"I hope he thinks over what I said. I told him the things I would have said to our own boy if we'd had one."

"I know, David. I know how much you enjoy him. That is why I didn't disturb you two out there."

"Yes, he is a fine young man. Yesterday as I watched him work, I couldn't get it out of my mind how capable he is for his age. You know, Anna, business has improved so much since Henry started working for us, I wonder if he wasn't sent by the Lord as the answer to our prayers for help."

"The Lord works in mysterious ways, David ... in more ways than one."

David looked at his wife with love. "Come, Borden's Bakery brought some fresh sourdough bread this morning. I'll cut some salami and a ripe Roma tomato, and we will sit down for a sandwich. What do you think, Anna?"

"How can I say no, David, when you say it so romantically?"

CHAPTER ELEVEN

THE BAD NEWS WAS there were only two days of summer holidays left, the good, that it would be Henry's first year in high school. Even better was that Jenny would be in the same grade as he was and going to the same high school. It sure would have been great if they'd been assigned to the same form, but the notices the school had sent out a week ago said otherwise. Both Henry and Jenny were very disappointed.

On this, the second-last day of summer holidays, Henry and Jenny planned to go to Wascana Park for the afternoon. They had talked about having a picnic, but neither of them wanted to ask their parents to pack them a lunch, considering the by now oft-mentioned concern that the teens were already spending too much time together.

Henry stocked shelves for two hours and delivered a grocery order, then asked Mr. Engelmann if he could have the afternoon off. It was a beautiful day, perfect for bike riding with Jenny before school started on Friday.

Mr. Engelmann peered over the top of his glasses and met Henry's gaze. After studying him for a long moment, Mr. Engelmann nodded.

"Have a good time, Henry. You deserve it."

The aroma of fried onions and potatoes filled Henry's nostrils when he arrived home for lunch. It was the start of a perfect afternoon as far as he was concerned.

"Hi, Mom. Smells good." He dragged out the last word and she smiled.

"How was work this morning?"

"Pretty good. We're starting to get more and more deliveries and it's helping our sales. Mr. Engelmann is very pleased." After a short pause Henry casually said, "I think I'll go out for a bike ride after lunch." He didn't say anything about Jenny.

"Oh, you're not going back to work this afternoon?"

"No, there are only two days left before school starts and we thought we'd go out for a ride." Henry cringed at his use of the word *we*, and hoped his mom wouldn't pick up on it.

"Well, you and Jenny have a nice time," she said approvingly, removing any guilt Henry had about not mentioning Jenny's name.

He'd hoped she would be waiting for him on the step, but Jenny was nowhere in sight when he got to her house. He got off his bike, leaned it against the fence and waited for her to come out. After five minutes he decided to knock on the door. As he started up the steps, he heard Jenny and her mom arguing.

"...Yes, but your father and I feel you are seeing too much of that boy."

"Mom, he's a very good friend. I'd be lost without him."

"As soon as school starts, we want you to make some new friends right away. It's good to have a large circle of friends."

"Oh, I will, Mom. Don't worry."

"Henry's a nice boy, but you're seeing far too much of him."

They were arguing about him. Tension rooted him to the landing. He so wanted Jenny's parents to like him.

"It's just a bike ride, Mom."

"But I still need your help with the last of the unpacking and putting things away. Besides with school starting, you should stay in during the week and only go out on Saturdays."

"I've always been a good student. Trust me, Mom."

A long silence followed. Henry didn't know if Jenny was coming out or not. He hoped Mrs. Sarsky wouldn't come to the door.

"Mom, *please*, we only have a couple of days of holidays left."

"Well, be careful and not too long, now."

"Oh, thank you, Mom!"

In his mind's eye, Henry saw Jenny's eyes brighten and the return of her bubbly self. With that, his tension melted away.

As Jenny came to the front door, he quickly backed down the front steps. He didn't want her to know he'd been eavesdropping. Just as he reached the bottom step, Jenny appeared.

"Oh, Henry, you're here."

"Yeah, just got here."

Jenny always looked lovely, but she was particularly radiant as she stood on the stoop, sunlight picking out bright glints in her hair. Usually when they went bike riding, Jenny wore jeans or slacks, but today she had on her black-and white-checked skirt and a white short-sleeved blouse. A white ribbon held back her hair. No matter what she wore, she always looked beautiful.

"It's so sunny out today; I thought I'd wear my straw hat, too." She brought it out from behind her and placed it firmly on her head with two hands, slanting it rakishly over one eye to cast a sharp shadow across her nose. She looked mysterious, sophisticated, like a movie star. And before Henry could think of who she reminded him of, she quickly thrust the rim of the straw hat up, her happy features instantly lit by the sun. Now she looked like a sailor, ready to pull up anchor. The straw hat seemed to capture Jenny's mercurial personality. Her eyes sparkled, and her smile was teasing.

"Oh, Jenny …" Henry was speechless. He shook his head side to side, trying to convey what words at that moment couldn't — how thoroughly he loved her. She had to feel his thoughts beaming at her like the light from a beacon.

"What's going on out here?" Mrs. Sarsky asked stiffly, shattering Henry's romantic reverie. It was as if the warmth of his tender feelings had been iced over with cold. He snapped to attention.

"Why aren't you gone yet?" Mrs. Sarsky demanded, her tone irritating Henry's raw nerves further.

"Oh, I was just showing Henry my straw hat." Jenny responded, her soothing, measured voice coming to Henry's rescue.

"Yeah, it sure looks cute on her." Henry couldn't think of what else to say. "Does it have a string, Jenny? It might blow off in the wind when you ride your bike."

"I forgot about that. Guess I'd better leave it at home."

Jenny took it off and handed it to her mom.

"I'll get your bike, Jenny." Finally, a reason to leave. Mrs. Sarsky looked so sternly at him that he began to feel guilty about taking her daughter out. Jenny was waiting for him at the gate when he came back with her bike. He caught Mrs. Sarsky looking at him through the screen door. Her penetrating glare sent a chill up his spine. He was really glad now that Jenny had wanted to keep quiet about the night those guys had grabbed her; how much more would Mrs. Sarsky hate him if she knew he hadn't been able to protect her daughter?

"Let's go." Jenny got on her bike and sped down the block.

"'Bye, Mrs. Sarsky," Henry called out as he hopped on his bike. She didn't answer as he pedalled away, hard, and quickly caught up to Jenny. He found it difficult to keep his eyes off her as they rode along.

To get to Wascana Park, they headed down College Avenue to Albert Street. Jenny was impressed by the stately homes.

"Are those houses ever gorgeous! This must be an older part of the city. I'd sure like to live in one of them."

When they turned into the park, the roadway was deserted. They rode past the Legislative Building and continued on through the park to the lakeshore. Jenny hadn't talked about that night since it happened, brushing off Henry's questions about how she felt the next day with, "I'm fine, Henry. Let's just forget about it, okay?" Still, he hoped today would erase any lingering memories of the last time she'd been here. With its jewel-like lake, the park really was a beautiful place.

They turned off the road onto a wide sidewalk that created a boardwalk of sorts down by the water, circled around the bandstand, and weaved in and out of large groves of aspen and elm, willow and pine. Once again, they were alone. They came to a section of the path with only a few slight curves and hills.

"Follow me!" Jenny hollered over her shoulder, gathering speed to race down the path.

In no time, Henry caught up to her, and by the time they got to the end of the path near the water's edge, they were both gasping from exertion. They got off their bikes and laid them on the grass. They walked along the edge of the lake, the embankment of which was elevated about three feet by a stone and concrete wall. Henry's dad had told him the lake was manmade, dug out by hand as a make-work project during the Depression. After walking a while, the path ended in a secluded stand of trees. Jenny sat on the grass and Henry sank down beside her.

"That was fun," Jenny said, catching her breath. "It's very pretty here. And I love the way the Legislative Building is reflected in the water."

It *was* pretty, Henry thought. Some of the trees had begun to change, their fall colours contrasting warmly against the tall, cool evergreens. A sailboat appeared further down the lake.

"Have you ever been in a sailboat?" Jenny asked him.

"No, have you?"

"Yes, when we lived in Vancouver, friends of ours had a huge sailboat with a cabin and all. I loved it when the wind caught the sail. It was exhilarating and scary all at once. At times I thought for sure the boat was going to tip into the ocean."

A few clouds had formed, masking the bright sun. Jenny lay back on the embankment and looked up at the sky, Henry beside her. Their arms touched, and instead of just holding hands like they usually did, their fingers sort of played with each other, gradually intertwining. A tingly sensation zinged through

Henry's body, and the yearning he sometimes felt for Jenny when he lay in bed at night waiting to fall asleep grew stronger by the second.

"Do you ever try and see things in the clouds?" she asked, breaking the silence and the growing tension.

"Yeah, lots of times," Henry replied, though clouds were the last thing on his mind. His thoughts were consumed by how it felt to have Jenny's lips under his, her body pressed close. The soft hint of lilacs and the scent of her own warm skin nearly drove him crazy. He rolled over on his side and propped himself up to look down at her. He watched the pulse beat at the base of her neck and imagined following the scoop of the silver chain she wore with his finger, shuddering eagerly at the thought. If only he were older and had a class ring she could wear on that necklace. He wanted her to belong to him. He wanted her more than anything in the world. They stared at each other for a long moment. He drew closer and their lips gently touched. It was a brief kiss. Henry pulled back slightly, only to be drawn back down to her tender smile, never wanting to leave her again.

Jenny's tongue touched his closed mouth. He instinctively parted his lips and when their tongues met, electrifying pulses surged through him. Slowly, he trailed his hand up her torso, coming to rest on the soft mound of her blouse-covered breast. Jenny quivered as his right leg moved almost of its own accord over hers, working its way between her legs. Her skirt was rucked up slightly by the action and Henry could feel the answering swell in his groin. He wondered if Jenny could too. He pulled her in tight, pressing against her warm body. Jenny moaned softly and the sound made him drag his knee up, but she held firm, unwilling to part her legs further. He was sure Jenny wanted him as much as he did her by the way she was kissing and responding to him, but that slight hesitation jarred his senses.

Only an hour ago Jenny had told her mother that she could be trusted, and here he was trying to get her to break her promise. He also recalled the long look Mr. Engelmann had given him that morning before saying he could have the afternoon off. Then Mr. Engelmann's words about Pavlov's dogs came flooding back, along with his warning to think things through, to have a plan of action in the face of temptation and to be aware of the consequences of one's actions.

Oh, but she was an assault on his senses, though; the sight, sound and scent of her made the blood thunder through his veins; the answering movements of her body fueling the desire in his own. He had to get closer, and he pressed his warm mouth to the tender spot on her neck beneath her ear, trying to breathe her in. Jenny gave a small, breathless sigh and her legs shifted, parting, signaling him to go on. His knee fell solidly between her legs and he pressed hard against her once more.

It was nearly his undoing. Henry leaned into her body, his breath coming fast, his entire body flushed and hot.

He felt like the sailboat in Jenny's memory, swaying first this way and then that, caught between the rushing winds of desire and the waves of reason washing over his mind. He struggled for control. As Mr. Engelmann's words pounded through his thoughts again, Henry knew he could go no further. He pulled back, and Jenny brought her legs together almost instinctively. She opened her eyes and looked at him, desire and hesitation warring within her. She seemed about to speak but didn't.

He slid off and rolled onto his back next to her, neither of them saying a word. Their hands touched, and their fingers immediately laced together. Henry knew he would look back on this moment and wonder *what if...*; he knew there would be times he would regret this decision. He'd had the opportunity to make love to Jenny; she would have let him, he could tell.

Controlling his desire was probably one of the most unselfish things he had ever done, the beginning of a conscious effort to live a life based on values he would start to believe in, of putting into action Mr. Engelmann's teachings.

Henry cleared his throat and tried to calm his body, still choked and swollen with need. "Uh, I see a two-storey house in that cloud. Do you see it, Jenny?" He pointed towards it with his free hand.

"Oh, sure," she said, her voice a bit raspy too. "There's the roof. And look, it has one of those dormers in the centre."

"Yeah, it's just like the ones we saw on our walk. I really like them, too. Someday when we're married, we'll own a house like that. And maybe the window in the middle will be Camilla's room," he added, hoping Jenny would be pleased he had remembered the name she wanted to give her daughter.

Jenny squeezed his hand, and Henry knew she understood why he had stopped.

They lay there, absorbed in their own thoughts. Jenny's forefinger brushed the top of his hand. He knew she was deep in thought, trying to figure it all out. He thought about talking about it, and he thought Jenny might want to, too. Yet, they remained silent. A dispassionate discussion would spoil the beauty of what they'd shared. Jenny shifted her body towards Henry and rested her head on his shoulder.

After a long pause, she murmured, "I really love you a lot, Henry."

Henry didn't know how to respond. He hadn't expected Jenny to say that, but his heart soared at the words. He tried to contain the joy bubbling inside him as he whispered back, "I love you too, Jenny."

Jenny squeezed his hand again as they lay there, oblivious to the world. There was nothing more to say. Henry would never forget the oneness, the ecstasy of being so close to another human being. He didn't feel cheated out of sex. They had done the right thing. There was no guilt, shame or worry—only pride.

They stayed in each others arms for a long time, dreaming of their future. When Henry opened his eyes and became aware of his surroundings again, the air had cooled and the sun hung near the treetops to the west. The moisture in the air told him that rain had fallen a few miles away. Huge cumulonimbus clouds reached high into what had been a clear blue sky.

"We better get going," Henry said.

"Yes, I guess we better," Jenny said, opening her eyes.

Moving to her knees, Jenny kissed his lips lightly and gazed longingly into his eyes. How her own could capture the blue of the sky and the warm radiance of the sun at the same time was a mystery to him. He could gaze into them forever. She tugged on his hand.

"Come on," Jenny coaxed him up, grabbing hold of both his hands and pulling him sharply towards her. Just as they were about to collide, she let go and threw her arms around his neck, burying her head on his shoulder. "Thank you, Henry."

Henry knew what she was thanking him for. He'd removed the pressure and freed her from worry. He felt like her knight in shining armour, a gentleman in the true sense of the word.

"I had a great time today," she smiled.

"So did I." Henry wrapped his arms around her. As he did, he noticed a huge elm tree directly behind her. Near the water's edge, its large trunk almost divided the view of the Legislative Building on the other side of the lake in half. "Come on, Jenny. I want to do something to remember this day."

Casting Henry a puzzled look, she followed him to the tree. He let go of her hand, reached into his pocket and pulled out his jackknife.

As she stepped back to give him room, she said, "Oh, great artist, are you going to carve out my heart?"

Henry just smiled and turned to the tree. Using the point of the knife as a pencil, he outlined the shape of a heart large enough to hold printing. Then, holding the knife with two hands, he carved away the protective bark, gradually exposing the bright wood of the tree's interior. He could smell the sappy first layer that had started out so many years ago as a single, tiny twig, protecting all ensuing layers as it grew into a fully mature tree. That was what their love for each other would be like, too; it would grow like the layers of a tree into a strong, everlasting love, weathering all the storms of life that came their way.

Finally, the entire shape of the heart was visible. It was almost three inches wide and four inches high, a little larger than he wanted. It contrasted sharply against the dark bark and was now permanently embedded into the large elm.

"Henry," Jenny breathed, entranced, "The tree will always share the beat of our hearts!"

Henry smiled. "What a nice thought, Jenny."

His gaze remained steady on the trunk as he carved their initials, HP + JS, into the heart.

Behind him, Jenny put her hands on his shoulders. She raised herself on her toes to peer over his shoulder at the tree.

"Oh, Henry, it's beautiful."

"There's just one more thing I want to add."

Since the heart was large, there was room beneath each of the curves at the top. With the point of the knife, he scratched in a tiny cupid figure, almost in a reclining position, first on one side and then on the other side of the heart.

As he etched the shape of a wing on each figure, Jenny exclaimed, "And there are our guardian angels watching over and protecting us."

Henry nodded, happy that they seemed to share the same thoughts.

Jenny slid her hands off his shoulders and wrapped one arm around his waist instead. He drew her close, allowing her to snuggle in next to him. They held each other, gazing at the inscription before them.

It was getting harder to pick out the details and Henry again realized how late it was. He'd been so excited to carve the heart in the tree he'd lost all sense of time. Shadows grew longer and the air cooler. Jenny noticed it, too.

"Yikes!" she said, looking at her watch. "It's quarter to six. We better start back."

"Yeah," Henry said, reluctant to do anything that would end their day until Jenny's lovely face lit with mischief, her eyes dancing. She startled him by putting her hands against his chest and giving him a quick shove, "Race you to Albert Street!"

She was on her bike before he realized he'd been challenged.

Albert Street was busy. They rode single file, not side by side as they had on the way there. Jenny was in the lead and pedalling as fast as she could. When they arrived at College Avenue, they turned east. Traffic wasn't nearly as congested now so Henry pulled up beside her. She turned and caught his gaze, smiling, and extended her hand. He reached up and grabbed it, and in almost perfect unison they rode down College Avenue together.

At Broder Street they turned north. Home was only a few blocks away. Their adventure would soon be over.

Jenny's mother was standing at the gate looking their way as they rode up.

"It's about time you got back." Her eyes flashed with anger.

"It's still early, Mom, and I said I'd help you all evening with the last of the unpacking."

"I'm sorry if I kept Jenny out too long this afternoon, Mrs. Sarsky. I guess we didn't realize the time."

Jenny's mom glared at Henry for a moment. "You better get on home, Henry." Her voice carried a tone of finality, almost as if she'd never let Jenny go out with him again.

Henry didn't know what else to say. Jenny smiled and winked at him behind her mother's back. She had just laid her bike on the front lawn when Mrs. Sarsky grabbed her arm and led her up the front stairs.

"See you tomorrow," Jenny called over her shoulder.

Henry thought it better not to say anything, but lifted his hand in a half-hearted wave. Sweat rolled down his back. He wiped away beads of perspiration from his forehead with the back of his hand before wheeling his own bike home. When he entered the house, his mom was in the kitchen, preparing supper.

"Is that you, Henry?"

"Yeah, it's me, Mom. I'm going to wash up."

Mary Pederson was peeling carrots when her son walked into the kitchen and sat down at the table. "How was your bike ride?"

"It was great. We had a lot of fun. We went to Wascana Park."

She turned and looked at him. "That far?"

"Oh, it's not so far. I showed Jenny the Legislative Building,"

Henry said. And before she could ask him any more questions, he added, "When's Dad coming home?"

"Oh, he said he'd be home late," his mom answered, in a voice that Henry knew meant she was still concerned that he had gone to the park with Jenny and wanted to talk about it.

Sensing her concern, Henry quickly put in, "I'm going to finish painting the inside of Mr. Engelmann's store tomorrow. Do you know if Dad can spare any more paintbrushes?"

"You'll have to ask him when he comes home."

After a short silence, Mary asked, "Did Jenny's mom know you two were going to the park?"

"Yeah, I think Jenny told her," Henry answered, trying not to feel as though he were being interrogated.

"Well, make certain you always tell her parents where you're going,"

"Yeah, I will, Mom." After a brief pause, Henry voiced something that had been bothering him, "Did you think we were out too long this afternoon?"

"No," his mom was thoughtful, "I don't think so. Why do you ask?"

There she went again, putting him on the spot.

"Well, when we got home, Jenny's mom seemed a little upset."

"She's probably concerned about her daughter being new to the city and all."

"Well, it seemed like she was more upset at me."

"Parents tend to worry more about daughters than they do about sons. Always tell her parents where you're going and always bring her home on time, and things should be all right."

"Why do parents worry more about girls?"

"Oh, it's just a parent thing. When you're a parent and have a daughter, I'm sure you'll understand."

She hadn't exactly answered his question but he sensed his mom was ready to drop the subject.

"Would you please set the table?"

"Yeah, sure."

Henry never really thought about how parents felt when

their children went out on a date. It occurred to him he was responsible not only to Jenny, but also to their parents. He had definitely seen worry on both his mom's and Mrs. Sarsky's faces.

His thoughts flashed to the gym locker room and the comments he'd heard from other boys. How would the guys feel if the parents of the girl they were talking about were sitting in the room too? Would they boast about stolen bases or what they'd done with her in the back seat of their car then? What if the girl they were talking about was sitting in the room and listening to how she was being used? It was awful. He was proud of himself for thinking things through earlier and honouring Jenny.

When his dad arrived home, he was kind of grumpy and hardly did more than grunt. Henry caught his mother's eye. Something was bothering his dad, but they knew from past experience it was best not to ask until Bill was ready to say what was on his mind. They ate supper in an uneasy silence.

Afterward, Henry went outside to sit on the steps. He wanted to visit Jenny but was afraid he would upset Mrs. Sarsky even more. Besides, his best friend Gary Franklin and his family should've been home late last night, so Henry decided to walk over to Gary's place, which was on the next block in the opposite direction of Jenny's.

Henry smiled as he thought about playing in Gary's backyard. They had discovered an old airplane cockpit at the junkyard one summer and had brought it home on a wagon. They'd heaved it onto an old mattress that had been discarded in the alley and had discovered great joy in pretending to be Canadian Air Force pilots being attacked by German planes. Of course, they won every battle. They'd played on that airplane every time Henry visited. Now that he was in love and thinking about getting married, Henry wondered if he was getting too old for that kind of thing. It was hard to believe that had only been a couple of years ago.

"Hi, Hank!" Gary called out as Henry turned into his driveway.

"Hey! How was the holiday?"

"Great!"

Gary told him about visiting his dad at the army base and the leave they took to Jasper and Banff, and all about his first time seeing the Rockies and glaciers. The way Gary described it, Henry sort of wished he'd been there.

Henry filled Gary in about working for Mr. Engelmann, how the old man had, surprisingly enough, become a good friend and about his own ideas to increase sales by offering a delivery service.

"By the way, would you like to work Saturdays delivering groceries?"

"Sure," Gary said, "how much does he pay?"

"Whatever he can afford. There's no standard amount."

Gary thought about it. "Yeah, sure, why not? It'll help pay for some of the school books."

That was Gary. Steady, practical and dependable. He was always there when Henry needed him.

From there the conversation turned to how they'd used to tease Mr. Engelmann about the squeaky floors in his store. Over the years, Mr. Engelmann had become attuned to the sounds each floorboard made and used this knowledge to keep a watchful eye on Henry and his friends. On several occasions, they entered the store as a group, spread out and jumped up and down on the floorboards all at the same time, trying to confuse the old store owner.

Henry and Gary's laughter brought Gary's sister, Sarah, out onto the porch. She sat down next to them on the steps.

Sarah was a bit overweight and had a large dark purple birthmark on the left side of her face. She didn't have very many friends, partly because of her appearance. But Henry liked Sarah and was as comfortable around her as he was with Gary.

Henry told them about Jenny, thinking she and Sarah would get along well, and told them he would introduce them if Jenny was around the next night.

After another few minutes of small talk, Henry headed home. The sun had slipped below the horizon and the corner streetlights came on, making him conscious of his shadow as he walked home. As he neared the streetlight, the shadow behind him grew shorter and shorter until it was just beneath his feet. When he passed, his shadow grew longer again, in front of him now, arriving at his house before he did. Just before he opened the gate, Henry stopped and raised both arms, curling his fingers, watching as the shadow before him morphed into a monster. He smiled to himself as he brought his arms down. Maybe he wasn't quite finished being a little kid.

Henry swung open the gate and made for the front steps, surprised to see his dad was sitting on one of them. He wondered if his dad had seen him fooling around with the shadow. He still seemed absorbed in thought.

"Hey, Dad."

"Hi, son. Over at Gary's place?"

"Yeah, they got home last night, and I thought I'd go and say hello. Sounds like they had a nice holiday."

When his dad didn't respond, Henry knew it was because his own family hadn't gotten away that year because of his dad's work. Henry wanted to sit down and talk with him, but it felt awkward.

"Well, good night, Dad. Think I'll head off to bed. Big day at the store tomorrow."

"G'night, son." As Henry passed him, his father added, "I left another paintbrush for you on the kitchen table. You can use it. Just make sure you clean it when you're done."

"I sure will, Dad. Thanks a lot." Henry left his dad on the stoop and went in.

His mom was mending some of his socks. She asked him about Gary and his family and he filled her in.

"Your dad left a paintbrush out for you."

"Yeah, I know, he just told me. Boy, I'm sure tired tonight. Think I'll hit the hay early."

"Well, you do have a busy day tomorrow, maybe that's a good idea."

With that Henry headed down the hallway to the bathroom.

His reflection in the mirror seemed older, he thought. He placed a finger above his upper lip and rubbed at the soft fine hair growing there. He wondered when he would be able to shave. He lowered his finger to his lips, trying again to feel Jenny's mouth on his, her tongue touching his. He wanted to savour the day, somehow store its memories and preserve them. He was reluctant to wash his face or brush his teeth because he wanted it to linger a little while longer.

In his room, he climbed into bed. The blinds were open and the light of the full moon cast shadows of tree branches across his blanket and up the wall. He thought of playing with the light to create another shadow, like he'd done with the streetlight, but he no longer wanted to play that game. He only wanted to think about the day, what had happened—and what hadn't.

Henry closed his eyes, letting his thoughts run free.

CHAPTER TWELVE

Henry arrived at work on the last day before school wondering how Mr. Engelmann would be able to keep up with things. Business had picked up considerably, and if the good service they had developed didn't continue, things could easily take a turn for the worse again. There was only so much Henry could do on evenings and Saturdays.

"'Morning, Mr. Engelmann."

"Ah, *guten Morgen*, Henry," Mr. Engelmann peered over the rim of his glasses. Keen hazel eyes beneath bushy brows read Henry's every move and gesture. "How was your outing with Jenny?"

"Oh, it was great, Mr. Engelmann. We sure had a good time."

Satisfied that Henry had done no wrong, Mr. Engelmann nodded once and lowered his gaze to the invoice in front of him.

After a brief silence, he said, "There are three deliveries this morning. Could you please look after them before restocking the shelves?"

"Sure, Mr. Engelmann. I'll do them right away." Henry studied the deliveries to plan out his route. Since they weren't large orders, all three easily fit in his bike carrier. "See you in a bit."

When Henry returned, Mr. Engelmann asked him to watch the store while he tended to Anna. She had not been feeling well for the last few days and it was clear Mr. Engelmann was worried about her. As Henry restocked shelves, a man wearing a dark blue suit, white shirt and navy blue tie with maroon stripes entered the store. Henry was impressed by the matching maroon hankie tucked into the man's breast pocket. Henry wished he could dress like that man someday.

The man looked around until his eyes settled on Henry standing in the centre aisle.

"Do you sell Players cigarettes?"

"Yes, we do."

"Good, I'd like three packages." He put $1.50 in quarters down on the counter.

Henry got the cigarettes for the man, who winked at him and left the store, tossing a casual "Keep the change" over his shoulder.

Henry wondered what he did for a living and jogged to the front door to see what kind of a car he was driving. By the time he got to the window, though, the man was gone.

As Henry returned to restocking shelves, his eye caught the glint of the quarters beside the till. He walked over to the counter and stared down at the money. He had forgotten to ring it in. He moved to the other side of the counter to do so, then hesitated. No one was in the store and Mr. Engelmann was upstairs with his wife. He looked at the six shiny quarters and thought how easy it would be to take them. He also thought about all the things he could buy with that money, especially with school just starting. He had worked hard for Mr. Engelmann and hadn't received very much in payment. He looked around to see if Mr. Engelmann had come back, but he was still alone.

Henry glanced over to the tiny opening in the wall behind the till. He had noticed Mr. and Mrs. Engelmann peek through it on occasion to check on customers in the store. They especially kept a watchful eye on young people to make sure they didn't take anything. If one of them swiped a candy bar or some other sweet, Mr. Engelmann would come out from the back and politely ask the boy if he wanted to include the pocketed item in his purchase. Even Henry and his friends had all been amazed that Mr. Engelmann seemed to know their every move, almost as if he had X-ray vision or the power to read thoughts or something.

Henry had that same kind of feeling now, even though he was sure Mr. Engelmann wasn't there. Then the toilet flushed above him and he knew Mr. Engelmann would be down in a minute.

Henry stared at the money. He wanted it, yet something inside rebelled. His heart raced as he covered all six quarters with his hand. The money felt cold against his hot sweaty palm. He pulled the coins towards him. *Quick, Henry, just take it and put it in your pocket. No one will know. No one. No one but me.*

Like a bolt of lightning, a flash of insight illuminated Henry's troubled mind. *Values,* Mr. Engelmann had said. *Principles to live by.* When they had talked about it out back, Henry hadn't quite understood how these thing applied to his own life. He remembered how Mr. Engelmann had struggled to find words and examples to more clearly define his meaning, and Henry remembered the day before in the park with Jenny—and why he'd stopped. Tempted for the second time in as many days, he understood the choice between right and wrong at a gut level.

Values to live by and choices based on values. Honesty, that's a value. That's what Mr. Engelmann meant. Are you honest or dishonest, Henry? Taking that money is stealing. That's dishonest. Sure—it was just another choice he had to make based on a value he believed in, but it wasn't just a one time choice. Life was a series of ongoing, daily choices! There was always a choice.

Henry felt the edge of a coin bite his hand and instantly knew the choice he had to make. Without lifting his hand, he simply pushed the entire six quarters back as far back as he possibly could towards the till where they belonged, then lifted his trembling hand off the silver. Two of the quarters stuck to his sweaty palm then dropped with a clang on the marble counter before rolling to a stop. At the sound, his face turned beet red and he held his breath. He glanced up to see if Mr. Engelmann had come down, but he was still alone.

Henry left the money there and went back to restocking shelves. He wanted to get as far away from the six quarters as fast as he could. His heart pounded and sweat had formed circles under his armpits and rolled down his back. As he placed a bottle of dish detergent on the top shelf, he looked past the neatly placed bottles and met Mr. Engelmann's gaze where he stood in the shadow of the back doorway.

How long had he been there? Had Mr. Engelmann seen him?

As Mr. Engelmann walked into the light of the store, Henry looked at him intently, studying his eyes for an answer. Mr. Engelmann only smiled. There was no anger, just a look of contentment ... or was it satisfaction?

"Did you sell a hundred dollars' worth of groceries while I was gone?"

Mr. Engelmann's laughter eased the tension gripping Henry. He took a deep breath.

"No," he replied, his throat dry and crackly. He tried to smile back and make light of Mr. Engelmann's question.

Mr. Engelmann took his spot behind the counter and noticed the six quarters.

"What is this, Henry?" He pointed to the coins with a bent forefinger.

"Oh that," Henry said nervously, trying to find the right way to explain it. "Yeah, a man came in all dressed up and bought three packages of cigarettes and said to keep the change. I ran over to see what make of car he was driving after he left, and ... I guess I forgot to ring in the sale. Sorry, Mr. Engelmann."

"Please, Henry, never leave money lying around. Always put it into the till. Money is a source of temptation. It is a good method of exchange and yet it can be the source of much evil." He peered over his glasses and stared at Henry, hard.

"Yes, sir," Henry replied, contrite. "I won't let it happen again."

And he meant every word.

Mr. Engelmann rang in the sale and took out fourteen cents.

"Here, Henry. This is yours. As the man said, 'Keep the change.'"

Henry hesitated. He didn't deserve it, after all he'd almost stolen it.

"Come on, Henry. Come. Here it is."

Henry walked over to the counter. He looked at the money, reluctant to take it.

"Henry!" Mr. Engelmann said, startling him somewhat. Henry's gaze snapped up to meet Mr. Engelmann's. "You deserve it. When I hired you, I said it and I say it again now: you're a good boy, no—a good man." And then with a look that penetrated Henry's very soul, he added, "I trust you."

They looked at each other for a long moment and Henry had the feeling that somehow Mr. Engelmann knew what had almost happened. It had felt like he was being watched, like he was being tested. How well had he learned Mr. Engelmann's lesson? Maybe that well-dressed man was even part of the test. Henry slowly picked up the money and put it in his pocket without a word. He went back to work, not wanting Mr. Engelmann to see how proud he felt or the tears welling up in his eyes.

As Henry filled the gaps on the shelves, Mr. Engelmann went through the invoices to be paid. The letter from the city tax department was still tucked beneath the till. Henry saw a corner of the letter stuck out. He thought about Mr. Engelmann's financial burden.

He gasped and raised a hand to his mouth. He had nearly stolen money that Mr. Engelmann desperately needed.

It really came home to him that a life lived on sound values was a life well lived, free of the burden of worry, shame and guilt. Had he taken the money, he might have been richer by $1.50, but how much poorer in self-respect, self-image and self-worth? Rather than pride, he would be riddled with guilt, worrying that Mr. Engelmann would notice the cigarettes missing from his inventory. And, having done it once and gotten away with it, he would be tempted to steal again. It made Henry remember what Mr. Engelmann had said about Pavlov's dogs: once rewarded, one can easily become conditioned to repeat his actions.

And even worse, had he given in to temptation, the entire truth of this experience—the enormous revelation of living a life based on truth and values—would have completely passed him by. It was all beginning to make sense now.

Mr. Engelmann's *I trust you, Henry* resonated in his mind for a long time.

Chapter Thirteen

THE NIGHT BEFORE SCHOOL STARTED Henry had trouble sleeping. Every hour or two he would wake in a cold sweat. He was a little nervous and excited about starting high school, but he was especially concerned about Jenny and him. Since they'd stopped seeing each other every day, Mrs. Sarsky seemed a bit nicer, but still wasn't nearly as friendly as when he'd first met her. And now, instead of seeing Jenny every second night, it was every third or more; Mrs. Sarsky seemed to always be able to find something for Jenny to do, as if she were purposely trying to keep them apart. Jenny had told him again not to worry about it, and that once school started and she made other friends, things would get better. His only consolation was the exchange of notes via the fencepost. It was the highlight of his day. The one Jenny had left for him the night before had said she would meet him at her gate at eight-thirty so they would walk to school together.

When morning finally arrived, Henry finished his breakfast by eight o'clock and stood by the front door, a new black leather case his mother had bought for him at Simpsons-Sears slung over his shoulder. She thought it would be easier for Henry to carry his books since he now would be walking almost a mile to school instead of six blocks

"Boy, you're sure up early!" Mary smiled at her son.

"Yeah, I'm kinda anxious to get going; just waiting until I meet Jenny. We're going to walk to school together." Then he added, "Timmy will probably walk with us and maybe Gary, too, but he was really sick last night. I'm not sure if he'll make it today. He said he would be here by twenty after and if he didn't show up by then, he'd be staying home today."

"Oh, that's too bad. The first day is so important. You get to meet your new teachers and the students in your class and sort of get oriented to high school"

"Yeah. I told him if he didn't come that I would try to see what class he is in and who his form teacher is."

"Well, that is good of you, son." She handed him a bag lunch. "You'll have to buy a soda pop or milk at the confectionary. Do you have enough money with you?"

"Yeah, I think so." He reached into his pocket and pulled out over a dollar in change. "Yeah, I have more than enough."

By twenty-five after, Gary still hadn't shown up so Henry decided to go ahead without him.

At his farewell, his mother emerged from the kitchen and kissed his cheek. He felt a little embarrassed—wasn't he too old for her to do that? But he still liked it. She was sending out her love, hoping it would guide, protect and comfort him as he faced a new day full of unknowns.

"Have a nice day, Henry."

"Yeah, thanks, Mom. You, too. I'll sure miss your lunch at noon." Henry caught her smile just before the storm door shut behind him.

Henry was glad to see Jenny already waiting for him at her gate. He hoped her mother wasn't peering out the front window. He was uneasy enough about school and didn't want to add to it by getting another stern look of disapproval from her.

Jenny beamed as he approached her.

"Hi, Henry. Am I ever excited about school—I can hardly wait to get there!"

"Yeah, me, too," Henry tried to match her enthusiasm. Jenny was always so adventurous, ready and eager to start new things, almost the opposite of his insecurity and tendency to hesitate. Once he got started, he usually adjusted pretty quickly, but he was anxious for the next few days to pass so he could feel surer about everything.

"I thought Gary was coming with us this morning?"

"He was pretty sick last night. He told me he might not be able to make it today."

"Oh, that's too bad. Hope he's feeling better by tomorrow. It'll be harder to start and fit in the longer he leaves it."

"Yeah, I know what you mean." Henry was already feeling that way himself.

As they passed Jenny's house, Henry noticed the curtain in the front window move. He didn't dare look or hold Jenny's hand, at least not until they were out of sight. Henry was also sure his mom was looking out their front window but he wasn't so worried about what she might be thinking.

"So, what about Timmy? Is he coming this morning?"

"I think so," Henry replied. He had hoped that Timmy wouldn't come until later so he and Jenny would have some time alone. "I really liked your note last night, Jenny. 'If you were a star in the heavens, I'd always know which one was you by its brightness!'"

"That has a double meaning you know," Jenny said. "Your personality just shines, and you're so clever and smart."

"Flattery will get you everywhere," he teased.

"Oh, it's not flattery," she countered, shifting her carrying case to her other hand and freeing up the one next to his. "I mean it with all my heart."

Henry had been waiting for her to do that and his hand found hers. She squeezed and he squeezed back before they relaxed into a more tender hold.

"I liked your last note, too, Henry—"

"Good morning, lovebirds," Timmy singsonged, having snuck up behind them on his bike. "Holding hands again, I see."

"Hi, Timmy," Jenny greeted him.

"And, what about you, Hank? Not glad to see me?"

"Oh no, Timmy, just a little nervous about school."

"Nothing to be nervous about. At least I won't have that shithead math teacher anymore, and besides, I hear some of the teachers are really young, and most of them are girls."

"They're too old for you, Timmy."

"Never too old for me, Hank. I'll have them eating out of my hand in no time."

"Yeah sure. They'll all wish you had enrolled at another school."

"Oh, I'm so excited!" Jenny exclaimed again, her eyes wide and sparkly, trying to take it all in.

"Yeah, I'm getting excited, too." Henry said, and this time he meant it. "I think the letter we received last week said to meet in the auditorium at nine to find out who our form teacher is."

Chaos reigned inside the school and out. The huge hall was packed with students. Three tones sounded over the PA system to get everyone's attention.

"Would all Grade 9 and 10 students please proceed to the auditorium directly across from the administration office."

The auditorium was already over half full when they entered. There were rows upon rows of seats, set on an incline so everyone could easily see the stage at the end of the huge room. Deep purple curtains hung across the back of the stage. Two long tables sat in front of the curtains, surrounded by several people.

"There are two empty seats over there," Jenny said, interrupting his thoughts. "Quickly, hold my hand."

With only a slight hesitation, Henry thrust his hand into hers as they rushed for the seats, hoping to beat whoever else might have had the same idea.

No sooner had they sat down than Principal Mitchell approached the podium. "Everyone please take a seat. We have to get started right away." Within a few minutes all the students were seated and the principal continued. "Good morning and welcome to Balfour. For many of you this is the start of high school and a totally new experience. We wish you well. For all the Grade 10 students returning this year, we wish you well, too, and ask that you help new students find their way to classrooms and answer any questions they may have."

A murmur rose from the crowd, and a couple of tenth graders said they'd be happy to show any newcomers to the furnace room or bathroom for their first class.

"Please, please," said Mr. Mitchell, raising his voice above their giggles and laughter. Once relative quiet had been restored, he swept a hand towards the table and introduced the vice-principal, the president of the student representative council and six teachers.

The vice-principal said a few words and welcomed them to the school. Then the president of the SRC came to the microphone and basically said the same thing. He talked about getting involved. They could expect to get out of high school what they put into it.

The principal got up again. "You received a letter in the mail about two weeks ago, telling you what form room you are in. We have asked the form room teachers to be up here to help you out. As I introduce them and the form to which they have been assigned, they will leave the auditorium. As they do so, all students of that form will follow their teacher to the classroom. Please, do this as quickly and quietly as possible."

Henry's homeroom teacher was the third one introduced, Mr. Dornan. He was also one of the science teachers. As Mr. Dornan walked down the aisle, Henry rose and squeezed Jenny's hand with a whispered, "I'll see you in the cafeteria at lunchtime."

Henry and about twenty-five other students followed Mr. Dornan to their homeroom on the second floor. Just before they entered the classroom, Mr. Dornan pointed out their lockers. As soon as the students were seated, Mr. Dornan took attendance. Some of the names were difficult and they laughed at his pronunciation, much to the embarrassment of those students. Henry didn't pay much attention to roll call—his mind was on Jenny—but that was immediately shattered when Mr. Dornan called, "Zeigler, Eddy."

Henry's heart skipped a beat. He slowly turned and scanned the classroom. There he was, glowering in the very back corner of the room.

Their gazes locked. Eddy made no attempt to look away. Rather, he tried to stare Henry down. He even purposely sat up and leaned forward in Henry's direction, lifting his chin in challenge. Henry had never realized how long and pointed Eddy's nose was, and, skinny as he was, with that big wave in his hair held in place by a ton of grease, Eddy gave Henry the willies.

Well, Henry sure wasn't going to be the one to crack. He twisted in his seat to position himself directly in line with Eddy's gaze. Although anyone could have beaten Eddy up, they didn't because most people were afraid of him. He exuded reckless bravado as if he could beat the crap out of anyone and never backed down from a fight. In fact, he often went out of his way to start one, proving that his size in no way prevented him from taking on the world.

"Let's see, did I forget anyone? Ah, yes, Pederson." The sound of his name broke Henry's concentration. He turned to see Mr. Dornan staring at him. "Well, do you want your lock or not?"

"Y-yes, sir." Henry rose from his desk to get his locker number and lock from Mr. Dornan's outstretched arm.

With the preliminaries finished, Mr. Dornan explained that their classes would be shortened just for the day so students could meet all their teachers and find their way around. He passed out blank timetable cards and instructed the students to copy out the schedule on the blackboard. He also reminded them to memorize the combination of their lock, and to destroy the slip of paper with the combination on it. "I don't want to see anyone coming up to me and complaining that someone got into his or her locker."

Just as Mr. Dornan showed them a floor plan of the first and second level of the school, the bell rang. Before he dismissed them, he reminded them that they were to return to homeroom every morning and afternoon for attendance before proceeding to their classes.

Henry's locker was two down on the right from his home-room. He put his lunch and carrying case in and took out a notebook for his next class. As he was about to close his locker, Eddy appeared. His locker was right next to Henry's. He bumped Henry out of the way.

"Don't hog the whole hallway."

Henry's blood boiled. He retaliated by thrusting a hip against Eddy's, almost knocking him over.

Henry slammed his locker door shut.

Once again, Eddy stepped forward and tried to bump Henry. As Henry turned to hit him back, Mr. Dornan emerged from the classroom, putting an end to their shoving match.

Henry glared at Eddy and shook the notebook at him. Eddy jerked his head back, not wanting his pompadour ruffled.

"I'm warning you, Eddy, next time I'll ..." Henry couldn't think of anything foul enough. He turned and walked away.

The hallway was very crowded. Henry looked around for Jenny and Timmy but couldn't see them. Behind him, Eddy booted the locker shut. Henry hoped Mr. Dornan would see him and kick him out of school. Two girls from Henry's home-room introduced themselves to him as Betty and Arlene and asked if he would help Betty with her lock.

The bell rang and like a herd of cattle students shuffled along to their next class. For Henry, that was art.

The art room on the main floor was spacious, with windows all along the north wall. The twenty or so tables were higher than regular desks and had tops that tilted up at an angle. Each had a stool with rollers. The tables were arranged in a circle around the perimeter of the room.

A male teacher who was working at his desk stood as they came in.

"Good morning, I'm Mr. Victor, your art teacher this year."

He gave the students a little of his background. Not only did he have an art degree but he had also worked for an advertising company at one time. Henry wondered if Mr. Victor might be able to help him advertise Mr. Engelmann's store. Henry liked the art teacher right away. He showed them where all the art supplies were stored, and what their first project would be. He had a still life set up in the centre of the room, positioned so they could all see it. They would learn some of the fundamentals of drawing using charcoal sticks.

At noon, Henry got his lunch and made his way to the cafeteria. It was packed. His head swiveled back and forth, looking for Jenny. Then he heard her call his name.

"Henry, Henry, over here! I saved a chair for you." The moment he was within earshot she recounted the events of her morning; her form teacher, the new students she had met, and the English teacher with the inch-thick glasses.

"Jenny, you're not going to believe who's in my form room," Henry said.

Jenny studied him for a moment, wanting to guess.

"Gosh, Henry, I don't know anyone yet. I couldn't possibly know. Who?"

"I'm glad you're sitting down. Eddy Zeigler."

Jenny's eyes grew large, her mouth wide. "No way!"

Henry nodded. "Yup, it's Eddy the jerk, all right."

"So, what did you do? Did you hit him? Tell me Tell me."

"So far we just stared at each other, and would you believe, his locker is right next to mine. When we were getting our books, he deliberately bumped into me. I bumped him back. I know before the week is out, I'm going to have to clobber that pipsqueak."

"And if I see him, I'm going to kick him in the shins. My wrists were sore for almost a week after his friends forced me into their car." Jenny's anger lasted only for a moment then her face brightened. "Oh, Henry, don't let him spoil your first day at school."

"No way, in fact, I'm glad he's in my homeroom. This way I won't have to look for him. He'll get what's coming to him soon enough."

"Well, let's have lunch and not think about him anymore, or

else you'll have indigestion for sure," Jenny said with a grin.

After lunch they found their way out to the west side of the school, Jenny ignoring wolf whistles from some of the other boys. Henry didn't like it. Sensing his feelings, Jenny took his hand, surprising him with her boldness and lack of concern for what others thought.

The afternoon passed quickly, especially with the shortened periods. Henry met his history, English and math teachers. His history teacher spoke very quickly in a commanding voice like a military officer. Henry wasn't surprised to later learn that he was a sergeant in the reserve force at the local armory.

Henry met up with Jenny after school and she told him about her afternoon classes and what she thought of her teachers. Timmy caught up to them on his bike and described his teachers as either idiots or old cranks, with the exception of his math teacher. She was young, on her first teaching assignment, and according to Timmy, was simply gorgeous. Henry could see lovesickness in his friend's eyes as Timmy took his hands off the handlebars to illustrate her luscious 36-24-36 figure. The front wheel of his bike suddenly turned, toppling Timmy to the sidewalk. Jenny and Henry laughed.

THE FOLLOWING MONDAY, Gary was able to join them, though he still looked pale. He had been assigned to Jenny's form, so she filled him in on everything he needed to know.

All that day, Eddy and Henry missed each other at the lockers. Occasionally they brushed each other in the hall, which, thankfully, resulted in nothing more than the exchange of a dirty look.

Henry learned the best place to get back at him, however, was in Phys. Ed. It was evident within the first fifteen minutes of basketball that though Eddy was fast, he had no idea what he was doing; he didn't know how to dribble, got called for travelling, missed the backboard completely on his shot, and fouled constantly. Whenever he thought he could get away with it, Henry bumped into Eddy so hard he fell to the floor. At the end of the period, Henry overheard Eddy talking to the instructor to see if he could get out of the class and take shop or anything else, but the teacher would have none of it.

By the end of the week, they all knew their schedules and had learned the names of the students in their classes. At the end of each day, Jenny and Henry walked home together, with Timmy and Gary tagging along.

As soon as Henry got home, he hopped on his bike and headed over to Mr. Engelmann's store to take care of the deliveries. After those were done, he told Mr. Engelmann about school and his classes. Henry missed working at the store and was glad that he could spend the whole day there on Saturday. Mr. Engelmann was glad, too. He was finding it difficult to keep up with all the work since Henry had gone back to school.

Henry wanted to take Jenny out to a movie on Saturday night, but her mother refused to let her go. They were expecting company for dinner that day, she said, and she wanted Jenny home to meet them.

On Sunday when he saw Jenny briefly after church, she told him she really hadn't needed to stay home. The guests were old, and she had excused herself right after dinner, gone to her room and read a book. Henry's stomach sank. He suspected Mrs. Sarsky had kept Jenny at home just to keep her from going out with him.

CHAPTER FOURTEEN

J UST LIKE EVERY OTHER MONDAY MORNING, Henry awoke to the drone of the washing machine drifting up from the basement through the wooden floor of his bedroom. The monotonous sound made it difficult for him to get up. It reminded him of the hum of the car engine after a late night visiting relatives on the farm and he lay half asleep in the back seat. However, on this particular Monday, Henry was eager to see Jenny. So he jumped out of bed and counted down the minutes to eight-thirty when he could hold her hand as they walked to school.

When he got to Jenny's, the front door, usually open behind the screen door to let in the brisk morning air, was closed. He waited a few minutes, hoping Jenny would come out, but with no sign that the Sarskys were even up, he decided to head to school. He would have knocked on the door, but Mrs. Sarsky had been so edgy lately, he thought it best not to irritate her or add to the growing distance between them.

As he walked to school, his thoughts oscillated between Jenny and Mr. Engelmann's business. Things had definitely been looking up at the store, and customers were very impressed by the improvements. The free Saturday delivery was a great success, as was the special delivery service after four o'clock on Mondays, Wednesdays and Fridays.

Another idea Mr. Engelmann and Henry had was to hand out flyers advertising upcoming sales. Not only were they able to sell more, but they'd also moved older stock and items that hadn't been selling well. One of the salesmen who came to the store once a week had offered to print their flyers; Mr. Engelmann only had to pay for the paper used. The salesman was really nice and was happy to see them improve business and get ahead. Of course, that also meant selling more of his product as well.

Most of their other suppliers wished them well too. Coca-Cola had agreed to deliver a new upright soft drink cooler like the one Henry had seen at the Golden Gate Confectionary. Mr. Engelmann had also asked the pop company to put up a new sign in front of the store that would advertise its name as well as theirs. Henry smiled as he recalled how excited they had been when the Coca-Cola salesman agreed to do it.

Henry wanted to paint the front of the store—it really needed it, and the interior looked so nice now. With so many deliveries, he didn't have the time and had offered to do it on Sunday, but Mr. Engelmann wouldn't hear of it. Sunday was a day to relax, go to church, and have fun with family or friends. They could paint without compromising the Lord's day.

But where was Jenny? Henry hoped she wasn't sick. She'd seemed fine after church yesterday, but he hadn't seen her for the rest of the day. Which, come to think of it, was sort of unusual.

Henry had yet to meet Jenny's dad and wondered if that might help thaw Mrs. Sarsky's frostiness. Jenny just joked about his uneasiness over her mother's concern about their relationship and he always chuckled at Jenny's imitation of her mother. Putting on a stern voice, Jenny shook a finger at him, "You're too young to be seeing so much of that boy—why don't you make some other friends?" Actually, it sounded reasonable to Henry and was probably what he would have said if he was a parent. Yet he was so in love with Jenny that he wanted to see her day and night, and no argument would sway him.

"Hey, Hank, what's your hurry?" Timmy yelled out, coming up from behind on his bike.

"Hey, Timmy."

Timmy slowed his bike to a wobble to match Henry's pace and asked, "So, where's the wife, Hank?"

Henry just looked straight ahead and didn't respond for a brief moment. He wished Jenny *was* his wife and not the subject of a Timmy Linder joke.

"I don't know," he finally replied. "She wasn't out this morning when I passed by her place. So, how are your classes going?"

"Geez, Hank, I really like math all of a sudden. I never thought I would but I can't wait for that class."

"Is it the math or that gorgeous teacher, Timmy?"

"Well, of course it's the math," he retorted with a smirk. "What do you take me for?"

As they neared the high school, students streamed in from all directions and converged on the main doors. Henry knew many of them by name. A school of 440 students wasn't really that big, and gossip spread quickly. He knew some of the students were already talking about him and Jenny and the fact that they held hands all the time.

The hallways were packed, as usual, and they had to swim upstream to the second floor and their lockers. Jenny's locker was also on the second floor and just down the hall, Henry glanced over to see if she was there. She wasn't, but Eddy was. Henry threw him a disgusted look and turned away. They had fallen into a sort of cold war, even when they played basketball in gym class. They often played on the same side but made no effort to work together. Still, Henry could see that though Eddy had no athletic training, he had a lot of potential for a guy his size. Henry could have helped him and offered suggestions but he preferred to make Eddy look foolish by throwing the ball slightly ahead of him or to make him fumble by throwing it too hard. It seemed that neither of them was prepared to forgive and forget.

Henry was always amazed by how quickly the hallways emptied when the bell rang. Just as he was about to enter Mr. Derkatch's English class, he heard Jenny call out his name. She was running down the hall, and as she drew closer, Henry could see she'd been crying. Henry hurried over to her and grabbed hold of her hands as she reached out to him.

"What happened, Jenny? Why are you crying?" he asked, trying to calm his racing heart. He had never seen her like this.

"Oh, Henry," she stammered, her voice trembling. "I'm leaving—I'm going away!"

Henry looked at her. Her eyes were red and fresh tears tumbled down her cheeks.

"What do you mean, you're leaving?"

"My dad," she sobbed, trying to catch her breath, "my dad has to go to Ottawa, right away." Jenny could barely get out the last word, then began to sob so hard she couldn't go on.

Henry took her into his arms and held her. Her chest heaved with her tears. She held onto him so tightly he had difficulty breathing. He didn't know what to say. He had to find out the details. He stroked her back, trying to calm her.

"Why does your dad have to leave?" Henry finally asked as Jenny settled a bit, swallowing her tears.

"The president of the company died yesterday morning. When we got home from church, the company called and asked my dad to replace him. He's flying to Ottawa tonight at seven and ..." tears welled up in her eyes and before losing control again, she blurted out, "and I have to go with him!" She started sobbing again.

"What do you mean you're going with him? For how long?"

"For-for ... ever."

Henry couldn't believe what he was hearing. How could Jenny be leaving forever? She had just moved here two months ago! This had to be something temporary. "That's impossible, Jenny. You'll only be gone for a little while, right?"

"No, no, Henry, I'm going with my dad, tonight. They don't

want me to miss too much school. This morning my mom phoned a high school close to where we're going to live and I'm already enrolled. They're expecting me tomorrow!"

A bright bubble of pain burst in his chest and his heart sank. Henry's whole world was crumbling. The thought of Jenny leaving—of not seeing her on the front steps anymore—was unbearable. He began to feel sick, his knees grew rubbery and he had trouble staying upright.

"Oh, Jenny," he finally said, "Tell me it isn't so."

"I wish I could, but it's true. We've already started packing. They're so anxious for my dad to get there, the company's sending movers and someone to drive our car to Ottawa. Mom was calling the real estate agent when I left." She took a long shuddering breath. "

Tears welled in Henry's eyes and now Jenny tried to comfort him as the reality of the situation finally sank in. He felt like he had been struck by a heavy weight and all his senses were suddenly deadened. He pulled himself away from Jenny and looked into her eyes for the mischievous spark that would let him know it was all a joke. The look she returned confirmed his worst nightmare.

Jenny was leaving. Really leaving. He couldn't bear to think on it any longer. No longer concerned about morning classes, Henry took hold of Jenny's hand and turned down the hallway. Jenny let him pull her along, then picked up her gait to walk close beside him. At the end of the hallway, they descended the stairs and made their way through the first door they came to. They walked out into the shadow of the building and the surrounding trees. Although it was a hot day, Henry shivered. Jenny leaned into him. The idea of not having the warmth of her body next to his from now on was unthinkable. He choked back what he was afraid was a sob.

"Oh, Jenny," he groaned, "I just don't know how to cope with this. The thought of you going away …" He didn't know how to finish the statement.

"I know," she replied, "but we'll figure something out. We can write to each other, and maybe when my dad comes to Regina on business, I can come with him. It'll be all right … somehow."

Emotions chased each other across Jenny's face as she spoke: hurt, sympathy, understanding, turmoil. Try as she might to regain composure, her pain and sorrow was plain. She had reassured him somewhat, but he tried to think of other solutions, too. His mind churned. When could he see her again? How could he get to Ottawa? Where would he get the money from? Could he go alone or would his mom or dad have to come with him? Rather than give him hope, however, these thoughts overwhelmed him. He couldn't think any longer. He felt only despair.

Henry started walking again, tugging a listless Jenny along. He couldn't stand still. Feverish emotion was building up inside and he had to expel it somehow. They walked for a long time, absorbed in their own thoughts and unsure what to say. They crossed busy streets and heard honks, not knowing or caring if they were directed at them. Maybe being hit by a car would be the best thing in the face of this tragedy.

"It just isn't fair," Henry burst out, breaking the long silence. "You've moved three times in the last four years, and now you've hardly been here two months and you're supposed to move again?!"

"They promised my dad this would be his last move," Jenny's words were quiet. "They're paying for all the expenses and even giving us a new house on the outskirts of Ottawa."

"But, Jenny," Henry reasoned, "that may be okay for your dad and mom, but it's not fair to you … it's not fair to me. You're just starting school, and now to have to move? What are they thinking?"

Henry was angry and ready to fight but he didn't know what to hit or whom to lash out at. Mr. Sarsky's company sounded inhuman. The whole thing was unreal.

"Who could I see there?" Could he talk to Jenny's mom and dad? What would he say? Who was he to tell them what to do? No one would listen to him. They'd probably just laugh at him and tell him to go away.

Jenny squeezed his hand.

"Don't worry, Henry, we'll work something out. There has to be a way," she said again, but Henry could hear the hollowness in her words.

"We could run away," he blurted.

"Yes, we could," Jenny replied, "but for how long? They'd find us. They'd send the police after us. They'd be so mad at us they'd maybe never let us see each other again. And what would we do without money?"

"I could maybe borrow money from Mr. Engelmann."

"But you told me he was already in financial trouble. And your parents don't have any extra money—even if they did, they'd never give us money to run away. It's no use thinking that way, Henry. I'm sure we will find some way to stay together. It might not be right now, but in time we'll find a way to be together again."

"Oh, Jenny," Henry stopped so abruptly he almost tripped her. He took both her hands and looked into her eyes, memorizing her face, "I love you, so much."

"I know, Henry. I love you, too." Oblivious to the traffic of downtown Regina and the people walking around them, they moved closer together. Jenny tilted her head to the side and parted her lips slightly as Henry's mouth pressed gently against hers. Henry didn't know how long they held each other, but in that moment, all his worries and concerns vanished. Jenny was his and he was hers. Their hearts beat as one. Had it not been for the sharp blast of a horn and a warning call from a passerby, they would have stayed that way much longer.

They turned towards home. Traffic was heavy and as they waited to cross the street, Jenny repeated the words that had so captivated Henry's heart on the first day he'd met her. "Quickly, hold my hand."

And take me along with you wherever you are going.

They'd walked all morning. As they turned onto Broder Street, Henry asked if he would see her that afternoon.

"I don't think so, Henry. Mom and I are packing. I packed most of my things late last night after mom and dad told me we were moving." A sheen appeared in her eyes once more.

"But, Jenny, I have to see you again. This just *can't* be the end."

So absorbed in their dilemma were they, neither noticed Jenny's mother marching towards them. At twenty feet away, Mrs. Sarsky could no longer contain her worry and anger.

"Jenny! Where on earth were you? We were looking all over for you. When you didn't come back right away, I phoned the school, and they said they hadn't seen you." And then she directed her fury at Henry, "And you, Henry, what on earth are you doing out of school, and what are you doing with Jenny?"

"We … we … were just saying good-bye," Henry stammered, taking a step back.

"Surely, it doesn't take hours to say good-bye," she sputtered. "Didn't you once think that we would be concerned?"

Henry didn't know how to respond. Silence was probably his best and safest defense anyway.

Jenny squeezed his hand and shot him a sad look of apology. Mrs. Sarsky stared down at their tightly joined hands and stepped between them, grabbing Jenny's wrist to pull her towards the house. Jenny kept looking over her shoulder at Henry, and each time she did, her mother yanked on her arm all the harder. Jenny pleaded with her mom to let her say good-bye once more, but Mrs. Sarsky would not relent. Jenny's tears turned to heart-wrenching sobs as they walked up the steps to their front door. Jenny turned, looked at Henry with love and desperation one last time, then disappeared inside.

Chapter Fifteen

Is that you, Henry?" his mother called as the screen door slammed shut behind him.

"Yeah, it's me." Henry could hardly speak.

She emerged from the kitchen. "What are you doing home?" Studying his face a little longer, she added, "Have you been crying?"

Her sympathy was all it took to bring the tears flooding to his eyes.

"Goodness! What's wrong, Henry?" she rubbed his arm, scanning for injury, but the hurt was too deep to see. "Why are you crying?"

Trying with all his might to control the tremble in his voice, Henry answered, "Jenny's leaving, Mom. They're moving away."

"What? Why? They just moved in!"

"I know, but Jenny's dad got this big promotion because someone in his company died, and he has to go and take over right away."

"Oh, dear." Not knowing what else to say, knowing there was no way to help, Mary opened her arms to her boy. Weak with fear and desperation, Henry fell into them.

He'd been ten or eleven when he'd started to feel embarrassed by his mother's hugs. It just wasn't manly, was maybe even a sign of weakness to show affection. When his father had problems, he usually bottled them up inside—he didn't want to be comforted; he put on a brave front. Henry wanted to be strong like his dad, but at that moment, he just needed his mom to hold him. He rested his chin on her shoulder and, unable to hold back the tears any longer, he sobbed out loud. The slow, steady beat of her heart and the even rhythm of her breathing contrasted his racing pulse and shuddering gasps. Gradually, her calm seeped into him.

They stood together in the dim light of the hallway. The sun had not yet travelled far enough to the west to flood it with light. In a way he was glad, there was some comfort to be found in the shadows instead of being exposed to the bright scrutiny of the sun. A sudden, cool breeze wafted through the screen door, adding to the chill of Henry's grief, and he wished the wind would carry his troubles away. But it wasn't possible. He was in the eye of a storm, having been tossed around by uncontrollable circumstance before having to get used to living in the destruction of its wake.

His mother stroked his shoulder. His anguish slowly released some of its hold.

"Things have a way of working out, Henry," she said now. "What seems impossible at the time has a way of resolving itself."

Maybe there was a glimmer of hope: if his mom understood, perhaps Jenny's parents would as well.

"Would you like some soup?" she asked as she let him go.

"I'm not really hungry, Mom."

"I understand."

"I can't go back to school this afternoon, either."

She let out a small sigh, then smiled gently. "It's okay."

Mr. Engelmann, he suddenly thought, *maybe* he *can help*. "I think I'll go to the grocery store. I have some work I want to do."

Henry rode his bike to the store. Whenever he was troubled, riding his bike and feeling the wind on his face somehow made him feel free, with no burdens or worries. And though a bike ride wouldn't fix the problem, it might help relieve a bit of the tension gnawing his guts.

There was no movement at Jenny's when he left his house. His gaze stayed pinned to her door for the longest moment. She'd be gone tonight. He wanted to see her, talk to her, but he knew better.

Mr. Engelmann looked up then at his watch when Henry walked in.

"It's not even one o'clock, Henry. How come you are here and not at school? Is there some kind of holiday?" As Henry got closer, Mr. Engelmann saw the expression on his face and his tear-stained cheeks. Before Henry could say anything or offer an explanation, Mr. Engelmann said, "Anna is feeling better today. Go out back and sit on the crate. I will be out shortly."

Henry looked at his feet as he walked past Mr. Engelmann, knowing if he caught the older man's eye, he wouldn't be able to keep from crying. He'd had enough of that already. But it was uncanny how Mr. Engelmann knew what he needed.

He heard Mr. Engelmann call out, "Anna, can you come down and watch the store for a little while? Henry and I need to talk." Mr. Engelmann's friendship and concern touched Henry. The tears perched on the raw edge of his emotions surfaced, spilling over his eyelashes.

He sat on the weathered crate like he usually did, closed his eyes and tilted his head towards the sun. The heat felt good and quickly dried his wet face. Henry quickly dashed a hand across it, wiping away whatever tracks remained. As much as he respected Mr. Engelmann's wisdom, Henry doubted there was anything he could say that would make him feel better.

The door handle turned and the back door swung open. Mr. Engelmann came out, glancing at him over the rim of his smudgy glasses before taking his usual seat. His brief look was both penetrating and analytical. In that split second, Henry knew Mr. Engelmann had figured out where Henry was at, both mentally and emotionally, and all he had to know was why.

Mr. Engelmann sat down on the crate next to him.

"I can see you are very troubled today, Henry. Can I be of some help?"

"You know how much I like Jenny," Henry said, staring straight ahead, his voice almost monotone with his effort not to rage.

"Yes, I know you love her very much."

He just cuts right to it. Henry's confidence in Mr. Engelmann rose a few notches. "She's moving away. Today. Her dad has accepted a big position with his company in Ottawa and needs to go there right away. They need him to take over immediately. Jenny is going with him tonight so she can start school as soon as possible. I don't know if I can ..." Henry hesitated, his voice now trembling so much despite his best efforts that he couldn't complete the sentence.

"Live without her?"

"Yeah!" he exploded. "What am I going to do?"

Mr. Engelmann nodded, considering. He turned to Henry, his expression as sorrowful as Henry's own. "This is a very sad and serious matter, Henry."

"Yes, it sure is! How can I stop it?" Henry looked up at him.

Mr. Engelmann returned his look but remained silent. They both knew there was nothing that would stop Mr. Sarsky from moving his family away.

"It's so unfair to uproot Jenny again, and just when she is making friends and ... meeting me ... and we like each other so *much*. Don't they understand how *wrong* this is?"

Mr. Engelmann didn't respond right away. He patted Henry's knee several times. "It's a very difficult thing when someone you love suddenly goes away. I understand the heartache you are feeling."

Tears spilled over again and Henry dashed them away angrily.

"You know that Anna and I are from the old country. We came to Canada halfway through the war. We used a lot of our money to get away from the Nazis."

What has that got to do with anything? Henry thought.

"Anna is of Jewish faith. We met just as the war broke out. Just before we left Austria, the Nazis started rounding up all the Jews and sending them to concentration camps. One day as I walked Anna home, we saw the Gestapo in front of her apartment. A minute later, two soldiers brought out her mother and father. If she had yelled out or tried to stop them, she would have been taken away also, or perhaps shot on the spot. So in silence, we watched as her parents were herded onto the back of a truck and taken away. They were not seen again. In the same way, I too lost a brother and sister in the war for sheltering a Jewish family."

Henry looked over at Mr. Engelmann, fists slightly clenched, anguish etched in his eyes. But Mr. Engelmann, more than anyone, understood this pain.

"Perhaps you are angry with Jenny's parents, for taking away your loved one."

"Yes, yes!" Henry raised his voice. "It's not fair, to Jenny or to me. Jenny was just barely getting settled, and suddenly she's forced to go away? *She* doesn't want to go and *I* don't want her to go!"

"Yes, yes, Henry, it isn't fair, and it is very painful when something like this happens. When Anna and I left Austria, we were devastated and thought we could never go on." Here it seemed that Mr. Engelmann, too, might get emotional, but he swallowed and went on, "But slowly we accepted what life handed to us and eventually even forgave the Nazis who murdered our loved ones. I know you are waiting for me to give you some answer that will immediately solve your problem, but I don't want to fool you, Henry. I don't have the answer you may want. But this I do know: time is a great healer, regardless of the outcome."

His words were not what Henry wanted to hear at all.

"It will be very hard for you to see Jenny go away tonight, but it is not the end. You can write to her. And time is not only a great healer, it also passes very quickly. I am a lot older than you, Henry, and I know this. You are just starting Grade 9. In a few years you will be graduating and then perhaps going off to university. This time will go very fast."

Henry tried to imagine where he'd be in three or four years. It seemed like an eternity.

"I don't know if I can even wait a day … or a week," Henry said, hopelessness transparent in his voice.

"I remember when I first bought this grocery store and used to walk around the block, seeing you on your tricycle. Do you remember?"

"Yes."

"And do you remember a time when you wanted to ride a two-wheel bicycle?"

"Yes, I could hardly wait for my mom and dad to buy me my first bike."

"And that's the one you have now, no?"

"Yes."

"Do you remember you could hardly wait? Here we are now, and you have it. See how quickly the time went?"

"Yes, I guess so."

"And now, what about driving a car? Are you thinking about that, too?"

"Yeah, sure. All the time."

"Well, when you are sixteen, less than a year away, you can apply for your license. Do you think that time will come soon enough?"

"I suppose so," Henry replied.

"Now that you look back, wanting a tricycle and then a bicycle and now a car, you see that time moves very quickly, and before you know it, you have it! The older you get, the more you will want time to slow down, Henry. That day will come all too soon." After a brief pause, he added, "The point, Henry, is that you and Jenny may have to be separated for a while. People are separated all the time. Men go away to war. Children leave their parents to go to school. Soon they are back together again. If it's meant for you and Jenny to be back together, you will be together again before you know it."

"And, what if it's not?" Henry asked, fearing the answer.

"Well, if it's not, then it's simply not, Henry. Sometimes people fall in love, and after a while, they realize they are not meant for each other. I know right now you may think that could never be the case with you and Jenny, but others who have felt the same way as you do now were proven wrong over time.

"Trust an old man. What looks so dark and heavy to you now will soon brighten up. Things happen that give us hope. I remember an old saying: 'Life by the yard is hard, but life by the inch is a cinch.'" Mr. Engelmann glanced at Henry to see if he understood. "Time is a great healer, but don't be controlled by it. If you focus too much on the future and how long things will take, you can become overwhelmed by it. Take one day at a time. Live fully in the present and a happy future will be in store for you."

Finally, Henry thought he understood. He and Jenny were at the mercy of time. Time was their greatest obstacle. They were so young now. If they were three or four years older, they would be more in control of the future, with more solutions at hand to realize the dreams they held in their hearts. But for now they needed to wait and take it one day at a time.

"Patience, Henry. You must be patient," Mr. Engelmann said.

"Yeah," Henry sighed, "I know, I need to accept—"

"Yes, yes, Henry, acceptance right now is very important for you to understand." Mr. Engelmann said it with such conviction, Henry had to turn and look at him. "There is another saying that applies not only to your situation, but to most of life's troubles: 'Lord, grant me the serenity to accept the things I cannot change, the courage to change the things I can, and the wisdom to know the difference.'" Mr. Engelmann paused for a long time. Henry knew he wanted to let what he had said sink in.

Mr. Engelmann was right. He could cry, rant, rave and scream, but it wasn't going to change anything. Mr. Sarsky was going to do what was best for himself and for his family. Henry simply didn't fit into the Sarsky's plans and he had to accept that fact—for now. And if Mr. Engelmann and Anna could forgive the soldiers who had killed members of their families, then surely he could forgive Mr. and Mrs. Sarsky for leaving and save himself from being consumed by bitterness and grief.

Relief inched its way into Henry's heart and he started to think more clearly. *Jenny's leaving tonight.* "I'm not ready," he muttered.

"What was that?"

"Oh, I just feel so unprepared," he repeated.

"That's how life is sometimes, Henry. Things can happen very quickly. We have to learn to *accept.* That's the key. We have to accept troubles that come our way, and trust in the Lord to make good out of it. Look at the tragedy of the cross, our Lord tortured and crucified. How horrible a crime, and yet out of all this came such good. Through the death of His son, God forgave us our sins and opened the doors to heaven for us!"

How can good come from Jenny leaving? Sometimes Henry just didn't understand things.

Again, Mr. Engelmann read Henry's mind. "The older you grow, the more you will see how the Lord works and turns the seemingly most cruel things around to make good of them. Trust in the Lord with all your heart, Henry, and don't lean on your own understanding. He will look after you. After all, hasn't He already sent His guardian angels to look after us?"

Henry liked those last few words, and hung onto them. Their guardian angels would bring him and Jenny together again, he just knew it.

From inside came the faint tinkle of the bell that indicated someone had just entered the store. Mr. Engelmann patted Henry's shoulder. "I have to go in now. Anna needs her rest. I know this will be difficult for you, Henry, but you will adjust. You will be able to handle it and it will all work out for the good."

"Thanks for taking the time to talk, Mr. Engelmann."

Mr. Engelmann patted Henry's knee and pushed himself up, "You cannot share your heart in a hurry, Henry."

After Mr. Engelmann went in, Henry thought about what he had said. The old man hadn't given him a pat answer or definite solution, yet the way he spoke and the examples he gave put everything back into perspective somehow. For the first time since Jenny had told him the news, Henry actually worked up a smile, confident that he could now better handle the situation. The helplessness he felt began to lift. The huge block of ice that had weighed him down and chilled him to the bone melted and lightened, thawed not only by the hot rays of the sun, but by the reassuring warmth of Mr. Engelmann's words. Time, acceptance and trust in God were what he had to help him. He only needed to take one day at a time.

Mr. Engelmann was writing up an order when Henry entered.

When he looked up, Henry said, "I've decided to start painting the front of the store."

Mr. Engelmann nodded and smiled.

Henry headed out front and examined the weathered boards. Most of the paint had dried up and chipped away after years of exposure to the harsh prairie elements. Henry decided to start by washing the windows, then he'd scrape off the rest of the old paint clinging to the siding. He brought up the painting supplies from the basement and got to work.

BY FIVE O'CLOCK, Henry had cleaned the windows, scraped off the siding and painted half the storefront. People complimented him as they came and went. The transformation was incredible. One side was bright white and new, while the other side remained weathered and old.

Mr. Engelmann came out and gasped. "Henry, what have you done? It does not even look like the same store! It's like a magic wand has touched this side of the building." He patted his employee's shoulder, "Well done, Henry. You are renewing our store and making an old man feel happy and young again."

Now it was Mr. Engelmann's turn to hide his tears. Before he went in, Henry heard him say, "Wait until my Anna sees this— it'll put a spring in her step!"

Henry cleaned up and called good night to Mr. Engelmann. He hoped he could see Jenny again before she left.

CHAPTER SIXTEEN

WITH HIS MIND STILL ON JENNY, it took a few minutes for Henry to notice the darkly ominous sky above him. The distinctive smell of rain and the wall of water off in the distance told Henry a storm was headed their way. Clouds as black as night rolled overhead, leaving only a single pinpoint of sunlight. That tiny spark of light mirrored the hope he clung to for Jenny and him. No sooner had the thought entered his mind than the wind shifted and the clouds shut tight.

Henry hopped on his bike and pedalled furiously home. There was a taxi in front of Jenny's place. Wasn't it a bit early for Jenny and her dad to be going to the airport? He got off his bike, leaned it against the fence and walked towards the taxi. Jenny's front door suddenly opened and Mr. Sarsky stepped out, carrying a large suitcase. Jenny followed with a smaller suitcase, her mother close behind. As they made their way through the gate and onto the street, Jenny saw him.

"Henry, you came!" she cried, her eyes brightening. Her suitcase thudded to the ground.

Jenny's mother took her arm, "No, don't, Jenny. We have to go."

Ignoring her mother's command, Jenny broke loose and ran towards Henry. Mrs. Sarsky started after her, but Mr. Sarsky grabbed his wife's arm. "Just leave her be."

Tears streamed down Jenny's face as she ran to Henry. When she reached him, she flung her arms around his neck. Henry closed his eyes and held her tightly, imprinting her lilac scent in his memory, the feel of her body against his.

Jenny tried to catch her breath. "Oh, Henry," she said, the words coming in gasps, "I love you so much. I don't want to go. I'll write to you, right away."

"I will, too," he said, "I promise."

Jenny stood on her tiptoes for one last kiss. Mrs. Sarsky, face as angry as the dark sky above, appeared behind Jenny. She snatched at her daughter, jerking her back and breaking their embrace. "Come right this minute, Jenny," she ordered. "The plane is leaving in an hour and you still have to check in."

"Just one more minute, Mom," Jenny pleaded. "Please, we have to—"

"No! We have to go now!" She yanked again, hard, nearly tossing Jenny to the ground. Jenny stumbled and her mother tugged her to the waiting taxi her as if she were a rag doll, Jenny looking over her shoulder at Henry the whole time. He stared back at her, helpless, not knowing what to do.

"I'll write! I love you!" she called.

"I love you too, Jenny," Henry mouthed. This good-bye sure wasn't endearing him to Jenny's parents, he could tell. The Sarskys were already concerned about how close he and Jenny had grown in such a short time, and seeing him and Jenny kiss like that in front of them would probably only add to Mrs. Sarsky's conviction and determination to keep them apart. And Mrs. Sarsky proved it as she shot him another unfriendly glance.

By that time, Mr. Sarsky had loaded his suitcase in the taxi and had retrieved Jenny's from where she'd dropped it. The cab driver held the back door open, waiting for Mrs. Sarsky and Jenny to get into the cab.

Jenny's mother pushed her into the back seat. Jenny tried to see Henry, but the back seat was crowded and she had trouble turning all the way around. Henry ran forward, trying to say a final good-bye. He waved, hoping Jenny could see him.

Jenny leaned forward past her mother and looked out the window. Their gazes met and locked for the last time as the taxi sped off, dust from the road hiding the rear window as the car sped down the street.

By the time the dust settled, the taxi was gone and so was Jenny. Henry was numb. He stared straight ahead, his heart as empty as the street. He tried to recall the words of comfort his mother had said to him at lunchtime and the hope he'd felt after his talk with Mr. Engelmann that afternoon, but nothing could penetrate his utter despair. He was, quite simply, devastated. He could see no future without Jenny. The past few weeks had been so full, so exciting, and so loving. The only thing ahead of him now was emptiness.

Then the warmth of a soft hand touched his shoulder. His mother, watching from behind the curtain of the living room window, had held back until she, like Henry, could no longer carry the weight of the moment alone. So in tune was Mary with the heartbreak her son was feeling, she needed his comfort almost as much as he needed hers.

"It'll be okay," his mother whispered, hoping it would be true. At her words, Henry's dam of tears broke for the second time that day, just as the first drops of rain tumbled from the heavens.

Henry looked towards what had been Jenny's house. With both doors closed and no light inside, the life of the home was gone. What had brightened all his days would be only an empty reminder of what had been. There would be no more calling on Jenny for school or holding hands or the bright sound of her laughter.

A bolt of lightning streaked across the blackened sky, followed by a thunderous clap, as if the sky itself released a cry of gut-wrenching pain. The storm was almost upon them, growing more foreboding. Lightning and thunder alternated in succession so that it was no longer possible to tell which lightning streak was responsible for which thunder clap. The winds howled and drove the raindrops like pellets against their skin.

"Come on, let's get inside," his mother urged. "It's going to pour any second now."

They turned in unison, Henry with his mother's arm around him, guiding him. Raindrops fell faster and in greater numbers, providing a distraction and welcome relief from his troubled thoughts until it was raining so hard Henry couldn't see the front door only a few yards away. Tiny beads of hail mixed with the rain to bounce off the stairs and sidewalk. Just before Mary guided him through the door, Henry looked up at the sky, begging the storm to drive out the distressing thoughts so firmly rooted in his mind.

They were soaking wet, hair plastered against their scalps, clothes stretched and drooping. They stood in the hallway in a growing puddle of dripping water. In spite of the choking sadness, Henry smiled at his mom, soaked from head to foot. His mother chuckled through her tears. It was one of those rare moments when conflicting feelings coexist with ease. It was exactly the respite Henry needed; a momentary chance to stand back and allow the healing process to begin.

His mother put her arms around him and kissed his wet cheek. "You best go to bed early tonight," she said. "It's been a very tough day for you."

"Thanks, Mom," Henry murmured. He turned and walked down the hallway to his room, leaving wet footprints behind on the hardwood floor.

AROUND ELEVEN O'CLOCK as Mary headed to bed, she noticed a light shining under the bottom of Henry's bedroom door. She gently knocked and waited for an answer. When there was no response, she opened the door to find him slouched over his desk, head resting on his arm, sound asleep. She shook him softly, trying to wake him.

"Come on now, Henry. Time for bed." She tugged at him, gentle but persistent, until he finally wobbled to his feet in a sleepy daze. A pen dropped from his hand onto the desk, the chair he was seated on slid backwards and almost toppled over. Mary held him until he was close enough to the bed that he flopped onto it almost in reflex. *Poor boy,* she thought. At least he was so emotionally drained he couldn't help but sleep deeply. She covered him with an extra blanket, tucking it around him as she had since he was small.

As Mary reached to turn out his desk lamp, she hesitated for a long moment, then allowed her eyes to wander over the words he had written before falling asleep.

Dear Jenny,

I miss you so much already. I hated to see you go. I so wanted to kiss you just once more before you left. You are my one and only love. I don't know how I can live without you. Please come back soon.

I love you!

Love,
Henry

Mary clicked off the light and the darkness hid the stain of her teardrop that had fallen on Henry's very first love letter.

CHAPTER SEVENTEEN

HIS EYES FELT SWOLLEN and his stomach muscles ached, and at first he didn't know why. It took him a few moments to wake up and then the loss hit him.

Jenny.

She was gone and his life would never be the same. How was he ever going to get over it? Again, Henry felt himself slipping into despair; the day seemed doomed to be cheerless and miserable, and he was afraid he wouldn't be able to pull himself out of it.

Just as panic began to get a foothold, he remembered Mr. Engelmann's words: *there was always a choice.* He could choose to be happy or sad, to feel sorry for himself or focus on the bright things, on the possibilities of life rather than the negatives— which would only make him depressed and get him absolutely nowhere. Henry struggled to focus on that thought. For added strength he asked God and his guardian angel to help him, the way Mr. Engelmann did every morning.

What would improve the situation? Nothing. A life without Jenny was a life not worth living. *There I go again!* He wrenched his mind back to his decision to focus on the positive, on *now,* and then after a moment, it occurred to him that Jenny wasn't gone for good; they were only separated by distance. He started to think of her as being on vacation, away only for awhile. And it *would* be fun to write letters back and forth. Some things might even be easier to say in a letter. And, as Mr. Engelmann had said, time was a great healer and passed quickly. In no time, he and Jenny would be back together again, and he would just have to make the best of it until then.

He took a deep breath and started to feel better. Maybe he could make it through the day. He pushed himself to his feet and stumbled over to his desk. There was the first letter he would send to Jenny as soon as she wrote him with her new address. He looked it over. It expressed what was in his heart. There was a water stain on the paper and he rubbed it absently with his finger, thinking of the feel of her skin. *Yes,* he concluded, *it will be exciting to write back and forth to each other.*

Henry went to the bathroom, barely recognizing the face that stared back at him from the mirror. His eyes were still red and puffy from crying. He couldn't go to school looking like this. He splashed cold water on his face, hoping it would take down the swelling. It didn't. But the cold water felt good so he did it another couple of times.

His mother was washing dishes when he arrived in the kitchen. Henry was relieved that his father had already gone to work and wouldn't see how hard he had been crying, how unmanly he'd been.

"Hi, Mom."

"Good morning, Henry. Did you sleep okay?"

"Yeah, I guess I was really wiped out."

She came over and kissed his cheek, ruffling his hair a bit with her hand before smoothing it back. "Well, sit down and I'll make you your favourite breakfast."

Henry smiled at her. Her eyes were as red and swollen as his. She'd been crying too, sharing his loss and heartbreak.

"Thanks, Mom, I *am* a bit hungry. Guess I haven't eaten since yesterday morning."

"I know."

As Henry ate his eggs and bacon, he told her what Mr. Engelmann had said to him about choices and looking on the positive side of things, and that he believed he and Jenny would be together again.

His mom's eyes brightened as he spoke. Her boy was growing into such a thoughtful man. And she'd have to remember to thank Mr. Engelmann for his caring words; that job was turning out to be a real blessing for Henry. But all she said was, "That's pretty good advice."

"Is it okay if I don't go to school today? I look awful, and I don't think I can concentrate on anything right now anyway. Besides, I want to finish painting Mr. Engelmann's storefront. I started yesterday and it looks really good."

Mary reflected on his request for a moment before answering. "Well, I guess one day won't hurt. But you have to go back tomorrow for sure."

"I promise, Mom." He got up and kissed her cheek.

Henry got his bike and wheeled it out the front gate, glancing over at what had been Jenny's house. It looked silent, vacant, all the life …. Before his thoughts got the better of him, he hopped on his bike and peddled to the store as fast as he could. Maybe he could outrun his feelings. Maybe the wind in his face would blow the seeds of depression away from his mind so they couldn't take root again.

When Henry rode up to the store, Anna and Mr. Engelmann were standing outside, admiring the newly painted clapboard siding of the storefront. When they saw him, Mr. Engelmann called out, "Look, Anna. Here comes the master painter!"

"This looks so nice, Henry," Anna said as Henry got off his bike. "You are making us very happy and proud of the store again. And David tells me you get the paint at such a bargain. I never heard of such a thing."

"Thanks, Mrs. Engelmann. Getting the paint was no problem at all." Henry told them he had his mom's permission to work there for the day instead of going to school.

Mr. Engelmann took in his appearance but merely said, "That will be fine, Henry. If your mom says okay, then it's all right with Anna and me."

With that, Henry went to get the paint and brush from the basement. By noon he had finished the lower part of the front of the store. He'd need a ladder to do the second storey. A neighbour down the street had one that was tall enough, but Mr. Engelmann felt the second storey was too high for Henry to do; he'd hire another painter to do that part and asked Henry to paint only the sides and back of the store, going only as high as he could with the eight-foot ladder.

Henry began to work on the east side of the store after lunch. It was very hot. With no cloud cover, the sun burned down in all its fury; the wind seemed to have taken the day off, too. Not even the leaves on the trees rustled. The only consolation was that he'd be working in the shade for most of the afternoon.

As he painted, Henry thought of Jenny, wondering if it was this hot in Ottawa and how she was adjusting to her new home and school. He wondered what it would be like to live in Ontario. Cities there were much bigger than in Saskatchewan. And Ottawa was the country's capital—there was sure to be more to see and do there than here. He made a mental note to ask Jenny those things in his next letter.

The paint went on easily in the shade, and by five o'clock he had finished the first coat on the entire east side of the store. He could do the second coat the next day after school. The store looked a lot better already and again people had commented how nice it looked as they walked by. Henry got great satisfaction from seeing something transformed and become more beautiful.

The front yard of the store was about fifteen feet from the city sidewalk. A four-foot walk split the lawn area in front of the store in two equal halves. But the lawn had been neglected and trampled over. Scraggly patches of weeds and grass had grown tall and turned to seed. When Mr. Engelmann came out to assess his progress, Henry told him he'd clear it all out—he'd had lots of practice at Mrs. Goronic's over the years, after all. He also mentioned that a strip of flowers in front of the store would look good.

"Yes, yes, that would be nice. Anna loves to garden and could probably manage a small flowerbed. Why didn't I think of that?"

They walked around to the east corner of the building and admired the fresh paint. It looked pretty impressive.

When Mr. Engelmann spoke, his words were quiet and sincere. "Henry, you are changing the store. You are a good painter for such a young man. You are always thinking about how to improve things and make them look better. Someday you will be a very successful businessman."

"Thank you," Henry answered. He was just glad he'd had something else to think about. It was the best he'd felt in two days. "Well, I think I'll head home now, Mr. Engelmann."

"Yes, you have worked very hard and now need some rest. By the way, did Jenny and her parents get away yesterday?"

"Yeah, they left last night." Henry wasn't sure he wanted to relive their departure.

"You miss her?"

"I do." The words came out on a troubled sigh.

Mr. Engelmann put his arm around Henry and repeated almost the same words his mom had told him the night before. "It will be okay, Henry. Things have a way of working out." He patted Henry's shoulder.

"I sure hope so."

"Well, I'll see you tomorrow after school. Thank you again for the fine job you did today."

HENRY RAN INTO THE HOUSE, and before his mom could say hello, he asked, "Did I get any mail today?"

His mother just smiled. "No, not today. I don't think any mail from Jenny will come until at least next week, if that's what you're waiting for. How was your day?"

"It was very hot, but I painted the store on the shady side. It looks really good."

"Hello, son," his father called from the living room.

That was odd. His dad wasn't usually home this early.

"Oh, hi, Dad."

"Well, you better wash up and get ready for supper," his mom suggested.

"Sure, Mom."

After supper, Henry went outside and sat on the steps. A man came out of Jenny's house and walked towards his car. When Henry stood up he noticed the FOR SALE sign in the front window. Mrs. Sarsky hadn't wasted any time. *This is for real,* he told himself.

Henry turned and went inside, directly to his room. He sat down at his desk and began a second letter to Jenny. It was his only link to her now, the only way to be close to her. When he finished, he placed it in the top drawer of his desk. From the bottom drawer, he pulled out the twelve notes Jenny had left him on the fencepost over the summer and read and reread them, caressing each one.

Chapter Eighteen

FOR THE NEXT TWO WEEKS, the pattern repeated itself. Henry woke at seven, had breakfast, went to school with Timmy and Gary, came home, worked at the store, came home, asked if any mail had come for him, had supper, and wrote to Jenny. If time permitted, he studied too. Immersing himself in work and letter-writing and studying was the only way he could cope. Some days he took his frustrations out on Eddy in the gym, but that soon lost its numbing effect. *You can't solve one problem by creating another,* he thought. Yet he didn't know how else to deal with the fact that Jenny hadn't yet written. And he had no way to reach her to find out what was happening. His heart ached with each passing no-letter-from-Jenny day.

One morning as he passed Jenny's house on his way to school, he noticed the elastic that he and Jenny had used to leave each other notes under was still wrapped around the post. Soon the sun, wind and rain would weaken and break it, leaving no trace of the purpose that piece of rubber had served. It, at least, was a tangible reminder of Jenny's existence, of her feelings for him. He stretched it over the newel post, astonished to find a bit of paper twisted around it.

The note was partially torn and still damp from the series of showers they'd had, and the elastic snapped as he unraveled the paper. Henry was thankful it had held up this well. The thought of Jenny's last note blowing off in the wind without ever seeing it sent a chill down his spine.

He walked through the gate to the front steps of the empty house and sat down, pretending Jenny was beside him. His hands trembled as he opened the note. Some of the ink had run, smudging bits and pieces of the words. As Henry's eyes filled with tears the whole letter blurred.

"Oh, Henry,"

My heart just aches and I feel like it's being torn in two. Being with you has made this the happiest summer of my life. The thought of not seeing you anymore is more than I can bear.

Always remember:

True love lasts forever, it never says goodbye, "for you and I have a guardian angel on high with nothing to do but to give to you and to give to me love forever true."

Jenny

p.s. If you were a heart, I'd want mine to beat inside yours.

It was as if Jenny were right beside him. He could hear her singing the words from "True Love" in his imagination. Somehow Henry wasn't surprised that she'd remembered the song lyrics from their first date just as he had. And her postscript made him ache to hold her, to kiss her, to feel her warmth, and, yes, to have her heart beat next to his.

Henry wiped tears from his eyes. He brought the note up to

press it to his lips. A faint breath of lilacs rose from the scrap of paper and Henry recalled the walks they'd shared when they'd first met and how Jenny loved the smell of those blooms. It was her favourite perfume. He wished he had discovered the note earlier—the rain had washed most of the scent away.

He read the note again and again. It was a godsend, giving him something more to hang onto. The words of the song lifted him ... *for you and I have a guardian angel on high with nothing to do but to give to you and to give to me* ... "Yes," whispered Henry and silently sent a prayer of thanks heavenward. Henry sat on the steps for over an hour, unwilling to let go of the moment. It was the first time in days he had truly felt any kind of relief.

The morning sun peeked around the front corner of the house. The grass and fallen yellow and orange leaves glittered as the sun spread golden rays across the front lawn and sparkled off the tips of the white points of the picket fence like a row of candles, warming Henry's spirits.

Henry was so immersed in the world Jenny and he had shared that the thought of school never entered his mind. By the time it did, he was already very late and his eyes, he was sure, were too red. Besides, the Coca-Cola man was going to deliver the new sign for the store today. He decided to go see if he could help.

When he got to the store, the sign was already in the process of being attached to a steel rod workers had secured to the building. Mr. Engelmann was surprised to see him, but after one of his analytical looks, only asked that Henry call his mother right away to tell her where he was.

It took all morning and most of the afternoon to install the sign and get the electrical working. Finally, the sign flickered on. Oh, the Coca-Cola logo was part of it, but the highlight was the red and black lettering covering the centre of the sign: EN-GELMANN'S GROCERY & CONFECTIONARY. The sign lit up like a Christmas tree for all the neighbourhood to see. It was hard to tell whether he or Mr. Engelmann was more proud. As sick as she was, Anna came out to look too. She could hardly contain herself. Even before she turned to look at the sign, tears filled her eyes.

"Oh, David," she said. "Oh, Henry." She stood beside them, gazing up, speechless.

Henry admired the crisp clean look; the fresh white paint, the new sign. He wondered how it would look with red trim around the windows and a red door to match. When he'd picked up more white paint at the paint store the other day, he'd seen a gallon of red there, too. The red trim would be the perfect finishing touch.

The next day Henry went to Northern Paint. The gallon of red was still there and had been for a long while. The store manager was ready to throw it out.

"You know what? Just take it," he'd said when Henry asked if he could buy it.

When Henry opened the can back at the grocery store, he was amazed to discover that the colour almost perfectly matched the red in the sign. He painted the frame of one of the windows and then called Mr. Engelmann to see if he liked it too.

"Very good, Henry! How can anyone miss our store now?"

"That's the whole idea, Mr. Engelmann. We want everyone to know we're here." Henry liked the way Mr. Engelmann had said "our store" as if Henry was a part owner. And in a sense it was true. Henry *did* feel like the store was his and felt proud and motivated to improve it.

And so it went for the next week: painting and landscaping to enhance the store's appearance. Customers raved about the improvements. The red sign and the red front door drew most of the favourable comments. They were using colour to market the store and didn't even realize it until customers who'd been going to Safeway began to re-frequent Mr. Engelmann's store.

Only the old grey crate at the back of the store—Mr. Engelmann's school of life—remained untouched. Henry didn't want to disturb anything that might interfere with the way he and Mr. Engelmann talked back there.

Both were amazed how the business improved. It was like the neighbourhood, caught up in the store's revival, was proud to be part of it. Customers talked about Henry and how he'd helped Mr. Engelmann improve the store. Even Mr. Mahoney, the city tax man, heard what they'd done and came to check it out.

Henry was extremely happy to see Mr. Engelmann give Mr. Mahoney another cheque towards what he owed the city. Henry beamed with pride when Mr. Engelmann told the city official it was his good fortune that Henry had come along when he did: "He is my righthand man," Henry's boss had said. Henry, busy helping a customer, just beamed.

Mr. Mahoney looked at Henry for a long moment as he had on previous visits, then turned back to Mr. Engelmann. "I see what you mean. Perhaps my earlier assessment was premature."

Henry was more excited about going to work than going to school. He loved the business, and the challenge of improving it and making it profitable. If it hadn't been for his job, he didn't know how he would have coped with Jenny's leaving.

BUT WALKING WITH HIS FRIENDS to school during the last week of September, Henry's feeling of abandonment only increased.

"Geez, Gary, I'm really going to miss you! Why don't you wait until the end of the year to go to Notre Dame?"

"Well, Dad wants me to attend military college after Grade 12 and figures Notre Dame will toughen me up and better prepare me and 'the sooner, the better,' he says."

"Yeah, I heard the headmaster there has a reputation of being a really tough guy … and he's even a priest."

"But that's an all boy's school," chimed in Timmy. "That's no fun."

"That's not correct, Tim. Both girls and boys attend and students come from all over, not just Saskatchewan.."

"Well that's good, I'd hate to think the guys would have to invite their mothers for school dances," Timmy smirked, trying to cover up his ignorance.

The guys laughed.

"So when are you leaving, Gary?" Henry asked.

"This will be my last week here. Dad's coming home for the weekend and we're all driving out to Wilcox on Saturday."

"That sucks, Gary. Really sucks."

"We're sure gonna miss you, buddy," Henry added.

"Well, the one nice thing is that the college is only twenty-five miles from Regina, so I'll be home some weekends."

"That's good. Maybe when I get my driver's license Timmy and I can come out to see you."

"That'd be swell, Hank."

Henry wanted to talk about some of the great times they'd had in the past, especially the war games they played in Gary's backyard. But maybe they were getting to old to talk about that stuff. Still, if Timmy hadn't been there, he would have.

A silence fell over the boys as they walked along, each absorbed in his own thoughts about their impending separation, at least until Timmy blurted out, "Geez I can't *wait* for this morning's math class, I've really got the hots for that teacher."

At least some things never change, Henry thought as they laughed again. They turned onto the walk leading to Balfour's front doors. It didn't seem like Timmy really understood what was happening. The three of them had been together since grade school and now, just like Jenny, their best friend was leaving. It all made Henry's guts twist.

Ever since Henry had started working at Engelmann's store, he and Timmy didn't hang out as much. Even at school, Timmy seemed to chum around more with other guys. Funny, Henry thought, he didn't mind that they were drifting apart, but it did bother him that Gary was leaving ... he was a truer friend in more ways than one.

THREE WEEKS AND STILL no letter. What could possibly have happened? She'd promised to write.

Every night after work, Henry wrote a letter to Jenny. He had written sixteen so far, but with no address they just collected in his drawer. As he sat at his desk that night, almost at the end of another letter, he just had to pose the questions that troubled his heart.

Dear Jenny,

Have you found someone new? Are you just too busy with your new school or friends and that's why you haven't written? Not knowing is worse than knowing. If you want to break up, or take some time to see if you want to still want to be my girlfriend, please let me know. The silence is killing me.

As Henry sat there, he couldn't help but think how drastically his life had changed that summer. He'd been so bored before Jenny had entered his life. Then there'd been joy and love and new experiences. She had awakened a part of him that had been asleep. He bloomed into manhood when near her, soared like an eagle at the touch of her hand, ached when they had to part for the day. If only he hadn't needed sleep!

Then, almost overnight, those happy feelings of exhilaration had been replaced by loss and sorrow. It was as though a stone now grew in his heart, its weight swelling with each passing day.

Life is so unfair. Henry suddenly felt older and emptier. A whole lifetime of meeting and loving someone as beautiful and wonderful as Jenny had been crammed into two short months.

He let his head fall on his arms. Tears that had been dammed inside surfaced and filled his eyes to overflowing as if fed from an underground spring. His chest heaved and throbbed against the edge of the desk. Despair washed over him.

Oh, Jenny where are you? Where have you gone? What has happened to you ... to us? Where has it all gone?

CHAPTER NINETEEN

IT HAD BEEN THIRTY-EIGHT DAYS since Jenny had left and things were going pretty well at school. He enjoyed school and was even beginning to tolerate Eddy. In spite of Eddy's cocky attitude, he *did* have a knack for math. The math teacher moved Eddy to the front of the class, thinking Eddy couldn't see above the other students. Eddy protested and said that he didn't need to see because he understood the subject quite well. When he was moved up front, he put his head down or stared out the window, looking bored most of the time. But whenever the teacher asked him a direct question, he would raise his head and spout out the correct answer, much to Mr. Harder's chagrin. At times he even corrected the teacher.

But at their lockers, the cold war continued. They no longer bumped into each other but each knew the past wasn't forgotten. It was like they were treading water near the edge of a waterfall, waiting for the plummet.

Some kind of confrontation was inevitable.

Studying for exams, working for Mr. Engelmann and writing Jenny kept Henry totally occupied. He considered himself blessed to have so much on his plate; it distracted him from the reality of no letter from Jenny. His heartfelt words poured out into letter after letter to gather on his desk with no place to go. It was painful and frustrating.

As Henry wrote the thirty-eighth letter, he couldn't help but notice how much longer they had become. He went to the bottom of the pile of letters neatly stacked at the end of his desk and pulled out the first one. He reopened the envelope with his jackknife, pulled out the sheet of paper, and read it to himself. It was only two lines, but it expressed his loss and the pain in his heart over her sudden departure. It was even sealed with a tearstain that had caused the ink to run. The letter he had just finished, although it expressed his loss also, was more elegant and expressive. He read it again.

Dear Jenny,

I wrote an English exam today. I think I did okay. Tomorrow, I write a math mid-term. I didn't study for it—it's pretty easy. I'm glad because I have a lot of trouble concentrating on anything with you constantly in my mind. I think about you day and night and so want to kiss and hold you in my arms.

By now you must be fitting into your new high school. Are you writing exams too? What's your favourite subject? I'm sure it's English. I know how much you love books and like to read and write. How are you finding the students there? You would make new friends easily, I think. You're so easy to be with and so easy to love. I miss you so much, Jenny.

Two weeks ago I asked several questions in my letter to you that weighed heavily on my heart. With each passing day these unanswered ques-

*tions are becoming unbearable. Oh, Jenny, why
don't you write? Have you found someone new?
Are you just too busy? Jenny, please let me know.
I almost can't stand it.*

*In my last three letters I told you how much we
improved Mr. Engelmann's store. But now is it
ever starting to get busy! I just love working there
and the challenge of making it better. The only
thing missing in my life is you. Oh, Jenny, I love
you so much. Please write to me soon.*

He thought about the last note she'd written him and their
song.

*Ours is a love forever true, watched over by our
guardian angels.*

Henry

He folded the letter and slipped it into an envelope, adding
it to the pile.

THE NEXT DAY when there was a rare moment without any customers, Henry pulled Mr. Engelmann aside. "Is there any way
you know of that I can get Jenny's address?"

Mr. Engelmann folded his arms and raised his eyebrows.

"It is strange and not like Jenny not to write you, Henry. And
it would concern me very much, too, if Anna had not written
to me when we were separated at times. I'll think about it,
Henry."

What Henry didn't know was that Mr. Engelmann had been
trying to track down Jenny's parents and had contacted the real
estate agency that had sold their house, hoping to get a forwarding address. The real estate company was reluctant to give out
any personal information, but had offered Mr. Sarsky's new
business address and his work phone number.

Although Mr. Engelmann had the means of contacting Jenny's father, he was reluctant to interfere at this point, thinking it best to wait and see what happened.

ANOTHER WHOLE MONTH elapsed. It was the middle of November and the cold weather began to freeze out the warmth of the late fall. Along with the advent of the winter came increased requests for deliveries. Henry and Mr. Engelmann hadn't anticipated the large number of orders and the increased demands on their time. Mr. Engelmann even had to make a few of the deliveries himself.

It had been sixty days since Jenny had left. It was becoming increasingly difficult to keep writing; Henry was running out of things to say and had nothing to respond to. Even though he'd stopped writing every night, he still had at least forty-five letters, some on top of his desk and others inside his top drawer.

It was as if Jenny had vanished from the face of the earth.

Henry's parents suggested he stop writing and date a few other girls. He was only fifteen, with his whole life ahead of him, his mother said. And if it was meant for him and Jenny to re-unite, then time and destiny would do their work.

Although the logic sounded reasonable, Henry found it difficult to accept. There was undoubtedly some reasonable explanation for Jenny's continued silence. Maybe Jenny's letters had gone to some other address or gotten lost. But was that even likely? Maybe one or two, but all of them? Maybe she thought *he* hadn't responded? He needed closure. For better or worse, he had to know what had happened.

MR. ENGELMANN UNDERSTOOD that not knowing about Jenny was an open wound for Henry. It saddened him to see such a young man so lonely and heartbroken. As devastating as it might be if Jenny had found someone new, it would still be better to put Henry out of his misery.

Mr. Engelmann decided he could no longer remain uninvolved and dialed the long distance number he had received from the real estate agent.

"Mackurcher and Company. This is Elaine. How may I help you?"

"May I speak to Mr. Sarsky?"

"Whom may I say is calling?"

"David Engelmann."

"And what is the nature of your call, Mr. Engelmann?"

"Pardon me?" Mr. Engelmann asked, a bit flustered.

"Sir? What is your call in regards to?"

"It's ... it's personal."

"I see," said the secretary. "Please hold and I will see if Mr. Sarsky is able to take your call." An eternity later, the secretary came back on the line, "I'm sorry, sir, Mr. Sarsky is busy. If you leave your number, I'll have him get back to you."

Mr. Engelmann gave the secretary the number for the store then hung up. He waited for Mr. Sarsky to return his call. Although the store owner was very busy with orders and customers, he anticipated Mr. Sarsky's call anytime and tried to figure out a way he could talk in private. The telephone was just behind the till, attached to the back wall. He could turn his back on his customers, if any were in the store, but he was certain that they would overhear him. And he didn't want word to get back to Henry or his parents that he was meddling in Henry's personal life.

Mr. Engelmann was also concerned about what to say to Jenny's father. He had pulled together a couple of ideas earlier, but with so many interruptions over the course of the afternoon, he had lost his train of thought. He decided to leave it up to the Lord to give him the right words at the right time.

The afternoon passed with no call from Ottawa. Henry would soon be in after school and that would really complicate the privacy issue. Mr. Engelmann didn't want Henry to know he had even called Mr. Sarsky until he had an idea of what was going on. Once he knew, he could decide whether or not to tell the boy who had become like a son to him.

Henry entered the store right on schedule. Mr. Engelmann finished the order he was working on and handed it to Henry to deliver. When Henry left, Mr. Engelmann sighed with relief and waited for the phone to ring. Nothing. Henry returned twenty minutes later. As he entered the store, the phone jangled, startling Mr. Engelmann. His face flushed and his heart thundered in his chest.

The phone rang a couple of more times.

"Do you want me to get that, Mr. Engelmann?"

"No, no, Henry, I will get it," he answered, trying to decide how to respond. "Hello, Engelmann Grocery and Confectionary."

But it was only Mrs. Goronic calling in an order, which he gave to Henry to deliver on his way home. Mr. Engelmann felt Henry's gaze on him as he drew up an invoice for the order. He swiped beads of perspiration from his brow, hoping Henry didn't see them.

"Are you feeling okay?"

"Yes, yes, I'm fine. Maybe a little on the warm side. I was very busy today. Could you please go to the storage room and get supplies to stock up the shelves?"

"Sure." Henry checked the shelves to see what was needed, then went back to the storage area to get the products.

As soon as Henry went out back, Mr. Engelmann took the telephone receiver off the hook. He felt so tense he simply couldn't stand the uncertainty of whether or not Mr. Sarsky would call. He might lose orders by having the phone off the hook but decided he would be more comfortable losing an order or two than having Mr. Sarsky call when Henry was in the store.

Shortly after five the store was empty of customers and Mr. Engelmann told Henry he could leave early. After Henry left, he put the phone back on the hook, but it was now close to five-thirty; seven-thirty in Ottawa. David was sure Mr. Sarsky would be home by now and wouldn't call that evening. He walked to the back of the store to turn out the lights. He wanted to talk over the problem with Anna—it was becoming too burdensome to carry alone.

The cool fresh air felt good as Henry walked home. Normally the breeze cleared his mind, but not today. His preoccupation with Jenny had begun to take a toll. Weariness of heart and mental fatigue plagued him, sapping his interest in schoolwork. Henry knew his parents were concerned, as was Mr. Engelmann, and he knew they wanted to help but were unsure how.

IN HIS DESPONDENCY, Henry took his frustration out in gym … on Eddy. He ran into Eddy, throwing him hard to the floor.

Henry knew he had hurt the other boy, but instead of showing pain, Eddy only smirked. "The boys'll get you just like they got that blond chick of yours at the park. Bet they laid her before *you* did."

Henry's anger towards Eddy, which had been simmering like hot lava in a dormant volcano, erupted into an uncontrollable rage. He lunged at Eddy, grabbing him by the throat.

"Did they touch her?" Henry seethed through clenched teeth.

Eddy's smirk never wavered. He was obviously enjoying the moment despite his impending doom.

"Tell me!" Henry shook the little punk from side to side.

For the first time, Henry thought he saw a flicker of compassion in Eddy Ziegler's eyes.

"Hey man, just kidding, all right! *Geez!* They were just boasting. You know how guys are. A few beers and they think women are their slaves."

Henry looked long and hard into Eddy's eyes, searching for the truth. There hadn't been enough time for Eddy's friends to do anything to Jenny, had there? Henry shuddered at the thought and immediately tried to dismiss it. No! Surely Jenny would have known if she had been … hurt. He couldn't even think the word *rape*.

"Look, man, didn't you say you were right behind them that night?"

Henry wanted to agree with Eddy. Then again, Jenny had been kind of out of it when he'd found her. Henry shook his head, once again trying to dispel the thought. He gave Eddy's T-shirt a sharp tug. "Don't you ever speak this kind of bull ever again."

The other boys in gym class had gathered around, anticipating a fight.

Then, "What's going on over there?" Mr. Neader asked.

Henry got up. "Oh, nothing."

"I expect more from you, Henry. I don't want to see this kind of behaviour again."

Henry just nodded and walked away.

Eddy got up and straightened his T-shirt. Pete and John had told him that Pete had made it with the chick, but John didn't have time to before Henry got there.

Then again, maybe the whole story was all a lot of bull.

JUST AS HENRY WAS LEAVING the gym, Mr. Neader called him, into his office.

Oh, geez, now I'm in for it. That Zeigler's getting me in more trouble.

When Henry arrived at the Phys. Ed. office, the door was open and Mr. Neader was already sitting behind his desk piled high with paper and books, waiting for him.

"Sit down Henry." After a moment he went on, "I've been watching you and Eddy. I'm a bit surprised this altercation hasn't happened sooner. You've got it in for him for some reason … and that's none of my business. But trying to get students to get along and avoid that kind of behaviour is."

Mr. Neader got up walked around his desk pushed some of the paper along his desktop to make room for at least part of his butt and sat down on the edge.

Here it comes, thought Henry.

"Henry," Mr. Neader looked straight into his student's eyes and went on, "basketball season starts up next month and I was glad to see you signed up for it. You're a good player and students respect you. Frankly, I didn't expect to see that kind of behaviour from you today. But what I'm getting at is this: I'm going to appoint you captain of the team."

The teacher stopped and asked, "Are you willing to accept that role? It means it's your job to get the best out of your team, keep them in line, motivate them, keep their spirits high, be a leader and make them want to follow you. Right?"

Henry nodded slowly, confused. *What does this have to do with Eddy?*

"So, what do you say?"

Henry was quiet for a bit, having fully expected to get a blast, or possibly detention for his behaviour in the gym, and instead he was asked if he wanted to be the team captain. What a relief. And yet he was sure another shoe was about to drop. *Still ...*

"Yeah, sure, Mr. Neader, that'd be great!"

"There *is* one stipulation, Hank: I'd like to see Eddy Zeigler make the team."

And clunk, *there it is.* The blood drained from Henry's face. "You gotta be kidding, Coach! He doesn't even know the rules, he's short, and ... and, he's bad news!"

"Let's look at what you just said. I agree he doesn't know the rules. Yes, it's obvious he's the shortest guy on the floor, but did you see the way he deeked around Miller last period—"

"Yeah, but then he traveled and fouled—"

"But you have to admit, he had Miller going around in a circle."

"That's because Miller's used to playing with players as tall as he is."

"That's it Henry, exactly! Eddy's height is his advantage. Imagine, with a little training and coaching, we can turn that raw talent into a very good player. He may surprise all of us."

"I don't know, Coach. Eddy may have *some* talent, but to turn it into something may take a long time and ... I don't think that it's possible. And like I said, Eddy's bad news."

"That's my second point, Henry. He may be what you say, but it's our job to make every student good news." And with a gaze that had Engelmann written all over it he said pointedly, "Right?"

Henry looked at his instructor. Just then he sure reminded him of his mentor at the store. Reluctantly, Henry admitted to himself that Mr. Neader was right, and he did understand what his teacher meant; he wasn't just talking about Eddy, but Henry as well …

But to have to help that Eddy … *I can't stand the guy.*

"Henry, I know this is hard for you, I've been in similar situations from time to time in my life, but this I know: if you accept this challenge, it's going to change you for the better. And, to help motivate you, think on it this way …"

Mr. Neader got up and rubbed his butt, "Geez, I've got to clean up this mess one of these days—can't even sit comfortably on my own desk."

This time he rested both his hands behind him on the edge of his desk near the middle and slowly leaned back, positioning his butt between them.

"Oh yes, where was I? Oh yeah. Think on it this way, Henry: at the start anyway, as a team captain you have to lay aside differences you might have with any player on the team. When you're on the court, you're part of a team. There's no room for grudges or any kind of nonsense, no matter how justified you may feel. Right? You just may find that after a while you begin to feel that way off the court as well. So," he asked again, "what do you say?"

Geez, I don't know … help Zeigler? Who would ever have thought that I would even consider *such a thing?* And as Henry thought about it, other thoughts seemed to come out of nowhere, just like the time he'd gone to see Mr. Engelmann about working for him. He had every intention of turning down the job offer, yet words had come out of his mouth that morning that had totally surprised him. But now he knew that working for Mr. Engelmann was the best thing that had ever happened to him. Was it possible that the same thing might happen again? *No way.*

And just as Henry opened his mouth to politely decline the offer from his well meaning coach, the following words came to his lips.

"I'll give it my best shot, Coach."

CHAPTER TWENTY

TED SARSKY SIGHED as he closed the office door behind him. He stepped back and looked at his name painted on the translucent glass panel of the door. He gazed at the title below his name: *president*. It was much sooner than he had expected. At forty-seven, he'd made it to the top, and he still considered himself a young man.

Ted exuded an air of importance. He was tall and handsome and well dressed. His black hair had a natural wave, and streaks of silver grey had emerged through the sides, adding to his distinguished appearance. At six-foot-two, he towered over most people, which further strengthened his presidential status; people literally looked up to him. His dark brown eyes held a smile as he read the title once more. *How quickly circumstances change*, he marveled as he turned and walked towards the elevator.

Perhaps the main reason he had been promoted so quickly was because he was a man of impeccable integrity. He was honest and straightforward in all his dealings, and had received more contracts than his competitors because of that. His colleagues respected him, perceiving him to be fair and objective. He worked extremely hard and had high expectations of his staff.

He'd never burned a bridge. Ted Sarsky's only fault was his tendency to enjoy an extra drink or two. He was always careful not to overindulge in public and was even watchful at home.

But Ted was tired. He had been up since five and could hardly wait to get home and have a relaxing drink. Learning the duties and responsibilities of his new position had not been easy. At least three other executives had hoped to be selected for the position and were unhappy they had not been chosen. Although his rivals were cooperative and even helpful, at least two of them carried some degree of resentment. They were good at concealing it, but Ted had been in the business a long time and could read loyalty.

The first few weeks had been spent getting acquainted with the staff so he could position the right employees in the right roles based on ability and job performance. His choice, however, was always guided by his instincts. There were two executives he felt he could completely rely upon, and they became his righthand team. Fortunately, Ted and Elaine, his predecessor's secretary, had hit it off immediately, and she'd helped him adjust and sort things out. She had been with the company for over fifteen years and knew the business better than anybody, including the former president.

Ted let out a sigh as he walked out to the car. Besides having to deal with his new position and staff, he'd also had to cope with Jenny. She had been completely overwrought the night they'd left Regina and had hardly spoken a word during the entire flight, having cried most of the time. Jenny was very fond of that Henry, and had told him all about how nice the boy was and how he'd helped make improvements at Engelmann's Grocery. Ted was sorry he hadn't had time to meet Henry and see for himself what Jenny had found so appealing.

The last four years had been hard on them all. If the board of directors hadn't assured him this would be his final move, he wouldn't have accepted the position, great as the job was. Jenny had been reluctant to leave Vancouver; she loved the ocean and the West Coast scenery. She'd only accepted the move to Regina because the waving wheatfields of the prairies reminded her of the waves of the ocean. Also, she preferred smaller cities and Regina had reminded her of Kelowna, where she'd been born. Jenny had grown to love the small-town atmosphere of Regina and had immediately liked her new neighbourhood—and the boy three doors down in particular.

And that had been the start of the problem. Jenny wanted to be with Henry all the time, and the move to Ottawa had only made her feelings stronger. It was those darn letters. The very thought of them made him shudder. He inhaled, then exhaled slowly, hoping to dispel the guilt creeping into his chest.

The sky was overcast as Ted drove onto the freeway to the outskirts of Ottawa. It was almost a two-hour commute to get home. But the long drive gave him a chance to unwind and think about the day and the company. That evening, however, he was completely absorbed by thoughts of his daughter.

As Ted neared the Sarskys' new home—a stately Tudor two-storey on a five-acre plot of land—he recalled the day they'd arrived in Ottawa and the driver had brought them to look at their new home. The sight of the beautiful house, surrounded by incredible landscaping, had brightened Jenny's face if only for a moment.

Their first week had been extremely busy. While Edith began unpacking, he had spent almost an entire day with Jenny at her new high school, meeting the administration and some of her teachers. The teachers noticed immediately that his daughter seemed troubled. He blamed it on the move, rather than the separation from her boyfriend.

Now, as Ted drove up the winding, scenic road of their estate, he looked to the second floor of his home where the bedrooms were situated. On the first night they had spent in their new home, Jenny had wanted to write Henry a letter and had gone directly to the room she'd chosen as hers. She hadn't come out the entire evening. The next morning, Jenny had given him the letter to mail. But before Ted left for the city, Edith had pulled him aside and told him not to send it, that she would explain later. He'd tossed the letter into the glove compartment and for-gotten all about it. A few days later, Jenny gave him another to mail and he was reminded of the first. After Jenny went to bed, he and his wife had discussed the whole matter and agreed it best to destroy the letters.

It seemed wrong and yet he felt justified in terminating the relationship between Jenny and her young man. They'd been too close, too fast. His wife certainly felt that if they'd stayed in Regina, Jenny would have been pregnant before the year was out. Edith had been so relieved when the new position was of-fered to him, she hadn't complained once about the move. Ted also agreed with Edith that Jenny needed stability in her life, and new friends, not to be overburdened with a serious relationship at such a young age. Yet destroying his daughter's letters both-ered him deeply, even more so when Jenny began to ask if mail had arrived for her. Ted had hoped Jenny would soon be over it and adjust to her new life in Ottawa.

Ted was so deep in thought that he arrived in his garage without realizing it, the door closing behind him. It alarmed him somewhat that he couldn't remember opening the garage door and driving in.

"One of these days, I'll end up in no man's land," he muttered. And today Engelmann had called. Ted was too tired to discuss it with Edith tonight. Perhaps tomorrow.

ON THE WAY TO WORK the next morning, Ted decided to read one of Jenny's letters. He had thrown most of them out, but there were still a few from the previous week at his office and one in the glove compartment from the day before. He pulled his car into a roadside rest area and parked in front of a huge sign with a map outlining the main streets of Ottawa. Under the guise of studying the sign, Ted read Jenny's letter. He was, in a sense, looking for direction, not to the city centre, but to where his daughter's heart was heading.

Ted rolled down the window and was met by a blast of crisp morning air. The breeze momentarily cleared his troubled mind.

Uneasiness and uncertainty about opening his daughter's mail mingled with his guilt over having lied to Jenny about mailing the letters to begin with. Hopefully, something in this letter would vindicate their decision and convince him that what he and Edith were doing was right.

He opened the glove box but hesitated before bringing the letter out. Sweat broke out across his forehead. He knew on some level that it was cruel to let his daughter believe he was mailing her letters. It only encouraged her to write again and again, pouring her heart out. It devastated him to see Jenny's crestfallen face day after day of no reply. He heaped that guilt on top of the knowledge that Jenny had no idea her letters weren't even reaching Henry.

Before Ted could come up with a rationale to counter his guilt and shame, he thought about Henry. What was the boy feeling? Was he still hoping to hear from Jenny? He was probably writing letters as well, waiting to learn Jenny's address. Two lives were hurt by the choice he and Edith had made, and Ted felt an alarming surge of remorse that he did his best to tamp down.

"When Edith and I talked, it all seemed so right, so logical, so clear. And now ... I just don't know anymore," he muttered.

The whole dilemma weighed on him. It was exhausting. If only they hadn't interfered and had just let things run their natural course, Jenny would already be receiving letters. As he visualized the letters Jenny had written and the many he had already destroyed, he could no longer hold back his emotions.

What have we done? He hung his head. And that was probably why Engelmann had phoned. He must see the anguish in Henry as Ted saw it in Jenny.

Finally, he pulled out the letter Jenny had given him the previous morning, flipping it over and over in his hand, debating. He almost put it back in the glove compartment but he was in the wrong already. What was one further mistake? And perhaps the choice they'd made as Jenny's parents would be rationalized. He and Edith wanted only the best for her, after all. Maybe the letter would say she was getting over the boy, and they could all get on with their lives. Ted's hands trembled as he ripped the sealed envelope and pulled out the sheet of paper.

"Henry should be doing this. It's his letter," Ted sighed. He took a deep breath, unfolded the page, and lowered his eyes to his daughter's writing.

> *Dear Henry,*
>
> *It's been almost two months since I moved to Ottawa. This is the twenty-third letter I've written you. There's been not one letter in return. Every night I lie in bed wondering what happened and why you don't write back to me. My father says he's mailed all my letters. Maybe some have been lost, but you must have received some of them surely?*
>
> *If you're going out with someone else, I promise I'll be very happy for you. If you are afraid to write for fear that you might hurt my feelings, please don't be. Just let me know what's happened and how you feel about us. Each time I write to you, I find it harder to express my feelings. Perhaps you have another girlfriend and love her deeply, and when I write and tell you that I still have feelings for you, maybe you feel sad or guilty. Oh, Henry, if you have a new girlfriend, that's great.*
>
> *If I don't hear from you in the next week I'll assume you have either found someone new or no longer want me to be your girlfriend.*
>
> *Just to let you know, I went with Susan and Elaine, the two new friends I mentioned to you*

in my last letters, to a sleepover party at Susan's
house last night. We had a lot of fun. We laughed
and joked and talked about the boys at school. I
told them about you and how great you are, that
you're such a wonderful person and business-
man—and that someday you'll be a famous
artist. They thought that was so romantic.

I hope school is going well for you, Henry, and if
you have the time, please write soon.

I miss you ... so much.
Jenny

Ted lay the letter on his lap. He had tears in his eyes. Jenny still had feelings for that boy and desperately wanted some closure. *My father says he's mailed all my letters,* rang in Ted's mind. How could he have lied to his daughter over and over again? He had compromised his honesty, something he would never have done in business. He felt the wrongness of it in his heart and gut, and sighed. He would have to revisit the whole matter with Edith when he got home tonight. He'd ask her to read the letter too—surely she'd agree that their decision had been a mistake.

Preoccupied with the letter, Ted didn't notice the patrol car pull up behind him until he heard gravel crunching under heavy footsteps. The police officer tapped at the window. Ted quickly dashed a trace of tears from his eyes and tossed the letter aside.

"Everything all right, sir?"

"Oh, I'm fine," Ted countered, glancing quickly at the officer and then straight ahead. "Just stopped for a little break to enjoy the fine morning."

"May I see your driver's license, please?"

"Yes, of course." He took out his wallet, removed his driver's license and handed it to the officer, who was now studying him intensely.

"You're Mr. Sarsky, are you?"

"Yes, I am."

"And your address is correct?"

"Yes, it is. We just moved here. Is something wrong, officer?"

"No, just checking, sir. Routine procedure."

"I see," said Ted. "Is it okay for me to go then? I have an early meeting and an important phone call to make at the office."

"Are you sure everything's okay?" the officer asked once more, handing Ted his driver's license back.

"Yes, I assure you I'm fine."

"Well, you have a good day now."

"Yes, I'm sure I will," Ted lied, thinking of what he had to do. "And you too, officer."

TED FINGERED THE SLIP of paper with Engelmann's phone number. He'd have to wait; he had to talk to Edith first.

There was another phone message from the grocery store owner waiting for him when he returned from his meeting.

Ted buzzed his secretary. "Please call Mr. Engelmann back. Let him know that I am in meetings all day and will return his call first thing in the morning."

AFTER JENNY WENT TO HER ROOM later that evening, Ted found his wife in the living room and sat down next to her, holding out the letter he had read in the car.

"Edith, I think we need to talk about our decision not to mail Jenny's letters to Henry Pederson."

Edith's head snapped up. "Why do you want to bring that up again?"

Ted knew he was in for a battle. He looked Edith straight in the eye. "Edith, I feel very guilty about destroying Jenny's letters and I don't think we're doing the right thing. On my way to the city, I read the letter Jenny gave me to mail yesterday morning. Not sending her letters is hurting not only Henry, but our daughter, too."

"Oh, Ted, don't be so dramatic. They're just kids. They'll get over it. Someone has to be strong here and see the sense in all this. Don't worry. It will soon be over and forgotten."

"But, Edith, Jenny has a right to send letters and Henry has a right to receive them. Here, read this." Ted thrust Jenny's letter towards his wife. "See for yourself what a terrible mistake this is."

Edith rolled her eyes and yanked the letter from Ted's hand. As she read the letter, her expression of annoyance changed to one of triumph.

It wasn't exactly the reaction he had been hoping for.

"See, Ted, just another week and it'll all be over. I'm glad you read this—it confirms what I've thought all along: the whole thing was nothing more than a summer romance, Jenny attaching herself to someone to get some stability in her life after all the moving around we've done over the past few years. I can't believe you're talking this way. It's so near the end and you want to open it all up again? I don't think so." She quickly rescanned the letter and reiterated, "It'll be over and done with in just another week."

She tossed the letter on the coffee table, dismissive.

Ted picked it up again.

As he re-read it, Edith continued, "If you stir things up now, after all this time, God only knows what will happen. What if she wants to visit him, or he asks to come here for a week or so? What if she gets pregnant, Ted, then what? Would you admit I was right when it's too late and the damage is done? They're just kids, Ted. For God's sake, let it go. You have enough on your plate with your new job. And besides, can't you see the terrible mess we'd be in if we suddenly sent one of Jenny's letters? Their next question would be *Where did all the other letters go*? Are you willing to tell your daughter you destroyed them and have been lying to her all along?"

Ted sat back, confused again. The word *pregnant* resonated in his mind. If he got those kids back together again and Jenny got pregnant, he'd never hear the end of it. This morning he'd been so sure that Edith would see things his way after reading

Jenny's letter. But maybe Edith *was* right, after all. How had he allowed himself to get so emotionally involved? If Jenny found out that they had destroyed all the letters …

"My God, I hate to even think about it, but it really bothers me still," Ted murmured.

"What did you say, Ted?"

Ted was reluctant to share his feelings any further, afraid of what Edith might say, yet he still felt he should protest. "But, Edith, we're lying to her. She thinks I'm mailing her letters when I am, in fact, destroying them. I just took another six or seven down to the furnace room the other day and tossed them into the fire. You have no idea—"

"Ted, we've been over and over this. You have to look at the bigger picture, the overall good. We don't know much about this Henry. And the two of them are only fifteen! Besides, we're here in Ottawa now. Jenny has to make new friends and move on. Continuing a relationship with someone so far away, prolonging it by mail, will only stop her from going out with other boys and getting on with her life."

There was a long silence. Edith could see Ted was once again on track, but for added measure, she pushed her point. "Ted, sometimes we have to do things we don't like because it's best for all concerned. Look at the executive you had to fire back in Regina. Remember how you stewed about it for weeks, how difficult it was for you to let him go because he was married and had three children? Yet when you finally did it, remember how everything improved, how the atmosphere in the workplace immediately got better and sales went up."

"Yes … that's true; sometimes positives can come from negatives," Ted conceded.

"Exactly. And things worked out well for him, too. He started up his own business and is doing really quite well now, right?"

Ted was becoming more and more convinced that Edith was right. "You know, it's a good thing Jenny has only written to Henry. I'd hate to think what we'd have to do if she wanted to phone him. She'd find out immediately that he hasn't received a single letter she wrote."

"Don't worry about that," Edith said with confidence.

"Why not?"

"About two weeks ago Jenny asked if she could phone Henry or the grocery store where he worked."

"What!" Ted exclaimed. "Why didn't you tell me?"

"You have enough to worry about."

"Well, tell me what happened?"

"I simply told her that it was very expensive to phone long distance and we didn't want her to start doing that, that writing to Henry was best and put less pressure on him. That way she would be leaving it up to him whether or not to write back. Boys don't like to be chased, I told her. I didn't want to upset her, but she was going to have to face facts sooner or later."

"And Jenny just accepted that without any argument?"

"She seemed to. She said, 'Perhaps you're right, Mom.'"

"And she hasn't brought it up since?"

Edith looked away. After a long moment, she answered, "No…"

"Well, good. You may have convinced her. But something else has come up."

Edith looked at Ted quizzically, "Oh? What do you mean?"

"Yesterday morning, I received a call from a Mr. Engelmann. I believe he's the owner of the store where Henry works. Elaine told me he wanted to speak to me about a personal matter. I'm certain it has to do with Jenny and Henry."

"Well, it's hardly any of his business," Edith countered sharply. "And I'm rather perturbed he was able to get your office phone number."

"Hmm. You're right. We did leave instructions with the real estate company and the manager of our Regina office not to give out our forwarding addresses or telephone numbers. I will have to check on that."

"In any case," Edith continued, "if his call is in regards to Jenny and Henry, you can simply explain to him that Jenny is no longer interested in the boy and has found new friends. Certainly he will understand that."

Edith had it all figured out. He looked down at the letter in his hand and the sentence on which Edith had based her argument. *If I don't hear from you in the next week I'll assume you have either found someone new or no longer want me to be your girlfriend.* Ted hoped Jenny would be true to her word. He didn't know if he could take much more. In any case, he reasoned, things had already gone too far.

Edith was right. There was no turning back now.

Ted pushed himself up off the sofa and walked towards the fireplace. The fire was almost out, sputtering into nothing the way his guilt just had. He drew back the screen, took one last look at Jenny's letter and tossed it on top of the dying coals. He watched as the edge of the paper lit with orange and burned its way down, erasing each heartfelt sentence Jenny had written. Edith's eyes bored into his back and he shivered.

Slowly, the glow of flames reflecting on his face dimmed then died. The warmth was gone, leaving behind a troubled man.

Ted stared at the ash until the last spark of what had been Jenny's letter went out. He pushed his last doubts from his mind, took a deep breath and resolved to see the thing through. He'd decided how to respond to Engelmann in the morning.

Ted turned away from the fireplace, went directly to the liquor cabinet and poured himself a stiff drink.

WHILE HER LETTER turned to ashes, Jenny lay in her bedroom, crying. She hoped the letter she had sent the previous morning would find Henry swiftly and bring back the answer she desperately wanted to hear. Surely there would be some response. She couldn't go on like this.

CHAPTER TWENTY-ONE

As soon as Ted got to his office the next morning, he dialed Mr. Engelmann.

"Hello, Engelmann's Grocery and Confectionary, how can I help you?"

"Good morning, am I speaking to David Engelmann?"

"Yes, you are."

"This is Ted Sarsky, returning your call from two days ago. Sorry I couldn't do it sooner. What can I do for you?"

"Yes, yes! Thank you for taking time to call me back, Mr. Sarsky. I called concerning a young man who works for me. His name is Henry Pederson. I believe you know him as Jenny's friend."

"Yes." Ted steeled himself for what he had to do.

"Apparently when Jenny left, she promised to write to Henry and let him know her address so they could correspond. Up until now Henry hasn't heard from or received any letters from your daughter. I know this is not any business of mine, but Henry seems deeply troubled that he has not heard from Jenny at all. Out of concern for Henry, I thought I would phone you to find out what has happened."

Ted paused, his wife's argument replaying in his head. He took a deep breath.

"I understand your concern, Mr. Engelmann—and my heart goes out to Henry. But this is one of those things that happens in life. When Jenny got to Ottawa, she was faced with the challenge of starting in a new school and making new friends for the second time this year. We moved into our new home and before we knew it, a month had elapsed. Jenny expressed to her mother that she felt she should write Henry, but she's gotten so involved with her classes, extracurricular activities and music lessons, she's barely had any time to herself."

Before Mr. Engelmann could speak, Ted continued. He wanted to get this over with.

"My company assures me we will not have to move again; we're in Ottawa to stay. Jenny has had so many disruptions in the past four years and is finally experiencing some stability. Besides, she and Henry are both very young and there really is no future for them at this stage. To get right to the point, Mr. Engelmann, we are all hoping this little summer romance is over, and that Henry and Jenny—and me and my wife—can finally get on with our lives."

"I see," said Mr. Engelmann. "So, you are saying that Jenny will not be writing to Henry?"

"Yes, that's what I'm saying."

"And you do not want Henry to have your address so he can write to her?"

Once again Ted paused, Edith's words sharp in his ear: *Be firm with him, Ted. Just get it over with, once and for all. Let's not prolong this for another minute.*

"Yes, Mr. Engelmann. I am afraid this is the way it has to be. The three of us have given it a lot of thought and we feel that it's best for everyone concerned. I hope you understand," Ted's tone was final.

"Yes, I understand all you have said," Mr. Engelmann sighed. It was as he had suspected. "Yes, life has many problems, a series of ups and downs. We cannot avoid them or control them. I

won't trouble you again, but please know you can call me anytime if you wish. I will leave you with this thought, though. Is
this the right thing or the easy thing?" And then with some trep-
idation, he added with unexpected boldness, "Who are we really
protecting, Mr. Sarsky, our children or ourselves?"

Mr. Engelmann waited for some response from Ted, but
there was only silence. "Goodbye, then, Mr. Sarsky."

Mr. Engelmann hung up. He was frustrated and upset, but
relieved he had told Ted Sarsky how he felt about the entire
matter. Mr. Sarsky's use of the term *we* bothered him. He got
the feeling Mr. Sarsky had not been completely truthful just
now. Perhaps Mr. and Mrs. Sarsky felt that way, but not Jenny.
And Mr. Engelmann was not convinced that Jenny's father was
entirely comfortable with this solution.

Still, it wasn't his place to push the matter any further, although he could have added some choice words about not meddling in the lives of others and letting things unfold according
to God's will and not our own.

He sighed once more.

MR. SARSKY LISTENED TO THE CLICK of the receiver, the dial tone
aggravating his already troubled thoughts. He hung up, thinking of Mr. Engelmann's final words. He'd only met the grocer
once while they'd lived in Regina, but the old man had surprised
him even then with his ability to read people and situations.
Now, as he sat back in his leather armchair, he became aware
of the perspiration soaking the back of his shirt.

"Have we done the right thing or the easy thing?" Ted repeated. The question and its answer were painfully clear. He
wanted to be upset with Mr. Engelmann for having the audacity
to criticize the way they were raising their daughter, but that
feeling soon evaporated upon closer inspection of their motives.

Mr. Engelmann had been both accurate and astute. He and
Edith had done the convenient thing, not the right thing. They
were protecting themselves from the worry that went along with
raising children, especially a daughter. By thwarting Jenny's re-

lationship they had denied her the knowledge that she was loved and the life experience that went along with it. How was she to learn if they let her experience only the things they wanted for her? How was she to learn to trust others if they didn't trust her themselves? Worse, he and Edith had also denied themselves the opportunity to grow as parents, to help and guide their daughter. And their lack of trust and faith in Jenny was contrary to the values they had tried to instill in her.

If this was a test, they had failed.

A chill surged through his body; they might have avoided inconveniences and potential problems now, but what about in the future? His only real objection to the relationship was that the two of them were too young for such an intense relationship. But what if Jenny, in another year or two, chose someone completely unsuitable? Jenny had spoken with such pride about Henry, his artistic skills and business aptitude. She had said he was a good student, too.

Life was complex and hard at times, and yet parents still had to let go of their children. They couldn't protect Jenny forever. And he wanted her to grow into an adult capable of making her own choices, yet they'd given her no chance to be part of this decision. They shouldn't have tried to control her life.

Ted rose from his chair and walked over to the floor-length window. Not even the beautiful view of the Rideau Canal running its course behind Parliament Hill or the late fall colours of the maple trees could quell the unsettled feelings swirling inside him. When he was around Edith, her resolve quickly doused his feelings of guilt, but as soon as he was alone, they flared up to convict him.

Ted studied his faint reflection in the glass, superimposed on the cityscape of downtown Ottawa. He felt as if he stood naked before a very tough judge, a judge who knew his past—every nook and cranny—from whom he could not hide. A judge who lived by the highest standards and with whom there were no compromises. And before this judge, Ted knew he was guilty.

He felt like he was on a merry-go-round with headless horses, with no way to stop, no reins to pull in, and no way to get off. The right thing to do was to confess all to his daughter, but he would never be able to convince Edith. She was firm in her resolve and he'd left the bulk of the childrearing to her while he'd focused on his career.

My first responsibility should have been family, not work, he thought now. Then he would have had the leverage to challenge Edith on this. But how could he impose his will over Edith's now? It was too late. He would simply have to go along with his wife's wishes in the matter, caught between his value system and hers, his perception and hers, his conscience and hers. And there was a substantial gap between them.

Ted knew of only one way to fill it.

He walked over to the tall oak cabinet beside his desk and tugged open the two doors by their solid brass knobs. Presidency had its perks. On the glass shelves in front of him was every kind of liquor imaginable. The mirror in the back reflected every bottle, giving the illusion of an endless supply. With one hand he selected a glass and with the other he reached for an almost full bottle of Canadian whiskey. He poured himself half a glass and downed it in two swallows.

It was ten-thirty in the morning.

He set down his glass as softly as he could then returned the bottle to the shelf, avoiding his image in the mirror. He didn't want to see the guilt reflected in his eyes or watch himself in the act of washing it away. He shut the liquor cabinet and returned to his desk. He took a deep breath, sat down and reached for the call button on the intercom.

"Elaine, I'm ready for my eleven o'clock appointment."

"Certainly, Mr. Sarsky. I'll send him in as soon as he arrives."

DAVID ENGELMANN WONDERED whether he had said too much or not enough to Jenny's father. One thing was certain: Jenny's parents didn't want Jenny and Henry to continue their relationship. But what could he do? The Sarskys were only doing what they thought best for their daughter.

Perhaps the greatest sadness was that there would be no closure for either of the young people; Jenny had no way of knowing if Henry still loved her and Henry had no way of knowing if Jenny even thought of him at all. It was, the old man thought, a particularly terrible kind of torture. There was only one thing to do and David Engelmann did it.

He bowed his head and prayed.

CHAPTER TWENTY-TWO

"HI, MR. ENGELMANN," said Henry, a little more cheerfully than of late.

"Yes, hello, Henry! It's good to see you. It was busy today, and the shelves need restocking. How was school?"

"I'll tell you about it in a minute." Henry brought some canned goods out from the storage room. As he stacked cans of Campbell's soup, he said, "You know, you'll be glad to hear that Eddy Zeigler and I are getting along a little better." Mr. Engelmann looked up from writing an invoice. "What's that, Henry?"

"Well, a few weeks ago, Eddy and I had a fight in the gym and afterwards the Phys. Ed. teacher called me to his office."

Henry looked up to see if Mr. Engelmann was listening.

"And did you get a scolding?"

"Well that's the thing, I thought I would, but instead Mr. Neader asked me to be the team captain for the junior basketball team."

"That is wonderful news, Henry!" But after a little study of his young employee he asked, "And is there is anything else you wish to tell me?"

"I knew you would ask that," Henry smiled. "Yeah, the coach

said I could be team captain on the condition that I help Eddy Ziegler make the team."

Mr. Engelmann stared at Henry for a long moment and his eyes brightened. "That is a very wise teacher, Henry."

"I knew you'd say that too, Mr. Engelmann," Henry smiled from ear to ear. "You know, the teacher was right about Eddy. He does have talent; it just hasn't been worked at properly. Mr. Neader had Eddy and me practising together during Phys. Ed. and it's amazing how quickly Eddy caught on. And later when we had a scrimmage with the rest of the class, I threw him the basketball and set him up for a basket."

"I can only imagine that made young Eddy a happy player?"

"Yeah—I could tell he appreciated it even though he tried hard not to show it. And, you know, that's the first time in all these weeks I actually felt a bit better about Eddy and those other guys."

"That is so good to hear. You are freeing yourself from the bondage of anger. The Lord is helping you to forgive. You will see some good come out of all this, Henry."

"I sure hope so. It still really bothers me that those guys scared Jenny so badly."

"Oh?"

"Yeah. That fight I had with Eddy was over something he'd said. He told me his buddies had messed around with Jenny at the park. And then when he saw how upset that made me, he changed his tune and said he was just kidding."

"Well, but didn't Jenny say she was all right afterward? They didn't hurt her, did they?"

"Yeah, only the thing is, when I got to Jenny in the park that night, she'd fainted and was just coming around. But a girl would know, wouldn't she?"

Mr. Engelmann thought it over. "Yes, Henry, I think Jenny would have known. If she said nothing happened, then it probably didn't."

"Well, I sure hope not. I don't know why, but the whole thing just bothers me."

Mr. Engelmann smiled. "You love her and you're concerned for her. It's only natural you would feel this way."

"Yeah, I suppose you're right. Anyway, I'm trying to bury the hatchet with Eddy but I'm going to make darn sure I know where I buried it."

Mr. Engelmann looked up and shook his head. "Keep trying, Henry, and ask the good Lord for his help."

"I am, Mr. Engelmann," Henry said. "Actually, just as I was leaving my locker today, Eddy was coming down the hall. He looked at me funny when I said 'hi' to him."

"He may be suspicious of your motives, Henry. He may even test you a bit. Keep being nice to him. Soon he will see you are sincere and you will make a good friend out of him."

Henry rolled his eyes. *Him, Eddy Ziegler's friend? That'd be the day.* "It's strictly for the team's sake, Mr. Engelmann."

BUSINESS HAD PICKED UP exponentially since Henry painted the store, landscaped the front and kept the shelves stocked. In fact, Saturdays were so busy Mr. Engelmann had had to hire another two boys to help with deliveries, though they weren't as quick as Henry and Gary had been. Henry had really missed his best friend since he'd left for Notre Dame. Gary had been a fast and steady delivery partner, and Henry missed going to the movies with him after work on Saturdays.

To make up for Gary's absence, Henry had organized the deliveries so each boy had an efficient route. He'd also learned that when the boys were paid per delivery instead of an hourly wage, the deliveries were completed faster.

"You're a natural businessman, Henry," Mr. Engelmann often said.

THE FOLLOWING MONDAY MORNING, Mr. Mahoney came to the store to pick up another payment towards the back taxes.

"Good morning, Mr. Engelmann."

"And good morning to you, Mr. Mahoney."

"Your store looks very nice—I noticed the new sign outside.

You can see it from almost two blocks away! I trust business is good?"

"Very good," replied Mr. Engelmann. "The young man I hired a few months ago has been a big help."

"I can see that. You tell him if he ever wants a job at the city we'll have one for him."

"Oh, I hope not," Mr. Engelmann smiled, eyes twinkling, "I need him for as long as he can stay with me."

Mr. Mahoney glanced around. "I imagine the boy's in school?"

"Yes, yes. Henry's a very bright boy with a good heart. I believe he has been heavensent to us. He comes in every day after school and all day Saturdays. I know he is busy with schoolwork, yet he loves this business and is very devoted and loyal."

"I can see you are very fond of him."

"Like my own son."

Mr. Engelmann took out the cheque payment and handed it to the tax man. Mr. Mahoney smiled and looked at the cheque.

"Another ten payments and you'll be completely caught up, including this year's taxes."

"I know that only too well. It's a blessing to see out debts cleared up."

"Yes, I'm sure. See you next month, Mr. Engelmann. I wish you a pleasant day."

"And to you, too."

BUT THAT DAY, FOUR-THIRTY came and went with no Henry. Henry had always been on time, and at quarter to five, Mr. Engelmann began to worry. As he peered out the window, he saw the teen on the other side of the street waiting for a break in the traffic. But even when he had a chance to cross, Henry only stood there as if waiting for someone or deep in thought. Mr. Engelmann watched Henry for another five minutes and was about to go outside and ask if anything was wrong when the boy finally dashed across the street.

"Hi, Mr. Engelmann, sorry I'm late."

"Yes, yes, tell me what is going on. I saw you just waiting there and was beginning to get very worried about you. How long were you standing there?"

"Oh, I'm okay," Henry assured his boss. "I was standing there for about a half-hour."

"What on earth for?"

"Well, when I got to the corner around four o'clock, two ladies were waiting to cross the street but became so frustrated with the traffic and afraid to cross, they walked down to Safeway to get their groceries. Just think, Mr. Engelmann. They walked nearly three extra blocks so they wouldn't have to cross the street! They usually come to our store—but not when the traffic is busy."

Mr. Engelmann raised an eyebrow, the signal, Henry knew by now, for him to continue, which he did in a rush.

"We're losing sales because older people are afraid to cross the street. The main reason our sales are up is because of the deliveries. But when deliveries can't be made, some of our customers, as loyal as they try to be, just won't cross Victoria Avenue."

"You're very smart to notice that. It's come up several times over the years, but there is nothing we can do about it."

"Maybe there is!" Henry exclaimed. "While I waited to cross the street, I counted at least six people who wanted to cross but couldn't because there was no break in the traffic. And remember what almost happened to Jenny."

Henry swallowed, throat tight. Her name on his lips was still painful. A moment later he continued, "Mr. Engelmann, this is a very busy corner and the city should do something about it. There was a crosswalk at our high school, but because of the large number of students crossing the street, the city, at the request of the school board, agreed to install traffic lights instead. In fact, students and parents signed a petition to help the school administration force the city to do it quickly. It really got results."

"And so," Mr. Engelmann said, "you want to start a petition now, do you?"

"Yeah! Don't you see? When we make our deliveries and when customers come into the store, we can ask them to sign a petition to put traffic lights at the corner," Henry was nearly shouting with excitement. "If it works, our business will increase tenfold!"

Mr. Engelmann stared at Henry in disbelief. "My goodness, Henry, how your brain works—it's incredible. In all the years I have known of this problem, I never once thought about a solution." He beamed and shook his head. "Yes, yes, a petition just might work. *Gott in Himmel*, it just might work."

"But there's more, Mr. Engelmann."

"How could there possibly be more?"

"Well, Mrs. Tearhorst was one of the ladies who wanted to cross the street while I was out there."

"And?"

"Well, do you remember about three weeks ago when she was in the store, how proud she was of her nephew who was elected to city council?"

"Sure."

"Well, next time Mrs. Tearhorst comes in, why don't you show her the petition and ask her to give it to her nephew? Maybe he can help get the city to install at least a crosswalk at the corner. Mrs. Tearhorst knows how busy Victoria Avenue is. And maybe, Mr. Engelmann—"

"There's more?" Mr. Engelmann interrupted, his smile broad.

"Yeah! Maybe tell her how nice it would be to have traffic lights—cars sometimes don't stop for a crosswalk—and that would *really* ensure the safety of the people in the neighbourhood. If she and her nephew can get the city to do it, we could name the traffic lights after her: the Tearhorst Traffic Lights. Just think of it!" He and Mr. Engelmann laughed and laughed.

Mr. Engelmann gazed proudly at his young assistant, his laughter turning into one of his benevolent smiles. He loved Henry very much.

WHEN MRS. TEARHORST came into the store later that week, Mr.

Engelmann explained about the busy road and asked if she would help. As Henry had anticipated, the idea of Tearhorst Traffic Lights delighted Mrs. Tearhorst and she immediately took on the installation of a traffic signal at the corner as her mission. Mr. Engelmann later told Henry he thought Mrs. Tearhorst's nephew was in for some heavy-duty persuasion. She was further impressed by the fact that they'd collected sixty-seven signatures on their petition in just a few short days. She'd be pretty popular in the neighbourhood if she pulled it off.

Sure enough, within two weeks, Mr. Engelmann noticed a man at the corner, almost exactly where Henry had stood that day after school. The man kept a tally of some sort for almost the entire day. The next day he was back again, doing the same thing. While he was there, a senior crossing the street almost got hit by a speeding car.

In another two weeks, a city crew was out drilling holes for a set of traffic lights. Neither Mr. Engelmann nor Henry could believe their eyes. They jumped around the front of the store, unable to contain their excitement. At the end of the month, the lights were activated and Mr. Engelmann decided to have a "traffic light party." At the back of the store, Henry hung the huge sign he'd made:

Engelmann's Grocery & Confectionary
thanks Agnes and Jim Tearhorst
for their contribution to neighbourhood safety:
THE TEARHORST TRAFFIC LIGHTS

Mrs. Tearhorst beamed when she saw the sign and received the bouquet of flowers people in the neighbourhood had chipped in to buy her. She was so overwhelmed, she cried. Twenty-three people attended the party at the store—including, of course, Mrs. Tearhorst's nephew, who welcomed the publicity. Mr. Engelmann gave away free cheese, salami and soda pop. The party lasted for over an hour. Mrs. Tearhorst and her nephew were the last to go, shaking everyone's hands as they left and eagerly acknowledging their thanks.

The next week, just as Henry had predicted, the store was even busier than usual. Mr. Engelmann could hardly wait for Henry to get there after school—what with looking after Anna and trying to keep up with the business, he was run off his feet. But he wasn't too busy to notice that Henry hardly mentioned Jenny anymore. It seemed Mr. Sarsky had been right; it had been only a summer romance.

"Hello, Mr. Engelmann," Henry called out as he rushed into the store.

"How come you are so early today?"

"It's the traffic lights. I don't have to wait so long anymore!" Henry looked around the store, glad it was empty for the moment. "I have some news to tell you."

"Yes, what is it, Henry?"

"Jenny's house sold. The sign was up when I came home after school. The real estate man was just leaving and I asked him if he knew what the Sarskys' new address was, but he said he didn't know and that they weren't allowed to give out that information anyway."

Mr. Engelmann looked at Henry but said nothing, waiting for him to continue.

"I was wondering, Mr. Engelmann, if you could help me get her address? My mom tried over a month ago, and they wouldn't give her the address, either."

"I see," said Mr. Engelmann.

He had worried about what to say if Henry asked him for help. Would he encourage Henry to forget about Jenny and move on with his life or tell him that he had spoken with Mr. Sarsky? Now the moment was upon him and Mr. Engelmann hesitated. To hide his conversation with Mr. Sarsky from Henry was just as dishonest as perhaps the Sarskys had been with their daughter. *No*, he decided, *Henry must know the truth*.

And so Mr. Engelmann told Henry about his chat with Mr. Sarsky, explaining also why he had not told Henry sooner.

"I hoped Mr. Sarsky would reconsider and phone back, but

he hasn't. The Sarskys are very adamant that they don't want you and Jenny to correspond, and Mr. Sarsky seemed to indicate that Jenny was in agreement with this."

Henry was shocked by the notion. "She couldn't be! Jenny would want to hear from me!"

"Well, maybe you're right."

"I *know* I'm right, Mr. Engelmann!"

"Well, that may be the case, but unfortunately we can't do much about it. And so, rather than upset you further, I waited. I have noticed you seem to have accepted the situation over the last little while, and haven't mentioned it at all until today. I thought it best just to leave it unless you brought it up. And now, since you have, I felt it my duty to tell you what I know."

"Do *you* know Jenny's address, Mr. Engelmann?"

"No, I don't. I know where Mr. Sarsky works, but not his home address."

"I have forty-six letters at home, Mr. Engelmann. I can't just leave them there piled up on my desk. I have to mail them to her."

"I understand, Henry, but where can we send them? Mr. Sarsky was very firm, and now that almost another month has passed, I'm sure he will be even more adamant.

"But I just have to mail those letters!" Henry was desperate, hope flaring in him with even this remote contact with Jenny's family. "What can I do?"

Mr. Engelmann put his hand on Henry's shoulder, "The only thing you can do is box up all those letters and mail them to Mr. Sarsky's office. Then we will hope he will take them home to Jenny. That is the only option I can see for you."

Henry perked up immediately. He studied Mr. Engelmann, and Mr. Engelmann returned his steady gaze.

"Let's try it, Henry, but for your sake, if it doesn't work, then you must get on with your life. Do you understand?"

It was Henry's only chance and he was going to take it.

"Yeah, I do—I just know things will work out somehow!"

Mr. Engelmann peered over his smudged glasses and looked

hard into Henry's eyes. "Henry, I will support you in this, but you must promise me that if you do not receive any response, you will let the matter go. To continue feeling so distraught over something you can do nothing about must stop. Time is a healer of even the most terrible experiences, and we must let it do its work. To fight it day in and day out leads only to despair and death. The only reality is the present. To live in the past and dream about Jenny and your relationship can no longer do you any more good."

The old man waited for some acknowledgement.

"Yes, I understand, Mr. Engelmann, but I have to try, just once more."

"Bring the letters to me after school tomorrow, and we will box and wrap them. I will send them to Mr. Sarsky's office."

"Thank you," Henry said, his eyes alive with hope.

CHAPTER TWENTY-THREE

H ENRY WALKED INTO THE STORE the next day carrying a brown paper bag.

"I see you brought the letters."

"Yes, I did. And I also wrote a letter to Mr. Sarsky."

Mr. Engelmann looked at Henry, his brow folding into deep wrinkles. "What sort of letter?"

"Well, I want Mr. Sarsky to know I'm responsible and that I would never do anything to hurt Jenny. And I told him I would be very grateful if he'd let me write to her, and ... well, why don't you read the letter, Mr. Engelmann? I'd like your opinion."

"Yes, yes, let me see the letter. I'm sure it's okay the way it is."

Henry handed Mr. Engelmann the note he'd written to Jenny's dad. It wasn't very long, only two paragraphs. "That is good, brief and to the point. Now let me see." Mr. Engelmann adjusted his glasses and began to read out loud:

Dear Mr. Sarsky,

Although we've never met, I did see you at church with Jenny and Mrs. Sarsky on the last Sunday

*you were in Regina, but you were so busy talking
to other people I never had the chance to talk to
you. I wish I had met you so that you would
know I am a responsible young man. I work very
hard for Mr. Engelmann at the corner grocery
store and am a good student.*

*I also want you to know that I like Jenny very
much and would never do anything to hurt her. I
have been waiting almost three months for Jenny
to send me her address so that I can mail the letters I have written. Since I have not heard from
Jenny in all this time, I have decided to mail them
to you and ask if you would please take the letters
home to Jenny. If she decides not to write back, I
will understand, but I do want her to know that
I kept my promise to write. Thank you for doing
this.*

Yours truly,
Henry Pederson

Mr. Engelmann laid the letter down and looked at Henry.

"That is a good letter. You have left it up to him to decide. If
you would like, I could perhaps also add a note at the bottom,
letting Mr. Sarsky know what a good employee you are."

"Yeah, that would be great, Mr. Engelmann. A word from you
might carry even more weight."

"We'll see," the old man replied. He pulled the letter closer
and reached for his pen. After a brief moment he touched it to
the page just below Henry's signature.

Mr. Sarsky,

*Just an added note to let you know that Henry is
a fine young man. Since he came to work for me,*

*my store—which was on the verge of bank-
ruptcy—has completely turned around. You
would be proud to have such a clever and hard-
working young man at your company. I sincerely
hope you will consider Henry's request; I believe
it is important these two young people communicate with each other, even if it is only to say
goodbye.*

Thank you for your kind consideration,
David Engelmann

Mr. Engelmann put down his pen and pushed the letter towards Henry. Henry read the addition.

"Boy, Mr. Sarsky will have to give Jenny the letters now for
sure!"

"Well, Henry, I meant every word I said, but Mr. Sarsky still
may not give the letters to Jenny—and even if he does, Jenny
may not want to write back to you. As I said yesterday, you will
have to accept whatever happens now. If no communication is
what the Sarsky family wants, we have to respect their wishes,
even though we may not agree with them."

Henry thought long and hard about what Mr. Engelmann
had said. The bright hope in his face dimmed a bit.

"Yeah, I understand, and I'll honour whatever Jenny wants.
Even if she doesn't write back to me, I know deep in my heart
it'll work out somehow."

"Well, come on, now. Let's find a box for these letters and
send them off."

"Yeah, let's do it!"

Mr. Engelmann found a small box in the back and Henry
tipped the brown bag upside down, pouring its contents onto
the counter. Mr. Engelmann gave a low whistle.

"You did a lot of writing, Henry."

"Yeah, there are forty-six letters there. I wrote for hours and
hours and I'm so glad they're finally getting sent."

"It is very touching, Henry," his boss said as he pulled the flaps of the box open. "There must be a lot of love in these letters."

Henry blushed but didn't deny it. "Yeah, there is. I love Jenny more than anything," he said, surprising himself by saying the words out loud.

He stuffed the letters in the small box while Mr. Engelmann held it open. The old man crumpled a few pages of newspaper to fill up the rest of the space and Henry set his letter to Mr. Sarsky on top so Jenny's dad would see it as soon as he opened the box.

"Only a very coldhearted man could turn down a box of letters filled with love and such a plea for understanding," Mr. Engelmann murmured under his breath. "I guess that's it," he said, louder now, folding over the lid then sealing the box with packing tape.

Henry helped wrap the box in a sheet of brown paper and watched as Mr. Engelmann wrote Mr. Sarsky's business address on the sealed package.

"Well, Henry, the rest is up to the Lord. We can do no more."

Henry stared at the box. It was his last chance to reach Jenny. All his hopes and prayers were in there.

Finally Mr. Engelmann patted the top of the box with a small smile. "I'll take this down to the post office first thing tomorrow morning, Henry."

Henry just nodded. Then he looked at his boss, mentor and friend. "Thanks a lot, Mr. Engelmann, for all your help and for always being there for me."

Mr. Engelmann waved his hand as if shooing away a fly and looked at Henry tenderly. "You're welcome. Let's hope things turn out for the best."

CHAPTER TWENTY-FOUR

ON A MID-NOVEMBER MORNING, the wind roared through the buildings of downtown Ottawa. Damp air rendered the day bitterly cold, cutting through clothing regardless of layers. Ted Sarsky walked briskly from the parking lot to the front door of his office building, hunkered down into his collar like a turtle. Not that it did much good.

As he entered the lobby, the doorman on duty put down his newspaper.

"'Morning, Mr. Sarsky."

"'Morning, John. That's quite a wind out there," Ted replied, pushing the elevator button.

"You bet. Snow in the forecast later this afternoon."

"I don't mind the snow; it's the dampness that cuts to the bone."

"That's for—" was all Ted heard as the elevator doors closed.

Ted was nearly always the first to arrive at work and often the last to leave. This morning was no exception. When he arrived at the 18th floor, he unlocked the main door and went directly to his office. He tossed his coat over the chair in front of his desk, then rubbed his hands together before walking over to the window to stand in front of the heat register. The heat was dry and helped melt the chill he'd carried in from outside. But it could do nothing to ease the frost that had settled within him since their move to Ottawa almost three months ago.

It wasn't so much the mounting pressure and demands of his job that were draining him, but rather his role as a father. Almost every day, Jenny greeted him at the door with *Is there any mail for me today?* He'd always answered in the negative. He knew the answer even before the day began. He was living a lie and, try as he might, he could not divorce himself from it.

In the same way, every time Ted received a letter from his daughter to mail to Henry, he destroyed it—along with her hope that the boy of her dreams would somehow answer her. Ted knew full well that could never happen and it bothered him immensely. If only he could look at all this from Edith's perspective. She believed they'd done the right and best thing for Jenny, and had no qualms about their decision.

Ted's ruthless conscience hadn't allowed him a good night's sleep in weeks. And his drinking had only added to the problem, though at first, it had seemed to help—numbing, as it did, the shame and guilt that weighed so heavily on his heart. But he'd found he had to drink more and more, and rather than being soothed, he had started to shake. He feared even his staff had begun to notice, especially Elaine, his secretary, who had begun to rearrange appointments on particularly bad days.

Ted returned to his desk and sat down. He tilted the chair back as far as he could and closed his eyes. A little rest was all he needed. That'd help. He began to daydream about the mess he was in and the possibility that it would all be gone when he woke up. From deeper recesses of his mind someone called his name, the voice soft and distant. When he opened his eyes, he met Elaine's gaze. He had dozed off. It was nearly ten-thirty.

"Good morning, Mr. Sarsky," Elaine said, her usual professional tone unruffled. "I came in earlier, but you were asleep, and since you didn't have any immediate appointments, I decided to let you rest."

"Thank you, Elaine. I only intended to have a little cat nap."

He noticed the box in her hand.

"The mailman delivered this for you this morning."

"Who's it from?"

"The return address is Broder Street, Regina, Saskatchewan, Mr. Sarsky. Isn't that the street you lived on?"

"Oh, I think I know who that's from. Just leave it on my desk and I'll attend to it."

Elaine set the box down, turned and picked her boss's coat up off the chair in front of his desk and hung it on the coat tree by the door on her way out.

Ted stared at the box in front of him. He had a good guess as to what might be in there, and the very thought sent an icy shiver throughout his body far more penetrating than the chill of the damp wind outside. Ted pushed himself out of his chair and opened the liquor cabinet. He poured himself a drink then returned to his desk, eyes on the box, unable to do anything.

As the liquor thawed a bit of his cowardice, he contemplated the options. Finally, he took scissors from the top drawer of his desk and ran the sharp edge of a blade firmly across the paper the box was wrapped in and then through the tape under it keeping the box shut.

The flaps sprang open almost as if they were glad to expose the contents. A neatly folded letter with his name on it lay atop of several handfuls of crumpled newsprint. Ted took the letter out and removed the crushed paper, revealing three stacks of letters beneath. Each letter had Jenny's name on it. In a tone filled with shame and sadness, he muttered, "This is unbelievable."

As much as he wanted to read them, he couldn't bring himself to do it. They weren't his. The whole situation spun before him like a giant merry-go-round, one he could not get off of. Telling the truth would destroy his family. Neither Edith nor Jenny would ever speak to him again.

Ted reached for the letter with his name on it. He opened it and read the first line, "Dear Mr. Sarsky," then he let his eyes fall to the bottom of the page to see who had sent it. *Yours truly, Henry.* At the very bottom was another signature: David En-

gelmann. Guilt splashed acid in his guts as his gaze inched back
to the top of the letter. His eyes rested on the second paragraph:

> *I also want you to know that I like Jenny very*
> *much and would never do anything to hurt her. I*
> *have been waiting almost three months for Jenny*
> *to send me her address so that I can mail the let-*
> *ters I have written. Since I have not heard from*
> *Jenny in all this time, I have decided to mail them*
> *to you and ask if you would please take the letters*
> *home to Jenny …*

The boy's words cut through him and Ted closed his eyes. He
didn't want to read any more, it would only haunt him further.
But the anguish in those words was already emblazoned on his
mind. And that last sentence, "*… please take the letters home to
Jenny …*" echoed in his brain. Wave after wave of shame swept
through him. He shook his head, trying to loosen its hold but it
gripped all the harder. He tossed the letter down and returned
to the liquor cabinet, twisting off the cap of a fresh bottle of
Canadian Club to pour himself another drink.

Then another.

Without realizing it, he had crossed a line. The fortress of
high standards and principles he had so steadfastly built over
the years crumbled beneath the weight of the conflict with his
wife, feelings of shame and guilt, excessive drinking and poor
job performance. Without help—or a miracle—he would never
find the man he had once been, or regain the direction and focus
he had once held.

After a long while the liquor finally took effect and he
straightened up. He'd decided. *It's too late; it's all just too late.* He
refolded Henry's letter, tossed it into the box with the others,
and closed the lid. As Ted removed his hand from the box, the
flaps sprang open again, almost as if begging him to reconsider.
He took hold of the flaps, overlapping them brusquely, warping
them in the process. Ted shook his head and blinked several

times, trying once more to shake the image of all those letters and Henry's plea for compassion. For the sake of his own sanity he had to get rid of the whole thing. *Out of sight out of mind.*

He sat down heavily, emotional fatigue and whiskey taking their toll. Groggily he pushed the box to the far end of his desk, and with the same motion, reached for the intercom.

"Elaine, could you please come in here?"

His voice came out unusually loudly and he winced, hoping she wouldn't notice.

He was leaning over his desk when his secretary knocked briefly to announce her presence. He held a pen in his hand, pretending to take notes. "Come in, Elaine. I have a task I'd like you to carry out for me personally."

"Certainly, Mr. Sarsky. What is it you'd like me to do?"

"There are some papers in the box you brought in earlier—they're no longer required. They … have to do with our move to Ottawa and the sale of the Regina house. Could you please take them down to the boiler room and give them to the maintenance man? See that he throws them into the furnace."

Elaine looked at Mr. Sarsky for a moment, somewhat startled by his request, then picked up the box and simply said, "Right away, Mr. Sarsky."

She left the office, worrying about her boss. It was obvious he'd been drinking again. And his breathing had been short and shallow. Inwardly, she shook her head at the turn her boss's life seemed to have taken in the last few weeks; she felt helpless to do anything.

As she walked out to the elevator, she wondered what was really in the box. It didn't contain papers regarding the sale of their house—those had come in almost two weeks ago. No, that wasn't it. But it was likely, wasn't it, that the reason the career of a strong administrator like Mr. Sarsky had taken an ominous U-turn had something to do with what was inside? Perhaps, she mused, if she knew what the box held, she could help him.

As the elevator descended to the basement with its lone occupant, Elaine tugged on one of the box's flaps. It flipped open with unusual ease. On top was a folded sheet of paper and a bunch of envelopes addressed to Jenny Sarsky. She had met Jenny when the Sarskys had first arrived in Ottawa. It seemed odd that the envelopes had no address on them. And there were so many.

Elaine had just unfolded the loose sheet of paper when the elevator bounced to a stop at the basement. She stuffed it back in and quickly closed the box, holding her hand over the flaps to keep them shut. The elevator doors opened and she stepped out into the musty basement hallway. She really didn't like being down here. The lighting was poor and it always smelled of fuel oil and burning coal.

"Michael?" she called out, but there was no response. She went further down the hall, taking care not to bump her head on the pipes and valves running along the walls and low ceiling. "Michael?" she called again, this time a bit louder.

"Who's there?" the maintenance man asked, emerging from the darkness. His dark hair, black overalls and soot-streaked face were perfect camouflage in the dimly lit hallway.

"Michael, Mr. Sarsky asked me to have you burn this box and its contents. He wants me to make sure it's done. Do you have time to do it right now?"

"Sure. Furnace room's this way."

As Elaine followed Michael down the hallway, she was again tempted to read the folded letter. Perhaps she should take one of the envelopes, too. If she was going to help Mr. Sarsky, she'd have to act before it was too late.

They came to the end of the hallway, and as Michael fiddled with the key to the furnace room, Elaine reached into the box and took out the folded sheet of paper. While Michael headed inside, she surreptitiously tucked it into her pocket and hoped she'd have an opportunity to take at least one of the sealed envelopes. Michael struggled to open the heavy metal door

Finally he shoved it open and a blast of unbearable heat whooshed into the hallway. Instinctively they stepped back, waiting a moment for the heat to dissipate.

"It's pretty warm in here, Elaine. You sure you want to stay?

It's gonna get even hotter when I open the furnace door."

"Yes, I told Mr. Sarsky I would, so we better get on with it." Elaine moved inside, the searing heat startling her so much that she forgot to take out another letter from the box.

Michael said, "Here, hand the box over."

Elaine paused, reluctant to give it up. She looked down at the box, then up at Michael, and handed it over.

Michael wrestled one-handed with the door to the furnace and the box slipped out of his grip. Letters spilled across the floor. The intense heat scorched the maintenance man's hand as he tried to slam the door shut and catch the letters at the same time. He snatched here and there at the envelopes, walking on some of them and slipping on others.

Elaine watched, helpless. She dared not venture any closer than she already had.

Michael finally resorted to tossing the letters into the open furnace as he retrieved them from the floor. One after the other, the envelopes disappeared into the blaze. He was perspiring profusely as he picked up the last three and flipped them into the furnace. All that was left was the empty box.

"I guess that's all of them," he said, shrugging as he tossed the box into the furnace as well.

Michael's words rang sharply through Elaine's mind. That *wasn't* all of them. She reached into her pocket and felt the crackle of paper. Should she toss the letter into the fire as directed by her employer or should she keep it and hope she could help? It was a split-second decision.

Michael closed the steel furnace door with a clanging clunk that startled her and she shivered despite the heat.

"Oh, Michael," she said, a tone of urgency in her voice, "Looks like one more letter flew back this way." She pulled the letter out of her pocket and thrust it towards the maintenance man. "Here, please toss this in too."

That had been close. She'd been about to do something she'd never done in all the years of her employment. Although whatever the letter said might have helped her understand Mr.

Sarsky's problems, she was compelled to honour her promise to see his request through to the end.

Michael took the letter and reached for the furnace door again. He and Elaine braced themselves for a repeat of the fiery blast, but as Mike opened the door, they were surprised to see that the fire had settled, as if the envelopes had somehow tamed the burning hell raging behind the heavy steel door. They could scarcely believe their eyes; the gentle flames seemed almost peaceful.

They watched as the last letter landed at the base of the brick-lined opening and slowly lit up. As the letter burned, it twisted open, arching itself towards them as if it wanted to be read.

The name *Henry* glowed and grew clear in the last moments before the letter fell to ash.

She recognized the name. Jenny spent a few minutes waiting for her father from time to time and had been quite talkative about a boy named Henry back in Regina. It was clear she hadn't wanted to leave Regina because of him. But what did a boy two provinces away have to do with Mr. Sarsky's drinking problem? If only she had kept the letter, the pieces that puzzled her would have quickly come together.

Unsure if Michael had also seen the name, but unwilling to take the chance of anything private being leaked, Elaine cautioned him, "Thank you for your help, Michael. Please don't mention this to anyone."

Michael led her back to the elevator, pausing only to say, "Well, I hope that's the last of it."

"What do you mean?"

"Well, Mr. Sarsky was down here last week burning another bunch of letters. And that was the third time in the last three months."

"Did he do it himself?"

"Yes, he insisted on doing it himself."

Elaine only nodded but inside she was nervous. What was going on? She regretted more than ever not keeping that last letter. It might have made all the difference.

CHAPTER TWENTY-FIVE

EACH DAY HENRY RUSHED HOME, hoping a letter was waiting for him, and each day his mother had the difficult task of telling him that none had come. Each time Henry went to work he asked Mr. Engelmann if he had heard from Mr. Sarsky, and Mr. Engelmann always gave him the same answer his mother did.

If it weren't for school and the demands of his job at the store, he would have easily slipped into another serious state of despondency.

One afternoon Mr. Engelmann reminded him of their agreement. "Remember your promise to me when we decided to send the box of letters?" Mr. Engelmann asked, looking into Henry's eyes.

"Yeah, I know," Henry replied, recalling the details all too well. "I won't ask you again."

"No!" Mr. Engelmann said. "You can ask me over and over again, but be prepared for an answer you may not like or want to hear. The fact that you have received no reply from either Jenny or Mr. Sarsky might, in fact, *be* your answer. And you will have to accept it."

Mr. Engelmann paused before continuing. "Life has no guarantees and makes no promises. We cannot control the lives or actions of others, only our own. We may be frustrated and disappointed by others, but in the end it is futile to try to make others do what we want or expect them to. I have learned this over and over in my life. Furthermore, who is to say what is right or who is right? What you think is right might be very wrong to someone else, based on their life experience. Do you understand what I am saying?"

Oh, he understood what Mr. Engelmann was saying, all right, he was just reluctant to accept it. And saying it out loud somehow made it permanent. "Yeah, I understand, Mr. Engelmann."

"I know it's a very hard thing to accept, Henry, but that's the reality of life. When the Nazis came to Austria and tortured so many people, their thinking was so distorted they believed what they were doing was right. I know that is far different from what we think Mr. Sarsky has done, but it is very possible he and his wife feel absolutely certain they are doing the right thing, too. And sometimes, the best thing to do is simply to accept."

Mr. Engelmann was gearing up for one of his lessons.

"Deal with your own life, Henry, as best as you can. It's the only life you have control over. Live in the present and try not to crowd it with worry over your past or the future. The present is the only reality. I can predict how you are going to feel if you continue to think about Jenny, how her parents are so unfair, how life is so unfair. Continue to think this way, and an hour from now, you will be in the same boat as you are now ... and slowly sinking.

"Abandon those thoughts and move on. The way you live in the present—today—will determine your future and shape your view of the past. To live otherwise is a waste of time and results in absolutely no gain. It's a very wise man who can accept what he cannot change, change what he can, and get on with his life."

Mr. Engelmann studied Henry for a moment, and then with a twinkle in his eye, added, "There is an old Chinese proverb: 'You cannot prevent the birds of sorrow flying over your head but you can prevent them from building nests in your hair.'"

Henry forced a smile as his vivid imagination quickly painted a picture of birds nesting in his hair. He'd been spending almost every moment thinking about Jenny, the letters, and life without her. He understood it was self-defeating to blame the Sarskys for not doing what he wanted. Yet he couldn't seem to stop. Then he remembered what Mr. Engelmann had told him over and over: when all the reasoning in the world doesn't help, turn to God.

Please God. Please help me to trust in You, that You will somehow turn this sorrow and heartache into good.

How many times had Mr. Engelmann told him to trust in the Lord and not lean on his own understanding? Just saying that helped settle Henry's feelings. He was not alone. A wave of strength and conviction welled up in him. He would get on with his life and put more faith in God.

"But this much I know," he said aloud without thinking, "regardless of what happens, someday I'll see my Jenny again."

Mr. Engelmann looked at Henry with concern. "Henry, are you okay?"

"Yeah, I think so." Then, more firmly, "Yes, I will be."

"Well, then, let's get back to work. I received eight orders this morning and they're not going to deliver themselves."

THE INSTALLATION of the traffic lights not only brought in their regular customers more often, but also new ones who had avoided shopping there before because of the traffic. And once they came and experienced the personal service Mr. Engelmann and his young partner provided, they just kept coming back.

One day, Henry commented on Mr. Engelmann's uncanny ability to remember most of his customers' birthdays.

"You know, Mr. Engelmann, people are so surprised when they come in and you wish them a happy birthday. They can't believe that you actually remember—some of them even say that you're the only one who remembered at all!"

"Well, I like to make a point of such things, Henry, just like I want to remember each person's name. People want to be recognized, appreciated and, most of all, loved. I may be just a simple grocery store owner, and my job may not seem very important, but I know my purpose in life is to serve my fellow man the best way I can. There are many important people out there who have much bigger and better jobs than I do, yet fail because they are only interested in themselves or in making money. True, we need to make money to live, but that is only secondary to what should be our main goal: to be kind, giving, caring and concerned, which all adds up to loving each other." After a reflective moment, he added, "And isn't that what the good Lord commands us to do, to love Him with all our strength and mind and heart, and to love our neighbour as ourselves?"

Henry gazed at Mr. Engelmann, thinking. Mr. Engelmann was always saying and doing things like that. Henry tried to store those moments away in his mind, not wanting to forget one precious word.

"I'm sorry for going off like that. What were you saying about birthdays? Are you going to tell me another way to improve my business or not?" Mr. Engelmann probed, snapping Henry out of his reverie.

"Well, yeah," Henry said, trying to organize his thoughts again. "It makes people so happy when you wish them happy birthday, and then when you give them a little extra salami or bologna, you can just see the way they love it, and how their eyes light up. Even though it's such a little thing, it's like you've given them the world. I know you do it from the heart and—"

"Yes, yes. I never try to manipulate people in that way, Henry. In whatever I do, I try to be genuine."

"Yeah, I know, but what I am getting at is this: if it makes some of the customers so happy, why not try to do it with *all* the customers? And if it increases the business, so be it." He quickly added, "What's wrong with that?"

"Goodness, Henry, sometimes you are just too smart, too good of a businessman. Let me think ... Yes, yes, there is nothing wrong with trying to remember everyone's birthday, but how is that possible?"

And Henry had the answer.

"Remember the copy you made of that petition? The people who signed had to write down their age and birthdays to show they were of voting age."

The light in Mr. Engelmann eyes flickered on and almost glowed. "How do you think of such things?"

Mr. Engelmann rushed behind the counter, opened the drawer and pulled out his copy of the sheets of paper people had signed. He rifled through them and kept repeating, "Yes, yes … yes … yes. Henry, almost everyone has put their birthday on the sheet! Can you imagine how surprised and happy we will make all these people? I cannot wait to tell Anna."

Mr. Engelmann looked at Henry with an appreciative smile. "The Lord has blessed you with the gift of insight. This idea, Henry, will bring us and our customers both much joy."

Henry was so overwhelmed by Mr. Engelmann's gratitude that his eyes teared up. He beamed.

Just an hour earlier he had felt terribly low because he hadn't heard from Jenny or Mr. Sarsky—and now here he was, on top of the world. He was living in the present, serving others and not thinking of himself, just like Mr. Engelmann had encouraged him to do.

"There's just one more thing I'd like to talk to you about before I go home for the day, Mr. Engelmann."

The old man smiled again, "Oh, Henry, what more could you possibly share with me today than you already have?"

"My dad gave me a huge calendar with large squares around each date. His company gave them out. If you give me the petition list, I'll go through it and write the names of the people and their birthdays in the right square. Then all we have to do is just look at the calendar to know whose birthday it is. And we can even check ahead of time and phone them to see if they have the time to come in, maybe for a little extra salami or something like that."

Mr. Engelmann was beaming and laughing so hard he hopped from one leg to the other. He threw his arms up in the air and raised his head, exclaiming, "*Wir danken dir, lieber Gott,* we thank You, for sending this fine young man to Anna and me!" He rounded the counter and gave Henry a big hug. After a long moment he patted Henry's shoulder and pulled away. "And thank you, Henry, for being the son we never had."

Henry was glad he could help Mr. Engelmann almost as much as Mr. Engelmann was helping him.

But what Henry loved the most was the feeling of love between them; and it occurred to him that he truly felt like the Engelmanns' son.

Chapter Twenty-Six

I T WAS THE MIDDLE OF DECEMBER; it had been snowing virtually non-stop for more than two weeks, leaving large drifts of snow in front of the Engelmanns' store. Henry had been shovelling for over an hour after the latest accumulation and decided to take a break.

Bing Crosby was singing "I'm Dreaming of a White Christmas" on the radio when Henry entered the store. Henry looked at the thigh-high heaps of snow and silently told Bing he could stop dreaming—it was definitely going to be a white Christmas. For a fleeting moment Bing's voice made him think of "True Love" and Jenny. But only for a moment. He knew that *was* just a dream.

It had been almost four months since Jenny had left and Mr. Engelmann's observation had proven correct. The answer Henry had been waiting for lay in the fact that neither Jenny nor her father had responded to his letter or any of the letters in the box. It was over ... for now.

Yet, the thought of going into Christmas and the New Year without Jenny was terrible. Henry tried to push the thought out of his head. "I'll be Home for Christmas" came over the airwaves. *Boy, can't they play someone other than Bing?* It was hard not to conjure a fantasy of Jenny returning home to him. He could picture it: waiting at the train station, watching Jenny step down from the locomotive. She'd wear a white fur coat with a thick collar turned up so only her beautiful heart-shaped face and blond curls peeked out. Her blue eyes would sparkle when she saw him. He raised his arm, reaching out for her as she came down the last step …

"Here, let me have that," Mr. Engelmann said, taking the dripping shovel from Henry's outstretched hand. "Anna made some hot chocolate. Take your coat off and go have a drink. It's in the thermos on the table in the storage room."

It took Henry a moment to return to real life. He walked to the back of the store, the Christmas songs on the radio reviving all his tender feelings for Jenny. He'd been going along all right, but suddenly he knew that before the New Year began he had to try to reach his girl one last time. With Christmas and all, maybe Mr. Sarsky would have a change of heart. He still had Mr. Sarsky's business address tucked away in his wallet, carefully memorized from the box Mr. Engelmann had labelled and mailed. But this time, Henry wasn't going to tell anyone that he planned one final letter—except perhaps his guardian angel.

And he could send a gift for Jenny along with the letter, too! He already knew what he wanted to give her, and even though he'd just come up with the idea, he could hardly wait to get it and send it off. It was four-thirty and the stores downtown would be open until six. It was still snowing and rather cold out, and not many people had been out grocery shopping … maybe he could go right now!

"Would you mind if I left now, Mr. Engelmann? I shovelled the sidewalk and I think it'll be fine until the store closes. I need to go downtown and do some Christmas shopping."

"Yes, yes," Mr. Engelmann replied without looking up from his invoices, "of course you can go. A present for your parents would be very nice."

"Yeah." Henry didn't tell Mr. Engelmann that he had bought something for his mom and dad almost a month ago.

As Henry sat on the trolley, tossed about as the steel wheels bumped through the snow, he thought that the likeliest place to find the gift he was looking for was Eaton's. It was the largest department store in the city. As the trolley crossed Broad Street and came within half a block of his destination, Henry reached up and pulled the cord. He stood up, grabbing the steel bar that ran parallel to the signal cord, and worked his way to the trolley's back door. Finally, the trolley halted, the doors squeaked open, and he jumped off, exchanging the relative quiet of the trolley for the holiday sights and sounds of downtown.

Cars coursed up and down both sides of the street, horns blasted, and people walked to and fro. Snowbanks were piled high on each side of the road. Bright lights and Christmas decorations hung everywhere. Large holiday ornaments adorned each streetlight, each one a candy cane or a wreath or something Christmassy. Every store had a beautifully festive window display. He stopped to admire a nativity scene depicting three wise men standing with Mary and Joseph, overlooking the baby Jesus.

Henry couldn't believe he and Mr. Engelmann hadn't thought to put up a display or even lights. He vowed to mention it to Mr. Engelmann first thing.

As he approached Eaton's, he heard the sound of ringing. By the front door stood a Santa Claus, jingling a small circlet of bells. Beside him was a huge pot suspended from the top of a tripod. Attached to the pot was a red-lettered sign that read SAL-VATION ARMY. As people walked by the *ho-ho-ho*-ing Santa, some dropped in a coin or two. For each donation, Santa nodded his head and said, "God bless you."

Henry reached into his pocket and dropped five cents into the pot.

Santa responded, "Thank you, son. God will bless you."

Henry looked at the Santa and smiled. As he turned away, a sparkle on the Christmas tree in the window display caught his eye. He moved closer. Light reflected off a tiny metal angel near the top of the tree, giving it a halo. There was his gift to Jenny— an angel to keep her safe and protect her from all harm, and to remind her of his love for her always.

What luck to have found what he wanted so quickly among the hundreds of other ornaments on display! If he hadn't come by the Salvation Army Santa, he might never have seen it. Henry turned to thank the man before going into the store, but he was no longer there. Henry looked up and down the street, but Santa was gone and so was the pot—vanished behind the veil of heavy snowflakes now tumbling from the sky. Maybe he'd been looking at the tree longer than he remembered. *Oh well.*

Henry rushed into the store and approached the nearest cashier. "I'd like to buy the little angel ornament hanging under the star on the Christmas tree in the window display, please."

The cashier looked at him and replied, "Oh, I'm sorry, but those ornaments are for display only. They're not for sale."

Henry couldn't believe his ears. "But they've got to be!" he insisted.

A supervisor walked over just then. "Is anything wrong here, Miss Downs?"

"I was just telling this boy that the ornaments on the tree in the window display are not for sale."

"Perhaps we have a duplicate on the shelf?" the supervisor inquired.

"No, I'm afraid not. We sold the last one yesterday."

"I see," the supervisor nodded.

"But I just have to have that one. Please?" Henry pleaded, unable to believe he'd found the exact right thing but wasn't allowed to buy it.

The supervisor looked at Henry and Henry hoped he looked desperate enough to convince her to sell him the ornament.

"Could you show me the item you are referring to, young man?"

"We'll have to go outside," Henry said, "unless we can go into the window."

She thought for a moment, then said, "Perhaps it's best you show me outside."

Once outside the display window, Henry pointed excitedly.

"Look, there it is at the top, the angel for my girlfriend, Jenny!"

The supervisor's gaze followed Henry's finger to the angel. Her eyes widened and she smiled.

She looked at Henry, "The tree won't be nearly as pretty without that angel, but it's Christmas and giving is what it's all about … especially to a girlfriend." She winked at Henry. "Come on. Let's go in and get that angel off the tree before it flies away."

Henry laughed as they re-entered the store. "I just knew I was going to find my gift for Jenny here."

"Well, of course! We're the best place in town to shop," the supervisor replied. "Please, wait here at the counter while I try to catch your angel."

Henry nodded and smiled, then watched as she carefully climbed into the display window and stood on her tiptoes to reach the angel. The branch of the tree bent slightly as she released the beautiful ornament from its perch. As it rested in her hand, she looked at it and smiled again.

"It's made of pewter," she murmured. Henry could tell that she thought it was beautiful, too.

She brought the angel over and handed it to Henry. It was about two and a half inches tall, but quite heavy for its size. It was the first time Henry had seen pewter, a very smooth metal with a silvery satin finish. The arms of the angel stretched before her in a gesture of love and protection, just what Henry wanted Jenny to feel. It was so pretty it could be jewelry; *Jenny might even wear it as a necklace,* he thought. At the bottom of the angel's garment was an inscription: WATCH OVER MY BELOVED. It was perfect. He rubbed his thumb over the engraved letters and felt the shiver of goosebumps.

Henry sensed the two employees watching him with knowing smiles and suddenly felt self-conscious. He handed his treasure back to the cashier to wrap up.

"Yes, this will be just fine," he said. "Thank you very much for getting it for me!"

The older lady smiled. "Glad to be of help."

The cashier put the angel in a box and covered it with a cloud of white cotton. "That will be $1.79."

Henry handed her a five-dollar bill and thanked her as she handed him his change.

"You're welcome, sir. Merry Christmas!"

Back outside, Henry stopped at the display window and looked in. The Christmas tree, festooned with hundreds of ornaments, simply did not look the same without the sparkle of the angel. Henry had stolen the heart of the tree and clutched it in his hand.

The streets were just about empty as Henry hurried to the trolley stop. It had started to snow again and he hoped it wouldn't be too long of a wait. In spite of the cold and blowing wind, he felt warm and hugged the bag closer as if to protect it, although he knew it wasn't the angel who needed protection.

The trolley arrived just as the snowfall sped into a full-blown blizzard. Henry got on gratefully and took a seat near the back. The moment he arrived home he would write the letter then mail it the next day so Jenny would be sure to receive it and her angel before Christmas. As he looked at the bag on his lap, the Eaton's logo caught his eye and he wondered how he could get the name of Mr. Engelmann's store on the bags they used. More advertising certainly wouldn't hurt. He would have to run it by Mr. Engelmann. And for sure they should put up Christmas lights and maybe even a Christmas tree.

Because of the snowstorm, it took the trolley almost an hour to reach Broder Street rather than the usual twenty minutes. Once Henry stepped off the trolley, he ran home as fast as he could down the snow-clogged street, knowing his parents would be worried. His mom was upset but relieved he'd made it home safely.

"Where have you been all this time?"

"Sorry, Mom. I went shopping."

"Well, please phone or something to let us know if you're going somewhere after work. We were very worried about you out in this storm and all."

"Yeah, I know, Mom. I'm sorry."

"Well, tell me, what on earth was so important you had to go shopping in this weather?"

"Sorry, Mom. It's a secret."

When she didn't question him any further, Henry knew she thought the gift was for her.

"Well, come and eat your soup, Henry. It's already on the table."

As he ate, he told his mom about the birthday idea he'd thought of for the store.

"What a clever plan," his mother said. "You sure are a businessman at heart."

Suddenly thinking of an excuse to go to his room early, he added, "You know, I'm almost finished putting everyone's name on the calendar. Think I'll go to my room and finish it off."

"How was work today?" Henry asked his dad as he passed the living room.

"Oh, it was all right. It was quite cold in the plant today. It's not insulated enough to withstand this weather."

"Yeah," Henry agreed. "Mr. Engelmann's store isn't that warm either, even though the furnace hardly shuts off."

Henry told him about his schoolwork and promised to study for his upcoming exams, then excused himself. He could hardly wait to get to his room and begin writing what might be his most important letter to Jenny.

His desire for Jenny was still so strong he ached inside. After all these months his feelings for her hadn't waned in the least. In fact, they were stronger than ever. Henry sat at his desk and pulled out a blank piece of paper. For once he was unable to think of the right words.

So many things had happened lately that just seemed beyond coincidence. Like that Santa Claus in front of the Christmas display that held the angel—the very last one in the store. And then for the supervisor to be there just when the cashier told him he couldn't have the one on the tree, and how kind she'd been to let him have the ornament … very strange.

The words he usually prayed each night flowed into his mind, "Angel of God, my guardian dear—it is you who is watching over me and directing my life, isn't it?"

Henry got up and walked over to the window. The wind had died down, the snow fallen into sweeping drifts, but clouds still blocked out the moon. The sky looked somber without it, just like his life was joyless without Jenny. Yet he knew that behind the clouds was a silver lining. The moon was up there, somewhere, reflecting the light of the sun. And up there, too, was the brightest star, off to the east. He wondered if Jenny was looking out at the same star tonight?

He made a wish. "Oh, bright star of the east, carry my love in a ray of light to Jenny's heart. Let her know how very much I miss and love her."

Henry then returned to his desk and put his pen to the page in front of him.

Dear Jenny,

It's almost Christmas, and just about four months since you left. I was thinking today that the only gift I would ever want for the rest of my life is to receive a letter from you.

I sent a box to your dad's company address almost a month ago. It was filled with all the letters I've written to you since the day you left. I hope you received them. If you did, could you please tell me why you haven't written back? Even if you no longer care or have found someone else, just let me know. It is so hard not to hear from you.

I wanted to send you one last letter, along with a little Christmas gift. I'll always remember how much you love your guardian angel. I went shopping after school today and as I walked past

Eaton's, I saw this shining underneath the star at the top of their Christmas tree. It was exactly what I was looking for—a guardian angel to protect you always and to remind you of my love for you. I hope you like it and will wear it around your neck all the time.

How do you like living in Ottawa and how are you doing at your new school? Have you made a lot of friends? I like Grade 9, and maybe you won't be surprised to hear that of all the subjects I am taking, I like art the best.

Oh, Jenny, I sure miss you. I miss your smile, your sparkling eyes, the way you talk and the way you walk. I especially miss holding your hand and just walking along with you. I often find myself dreaming you are beside me as I walk to school, but it's just a dream and so empty without you.

I am looking forward to the Christmas break and working full-time in Mr. Engelmann's store. I just love working there and seem to keep coming up with ideas to increase business. Mr. Engelmann is great to work for and I am learning so much from him.

I made a special wish to the bright star of the east tonight to send out my love to you. I hope and pray you get this letter and my gift. Every night I pray for my guardian angel to talk to yours, so that together they can find a way to bring us together again.

Even though we are far apart, you are forever in
my heart. I will love you always. Have a merry
Christmas!

All my love,
Henry

After Henry read the letter over, he folded it and tucked it into an envelope. Henry picked up the box with the angel and took the angel out. He pictured it resting near Jenny's heart. He took one last long look, brought the angel up to his lips and tenderly kissed the metal, warm from his hand.

"Take this kiss, guardian angel, swiftly to my dear, sweet Jenny," he whispered as he slipped the angel into the envelope. It added a small heft to the envelope but its slim form was nearly undetectable from the outside.

Henry closed his eyes and imagined Jenny receiving this letter. Her eyes would brighten with excitement as the angel flew out of the envelope. Tears of joy would flow down her cheeks. She would kiss the angel over and over, knowing he had kissed it too. Jenny would remove the silver necklace from her neck and thread the pewter angel onto it. She would wear it always.

Tears came to Henry's eyes. He wished Jenny were beside him. He reached out for her hand but felt only emptiness. Emptiness he could fill only with imagination and dreams.

CHAPTER TWENTY-SEVEN

THE NEXT DAY AT SCHOOL, all Henry could think about was mailing Jenny's letter. He had left it at home so he wouldn't lose it during the day. The mere thought sent a spike of fear through him. He could just see the guys in the locker room reading his letter aloud and teasing him unmercifully. His plan was to leave school right at quarter to four, pick up the letter at home and drop it into the mail box near the pharmacy about two blocks from Mr. Engelmann's store. Then he would go directly to work.

Henry was going over his plan for the umpteenth time when he saw Eddy coming towards him. Bitterness still tugged at Henry whenever he saw Eddy or one of his crew, but he'd learned to turn it over to the Lord, and purposely made an effort to greet him. In a way Henry was glad; it really wasn't in his nature to hold a grudge forever, and he didn't think it was in Eddy's makeup, either. Pride more than anything else was the real barrier. That was what Mr. Engelmann always said and Henry knew he was right.

Henry smiled as he thought about how Mr. Neader had got him to help Eddy and indirectly work out their differences. In many ways, Neader reminded Henry of his mentor at the store, always figuring out a way to make things better.

Anyway, Henry had to admit his coach was right. In no time at all, Eddy had picked up the game of basketball and Mr. Neader had talked him into signing up for the team. Henry actually felt proud that Eddy had learned so quickly. When they'd played Scott Collegiate two weeks ago, Eddy had been amazing. Eddy dribbled the ball and kept control of it like a seasoned player. And his size, as the coach had observed, was definitely an advantage. Many of the tall players couldn't keep up with Eddy's speed and agility, and they'd had trouble getting down to his level and fouled often, much to the delight and cheering of the crowd. Henry couldn't help but feel good inside that Eddy was getting such positive attention—sure beat having Eddy swagger around looking for trouble. Yep, he had to hand it to Coach Neader, who'd seen the potential right from the start. And Henry also had to admit that the coach had been right about another thing; he and Eddy *were* more comfortable hanging out together; in fact, they'd planned to take in the seniors' basketball game against Central Collegiate the following Friday night.

"Hey, Eddy. Still on for the game Friday?"

"Wouldn't miss it, Hank. Should be a good, close game. I'll meet you at seven at the corner of Winnipeg and Vic."

"Sounds good. See you tomorrow."

After school Henry carried out his plan and mailed the letter to Jenny's dad then headed towards the store. The air was crisp and chilled his cheeks to a Rudolph red. The overcast sky let loose a few snowflakes. An earlier snowfall had left a couple of inches on the ground. Henry knew he'd have to shovel the walk to the store as soon as he got there. Mr. Engelmann always liked the walk cleared, saying it showed they cared for the safety of their customers and that the store was open for business.

When he got there, Mr. Engelmann's store was filled with customers and Henry could tell he was relieved to see him.

"Ah, here's my assistant," he remarked, a big grin splitting his face. "Come. Please help Mrs. Forrest with her order. She has been very patient with me."

"Right away, Mr. Engelmann." Henry shed his coat and helped Mrs. Forrest. Other customers kept them busy until almost six.

"Whew," he declared after the last of them had left. "I've never seen it so busy."

"It's been like this all week, Henry. Only today it continued until the last minute. I think I might need someone else to help us. Anna is too sick to come down."

"Yeah," Henry agreed, "We do need someone else. If I didn't have to go to school, I could help all the time."

"Yes, yes, of course, but I would never want you to stop your education. It is far too important. I was thinking about Mrs. Schmidt. She's a very nice lady. Her husband passed away two years ago, and she came in shortly afterwards, asking if I had any work for her."

"Yeah, I remember her. She comes in a couple of times a month, usually on a Monday."

"That's right. She has a part-time job but could maybe work here too, if she's still willing."

"Sounds good to me," Henry said.

"I will give her a call tomorrow then," Mr. Engelmann said.

Although it was time to go home, Henry noticed how empty the shelves were. And Mr. Engelmann looked worn out. "Mom is probably going to be a little slow with supper tonight, Mr. Engelmann," Henry lied, "is it okay if I stay a little longer? I could use the extra money for Christmas presents."

"Yes, yes of course," Mr. Engelmann agreed. "That would be wonderful."

Mr. Engelmann went upstairs and Henry phoned his mom to tell her he'd be late. He stocked the shelves, swept the floor, and shovelled the steps and walkway. By seven-thirty, things looked ready for the following day.

His mom had supper waiting for him when he got home. After he explained why he had stayed late, she smiled at him with quiet pride. "That was very nice of you, Henry," she said.

He told her about all the lights he'd seen downtown and how he wanted to put up some at the grocery store.

His mother's eyes brightened and she said eagerly, "Oh, that's easy, Henry. There are two sets of old lights downstairs behind the furnace. They were on sale when Bill and I bought them then we found they were way too long for our house."

"That's great!" Henry said, almost spilling his soup. "Should I tell Mr. Engelmann we'll sell them to him? I know he won't just accept them—he's too proud."

His mom thought it over, then winked, "Tell him I won't take less than a dollar."

Henry winked back.

After supper, Henry went downstairs and rummaged behind the furnace. Sure enough, just as his mom had said, there were two dusty bundles of brand new Christmas lights. What a stroke of luck. No, it wasn't luck. He looked up and acknowledged his guardian angel for giving him such a generous gift.

Henry went back upstairs. His mom was in the kitchen cleaning up and his dad had gone bowling. Henry was glad he was out because his dad had been so moody lately. It was good for him to get out and do something he enjoyed.

After Henry helped with the dishes, he headed up to his room. No sooner had he sat down at his desk than his thoughts went to Jenny. He couldn't wait for her to get his letter. He wished he could speed up time like they did in the movies.

It was astonishing how quickly his outlook had changed. Only two days earlier, he had given up all hope of reconnecting with Jenny, but writing and sending off one last letter had restored his faith that he would hear from her again. It was amazing how positive thinking changed his whole perspective.

With nothing to do but wait for her reply, he tried to decide how he would decorate the storefront, and how he might reach the second storey to put the lights up. He took a sheet of paper from his desk and sketched the outline of the store. Once he saw it on paper, the solution presented itself. He would string the lights across the front of the first storey, and if there were enough left over, he would keep stringing them down the side of the store. He remembered seeing a hammer and some nails in Mr. Engelmann's basement. He'd use those to secure the lights to the building. He also hoped the neighbour down the street would let them use that tall ladder of his.

Henry was so excited about decorating the store he had trouble sleeping. Mr. and Mrs. Engelmann were going to be thrilled when he put up the lights. Mr. Engelmann's words ran over and over in his mind: *When people try to please others and make them happy, they are serving others. When people do this, they receive unexpected joy beyond their wildest dreams."*

HENRY WOKE A LITTLE LATER than usual, trying to make up for getting to bed late the night before. It was the last day of school before the holidays and he was looking forward to helping Mr. Engelmann full-time.

He didn't even know why they bothered having classes at this time of year. Everyone was so excited about Christmas and the holidays they hardly did any school work. As if to bear this out, the teachers decided to let the students out an hour early.

Henry picked up the lights from home before heading over to the store. Mrs. Schmidt greeted him when he entered. She was a stout, grandmotherly type of woman with a generous smile that never left her round face. She was perfect for the store. She looked as jolly as St. Nick, and when she laughed, as she often did, her tummy jiggled.

"You must be the Henry Mr. Engelmann never stops talking about."

"That's me," he smiled back, taking the compliment in stride. "This is your first day, right? How do you like it so far?"

"Very much. Mr. Engelmann phoned me early this morning and I rushed to get here by ten-thirty. The store has been very busy and Mr. Engelmann stayed with me as long as he could, but I think I can serve customers by myself and ring in the sales."

"That's great. It doesn't take long. Another day and you'll be so busy it'll look like Mr. Engelmann and I are standing still."

She laughed.

"Where is Mr. Engelmann?"

"Oh, he's upstairs with Anna. She is not feeling well again today."

"What a strain all this must be for the both of them."

"Yes, Mr. Engelmann looked pretty tired himself."

"Why can't the doctors do something for Mrs. Engelmann?"

Mrs. Schmidt didn't respond. She just frowned, glanced at the floor and shrugged.

"Well, I brought some Christmas decorations from home. My parents don't need them anymore so I'm going to go outside and start stringing them up. I'll try to surprise Mr. Engelmann."

Henry knew he was taking a chance putting up the lights before getting Mr. Engelmann's approval but he was so excited to give the store a bit of the glitz of downtown, he just had to do it.

He worked for over an hour putting the lights on the front and side of the store. There were about twenty feet left over but even with that, he'd still needed extension cords to plug the lights in. Luckily there were electrical outlets at both the front and rear of the building. When he went in, Mrs. Schmidt had the solution.

"Oh, my son's an electrician and we have lots of extension cords at home. I'll bring you three or four tomorrow."

"That's great!" Henry exclaimed, seeing his plan come together.

"And, you know what? When Mr. Schmidt was alive, he made a wooden tree that he outlined with lights. And at the top of the house, he put up a big Santa Claus made of plastic with lights inside. The whole neighbourhood could hardly wait for him to decorate at Christmastime." After a long pause she continued, "But now that he's gone, I can't do it, and my Ronny is too busy to decorate. It's a shame that it all just sits there in the garage collecting dust. Come over after school or even after work tonight, and pick it up if you want."

"If I want?" Henry said excitedly, "You bet I want! That's just great, Mrs. Schmidt." He visualized the Santa Claus ensconced right above the Coca-Cola sign.

It was past five-thirty, and since Mr. Engelmann had yet to come downstairs, Henry told Mrs. Schmidt that he'd check on him before heading home for the day. He went to the back of the storage room, and called up the stairs as softly as he could. There was no answer. He climbed to the top of the stairwell, and whispered in a low voice, "Mr. Engelmann? Mr. Engelmann?"

An unnamed fear choked him. What if something dreadful had happened? *Mrs. Engelmann has been so sick lately and Mr. Engelmann so weary and stressed out, maybe they are both too sick to move or maybe—* Henry didn't want to finish the thought.

He had gone upstairs many times before, but never beyond the bathroom area. He tiptoed to a room from which a dim glow emanated, holding his breath as he approached the door and peered inside. What he saw immediately touched his heart.

There lying in bed was Anna, her hair spread across the pillow. Mr. Engelmann knelt by her side, holding her hand, his head bowed and lips moving, deep in prayer.

Henry recognized the emotion. *That's the kind of love I have for Jenny,* he thought. He was relieved to see the blanket gently rise and fall.

Henry decided not to disturb them. He tiptoed back down the stairs. Mrs. Schmidt was just getting her coat on.

"Is everything okay?"

"Yeah, they're fine. I think I'll just lock up and turn off the lights. I've done it lots of times." Henry asked Mrs. Schmidt where she lived. It was only two blocks away from his house and he offered to walk her home and perhaps pick up the tree and Santa Claus.

"Well, you can walk me home, but the tree and the Santa are too big for you to carry. I'll have Ronny drop them off at the store tomorrow. He has a big van. It should all be here when you come to work."

As they walked, Mrs. Schmidt told Henry how happy she'd been to get Mr. Engelmann's job offer. Ever since Mr. Schmidt had passed on, she'd had trouble filling the long lonely days.

Henry could sympathize, though he didn't say anything about Jenny.

"Anna is such a good woman," Mrs. Schmidt went on, changing the subject. "She helped me so much when my Joseph died. She always had a kind thing to say to me and often called to see how I was doing before she became so sick. My heart just goes out to them. My Joseph was ill for a long time, too, before God took him home. It is very difficult watching someone you love be sick and in pain day after day. I'm sure David feels the same way."

After that they walked in silence, the rising moon reflecting off the snow. Henry's gaze turned to the east and there it was, the first bright star in the sky. He thought of his letter.

"I wonder if Jenny is looking at the same star tonight," he murmured.

"What did you say, Henry?"

"Oh, nothing, Mrs. Schmidt."

"Well, here's my stop. Do you want to see the tree and Santa?" There's no light in the garage, but I have a flashlight."

"Oh, I think I should probably get home. My mom's probably already got supper waiting for me. I was late last night too. Good night, Mrs. Schmidt, I'm glad your day went okay ... and thanks for helping out the Engelmanns."

"It was just fine, Henry. I'm already looking forward to work tomorrow."

CHAPTER TWENTY-EIGHT

A S MRS. SCHMIDT HAD PROMISED, the plastic Santa Claus and the wooden tree were waiting for Henry against the side of the store when he arrived after school. It was unbelievable that he had visualized something and circumstances had come together so quickly to make it happen.

The tree frame was painted green, stood about six feet high and had a star cut-out at the top. The plastic Santa Claus was a real prize. It looked almost new. Made of formed plastic, it was only a few inches in depth, but was at least four feet tall. When it was plugged in, red and white lights would make it just as jolly as any of the decorations downtown. A few nails through the white plastic border would anchor it above the store sign.

If he could get it up there.

Henry looked at the two decorations, glad Mrs. Schmidt's son had delivered them. But how he was going to hang that Santa Claus above the store sign? The ladder he had borrowed might be tall enough, but the Santa was too unwieldy for him to handle alone. And Mr. Engelmann couldn't really help him, he knew. Just as he was contemplating whether or not he could get his dad to help him, a black van with "Tibbets Electric" written on the side pulled up in front of the store. Out jumped a young man in his late twenties. He was stout with a round face and a beaming smile. He could only be Mrs. Schmidt's son.

"Hi. Are you Henry?"

"Yes."

"I'm Ron Schmidt. Mom said you might need some help."

"Thanks for bringing the tree and Santa over earlier. I really appreciate it."

"No problem, Hank, glad to help."

Henry liked the way Ron just cut through all the formalities and called him Hank. He'd known Ron for less than a minute and it was obvious he was a good guy.

"Mom asked me to drop by when I was done for the day and I got off work early, so here I am. Where do you want to put the Santa?"

"Well, I thought just above the sign under the second floor windows, but—"

"No problem, Hank, let's get to it." Ron went to the van, tugged out a ladder and leaned it against the store beside the spot where the Coca Cola sign protruded from the building. "You can put your ladder on the other side.

Henry quickly obeyed. Ron hung a hammer in the pouch he had strapped to his waist, put a bunch of nails in his mouth, and mumbled, "Let's go, Hank."

He picked up the Santa. Henry grabbed it too, and together they walked over to the ladders. They climbed up, and when they reached the Coca-Cola sign, Ron reached over and pulled the Santa from Henry's hands, holding it in place against the building above the sign.

"Okay, Hank, climb up a little higher and just hold it steady," he said, talking from one side of his mouth and keeping a tight hold on the nails with the other. Locating the holes where the nails should go, he secured Old Saint Nick to the top of Mr. Engelmann's store.

"I'll get an extension cord to plug it in," Henry said, climbing back down the ladder.

"No need to. I'll just wire it up to the sign," Ron said.

"Can you do that?"

"No problem." Ron unscrewed a small plate on the top of the Coke sign, looked inside, and said, "Uh huh." He went down to his van, brought out a piece of wire about four feet long, and climbed back up. He connected one end to the bottom of the Santa Claus and the other end to the Coca-Cola sign.

"Should I go turn off the power?" Henry asked.

"No problem, Hank. As long as I work with one wire at a time and don't touch the two wires together, it'll be okay. But don't you try this." When he connected the second wire, there was a tiny spark, then Santa Claus lit up.

"Wow! Does that ever look good! It lights up the whole store and looks so Christmassy."

"Glad you like it."

Henry liked Ron, too. He remembered what Mr. Engelmann had told him over and over again in their talks. No matter what job a person was assigned in life, if he used it to serve others, he would be happy. It was obvious Ron knew how to serve.

After Ron came down from the ladder, he hoisted it over his shoulder in one smooth motion and fit it back onto the van. "Okay, Hank, where do you want the tree?"

"Well, I thought it would look nice somewhere out front here, maybe on top of that snowbank?"

"No problem." Ron picked up the tree and walked knee-deep through the drifts Henry had made clearing the walk. He raised the wooden tree and thrust it deeply into the snow.

"Good thing you have all this snow," he said. "Dad and I usually had to nail a support board on the back to keep it upright before the snow came, but I think this'll work fine. I guess you want to light this tree, too, Hank?"

"Yeah, I do, but the lights on the roofline ended up at the back of the store on the east end of the building. There's about twenty feet of string there, but it's way too far to reach the Christmas tree."

"No problem, Hank." Ron pulled out his wire cutters and

walked down the side of the store to where the lights ended. He separated the wire with his fingernails, cut each one, then pulled out a roll of electrician's tape and wrapped the end of each cut wire. He then brought the cut section of lights to the front of the store. Next, Ron got a stapler from his van and, starting with a light at the very top of the tree, worked his way down, going from one side to the other.

"Looks like you've done this before," Henry commented, watching Ron's efficiency with awe.

"Oh, lots. Dad and I decorated this tree at least twenty times while he was alive."

Once again, Ron went to the van, this time bringing out a plug for the end of the wires on the now light-draped tree. He stripped the wires of their rubber insulation and in less then two minutes, a plug was securely attached to the string of lights.

"I hope you have extension cords. Your mom thought you would have some."

"You bet. Not a problem, Hank." Another visit to the van produced two long extension cords.

Henry marvelled at how quickly Ron worked, and without complaint. He admired the electrician's attitude. Henry wanted to have that kind of outlook, too.

"You just about ready for the show, Hank?"

"For sure," Henry said, rubbing mittened hands together.

Ron plugged in the extension cords, and the lights sprang to life, outlining Mr. Engelmann's store like a set of lit candles around a white cake. Henry's mouth hung open as he stared at the magic Ron had performed so quickly. He couldn't believe his eyes. It was every bit as beautiful as the downtown stores.

"Oh, Ron, it's unbelievable! Thank you so much for doing this. I could never have made it happen on my own!"

"No problem, Hank. Glad you like it."

Suddenly realizing this was what Ron did to earn a living, Henry dug in his pockets. "Is there any cost, Ron?" He hoped it wouldn't be any more than the three dollars he had.

"Consider it my Christmas present to you and Mr. Engelmann.

I really appreciate Mr. Engelmann hiring my mother. She needed to get out of the house."

"Thank you so much! And Mr. Engelmann and I are really happy your mom's working here. I like her; she's a very nice lady."

"None better than her; has a heart of gold, Hank. But you'll find that out soon enough."

"Well, thanks again, Ron, for doing all this. It's really nice of you," Henry said, extending his hand to Ron, who quickly took it and squeezed it so hard Henry thought his bones had been broken.

"No problem, Hank. Well, got to go. Have a date tonight. Can't leave the little gal waiting."

After Ron drove away, Henry turned back to admire the store. When he'd seen how beautiful downtown looked with all the lights and everything, he'd prayed to be able to do something similar to Mr. Engelmann's store … and here it was right before his eyes. It wasn't just haphazard circumstances coming together out of nowhere to make his wishes come true. He glanced heavenward in thanks and quickly asked for assistance in another matter.

How was he going to tell Mr. Engelmann what he had done? Mr. Engelmann was a proud man who liked to pay his way for everything. Though he was always quick to give charity, he sure didn't like to receive it.

Then it occurred to Henry how best to tell him. Plan set, Henry entered the store.

"Hi, Mr. Engelmann. Hi, Mrs. Schmidt."

"Hello, Henry," they replied, almost in unison.

"How's Mrs. Engelmann feeling?" Henry wanted to know.

"Oh, she's a little better today," Mr. Engelmann replied, "I heard her walking around upstairs a few minutes ago." Just then Anna appeared at the entrance to the storage room.

"What are you doing up?" Mr. Engelmann asked, rushing to her side.

"Oh, don't fuss over me, David. I'm fine, maybe a little tired, that's all."

"Why are you down here?"

"Well, I heard all this hammering under my window, almost like someone was trying to break in. I thought I'd better come down to see what was going on."

Mr. Engelmann turned to Henry. "Is something going on?"

The moment of truth had arrived. Henry looked into his boss's eyes. He knew Mr. Engelmann liked to be acknowledged that way. He had often said, "The eyes are the windows to the soul. A man who's truthful can look you straight in the eyes." And that was the way it usually started. First came the look and then the teaching. Henry was going to show Mr. Engelmann just how much he had taught him over the past several months. The student was going to test the master.

Mr. Engelmann waited.

"Over the last few months, you've taught me it is as important to know how to receive as it is to give."

"Yes," Mr. Engelmann nodded.

"You've also taught me that our main purpose in life, regardless of what we do, is to serve others."

"Yes," Mr. Engelmann nodded again.

"You also said that when we serve others, we often receive great joy ourselves, simply as a result of our service," Henry continued, surprising himself. The look in Mr. Engelmann's eyes told Henry he was surprised too.

"Tonight, Mr. Engelmann, a few of us wanted to show our appreciation to you and Mrs. Engelmann. My mom and dad want to express their thanks for hiring me and being so kind and good to me. And although Mrs. Schmidt just started here, she also wants to let you know how much she appreciates working here. And I want you to know how much I appreciate all you've done for me. I love working here, and I'm really lucky to have you as my boss and friend."

Mr. Engelmann stared at Henry, clearly at a loss for words.

"Tonight, Mr. and Mrs. Engelmann, we want you to accept our gift. It came from the heart and is waiting for you outside."

They turned to look at Mrs. Engelmann, unsure if she should go outside.

"Oh, don't worry about me!" she said, and snatched up a coat from the back door. Henry thought the coat was Mrs. Schmidt's; it looked as if five of Mrs. Engelmann could fit in it.

"Well, let's go see!" Anna exclaimed, excited and curious now.

Henry led them all outside, down the steps to the sidewalk.

"Okay," Henry said, "here is our gift to you both."

Mr. and Mrs. Engelmann and Mrs. Schmidt turned around together. Henry didn't need to look at the storefront; he could see it mirrored in the expression on their faces. They were awestruck by what they saw, but the lights on the store could not compete with the light of happiness that sparkled in the Engelmann's eyes and filled the tears that flowed down their cheeks.

Overcome, Mr. Engelmann could not speak. He just shook his head from side to side. Mrs. Engelmann cupped her hands together under her chin, almost as if she were praying, the oversized coat around her shoulders flapping in the wind like a pair of wings. Her face beamed, and for once the threat of her illness receded a bit. And Mrs. Schmidt looked a bit like Saint Nick herself: round and jolly and smiling from ear to ear.

"It's wonderful, Henry," she said. "It looks so beautiful."

"Thanks," Henry replied. "And thank you, too, for getting your son to help." Henry expected her to say, "No problem, Hank," like her son would've, but she just broadened her smile.

Henry waited for some response from Mr. Engelmann, a bit nervous about what he might be thinking. He hoped the Engelmanns would accept the gift and not argue about who owed what. Henry studied the old man, trying to decipher the look in his eyes. At first it seemed like he was trying to swallow his pride, but slowly Henry came to realize that Mr. Engelmann saw their offering for what it was—a gift of love.

When Mr. Engelmann finally spoke, he said, "Henry, this is the most beautiful Christmas gift anyone, besides my Anna, has ever given to me. Thank you from the bottom of my heart."

He came over and gave Henry a fatherly hug. Henry had never dreamed he would ever be able to teach anything to someone as wise as Mr. Engelmann.

No sooner had Mr. Engelmann let go of Henry than Mrs. Engelmann came over and opened her arms. Henry bent down a bit and stepped into them gladly, surprised by the strength emotion had given the usually frail woman. He held her lightly, gingerly, afraid to hurt her. Her heart pounded and between sobs of joy she thanked him over and over again. When they parted, the side of his face and his shirt collar were wet with her tears.

"You're welcome, Mrs. Engelmann," he said softly, tears shining in his own eyes.

CHAPTER TWENTY-NINE

THE SCENT OF BURNING LOGS rising from two of the three brick chimneys lingered lazily in the moonlit sky. There was not a breath of wind. It had snowed earlier in the day, blanketing the tall pines and maple trees surrounding the Sarsky residence in a soft layer of snow. The Christmas lights outlining the huge Tudor-style home sparkled in the snow crystals that still hung in the air. The ground spotlights peeking through the snowbanks highlighted the front of the dwelling, making the dormers cast long shadows that swept up and jumped over the peak of the roof, while the moonlight made silhouettes of the two slender gothic pillars shouldering the canopy over the entryway, stretching them down the front steps and across the freshly cleared driveway.

A snowplow operated by one of several groundskeepers headed towards the entrance gate of the Sarsky estate. The shrubbery outlining the lane on either side guided the tractor as it trundled through the heavy snowfall. The tractor turned into a bend in the winding lane and disappeared, taking with it the drone of its engine. The only evidence of the plow was an intermittent spray of snow into the night between the trees.

Skeletons of maples caught the falling snow and glistened in the moonlight.

A group of deer burst into a clearing behind the Sarsky home. Startled by the snowplow, they leaped effortlessly over the snow as if taking flight. It would be easy to imagine Santa Claus following closely behind, calling each one by name.

The Sarsky estate was a winter wonderland, a postcard picture of aesthetic beauty and charm. More than anything else, it was this enchanting setting that helped assuage Jenny's grief since leaving Regina.

Of the four dormers on the second floor, only the one furthest to the west had a light on inside. The incandescence from Jenny's bedroom warmed the snow caught on the ledges of her window. Just behind the frosted panes, Jenny sat at her desk, deep in thought. She was writing her very last letter to Henry. She hadn't planned to write anymore, but recent circumstances had made her change her mind. Oh, all the Christmas music on the radio had stirred up nostalgic feelings for Henry and her time with him, especially anything sung by Bing Crosby, but her decision was mostly based on what had happened that afternoon at school.

The students in her class had each been asked to bring an ornament to put on the twenty-foot high Christmas tree in the main foyer of the school. When one of Jenny's friends opened up the box containing her ornament, Jenny had been struck by the sight of a beautiful pewter angel. She'd had to get a closer look.

"Can I please see that, Tammy?" Jenny had asked, already reaching for it with excitement.

"Sure," Tammy had replied, placing it into Jenny's eager hand.

"It's so heavy and smooth," Jenny commented as she ran her fingers over it. "And the inscription on the bottom is perfect: WATCH OVER MY BELOVED."

A surge of pure exhilaration swept through her, "Oh, it's beautiful, Tammy! It reminds me of … of someone I really liked. We used to talk about guardian angels all the time."

After a brief moment, Jenny cupped her hands around the

tiny angel and brought it close to her chest. Maybe ... "Oh, Tammy, could we please trade ornaments?" she blurted.

"Sure," Tammy had shrugged. "Why not."

Not daring to let the angel go, Jenny handed Tammy the ornament she herself had brought, a medium-sized Christmas ball of metallic blue with a hand-painted scene of Santa Claus and his reindeer flying through a star-studded sky.

"Oh, Jenny, this is gorgeous! Are you certain you want to trade?"

"Absolutely, Tammy. I'll bring another one tomorrow. I'm going to send this angel off to Henry right away!"

Tammy looked at her in some confusion. "What?"

"Oh, never mind," Jenny had said excitedly, already running down the hall. "Thanks again, Tammy!"

Now she rose from her desk and walked towards her bedroom window, the warm weight of the tiny metal angel heavy in her hand. As she looked out, she caught the first bright star in the east and, as she watched it glow more brightly than all the millions of stars in the sky, Henry's warmth and love seeped through her as if he were holding her in his arms. Words formed in her mind and then on her tongue:

> Oh star of wonder, star so bright
> I beg you hear my wish tonight.
> Send your light to Henry's heart
> and let him know I've done my part.
> In a letter of love I've signed
> I send an angel to search and find
> a letter from Henry just for me.
> Oh, please let there be one under our tree.

Jenny returned to her desk, picked up her Parker pen, and allowed the bright blue ink to flow out and create, on a blank, lilac-scented page, a letter filled with love, hope and longing. As Jenny wrote the last two paragraphs, she was sure something beyond her heart guided the pen:

I made a special wish to the bright star of the east tonight to send out my love to you. I hope and pray you get this letter and my gift. Every night I pray for my guardian angel to talk to yours, so together they can find some way to bring us together again.

Even though we are far apart, you are forever in my heart. I will love you always. Have a merry Christmas!

All my love,
Jenny

Jenny read the letter over, folded it twice, and stuffed it into a pink envelope. She held the angel and stared at it for the longest time. It was the perfect gift. She kissed the angel tenderly and, as she dropped it into the envelope, whispered, "Guardian angel, please watch over my beloved." Jenny sealed the envelope, locking in the lilac scent to be released when Henry opened it. She placed it on the edge of her desk, ready to give to her dad to mail to Henry in the morning.

"'MORNING, MOM. 'MORNING, DAD," Jenny greeted her parents a little more brightly than she had of late. The letter was a hard rectangle in her sweater pocket. She was relieved to see her dad was still at home, having breakfast.

"You seem extra cheerful today," her mother observed.

"Well, it's just about the start of Christmas holidays, and last night I decided what I would like most for Christmas." She looked at her mother and father, not sure if she should say what was on her mind. As her parents looked questioningly at her, she finally blurted, "What I want most is a letter from Henry."

The blood from her parents' faces drained as they looked at each other then back at her, barely believing what they had heard. Over the past month, she hadn't once mentioned Henry, and they'd thought, with great relief, that she was finally over him. Now, out of the blue, she was back at it! The mood in the kitchen changed instantly.

"Jenny," her father started. "Jenny," he repeated, searching for the right words to say. "Henry hasn't replied to any of your letters. Please … stop this. You're only hurting yourself."

And me.

As Edith opened her mouth to no doubt reinforce what her father had said, Jenny cried out, "Stop! Please just stop, both of you, right now." Tears rolled down her face. "You might be right—but can't you see I have to try one more time? It's Christmas and I miss him, and I want to see him and … and … and I *love* him!"

Neither Ted nor Edith knew what to say. All they could hope was that this was the last time. The three of them sat in the kitchen, trying to soothe themselves in the warmth of the sunlight streaming through the eastern windows. They ate the rest of their breakfast in silence, each afraid to say anything further lest it lead to another outburst.

Ted rose first. "I best be on my way," he said. He kissed Edith lightly on the cheek and headed for the front door.

Jenny jumped up and ran to the front entrance, getting there just as her father finished buttoning his coat.

"Don't forget my letter, Dad," she said as she handed it to him. Jenny leaned closer and kissed him on the cheek. "Please promise you'll mail it today," her words were quiet, but she looked directly into her father's eyes.

"Yes, yes, Jenny." Then reluctantly he added, "I promise."

As Ted looked up, his gaze met Edith's. She gave her head a slight shake and Ted knew he had just broken another promise to his daughter.

CHAPTER THIRTY

TED WAS LATE ARRIVING at his office that morning. An accident on the highway had held him up for over an hour. Elaine was already at work when he entered the office.

"'Morning, Elaine," he said as he strode through the reception area.

"Good morning, Mr. Sarsky."

Ted entered his office, closed the door and headed for his desk. He set his briefcase down and stared at it. All his troubles stemmed from Jenny's letter, he tried to tell himself. But he knew better; his problems were locked inside himself and not in the case. His faltering leadership as company president, his drinking, his marriage, his role as a father all weighed on him with the accumulated guilt of those damn letters.

He removed a set of keys from his pocket. He unlocked the briefcase and took out Jenny's letter to Henry, lowering himself into his chair. The envelope smelled faintly of lilacs.

This letter was a bit heavier than the others and Ted hefted it in his hand. Something shifted inside. He ran his fingers over it and tried to feel the shape of the object inside. It eluded him. He replayed the conversation that had taken place in the kitchen earlier that morning, but couldn't recall anything Jenny had said that might give a clue as to what she might want to send to that boy.

As Ted contemplated what to do, Elaine knocked on his door. He sat up, sliding Jenny's envelope back into the briefcase. "Come in."

His secretary carried a small stack of papers with a letter on top. She stopped in front of Ted's desk. "These three documents require your signature, Mr. Sarsky. I'd like to get them off before noon to ensure they will be in today's mail. And a letter also came for Jenny Sarsky, care of your attention." Elaine laid the letter on top of the other documents she'd just spread out before him and Ted sighed inwardly at the sight of Henry Pederson's return address. "Is there anything you need me to do?"

"Not right now, thank you. That will be all, Elaine."

After she closed the door, he picked up the letter Henry had sent. It was nearly identical in size and weight to the one Jenny had handed him that morning. The extra shape in Henry's envelope felt almost the same as the one in Jenny's, too. *Odd.* He opened his briefcase, took out Jenny's letter to Henry, and laid it down beside the one Elaine had just brought in. Except for the colour of the envelope, the size was the same. And whatever the objects inside were, they seemed identical as well. A shiver tickled Ted's spine.

"Incredible," he murmured. "How can this be?" He picked up Henry's letter once more, tipping the envelope on its end. The object fell down the length of the envelope with enough force to make a tiny hole in the well-travelled paper and protrude slightly through it.

It looked like … pewter? He poked at it with his fingertip and overcome with curiosity, pinched the metal. He hesitated before extracting it entirely. Whatever it was could very easily have fallen out already, that much was clear, and the envelope needed to be taped regardless. That was all the rationale he needed. Without further ado, he pulled out the metal object.

"It's an angel!" He looked at it for a long time, running his fingers over the smooth metal. As he did, his troubled soul quieted. Finally his eyes wandered from the beautifully carved face of the angel down to follow its outstretched hands to the words at the bottom: WATCH OVER MY BELOVED.

The words sent an instant ache to his heart. He considered Jenny's envelope, eyeing it carefully. Could Jenny's letter contain the same angel? It defied coincidence.

Ted put the angel Henry had sent down beside Jenny's letter and ran his finger over the object inside the still-sealed pink envelope. He closed his eyes, visualizing the shape. A blind person, used to seeing by touch, would have been able to tell instantly. Another chill shot through him as he concluded that his daughter and that boy in Regina had, with no means of prior communication, sent each other the same gift. Uneasiness trickled through him. Was he toying with fate? Did God commission His angels, His messengers, to forge a union that was meant to be?

More importantly, was he going to be punished for his interference? Fear gripped him. The only way to alleviate it was to get rid of these letters as he had all the others. He couldn't bear any reminder of what he and Edith had done to Henry and Jenny. And feeling the finger of God upon him was just too much.

"Yes, that's what Edith would want. It's the right thing to do. Out of sight, out of mind." Without thinking it through any further, he pushed the button on the intercom.

"Yes, Mr. Sarsky?"

"Could you please come in here, Elaine?"

Ted suddenly wondered what she'd think. He didn't want her to see to whom the letters were addressed. Quickly he scrabbled through his desk drawer for a large brown envelope. He'd stuffed Henry's letter into it and was about to pick up Jenny's when Elaine walked in and approached the desk.

Uh oh, more letters, she thought. The name *Henry Pederson* was clear on the pink envelope on her boss's desk, but he snatched it up too quickly for her to make out any part of the address beyond "Saskatchewan."

Ted sealed the large envelope and pushed it towards his secretary. It skidded across the desk.

Ted swallowed hard, trying to calm his racing heart as he said, "Please take that down to the furnace and see that it gets burned."

"Right away, Mr. Sarsky."

Ted sat back in his chair as Elaine left with the envelope. *Thank God that's over.* As Ted reclined further back in his chair, he caught a glimpse of metal—the shiny pewter angel hidden behind his briefcase. In his haste to get both Henry's and Jenny's envelopes into the larger one before Elaine came in, he had forgotten to include it. Just the sight of it left him cold. Now what? He could hardly ask Elaine to toss an angel into the flames! Hell, he could hardly even think of doing so himself.

IT JUST DOESN'T SEEM RIGHT *to destroy someone's letter.* Elaine thought as she waited for the elevator to reach the eighteenth floor. "Oh, I pray Mr. Sarsky realizes it's a mistake before it is too late."

The elevator doors were just closing when Mr. Sarsky called her name and ran down the hall towards her.

"Elaine, wait! Don't close the doors. I'd like that envelope back." Out of breath, he waited for Elaine to extricate herself from the elevator, which had retracted its doors when she'd stuck her hand between them at the sound of her name. "I'm sorry, Elaine. I just realized this is something I must do myself."

It was as if her prayer had been heard. Elaine studied Ted, relieved that she didn't have to follow through on an order she didn't agree with yet felt duty bound to carry out. But she was also worried for Ted. Sweat had popped out across his brow. Clearly this must have been a difficult decision for him. And she couldn't shake the feeling that somehow his growing drinking problem revolved around these letters. If only she'd kept the one she'd had in her hand, perhaps she could've helped by now.

Trying to keep her thoughts from showing on her face,

Elaine handed the brown envelope back to her boss and merely asked, "Is there anything else you need me to do?"

"No, that's fine. Thank you, Elaine."

Elaine smiled, trying to cheer him up, but Ted didn't notice. He just took the envelope and hurried back to his office. Elaine watched him walk away. His shoulders slouched; his head was down. He looked troubled, haunted. How long until the board called him on it? For the hundredth time, she wished she could help him.

TED WAS RELIEVED HE'D CAUGHT Elaine in time, though now he felt weak-willed. He was right back where he'd started. He stared at the brown envelope in front of him. He picked it up and tore open the end, dumping both letters onto the shiny mahogany desktop. He tossed the brown envelope into the waste basket. Picking up the pewter angel, he began to talk to it.

"If it hadn't been for you getting out of that envelope, you and the letters would be burning in the furnace by now. Are you some kind of warning, an omen of some kind?"

Shivers finger-walked down his spine. His nervousness returned, and a pervasive fear that he didn't understand settled in. It made him want to get up and flee, but there was no rational reason to do so. He had to get the angel out of sight. He picked up Henry's envelope, reinserted the angel through the tear he'd made earlier and sealed the edge twice with tape to make sure it wouldn't come out again. He laid the letter down on top of the other one. Then he sat back, wondering what on earth he was going to do with letters that seemed controlled and destined by heaven itself.

A good half-hour elapsed as he sat absorbed in his thoughts, staring at the two letters. He chuckled humourlessly; it appeared that no matter how hard he and Edith had tried to end Jenny's relationship, the force of fate—or, or whatever—kept overcoming the obstacles they put in its path.

Here they were, a letter from Jenny and one from Henry, lying on his desk, almost hugging one another, in spite of his and his wife's efforts to keep the two teens apart. He hated to admit it, but he was actually touched by the whole thing. If he hadn't felt so despondent, he might have laughed at the entire matter.

Although he desperately wanted a drink, he refused to allow himself to be dulled by alcohol. He had to contemplate the possible consequences of his actions. Could *that* be the reason he had forgotten to put the angel back inside the envelope? Was it somehow meant to get him to take a closer look at his motivations?

Ted thought over the reasons he and Edith had chosen to keep Jenny and Henry apart. He understood Edith's worry and concern, yet he knew in his heart their actions, especially his, were wrong. Edith, after all, hadn't stood in front of a roaring furnace with a batch of love letters in her hand. He mulled that over, spiraling further into confusion and bewilderment. He tried to look at the situation the same way he would an important business decision, probing for all the possible alternatives and all the possible consequences. He freed his mind and allowed it to come up with a solution his instincts would acknowledge as right.

The words *honesty* and *truth* came to him. Ted had lied to his daughter repeatedly. What could he do to correct the situation? Tell her the truth. Explain why they had taken the action they had. Jenny would understand, eventually, and even if she didn't right away, she would be in communication with Henry and would forgive them in no time. They could then be supportive rather than manipulative and untruthful.

But just as the light of truth started to take hold of him, an image of Edith's disapproving face popped into his mind. When Edith was firm in her resolve, there was no way he could go against her wishes. It always carried devastating consequences when he tried.

For a brief moment, Ted had known what to do. If only he had reinforced those thoughts with the knowledge of how his decisions would affect Henry and Jenny's lives. But it was the imagined look in Edith's eyes that tipped the scale between doing what was right ... and what was easy.

Besides, would Jenny really understand? Would she forgive him? Would Edith still love him? What if Edith left him? What if his wife's worst fears were realized and Jenny became pregnant? Slowly, the arguments built up to blind him; a fog settled over him and clouded his previous clarity.

Ted took a deep breath and let it out slowly, trying to expel the tension growing within him. As soon as he'd imagined Edith's stern face and her harsh reprimands, his actions became predictable. He began to sink fast; he couldn't carry the load any longer.

Almost like an automaton, Ted rose and went to the liquor cabinet. He pulled out the vodka; it gave off the least odour. The bottle was less than half full. He opened the bottle and poured out a splash, trying to ration himself. He didn't drink it in one gulp the way he usually did. He just sipped at it.

Ted returned to his chair, tilting it back. It amazed him that Jenny had never tried to mail one of her letters herself. She'd had many opportunities when she and her mother went shopping in the city, but she had always left it up to him to mail the letters for her. Because she so loved and trusted him, she never once suspected he was destroying her letters. Guilt gnawed at him and he took another swallow to drown it.

He stared intently at the envelopes, wondering what the letters said. He tried to recall the love letters he had written to Edith when they were apart for a time. But it was too long ago, and the vodka had begun to work its magic. He wanted to read the letters to see if they were as similar as the angels, but that whole thing was eerie. It was as if the letters were protected by angels themselves .... The feeling that he was playing with destiny returned, and he didn't dare tamper with it any longer.

Ted finished the liquor in his glass and set it down. He reached for the envelopes and restacked them, one on top of the other. He took an elastic band from his desk drawer and slid it, like a ring over a finger, around the letters, then reached for another one. As Ted held the elastic, he noticed it was quite frayed, ready to break. He was going to replace it, but felt prompted to leave it. He slipped it over the letters next to the other elastic. It held. The letters were joined, even if his daughter and the boy weren't, and Ted took a kind of maudlin satisfaction in that.

Behind the large picture beside the liquor cabinet was a wall safe. Ted swung the painted landscape aside and entered the combination. The heavy steel door swung open. If only he could find the key to all his troubles and unlock them as easily.

Ted looked down at the two envelopes in his hands one last time. "Someday, perhaps, you will find your destinations, but for now ..." He put the envelopes at the back of the safe behind other important documents, then shut the door with a thunk of finality, hiding it behind the picture once more.

So be it, he thought.

He gazed at the picture thoughtfully. The serene landscape seemed to have captured more light somehow. Was the painting ... glowing? *Nah, it's gotta be the vodka.* Still, the thought that the angels somehow had the power to escape the confines of their chamber to fly to their intended recipients wouldn't leave his mind—and for a split second he imagined he saw them streak across the painted sky. Ted immediately pivoted on his heel and strode to the liquor cabinet.

This was getting ridiculous.

He poured the remaining contents of the vodka bottle into another glass and raised it to his mouth, downing it in one gulp. He hesitated, then cracked the seal on a bottle of Canadian Club, filling the glass halfway. He hoped a third drink would settle whatever demons were swarming around him.

In a way, he thought muzzily, he *had* done the right thing. He hadn't sent off the letters, but he hadn't destroyed them either. He'd found a kind of balance. It would be his secret.

And he consoled himself with the thought that at least the letters and their angels were together.

CHAPTER THIRTY-ONE

E VERY DAY IN JANUARY, when her father arrived home, Jenny asked him, "Is there a letter from Henry?"

And the answer was always the same. "No, Jenny, I'm sorry. There's nothing for you."

Jenny couldn't believe that Henry hadn't responded in some way to her letter and her gift. She'd been so certain there would have been *something*. Not even praying to her guardian angel could appease her longing heart. It was as if Henry had vanished from the face of the earth, his love for her as temporal as mist in the wind. Some days Jenny wondered if he had even been real.

The only things that reminded Jenny of their relationship, and the fact that one had actually existed were the little notes Henry had secured under the elastic on her fencepost. Without them, there was no concrete evidence of their time together. Jenny read and reread the notes almost daily; they'd become worn and ragged.

Having not heard from Henry by the end of January, she was so frustrated she decided to tear the notes to shreds. All they did was remind her of broken promises, and kept alive a memory that only added to her pain and longing.

In the end, however, Jenny couldn't bring herself to do it. They were just too precious. She still felt Henry's words so deeply, and the thought of his touch on the worn and tattered paper was her sole small comfort. Most days she hardly ate her dinner, and afterwards went directly to her room, not emerging until the next morning for school. Her appetite was nearly gone and she was as fatigued as she was apathetic. Lately the only thing that roused her curiosity was why her school clothes suddenly didn't seem to fit.

Her mom and dad had noticed the change in her and made an appointment with the family doctor. Surely Jenny's problem was more psychological than physical, or perhaps it was simply hormonal. Jenny was reluctant to see the doctor but gave in to make her mother leave her alone.

Her dad drove them into Ottawa on his way to work. After a morning of shopping and a brief stop for lunch, they walked over to the doctor's office. No sooner had they sat down than the receptionist called for Jenny. Her mother looked up from her magazine to say she would wait in the reception area unless the doctor wanted to talk to her.

Jenny attempted a small smile, "I'm sure everything's fine. Don't worry, Mom."

Edith smiled back, but Jenny could tell she wasn't convinced.

Jenny followed the nurse to an examination room and plunked herself into the chair indicated by the nurse. She tapped her feet as she waited for the doctor.

Dr. Breck was middle-aged and completely bald. He looked at Jenny and smiled warmly. The wide gap between his two front teeth made him somehow less intimidating and Jenny began to relax.

"Hello, Jenny, I'm Dr. Breck. What seems to be the problem?" He flipped through a couple of pages in his chart. "Says here your mother thinks you're not yourself lately. Is something bothering you?"

Jenny looked at the doctor, reluctant to tell him about Henry and how much she missed him. Instead, she decided to talk about something else that had been bothering her. "Well, I *am* concerned about the fact that I seem to be gaining weight, even though I haven't felt like eating much lately. Actually, I haven't been feeling too well for a little while now."

Dr. Breck looked at Jenny for a long moment. "Would you please take off your sweater and lie down on the table?"

When Jenny complied, Dr. Breck pressed down on her abdomen. "Does it hurt here? Here?"

Each time Jenny said, "No."

Dr. Breck stopped and looked down at Jenny. "When did you start menstruating?"

"Oh, about two years ago—"

"And when was your last period?"

Jenny thought for moment. She had been so preoccupied with the move and not hearing from Henry she hadn't given it much thought. It had all been so stressful… "Now that you mention it, I don't think I've had a period this month yet … and maybe not last month either … I'm not sure. I can't remember. And sometimes it's so minimal."

Dr. Breck's next words shocked her to her core. "I'd like you to have a pregnancy test."

"A … *what?!* Are you serious?" Jenny sat up.

Dr. Breck didn't answer right away. He could see Jenny was truly surprised. "Jenny, let's just do the test and we'll go from there, okay?"

"But, Doctor, I assure you …"

Jenny's words trailed off as Dr. Breck filled out a form and handed it to her.

"Here, Jenny, go to the lab for both blood work and a urine test. The results will give us an idea what may be going on here. Have the receptionist make an appointment for you next Friday. We should have the results back by then."

"Are—are you sure that there isn't something else that might cause weight gain and prevent my period?"

Dr. Breck considered, but Jenny could see he didn't think it likely. "Well, let's rule this out first, shall we? Perhaps after we meet next week, we might need to look at other possibilities. For now, go down to the lab on the second floor and get these tests done. Take this form with you."

The paper trembled in Jenny's hand. She slid off the table and pulled on her sweater.

"A pregnancy test is just ridiculous. It's just impossible. I've never ..." Jenny looked at the doctor. Their gazes met for a brief moment and Jenny felt heat rush to her face. She turned and walked briskly out of the office.

Her mother's eyes brightened when she saw her. "So? What did he say?"

"Dr. Breck wants me to take some tests down at the lab on the second floor. He'll tell me the results next Friday. I'm supposed to make another appointment and go to the lab right now."

"Did he say what the trouble might be?"

Jenny couldn't even say the words. It was just too absurd to discuss.

"No, he just wants me to have these tests done."

"What kind of tests?"

"Oh, just a blood test."

Jenny approached the receptionist before her mother could ask anything more. She made an appointment for the following Friday and walked out the door to the elevator. Her mother followed.

THAT NIGHT JENNY FLUNG HERSELF on her bed and cried. She was so upset with Henry for not writing, and now something was really wrong and she didn't know what. That pregnancy test had been a complete waste of time. She rolled on her back and felt her stomach. It seemed normal. What on earth could Dr. Breck have felt?

Jenny thought back. She hadn't had sex with Henry, even though she'd wanted to ... but what about that night when those guys dragged her off after the movie? She'd always felt a little uneasy about that night, and not entirely sure what had happened after they'd forced her into the car. She didn't even remember it very well, though sometimes she dreamed of a heavy weight on top of her, pushing ... but she'd *know* if he'd been inside her, wouldn't she? She shuddered at the thought. Sure she would know. And Henry had been so quick to find her, after all. As soon as he had, the guys had taken off. There hadn't been any blood on her panties when she'd taken them off later that night—she'd have remembered that for sure.

But the doctor's question about when she'd had her last period burned in her mind and her heart twisted in her chest. She hadn't had her period since then. *Was I ... raped?*

Nausea overcame her and she rushed to the bathroom where she threw up in the sink. She fell to her knees and threw up into the toilet again and again. She gagged until she was out of breath. The full impact of what had happened to her simmered in the recesses of her mind, but the thought of carrying that awful guy's child inside her was unbearable. She wanted it *out*. She heaved and retched until she was totally exhausted.

Her stomach ached. Her chest ached. Her heart ached.

AN ICY TENSION HUNG OVER the car as Edith, Ted and Jenny drove into the city the following Friday.

Over the last week, Jenny had sometimes wondered if her mom suspected she was pregnant. She had asked several times about the blood tests, and Jenny had done her best to put her off and protest her ignorance.

But she knew her mother didn't believe her.

Jenny was so nervous she could hardly walk when the nurse called her into the doctor's office.

When her mother asked if she could come in too, Jenny's response was an immediate "No!"

As soon as she was in the exam room, she collapsed on a chair. Her legs felt rubbery and weak. Jenny crossed and uncrossed her legs and tapped her fingertips against the arms of the chair as she waited.

Footsteps stopped outside the room and the doorknob

turned. Jenny's heart nearly burst with anxiety as Dr. Breck walked in. *At least if I have a heart attack, I'm in the right place,* she thought with a humour born of desperation. She gazed long and hard into the doctor's eyes, searching for some clue that would deny what she already feared was true.

Dr. Breck wheeled his chair in front of Jenny. He sat down and looked at her compassionately.

Jenny's mind flashed back to the park that night, and in a sweeping replay, she saw it all. All doubt and questioning were gone. The naked truth of what had happened was written in Dr. Breck's eyes and Jenny fell forward in a dead faint.

Dr. Breck called loudly for a nurse.

Edith heard the urgency in the doctor's voice and hastened after the nurse to find Jenny unconscious in the doctor's arms.

"Help me get her onto the table, Betty. This young lady fainted."

"What's wrong?" Edith cried.

"Please, Mrs. Sarsky, wait in the reception area."

"No! I want to know what's going on. I'm her mother for God's sake!"

Dr. Breck and the nurse lifted Jenny onto the exam table. Edith stood there, waiting for an answer, scanning the doctor's face much as her daughter had only minutes earlier. Dr. Breck avoided her eyes. He went to the sink, wet a cloth and brought it back to Jenny. He put it on her forehead and silently waited for the girl to revive, hoping she would tell her mother that she was with child.

"Are you sure she's asleep up there?" Ted asked later that evening, waving his drink in the direction of the staircase.

"Yes." Edith's voice was tense and weary and mechanical. Her nerves were just about shot. Ted wasn't the only one who could use a drink. Her greatest fear had come to pass and there wasn't a damn thing she could do about it. "I gave her the sedative the doctor prescribed," she added, "but she was so exhausted she probably didn't need it."

"And what's this story she was trying to tell you? It wasn't Henry, she was *raped*?"

"Yes," Edith sighed, shaking her head in disgust, "she said the night she and Henry went to the movie, some boys attacked them and took her to the park and raped her. How she could possibly come up with such a ridiculous lie is beyond me. I told you this would happen!"

"Surely if there was any truth to it she would have told us when it happened," Ted said.

"That's what *I* told her. I've confronted her over and over with the fact that it had to be Henry. But she's adamant that it wasn't and got so upset she was nearly hysterical. She claims she was so frightened that night in the park she fainted. By the time she came to, Henry and some man and woman had rescued her. Jenny said she didn't really think anything had happened, it'd all been so fast. Apparently she was more worried about upsetting us than what happened—can you imagine!—and didn't want to cause any trouble so she and Henry decided to keep it to themselves. I don't believe a word of it!"

Edith paused for Ted to agree with her and when he merely tossed back another swallow she went on, words clipped and tight. "Actually, I don't know what to believe. After her fainting spell in the doctor's office, the doctor did a thorough examination and couldn't find anything out of the ordinary, and he told us that even Jenny's hymen membrane was still intact!"

Ted got up to refill his glass, waving a hand at his wife as if to stop the flow of her words. He didn't really want to know this. Any of it. And yet it didn't make any sense to him either. "But how could she conceive if the boy didn't penetrate her? How is that even possible?" he finally asked.

Edith shook her head in disbelief at her husband's ignorance. *This* was why she'd taken charge of protecting Jenny, *this* was why she had tried to nip things in the bud; the man knew nothing!

"Ted, all it takes is proximity. And apparently," and here she gave a shudder of distaste, "there was proximity aplenty.'"

"But even so, how could his sperm pass through the membrane?"

"For heaven's sake, Ted, don't you kno—"

"Now Edith, I'm sure most men and probably even a lot of women wouldn't understand that. Why get so riled?"

Edith took another deep breath and looked at her bewildered husband. "I'm sorry Ted, I'm just so upset and annoyed by it all … the membrane is porous to allow menstrual fluid to come out—obviously, Ted, it's porous to sperm as well."

Ted stopped still, drink halfway to his mouth. He lowered it, words unfolding as the thought bloomed in his mind. "So, what you're saying is that there was no physical violence or trauma, that Jenny passed out and was unaware this even happened, that—horrible though it is—she has no memory of it.

"That's what I'm saying."

"Well, let's at least be thankful for that. To think what Jenny went through, it's best that she's been spared that awful memory … it's actually … kind of a blessing."

"*Blessing?* Blessing! Ha! You sound like Jenny. She claims her guardian angel saved her from all that. God! I don't understand either of you! This whole thing is a nightmare and the sooner she's out of it, the better for all of us. After all we've done—"

Edith's rant continued, but all Ted could think about were the pewter angels locked in his safe. A cold chill shot down his spine and he swallowed another mouthful to quell it. "Yeah, that's some story, all right. Jenny sure trusts this guardian angel," he muttered to himself. After reflecting on it a moment longer and wanting to make certain he had heard correctly, he interrupted, "So really, if it hadn't been for the fact that she conceived a baby, Jenny wouldn't have any memory of a rape even having occurred?"

"That's what she says," Edith huffed. "But I *still* think she's making it all up. Jenny has quite an imagination—and she's obviously protecting that boy."

"You'd think, though, that if it was Henry she'd say so. At least then she'd have an excuse to contact him, to tell him he's the father and has some say in all this. Especially with the way she feels about him, you know? And yet she doesn't … maybe she *is* telling the truth."

"Oh, Ted, don't you start in with this nonsense. You can't believe her for a minute! She was with that boy every blessed day. They were probably fooling around and he got too close to her. This whole story about being raped then saved by an angel so she can't remember a thing is next to impossible, Ted. She's just protecting that boy. I'm so glad we got her out of that city when we did!"

"But, it doesn't make any sense, Edi—"

"In any case," Edith lowered her voice, "perhaps it's a good thing she denies Henry's the father."

"What do you mean?" Ted asked, bewildered. Four drinks and he was having trouble following his wife's train of thought.

"Well, look at it this way, if she won't tell us who the father is, we don't have to search him out or concern ourselves with him at all. And she's far too young to raise a child on her own. That leaves two options: abortion or adoption."

"My God," Ted set down the glass and put his head in his hands, "What's happening to my little girl? How could her life get so complicated so quickly? These damn moves of mine have been so hard on this family."

Edith's tone grew hard and brittle once again. "This isn't *your* fault, Ted. Jenny should have known better. Always so lively, so full of life, always so ready to try everything out. Well, it finally caught up with her."

He looked up. "Now, Edith, that's not fair. Her liveliness and—and sparkle are why I love her so much. But she just hasn't been herself since she left Regina. She's hurting, and I think we've only added to that hurt by destroying the letters she gave me to send … and destroying the letters that boy sent, too." Ted lifted his glass and took a final swallow.

"Ted," she said, and the word was a shard of ice, "I'm not going there anymore. It's done. We have a much bigger problem to deal with now."

DR. BRECK SET UP an appointment for Jenny to see a psychologist. Jenny, already so despondent over the loss of her boyfriend, and now carrying the child of a boy who had forced himself on her, could easily have compounded her dilemma by slipping into seductive thoughts of suicide. Yet something within her, perhaps her spirit for life, came to her aid.

She knew the baby in her womb was already developing, was already establishing its identity. The more she thought about it and felt its shape, the more her maternal instinct emerged. She began to love the child, sweet and innocent. How could she possibly abort it or reject it? It wasn't the baby's fault. This child hadn't asked to come into the world. And with each of her letters to Henry going unanswered, she knew all too well what it was to be unwanted. She couldn't do that to a baby. Her baby.

In the end, after counselling, and repeated and heated discussions with her parents, they all agreed that if she wanted to give birth to the child, then it was best to give the baby up for adoption. Jenny had only one stipulation: whoever adopted her child must agree to the names she had selected—Henry, if it was a boy and Camilla, if it was a girl.

In all the heartache and emotional turmoil, three small things were in her favour: the baby was small and didn't show very much, even by the end of February—February was a cold month and Jenny could easily conceal her pregnancy under heavy winter sweaters; and, since the night she'd discovered she was pregnant, she hadn't suffered any morning sickness and so hadn't had to miss school.

The Sarskys decided to keep Jenny's pregnancy a secret, even from the school. The fewer people who knew about it, the better. When Jenny could no longer conceal her condition under winter apparel, her parents would simply tell the school she had mononucleosis and needed to stay home. Dr. Breck had agreed to write a letter indicating Jenny was not well and required home care and rest. Ted would pick up her homework every day on his way home from work.

Devastated, deprived of Henry and now completely dependent on the wishes of her parents, Jenny didn't confide in any of her new friends. She felt more alone than ever.

She yearned for Henry now even more than before. Her heart broke a little more with every day that passed with no letter. The support of her parents wasn't the same as having Henry's love. *Oh, if only the child was Henry's.* If only Henry had made love to her, she would keep the baby and raise it.

Jenny thought about phoning Henry and telling him. But what would he think of her? She been dirtied, sullied by someone whose name she couldn't even remember. Perhaps that was why Henry didn't write. Maybe he'd heard that guy had had sex with her that night and was disgusted with her. And now that she had a baby ... another man's baby ... surely that would scare him off. The more Jenny thought about it all, the stronger her conviction that Henry probably wanted out of their relationship.

Deep down, however, she knew it wasn't true. Henry still loved her. She knew it. But the only one she could tell, the only one she could cry her shattered feelings to, was her angel.

CHAPTER THIRTY-TWO

PEOPLE WHO ARE NOT FROM THE PRAIRIES don't know what cold is. February passed in a deep freeze and it looked like March would be just as cold. Each day seemed more frigid than the last. Thirty below, and with the wind chill, it was almost sixty degrees below zero. Spit froze before it hit the ground, and the snow was so frozen and packed that it squeaked when Henry walked on it. No car engines roared to life, they just laboured and groaned. How cars even started and moved through the glacial temperatures was a mystery to Henry. An Arctic cold front had swept down from the north to settle over the prairie provinces and it showed no signs of moving on.

"Make sure you wrap a scarf around your face, Henry," his mother hollered from the kitchen. "Skin freezes in less than thirty seconds."

"Yeah, I did," Henry called back, his words muffled by wool.

"They should close the schools when it gets so cold," Mary said as she walked out into the hallway.

"I'm all for that," her son replied.

Henry wore long underwear, winter boots, three sweaters, a toque, deerskin mitts lined with sheep's wool and, at his mother's insistence, a scarf wrapped twice around his face. He'd worn the same thing for the last six weeks to survive the walk to and from Balfour.

"Well, see you after school, Mom."

"'Bye, hon, have a nice day," his mom replied, ready to close the door behind him.

As Henry walked up Broder Street towards College Avenue, he passed Jenny's old house. An elderly farm couple had bought it about two months after the Sarskys had left for Ottawa. They were nice, but he wished with all his heart that Jenny still lived there.

Over ten weeks had passed since he'd sent his last letter to Jenny and still there had not been one word. Every day he rushed home to look at the table in the hallway where his mom usually put the incoming mail; each day he had to swallow his disappointment.

He wanted to tell his mom and Mr. Engelmann he'd written Jenny at Christmas but was too afraid to admit he'd done such a foolish thing. And he was reluctant to admit he'd broken his promise to Mr. Engelmann: if no reply came after he sent that box of letters, he was supposed to accept the fact that it was over and get on with his life. But with all those Bing Crosby songs at Christmastime, he had felt compelled to try one final time. He had been so sure that his guardian angel had prompted him to send off another letter … and finding that pewter angel had seemed like a miracle at the time. But she hadn't replied.

Had he imagined the whole thing?

Henry kicked at the snow and cursed the cold as he walked along, anything to expel the hard knot of anger growing inside. He knew what Mr. Engelmann would say to counter the negative thoughts he was entertaining but wasn't quite ready to let go of his pain.

God's ways are not our ways. His will for us may not be our will or what we want. God's time is not our time. "Yeah, well, then, when *is* God's time?" Henry muttered through his scarf, "when I'm dead and gone?" His heart ached for Jenny. "What good could possibly come from all this?"

Mr. Engelmann often said that if people trusted God, all things would turn out for the best. How could that be? Was God planning some big reunion? Henry kicked at the snow again. That was just false hope, he wasn't really accepting things and moving on. If some good came from it, fine. But it was just too painful to keep his hope alive.

Henry was surprised to realize he didn't feel as cold. The wind had abated somewhat, but it was more the heated debate churning through his mind that was keeping him warm. He could see his breath through his scarf before the exhaled air dissipated. Frost formed on his scarf so he looked like he was wearing a white beard. Spiky lines of hoarfrost clung to tree branches, which appeared brittle, ready to snap if touched. Yet the snow and frost made everything around appear like a fairyland, so pure, clean and white.

Henry took a deep breath of frigid air. It warmed a bit as it passed through the two layers of woolen scarf before entering his mouth and lungs. It still stung but it made him pay attention to where he was. Without realizing it, he had crossed College Avenue and was only another two blocks from school. The traffic wasn't that heavy, probably because a lot of cars hadn't started that morning and many people had decided to stay home.

As Henry neared the school, he studied the other students rushing towards Balfour. Everyone was all bundled up, concern over what they looked like finally taking a back seat to keeping warm.

Although Henry's love life was still in turmoil, everything else was in complete control and moving ahead better than he'd expected. He was a straight "A" student. He was popular enough with his classmates, although he didn't go out of his way to be. He was still sort of friends with Timmy and corresponded with Gary, who Henry felt was still his best friend, every second week.

And ever since Henry had accepted his Phys. Ed. teacher's

challenge to work with Eddy, Henry found his anger towards him dissipating; there was a dramatic change in their relationship. That in particular, just as Mr. Neader had predicted, had made a huge difference in his life in other areas too.

Henry tried to like everyone and treat them with respect whether they were popular or not. He spoke his mind honestly when asked his opinion, and questioned and challenged issues he didn't understand or that didn't seem right. His friends respected his sincerity and knew he wasn't an attention-seeker. It was just how he was. Others saw him as a leader, consistent in his behaviour and choices made based on sound values.

One of the results of Henry's attitude was his election as a student rep. He enjoyed being on the student council and the fact that he had some say in making important changes within the school. Irony of ironies, Eddy Zeigler had nominated him. Henry smiled when he recalled the day he'd told Mr. Engelmann, who had smiled and nodded. "See, Henry, how the Lord will bring good out of even the worst circumstance!"

The blast of heat when he entered the school felt good on his face, though his cheeks burned and he suspected they might have frozen. Henry put his hands over his cheeks to help warm them as he headed upstairs towards his locker.

He was looking forward to second period: art. It was his favourite class. The art teacher, Mr. Victor, was an amateur artist and displayed his work at craft shows. He was explaining his thoughts behind his work as Henry entered the classroom later that morning. His landscapes had very little detail, usually a clear blue sky and a strip of landscape that changed in colour from one painting to the next. "I'm trying to reduce the prairie view to its basics: land and sky."

Mr. Victor had told Henry he had a lot of potential and always commented positively on Henry's drawing skills, colour sense and element placement in his paintings. He often told Henry that his artwork had good composition and captured the life of prairie people and land.

Henry liked the graphic arts part of the class too. He used

that time to design a logo for Mr. Engelmann's store. When Mr. Engelmann had last ordered brown paper bags, the salesman had said it didn't cost too much more to put a logo on them. Henry thought it would help advertise the store. They were already very busy and Mr. Engelmann hadn't been too sure he wanted to advertise his name on bags that would be just thrown away, but Henry had convinced him that keeping the store's name in people's minds was a good thing. If they needed anything, chances were they would come to Engelmann's rather than Safeway. In the end, Mr. Engelmann had agreed.

Henry was also working on coupons they could hand out to their customers and put in mailboxes. He had just finished a coupon the day before. It showed a picture of Mr. Engelmann's storefront on the upper left hand corner, with address and phone number, the products on sale listed in the middle and their slogan across the bottom: *Your neighbourhood grocery store, where customers are family with free delivery and service with a smile.* Henry had made a coupon in January, advertising products left over from Christmas. They had sold most of the items simply by reducing them by ten or fifteen cents. Most people liked a deal and were happy when they could save some money. It made them feel like smart shoppers.

The day passed very quickly and Eddy was waiting for him at his locker after the last class. Lately, they had become a force to be reckoned with in their basketball games. They anticipated each other's moves and were always in the right spot to receive a pass. Eddy's size had proved to be a great advantage, especially against taller players.

It was funny; the one thing Henry liked most about Eddy now was the cocky, brazen attitude he'd so despised last summer. Although Eddy had become a little more respectful of others, he always spoke his mind, never fearing that he might offend someone. He didn't live for approval, something Henry was guilty of all too often. Henry always knew where he stood with Eddy.

Eddy also had his share of admirers and never had a problem getting girls to go with him to school dances. Because of his height, it looked like the girls were dancing with their kid brother. But that didn't bother either Eddy or the girls. There was something about his swagger that attracted girls like flies, and when Henry thought about it, he realized it all came down to how Eddy saw himself.

Eddy had never considered his size to be a disadvantage, had never felt shy or that he wasn't good enough. His cocksure manner somehow wooed the girls—one girl in particular. The school was still buzzing about how Eddy had hired a florist to deliver a bouquet of flowers to Hilda Spooner in front of the school during lunch. The very next weekend, Hilda and Eddy went to a movie. Girls glared at Hilda with envy as she and Eddy strolled down the hallway holding hands. Heck, Henry envied Eddy the hand-holding too, and he had to push away thoughts of his walks with Jenny.

"Hi, Eddy," Henry said as he landed at his locker.

"Hey, Hank, how ya doing? Geez, did this day go fast."

"Yeah, I know what you mean. Are you heading home?"

"Yeah. Ready to face that cold?" Eddy said. "I hear the wind is down, which makes it a bit better."

"Wait up. I'll walk with you."

They walked down Winnipeg Street, talking about the previous Friday's basketball game. The conversation lagged when Eddy reached for a package of Black Cat cigarettes

"There's something I really need to know, Eddy," Henry finally said, shrinking further into the hood of his jacket. "I won't hold it against you. I just want to know the truth."

Eddy shook a cigarette out of the package a bit clumsily with his gloves, put it into his mouth then looked up. Their gazes met.

"I want it straight, Eddy."

Eddy pulled out a lighter and lit the cigarette. He inhaled deeply, and as the smoke streamed out of his mouth, he said, "Okay, Hank, whaddya want to know?"

"I want to know what really happened that night your friends took Jenny to the park. Did they really do it to her?"

Eddy sighed another stream of cigarette smoke into the

frosty afternoon. "Okay. Here's the way it went down. Pete said he did it to the blond chick, but John said that just as Pete was about to start, a car pulled up—which turned out to be you guys. John said he grabbed Pete and pulled him away and they took off. John didn't think Pete had enough time to do anything, but Pete says he did. Pete was pretty drunk that night, Hank," Eddy snorted. "Personally, I think it's all bull—big talk and nothing more." Eddy took another long drag of his cigarette. "And that's it, Hank." He coughed as the smoke and the cold air irritated his throat. He shrugged; there was nothing else to say about it— except …. After a long pause, he asked, "Did she … Jenny, did she tell you what happened?"

"Yeah, she said nothing happened. Her wrists and arm were sore from being dragged into the car, but that's about all she said—"

"Well, what are you worried about then?"

"Yeah …"

"Whatever happened to that chick, Hank?" Eddy asked. "I remember seeing you and her talking in the hallway last fall. She looked like she was crying."

"She moved away to Ottawa."

Henry was going to tell Eddy that he had written and written to her and hadn't heard from her since, that he missed her and loved her, but decided he really didn't want to get into it.

"Well, if she's gone, I'd just forget about it. Find someone else."

"Yeah, that's probably the best."

Henry changed the topic back to basketball.

When they reached the corner of Victoria and Winnipeg, Henry turned east towards Mr. Engelmann's store while Eddy continued on home. He'd sounded so sure that nothing had happened to Jenny, but Henry was still uncertain. What if Pete *had* done it? What if Jenny was even pregnant? If she was—he did some fast adding—she would probably have the baby around the beginning of June. He shook his head to rid it of those thoughts. *Don't be ridiculous.*

He was creating a problem out of nothing.

CHAPTER THIRTY-THREE

HENRY ENTERED THE STORE to hear Mr. Engelmann wishing a customer a happy birthday.

"So, forty-two years old today, Martha, and you look so good, much younger than your age."

"Why, thank you," the lady replied, a blush tinging her cheeks.

"And look, here is my business partner," Mr. Engelmann said, gesturing at Henry.

"Hi, Mr. Engelmann. Hello, Mrs. Guloff. Happy birthday!"

"Thank you, Henry; it's so nice that you all remember."

"Don't take your coat off, Henry," Mr. Engelmann said. "Deliveries?"

"Yes, yes, there are four—all in the same area, fortunately. I have them all ready for you to take."

Henry packed the bags in his delivery satchel and slung it across his shoulder. After reviewing the addresses and deciding the most efficient route, he set off.

When Henry returned and removed his heavy overcoat, his shirt was soaked with sweat. He was always amazed how hot he could get even when it was extremely cold out. He set to restocking the shelves.

"Where's Mrs. Schmidt today?"

"She was in helping me this morning but had to leave early."

Henry worked the rest of the hour stocking shelves in silence, then dressed in his winter gear and went outside to sweep away bits of snow and debris from the sidewalk. When he went back inside Mr. Engelmann was going through purchase orders.

Henry propped the broom by the front door. "Guess I'll be going home—oh! I almost forgot. I have the new coupons." He rushed over to his bag and pulled out coupons advertising soup, corn and meat specials.

Mr. Engelmann looked at one and nodded his head. "My, my, Henry, this is very good."

"I'll start delivering them tomorrow on my way home from school, and we can include them in the delivery packages. We can keep a few on the counter, too. Here's the bill for the cost of the paper from the school."

"Very good," Mr. Engelmann said, taking the invoice from Henry's outstretched hand. "What would I have ever done without you?"

"Thank you, Mr. Engelmann. And there's one more thing I thought of. You know the birthday calendar we have in the back?"

"Yes," replied Mr. Engelmann, raising his eyebrows.

"Well, there are a lot of people whose birthdays we don't know, who weren't on that petition."

Mr. Engelmann nodded. Henry handed him another set of pages he'd copied at school that day.

"This form asks for the customer's name, address, phone number and birthday. As an incentive to get customers to fill out the form, we could give them some kind of a prize ... maybe, oh, a hamper, using the wooden crate the grapes come in. When customers fill out the form, they put it into one of our empty candy jars, and at the end of the month we draw a winner. Mr. Victor said it was good business to get information about customers because it allows businesses to carry out promotions."

Mr. Engelmann was speechless. He stared at Henry, his jaw

almost dropping to the floor. Henry always liked that look because he knew Mr. Engelmann was happy.

"Henry," Mr. Engelmann finally said when he could talk, "just when I think you cannot come up with another idea to improve this business, you prove me wrong again and again. And yes, it is true, this would help us to get to know the birthdays of everyone who comes into the store."

"And look how happy it made Mrs. Guloff when we wished her happy birthday today," Henry replied. "Now, we'll be able to do the same for almost every customer we have. And I bet it will even bring us more customers."

Mr. Engelmann just shook his head again. "I will have Mrs. Schmidt make up a hamper tomorrow, and I can hardly wait to go up and tell Anna. She gets such joy from hearing your new ideas."

"Well, good night, Mr. Engelmann. See you tomorrow."

"Yes, good night, Henry."

WITHOUT THE WIND, the temperature outside seemed warmer. And without the clouds, the sky was full of thousands of tiny stars. Smoke billowed from virtually every chimney as people snuggled in their homes, trying to stay warm. Henry felt surprisingly good as he walked home. He resolved to try and put Jenny into the background of his life and concentrate on school, art, and his business venture with Mr. Engelmann. He walked with new assurance, daring the cold to just try and slow him down.

When Henry got home, the usual aroma of supper was missing. He almost wondered if he was in the right house. He passed the living room on his way to the kitchen and was shocked by what he saw. His mother sat in the corner chair with the parish priest beside her. It was difficult to see her fully with only the one lamp on. But it was clear she'd been crying—perhaps still was. Henry's first thought was that something had happened to his dad.

"What's wrong, Mom?"

She didn't or couldn't answer, only shook her head as the tears rolled.

Finally, Father Connelly said, "Henry, I have some sad news to tell you."

"Is my dad okay?"

"Yes, we believe he's okay," the priest answered.

"Is he hurt?"

"No."

"Well, what then? What's going on?"

"Your father has left Regina and gone somewhere. We think he might be on his way to Vancouver."

"Why would he go to Vancouver?"

"He left with one of the other employees," Father Connelly said.

"Well, when will he be back?" Henry didn't quite understand why this was such a big deal ... and why their priest was here.

"Henry," the man sighed, "you don't understand. It seems he's gone away with a female friend."

"But, why?"

Father Connelly hesitated a moment. "I hate to tell you this, but it sounds like your dad has been seeing a female employee at the plant, and they've now gone away together to Vancouver."

Henry heard what Father Connelly had said but couldn't believe his ears. He stared at the priest and then at his mother in total disbelief.

"My dad went away with another woman? Impossible! This can't be true. Mom, is this true?"

She didn't look up, but kept sobbing and nodded. Her expression confirmed the awful truth.

Henry stepped back, unable to comprehend that his dad—who went off to work every day, who fixed things around the house, who answered his questions, who sat at the kitchen table every night—was going out with another woman. He turned and kicked the nearest chair.

"This can't be true. Dad wouldn't do something like that."

Father Connelly tried to put his arm around Henry, but he thrust it off and stalked away to another corner, wanting to lash out at something else and not knowing what.

Henry tried to piece it all together. His dad *had* been quiet lately. He hardly spoke at the supper table and went to read the paper right after. He'd been going out more and more often for a beer or bowling with his buddies. Could he have been lying about that? Seeing a—a girlfriend instead?

In that moment Henry hated his dad. *Betrayer.* He didn't want to be near him ever again. He couldn't believe that his dad would do that to his mom. She always looked after him so well, was always there for him, totally faithful to him. Why would he do such a terrible thing? *There must be some explanation,* he quickly reasoned, trying to reassure himself. Like Father Connelly's attempt to soften the blow, Henry tried to cushion himself from the reality of this crisis. To delay experiencing the full impact of what this would do to mom and to him, to their family—or what once had been their family.

"Are you okay?" Father Connelly inquired softly after a while.

Is he serious? Tears of anger erupted in his eyes. "Where is he? I want to find him right this minute!"

"We don't know where he is," the priest answered calmly.

"Well, I want to know, right now. I want to tell him what a terrible man he is. I … I want to hit him."

It was obvious Father Connelly and his mother could see the rage in his eyes. Henry didn't care. He was glad they didn't try to console him. He only wanted to be alone.

It was just like when Jenny had left. His world of love, trust and happiness crumbled around him. One minute things were fine and the next they were gone, disintegrated. He didn't know how to handle this. Dads weren't supposed to leave. It felt like the walls were closing in around him. He needed to get out. He headed to the front door and opened it, wanting to run out and freeze these horrible feelings and thoughts. Then maybe as they slowly thawed, he would able to cope with them. Better yet, he'd like to go out and come back in and maybe none of this would've happened.

The cold air hit him hard.

"Where are you going?" Father Connelly asked. "You can't run from your feelings."

The cold pouring in provided Henry with a brief moment of relief, the way the storm had on the day Jenny left. He closed the front door with a force that was just short of a slam.

"Come. Sit down, Henry. Let's pray about it," Father Connelly suggested.

"I don't want to pray about it. I can't pray. I'm too upset."

"I understand," the priest said. "It's okay."

And that was the turning point.

Henry repeated Father Connelly's *I understand* over and over to himself, and with that he no longer felt the need to hit something. He walked back into the living room. His mom had dried her eyes but looked so lonely and hurt. He knew he should go over there and put his arms around her and console her as she had him when Jenny left, but he was so angry with his father, he couldn't feel compassion at that moment.

Finally, his mother said the words he so needed to hear.

"Everything will work out, Henry," she said, a kind of calm assurance in her voice. "I'm not sure how, but we'll be all right."

Henry tried to swallow the anger and tears welling inside him. He nodded his head as if to agree. Slowly he focused his attention on his mother's pain and how, in spite of everything, she was trying to bring order and peace back into their home.

He went over and put his arms around her.

"I love you, Mom," Henry said, and now the tears did come. "Dad made a huge mistake."

After a few more moments of tears, Mary wiped her face with the back of her hand and steadied herself. "We have had sorrows before and we dealt with them." She got up slowly. "I'll go wash and get some supper on for all of us."

"No, Mom! That's okay," Henry said. Father Connelly echoed Henry's protests, but his mother insisted.

"No, I'll fix something up. It will help me get my mind off all this."

Henry and Father couldn't argue with that and let her do the thing she had some control over.

In the dim light of the living room, Henry looked around. It all looked the same and yet his world had spun upside down. He still couldn't believe it. His dad. He recalled what his father had said to him on several occasions: *A man is only as good as his word. Always remember that.* The thought made him scoff with derision and his anger flooded back. *Yeah? Well you broke your word, your vows!*

He stared down at the carpet, not knowing what to think, not even *wanting* to think. He studied the pattern in the carpet, noticing how it repeated itself, how the many colours worked together somehow to create a harmonious whole. Why he would notice that now was beyond him.

Father Connelly stood there like one of the statues in his church, waiting for Henry to say something. Finally he asked, "How is school going?"

"Fine," Henry answered, shrugging.

Henry was glad when the priest didn't ask any more questions but headed into the kitchen. Henry didn't want people around, didn't want to talk to anyone. He didn't want to be concerned about how to react or what to say. It was distracting and awkward and uncomfortable. Perhaps Father Connelly understood and that was why he had left.

His mother made grilled cheese sandwiches and opened up two cans of Campbell's tomato soup. When Henry finally went into the kitchen, the soup was beginning to bubble. It didn't give off the same full aroma as his mom's homemade soup, but for the first time that evening, the house smelled like a home again.

"Please sit down, Henry, and have a bowl of soup and a sandwich," his mother suggested softly.. Although Henry was hungry, he found it almost disrespectful to eat. He should be crying, not eating; mourning, not biting into melted cheese. He had often thought the same thing at funerals. How could people bury a loved one, go back to the church hall and drink and eat? Somehow it just didn't seem right to him.

Father Connelly picked up a spoon and stirred his soup to cool it. Henry picked his spoon up too. His mother had sat down between them but couldn't bring herself to do anything. She just stared into the bowl and didn't say a word.

Father Connelly broke the silence. "I'll say grace." He made the sign of the cross and said a short blessing.

Henry didn't want to thank God for the food or for anything else. He was still mad at Him for not having received a letter from Jenny, and now for allowing this ... this tragedy to happen to their family.

Father Connelly ate half his sandwich and more than half a bowl of soup before he said, "I am so sorry, Mrs. Pederson." Henry saw his mother wince at the title and he wondered if she was still Mrs. Pederson if his dad no longer loved her. "You will have to excuse me. There's a service tonight, and I have to get ready for it."

"Of course, Father," his mother said. "Thank you so much for coming over. I don't know what I would have done without you."

"Glad that I could be of some help," he said. He got up and pushed his chair back. Then turning to Henry, he said, "Good night."

"Good night, Father."

The priest walked to the front hall closet, put on his overcoat, boots, black hat and black gloves.

"God bless you all," he said, making the sign of the cross to bless the entire house and those within. "I'll call you tomorrow, Mary." He turned and hunched his shoulders, bracing himself for the bitter cold outside.

Henry was relieved to see him go. He didn't like Father Connelly sitting in his dad's chair, eating his dad's supper. His *dad* should be here. Henry wanted to know where he was. He screamed the thought so loud in his mind that he looked up at his mom to see if she had heard him. Her back was to him at the sink. She had not sat down again. Her soup was untouched.

She turned on the water to fill up the sink. Henry rose and took his dirty dishes to her.

"Is there anything else I can do, Mom?"

"No, that's all right, Henry," she answered. "Why don't you go listen to the radio or read a book?"

Henry walked towards the living room and then stopped. He went back to the kitchen, picked up a towel and began drying the dishes.

They stood there silently for awhile, then Henry asked quietly, "Why do you think dad did this?"

Henry's mom thought for a long moment, then sighed. "I really don't know, Henry, and perhaps even your father doesn't know. Sometimes the grass looks greener on the other side of the fence. And maybe he just wanted to find some way to get out of it all."

"What do you mean, Mom?"

"Well, he doesn't like his job very much, and he was complaining about how cold the plant has been lately. Maybe he just wanted to get away from it all. Go to a warmer climate and start over."

"But, what about us? What about you? Why not take you instead of that … that … other girl?"

"I can't answer that, Henry. I thought things were okay."

"How can you be so calm about it, Mom? I'm so angry I just want to hurt him as much as he's hurt us!"

His mother dried her hands on her apron. Without turning to Henry or looking at him, she put her arm around his shoulder.

"I feel angry and hurt, too. That's just the way life is sometimes, but things will work out. We still have each other." She patted his shoulder and pulled him towards her for a brief moment. "Thanks for helping me, Henry."

She turned, then went into the living room and turned on the radio before picking up a magazine, settling with it in her usual spot in the corner of the couch.

Henry followed, but stopped at the living room entrance. He watched his mom sitting under the tall lamp stand, pretending to read, pretending everything was normal, pretending her heart hadn't just been cut out of her. His heart went out to her. He wanted to say a prayer for her but he was still fuming at God.

Henry figured his mom needed to be alone and didn't need the extra burden of having to put on a strong front for his sake. He couldn't take much more himself.

"I think I'll go to my room and read for awhile. I have some homework to do, too. Do you need anything, Mom?"

"No, go ahead, Henry. That's a good idea. Try to get some sleep."

"Good night, Mom."

Henry made a valiant effort to concentrate on his homework but gave up and tossed himself on the bed. He grabbed his pillow and buried his head in it, trying to squeeze out the turmoil. He lay there for the longest time and eventually drifted off to sleep. He awoke a few hours later, cold from not having slept beneath the covers. The clock on the end table showed three-thirty. He got up and tiptoed to the bathroom. As he passed his parents' bedroom, he heard his mom. He stopped and listened. She was sobbing quietly. Tears immediately came to his eyes.

He went back to his room and this time snuggled under the covers, hoping the warmth would dispel both the cold outside and the cold in his heart. He tried to get back to sleep, but the idea of his mom lying there in bed without his dad beside her haunted him. His father was far away, sleeping with another woman.

Henry wished it were morning, so he could get up and do something to get his mind off it all. Not knowing what else to do, he started to pray for his Mom, for Jenny, for his Dad.

He decided to give God one more chance.

Chapter Thirty-Four

Henry had a terrible time concentrating at school the next morning, and by lunchtime he had such a headache that he went to the nurse's office and asked for a note to be excused. When he got home, his Aunt Darlene was there. His mom and Darlene were in the living room, reading a booklet.

"Why are you home from school?" his mother asked.

"Oh, I just have such a headache I can't concentrate on my classes at all. I saw the school nurse, and she excused me for the day."

"I see," his mother said. "Well, I haven't gotten lunch ready yet. Do you want me to make something?"

"Oh no, I'll make myself a sandwich and have a glass of milk when I'm ready." Henry walked into the living room. "What are you reading?"

His mother and Aunt Darlene looked at each other.

"Well, Henry," Aunt Darlene started, "I brought this novena prayer over for your mom. If you say this prayer for nine days in a row, followed by a Hail Mary and an Our Father, St. Francis will intercede for you and have God answer your prayers."

Henry looked at his aunt and then at his mom, not knowing

what to say. He still was upset with God for allowing this to happen in the first place, and now they were praying for some saint to ask God to end it. It just didn't sit right with him.

His mother was a woman of strong faith; she prayed all the time. She looked up at him with plaintive eyes and her words were soft. "I'd really like to try this, Henry."

"It's a good idea, Henry," Aunt Darlene added. "Prayers are answered all the time if the whole family prays together."

"So what are we going to pray for, that he comes back?" Henry asked.

"Yes, that's right," Aunt Darlene answered. "That he comes back, that he's sorry for what he did, that he gets his job back, and that we become a family again."

Henry thought about it. How could they become a family again after what his dad had done? He wasn't even sure he wanted his dad back at that moment. He looked at his mom. She was so lonely, and she had so much hope in her eyes. Maybe things could be reversed and their home life restored.

"Are you sure you want to do this, Mom?" he asked.

"Yes," she said, and a tear trickled down her cheek.

That decided it. "Okay, Mom, let's try."

"Well, we can start right now," Aunt Darlene said, trying to ocize the moment. She knelt in front of the couch. His mom slid off her chair and knelt beside Aunt Darlene, and reluctantly Henry joined them, resting his arms on the seat cushion of the sofa.

After a brief silence to foster a prayerful state, Aunt Darlene opened the booklet, made the sign of the cross, then read the prayer:

Father St. Francis, remember me and all your people, who are surrounded by so many dangers and difficulties. Help me to follow in your footsteps, even if it is from a great distance. Give me strength, that I may resist all evil. Purify me, that I may shine forth Christ. Cheer me in the Lord, that I may be happy. Pray and intercede for me in my intentions to bring back Bill and re-

store this family perfectly and better than it was before, with com-
plete trust and commitment to each other.

Pray, too, St. Francis, that God's spirit and grace may descend
upon me: that I may have the true humility you had; that I may
be filled with the charity with which you always loved Christ cru-
cified, who with the Father and the Holy Spirit lives and reigns,
world without end. Amen.

Aunt Darlene followed the prayer to St. Francis with an Our Father and a Hail Mary, then concluded with a Glory Be for good measure.

After she finished, she crossed herself, and Henry and his mom did the same. "We are to say this prayer for nine consecutive days, and on the ninth day, our prayer will be answered," Aunt Darlene said. "I'll come over every evening, and we will say the prayer together right after supper since everyone will be home at that time."

"Oh, that's so good of you, Darlene," Mary said, her eyes shiny. After a short pause, she composed herself and added, "I'll make us some coffee. Want a sandwich, Henry?"

Henry wasn't hungry but thought that maybe it would give his mom something else to think about, so he replied, "Sure, that would be great, Mom."

As Aunt Darlene and Henry sat at the table and waited for the meal, Henry was tempted to ask his aunt why she thought his dad would do such a thing, but changed his mind. They needed to talk about something else, the weather, her job or his Uncle Ron, but before he could decide on a topic, the sandwiches were ready.

"Is it okay if I go to the grocery store this afternoon?" Henry asked.

"I thought you had a headache and needed to go to bed?"

"Well, going to work is different than having to concentrate on math. It doesn't require thinking, if you know what I mean."

Mary looked at him and smiled for the first time in two days. "Sure, go ahead."

WHEN HENRY GOT TO THE STORE, it only took one look from Mr. Engelmann to know something wasn't right. When Henry did not go to school, something was amiss. Mr. Engelmann stood directly in front of Henry, studying him for a moment.

"What's troubling you, Henry?"

Henry didn't know how to say it. He was ashamed and embarrassed. He knew he had to tell Mr. Engelmann, wanted to tell him, in fact, but he was afraid. This went right to the core of his family and Henry wanted Mr. Engelmann to think he came from a good family, not one that ….

"My dad left with another woman, Mr. Engelmann," Henry said, exposing the whole truth in one fell swoop. Henry tried to gauge his boss's reaction and wondered what he would say.

Mr. Engelmann gazed at Henry, nodding as if he were scanning Henry's face and mind at the same time, reading every nuance. Finally, he said, "How is your mother, Henry?"

Henry was surprised by the question. He had expected Mr. Engelmann to ask how *he* was doing. "Oh, she … she's …" He was going to say *fine*, but that would be lying. "She's very hurt and upset."

"That is a sad thing to hear. It's very hard to understand how such a terrible thing can happen to a family." Henry nodded as Mr. Engelmann continued. "Unfortunately, these things can and do happen, even in the best of families." Then he added, "Your dad made a mistake, yes, Henry?"

"Yes!" Henry blurted. "I'd like to hit him!"

"Yes, yes, of course," Mr. Engelmann said. "It makes me upset just to hear it. Well, Henry, how do we deal with such a terrible thing happening to a family?"

"I don't know *what* to do! All I can think of is how mad I am at him. That I want to hit him, hurt him like he hurt Mom …"

"And you, too," Mr. Engelmann added.

"Yeah! Yeah, and me, too."

"I understand how painful this must be for you."

"Yeah, it is, Mr. Engelmann."

Mr. Engelmann was silent for a moment. Not once did he

tell Henry not to feel that way or make him feel defensive or guilty. Mr. Engelmann accepted where he was at and understood how he felt.

"Your dad made a mistake, we agree. But it's important to separate what he did from who he is as a person."

That was not at all what Henry had expected to hear.

"What do you mean?" he asked, puzzled.

"I met your dad, and from the way you've talked about him over the past several months, he is a good man." When Henry took a breath to interrupt, Mr. Engelmann continued, "But circumstances led him to do something that wasn't good. What I am saying, Henry, is that we must always try to separate what a person does from the person as a whole.

"If you look over your life, Henry, are there times when you did things or said things that may not have been right or true? To lie is wrong, but to condemn you as a person would not be the right thing to do, either. You are right to be upset with your father for what he has done but you can still love him—just like I can forgive you for perhaps lying in your past because I know you are a very good young man who maybe made a mistake in the journey of life.

"It's easy to judge or condemn, but if you were in the same set of circumstances, you might very well have done the same thing."

"Never!" Henry exploded, "I would never have done that to my mom or … my wife, rather."

"Well, that may very well be true, Henry, but all I am saying is for you to be open to the possibility that you might have done the same thing in similar circumstances. Perhaps, someday, your dad may explain to you why he did what he did. The moment of weakness, the temptation—"

"If you're saying I should forgive him, forget it … I can't."

"I understand, Henry. This is not an easy thing to deal with. There are many people involved here, many things to try and understand and sort out, but let's see what we can do." Mr. Engelmann came over to Henry and put his arm around him. "Let's go make some hot chocolate and talk a little more."

Both of them were thankful no one was in the store. It was too cold to go out back and sit on the old crate in their private classroom. So they headed back to the storeroom where Anna had set up a little coffee station months earlier.

"Hard working men need to take a break sometimes," she had said.

Mr. Engelmann turned on one of the burners of the two-element stove that sat on top of an old table. Beside the stove was a coffee pot and a teakettle, which was always filled with fresh water. Coffee mugs lay inverted on a clean dishtowel in front of it, and between the mugs and stove were all the usual fixings: tea, sugar, chocolate and coffee. Mr. Engelmann took two large mugs and set them upright, then reached for the tin of chocolate, scooping a couple of heaping spoonfuls of chocolate into each mug before putting the teakettle onto the now red-hot burner.

While they waited for the water to boil, Henry started the conversation again. "How do you forgive when you feel so much anger and resentment towards people close to you? I know I was able to let go of my anger towards Eddy, but this is different. I'm upset with my dad, and Jenny's parents, too. I think they're the reason Jenny hasn't written and why we're still apart. And now with my dad leaving, I feel like I don't even want to live anymore. It's not worth it for all this pain!"

Mr. Engelmann thought over his next words. "There are times in our lives when everything crashes in, when things completely overwhelm us. That's why it is so important, especially in such times, that we have each other, to have someone we trust and can share our deepest thoughts and emotions with, someone who understands and can help us carry the burden."

Henry nodded.

"And never forget, too," Mr. Engelmann added, "that we must turn to God for help as well. He says, 'Come unto me all you that labour and are heavy laden, and I will give you rest.' My biggest trial was to forgive the Nazis after they killed Anna's parents, and my sister and brother. For years Anna and I lived in hate and anger for what they did to our loved ones. And the more we hated, the more trapped we were in our pain, our unforgiveness.

"We prayed for release and to be delivered from our bondage and our hate. We knew deep down that this was the only way to be free and to live again. In a moment of anguish and despair, Anna and I cried out for God's help to deliver us. And our prayers were heard and answered. Since that day, Anna and I have known only peace and the true meaning of love."

Henry stared at Mr. Engelmann, trying to absorb his meaning.

"The Nazis, too, are children of God. I abhor what they did, but I love their being as much as I love you. We must always separate the person from their action. Love is what connects us all. You, me and everyone and everything in the world was made by God out of love and *for* love. Everything that God created is good."

"Well then, what happens?" Henry wanted to know. "Why do people do such cruel and hurtful things?"

"God gave us a free will, Henry. He didn't want to make us robots, one dimensional. He made us so we are free to choose His love or reject it. And the choices and decisions we make are based on our experiences, our interactions with others, what we have learned and what we are led to believe. It's complicated, but in the end, each moment we live is based on what happened before. And it is on that basis that we make decisions.

"We make millions of decisions and choices in a lifetime. That is why it is so important to develop sound values to live by. Honesty, kindness, truthfulness and forgiveness are important values and principles to live by. The more we adopt and ingrain such values into our lives, the easier it is to make the right choices. As we grow, we learn which decisions are good and which are not good for us. Which decisions help our Lord to make the world better and which hinder Him.

"Most of these learning experiences are not too harmful; most of the little bad decisions we can overlook. Unfortunately, Henry, some decisions we make are so big that we can't overlook it or forgive so easily. Your dad made such a choice. In a moment of weakness, his human frailty took over, and he made a decision that was not good for him or for those around him."

Before Henry could yell, "No it wasn't!" Mr. Engelmann said, "He succumbed to temptation, Henry. We don't know the circumstances that led him to make this decision. It is easy to judge others, but unless you walk in their footsteps and have the life experiences they had up to the time that caused them to choose as they did, we cannot judge.

"Even the cruelty of the Nazis, as terrible as they were, was a result of the experiences they had and beliefs they were taught up to that time. In their hearts they believed they were doing the right thing. It's difficult to understand and accept, Henry, but we must always try to separate the person from his actions and leave judgment of others up to God."

"But people have to be punished for the wrongs that they do, otherwise it's just not fair!"

"Yes, certain actions cannot be allowed. That is why we have courts and jails. But what I am trying to say, Henry, is that even when people do wrong or terrible things, they are still children of God. It is the *decision* that led to the bad action that is wrong, but because God loves each person, it is the *person* that we must always love and be ready to forgive. In short, Henry, we hate the sin, but love the sinner."

Mr. Engelmann looked at him earnestly and Henry thought he was finally beginning to understand. Mr. Engelmann pressed on.

"Have you always done the right thing, Henry?" Before Henry could answer, Mr. Engelmann made it even more specific. "Have you ever taken something that wasn't yours or said something that wasn't true?"

"Yes," he nodded, contrite.

"Well, they may be little things, Henry, but they, too, were wrong and not based upon right values of truth and honesty, yes?" He looked at Henry.

Henry nodded again.

"Well, if I know you did wrong, should I then see you as a bad person through and through, and hold it against you forever? Should I conclude that if you stole once, you are a thief forever and I should never trust or forgive you?"

"But," Henry protested, "what my dad did was really bad. It's a *big* mistake."

"Ah, that's right, Henry. It is just as you said, a big mistake." Henry was glad Mr. Engelmann agreed with him, but then the older man continued, "And a big mistake requires an even bigger amount of forgiveness."

That one-two punch caught Henry off guard. He could no longer justify his feelings. He'd been so righteous in his hate and anger but now he just didn't know anymore.

"Hate, unforgiveness, resentment," Mr. Engelmann went on, "holds others as well as ourselves in bondage, Henry. What about that boy, Eddy Zeigler? Look how he hurt you and Jenny. Just the other day you told me what a good friend he is becoming, and it's all because you let go of the anger and forgave him."

"Yeah, okay, but my dad is so much closer to me than Eddy. I never expected my dad to hurt Mom and me ..."

"Yes, when family hurts us, it is harder at times to forgive because we are closer and expect more from each other. In the end, though, it still comes down to forgiveness. We must separate the act from the person."

Mr. Engelmann paused for a moment and nodded before clarifying further. "The person who hurts us knows and feels our unwillingness to forgive, and therefore can't let go of it. In the same way, we also hurt ourselves for the sake of getting even and trying to make others pay for their mistakes and for hurting us.

"If you hadn't forgiven Eddy, you would still be hurting. You would still be a victim of your own unforgiveness. And Eddy, too, sensing your anger, would also be in bondage and unable to freely relate to you the way he does now. And it will be the same with your dad.

"Your hope lies in the love and forgiveness that unlocks the spirit and allows us to do the right thing. We must do what Jesus taught us: love our neighbour as ourselves. He showed us the way, the truth and the light. He forgave, even as they nailed him to the cross."

The whistling blast of the teakettle startled them both. They'd been so absorbed in their talk they had forgotten all about the hot chocolate.

"Ah, finally!" Mr. Engelmann turned off the stove, picked up the teakettle with a thick cloth pad and poured two steaming cups of hot chocolate. As Henry sipped the soothing drink, Mr. Engelmann said, "The big thing about the choice your dad made, Henry, is that it violated his commitment to your mom and to you."

"Yeah! Yeah, that's right. What about that?" And before Mr. Engelmann could answer, Henry went on, "He always told me a man is only as good as his word. How can I ever trust him again?"

"Well, your trust in your father has been put in jeopardy and that's equally as important as forgiveness. The two are very much connected. If your dad comes back, how will you know he won't do it again? How do you re-establish faith in him?"

Henry looked at Mr. Engelmann, anxious for the answer.

"Once again, Henry, it must start with forgiveness. You wipe the slate clean and start over, building up love and trust day by day. Look at the alternative. Look at how angry you feel now. You want to hit him, hurt him and get even. With such thoughts and feelings, how can you even begin to think about trust or love unless you forgive? If you don't, Henry, you will suffer along with your dad and your mom, the spirit of the family trapped in a web of anger and unforgiveness. This is one of the most important lessons in life, Henry. If you want peace, health, joy and happiness, then foster a spirit of forgiveness in your heart; it will give you all this and much more."

Mr. Engelmann's words were beginning to sink in. Henry did feel trapped, but sensed his anger loosening its hold on him. In a way it was like what he had done with Eddy. If he hadn't risen above their conflict, they would still be at odds with each other.

"Henry, we were meant to love. Only in the spirit of love can we grow. Love demands forgiveness or it is not love. Love is patient, kind, honest, truthful, forgiving and on and on, Henry. In turn we must constantly make choices based on those values. It's easy to make hard decisions when they are based on sound values."

At first Henry didn't quite get it, but the more he thought about it, the more he understood. If he really believed in his heart that it was important to be honest, truthful, forgiving and kind, and if he really accepted those values as the basis of his life, he could forgive his dad for what he had done. It was just like that time he'd almost made love with Jenny or stolen the six quarters that the well-dressed man had left behind when he'd bought those three packages of cigarettes. This was just another decision—only bigger and harder to make.

Henry looked up at Mr. Engelmann. He was such a wise man, kind and understanding. Henry hoped he could be like him some day.

"Anna and I are committed to each other. When we were married, we made a vow to love and to honour each other in sickness and in health until death do us part. And so it must be. In our lives we, too, have quarrelled. We, too, have been angry with one another—but at the end of each day as the sun goes down, so do our differences and anger. It disappears into the night, and with the sunrise, as the sun comes up to start a new day, so too does our marriage and our love for each other.

"As I said, in a moment of weakness fueled by circumstances, your father broke his commitment to his wife and to you, and now you and your mother face the challenge of forgiving and building up trust once again. It's up to you, Henry, to choose this minute. What do you want to do? Continue along the path of hurt, hate and anger? Or choose to forgive, to be an example to your mom, to lead your family out of this darkness?

"Even though you are much younger than your parents, you

can play a very important role in healing your family, whether your dad comes back or not. Parents are also weak and frail. They need help and guidance just like their children. It is up to you, Henry."

At that precise moment the phone rang. After Mr. Engelmann hung up, Henry looked at him.

"Thank you," Henry said, and he meant it. "I'll try."

"You have a good heart, Henry. I know you will do the right thing."

Mr. Engelmann set his empty mug on the counter, walked back to Henry, and wrapped his arms around him. Henry hugged back. As he did, his cup tilted and the little bit of hot chocolate remaining in the mug spilled onto the floor, barely missing the back of Mr. Engelmann's trousers. They looked down at the puddle and chuckled.

CHAPTER THIRTY-FIVE

THE COLD WEATHER CONTINUED until the middle of March and Jenny was still able to hide her pregnancy under bulky winter sweaters. She could have stayed in school longer, but she grew tired more easily, and so the Sarskys decided it was time for Dr. Breck to send his letter to the school.

Now that Jenny was home and had more time on her hands, she thought more and more about Henry and the baby. In bed at night, she was becoming attached to the baby, caressed her growing belly, thinking of Henry and her love for him. Day after day that love expanded to include her unborn child, and though the baby wasn't Henry's, she could no longer see how she could give it up for adoption. It seemed so cold. She knew, too, that the moment the infant was born, it would be immediately removed from the delivery room. She would not be allowed to see or hold her baby. *My baby.* She'd been told it was best for birth mothers to have no attachment or memory.

It seemed so harsh. Jenny wanted to see and hold the child she was carrying, for the baby to feel, at least once, that it was loved. Just like she knew Henry had loved her. Each kick and movement inside her solidified her connection to the unborn babe. She tracked its shifts and pushings with her hand on her bare skin, trying to touch it, to visualize it somehow. What it might look like. Whether it was a boy or a girl. Oh, she just had to see her baby, hold her child. It was hers. Tears came to Jenny's eyes just thinking about it.

If only it was Henry's baby, then she would have something to hold onto, something that would overshadow the horrible experience of that night. She imagined calling Henry to tell him they had a baby. It would be worrying, but joyful, too. He would come to her. They would make plans for the future, and she wouldn't have to give the baby away.

But there was no Henry, no letters. If only he would write and give her some hint that he still loved her. With each passing day, that hope had faded. Henry was gone and soon the child she loved within her would be gone as well.

At one point, Jenny had thought of writing her feelings about the baby and the pregnancy in her diary, but she just couldn't. The whole thing was so tangled and tortured she didn't want to see it in black and white. Or be reminded of what had happened. Instead she wrote letters to Henry, knowing she would never send them, telling him of the baby and how she felt it move under her heart. That she wished it would be a boy so she could name him Henry.

She wrote three letters. It seemed to help for awhile, but the very next week, in a fit of hopeless despair, Jenny tore them up and sobbed.

Jenny was alone one evening while her mother and father were in the city at the premiere of a new play. The quietness of the large house only enhanced her loneliness. *Oh, Henry,* she thought, and smiled sadly at the nickname. She missed him and wanted to talk to him so badly, to tell him what had happened—she wanted to phone him. She'd thought of calling lots of times before, but her mother had always told her the long distance charges were outrageous. *If only Mom understood how much I need to talk to him!* Jenny thought. And yet, she carried another man's baby. Why would he still want to talk to her, let alone care about her or her child? *But, oh, even just to hear his voice ...!*

Out of this anguish came a new thought. She didn't have to *talk* to him; she could phone station-to-station and take a chance that he'd answer. If he didn't, she would simply hang up. At least then she could hear his voice. She missed him so much.

Spurred on by loneliness, Jenny did the unthinkable. She picked up the phone and dialed the operator. The operator in Saskatchewan gave Jenny the number for Pederson on Broder Street. "Is this call station-to-station or person-to-person?"

Jenny paused for a long moment. She didn't want to say who was calling. She just wanted to hear Henry's voice.

"Station-to-station," Jenny replied, hoping against hope he would answer the phone. The operator dialed the Pederson's number. Jenny's heart pounded in her throat as she listened to the phone ring in Henry's house. After the second ring a male voice answered. Henry. His voice sounded a bit lower ...

"Hello?"

Tears slid down Jenny's face as she listened with all her heart to Henry's voice. She silently sent her love and yearning to him across the miles. She wanted to scream into the phone that it was her and that she loved him and that she wanted him to come to her...

"Is anyone there?" Henry thought he heard someone crying. He listened for another moment and then slowly hung up the phone.

"No! Wait!" Jenny yelled as she heard the click of the receiver. Hearing Henry's voice had sent her spirits soaring. Her eyes sparkled through her tears. For the first time in months, she finally had something to hold onto. She gripped the receiver, unable to hang up. It had been so good to hear him. She should have talked to him, told him about her pregnancy. Surely he would understand. But it was not his child. Would it be fair to ask him to accept the child along with her?

It was all too much to think about.

AFTER HENRY HUNG UP, he returned to the sofa and picked up the magazine he'd been reading. *That was a strange call.* Suddenly, an indescribable feeling swept through him. He got up and went to the phone again, picking up the receiver. There was no dial tone. The call hadn't been disconnected.

Again he heard sobbing.

"Hello? Who is this?"

HENRY'S VOICE STARTLED HER. Panicked, she lowered her voice, trying to disguise it, "Oh, I—I have the wrong number. Sorry to trouble you."

"It's no trouble at all. What number were you calling?"

Jenny looked at the number she had written down on the pad. She repeated it but changed the last digit.

"Yes, that's almost our number," Henry chuckled, "but you're out by one."

"Oh, I'm so sorry for troubling you," Jenny said again, fumbling for what else to say.

"Well, have a good evening," Henry offered, trying to end the call on a cheerier note.

"Yes, good night." Jenny almost added, "Henry."

"What was that all that about?" Henry's mom asked..

"I don't know. At first I thought it was some kid fooling around on the phone. I heard crying and hung up. Then, for some reason or other, I picked up the phone again, and there was a lady on the line, crying. She must have still been on the phone."

"Who was it?"

"I don't know. She seemed so unhappy. I wish I could have helped her."

Mary's expression reflected the puzzlement on his own face.

When Henry sat back down on the sofa, he couldn't get the sound of the lady's voice out of his mind. For a moment it had sounded like ... *Oh, that's absurd*, he finally told himself. She would have said who she was. But the thought gnawed at him. Henry now wished he had asked straight out, "Is this Jenny?" With that, Henry rushed to the phone. This time there was only a dial tone.

AFTER JENNY HUNG UP, she went into the living room, tossed herself on the couch, and cried. She felt so trapped, so confused and frustrated, so in love and unable to express her multitude of feelings.

Surely Henry would understand if she told him she was pregnant. Jenny just knew that he loved her. But if that were so, why hadn't he written? The same answer echoed through her mind— he had heard that she had been raped that night in the park and was no longer interested in her. *But if he really loves me, it shouldn't matter.*

"Oh, what should I do?" Jenny cried out loud. She had to talk to someone. She would share it all with her mother in the morning. Her mom would help her sort things out and tell her what to do. Besides, her parents were going to know she had phoned Regina when they got the telephone bill at the end of the month, anyway.

When her mom and dad arrived home shortly after midnight, they found Jenny asleep on the couch, her head resting on a tear-soaked cushion.

WHEN JENNY GOT UP in the morning, her mother was in the kitchen having a coffee. Her father had already gone to work. She knew it would likely upset her mother to talk about Henry, but Jenny couldn't help that. Jenny slowly built up her courage, and told her mother what she had done. Edith turned pale.

"You did what?!"

"I phoned him, but I didn't say anything. I couldn't. I just wanted to hear his voice. I miss him so much, Mom. I need to talk to him, so badly. Do you think it's okay to call him again?"

EDITH SARSKY GAZED into her daughter's eyes. For the first time, she glimpsed what Ted saw all the time: how much Jenny loved and missed Henry. It lasted for only a second. Long enough for her to see all the problems and complications that would result if she wavered from her decision.

If Henry got involved in all this, they would have to deal with the letters that Ted had destroyed. If he and Jenny got back together, they might decide to keep the baby and then what? Would Henry quit school? Would Jenny stay home and raise a child? No. Impossible. And besides, Jenny was just lonely and reaching out for someone, and Edith was certain that the two of them would get over it and move on. They were just kids, for God's sake. It was only puppy love.

"Oh, Jenny," Edith said, patting her daughter's hand. "I know how much you miss Henry, but you two are so young. Look how complicated your life is already. It would be unfair to ask Henry to share this responsibility, to carry such a burden at his age."

"Yeah, Mom, I thought of that, too, last night. That's why I didn't say anything to him."

"See, even you realize what's best. No, Jenny, it's hard enough that you have to go through all this. If it was Henry's child, then it might be a different matter. But you yourself have insisted he had nothing to do with it, and the circumstances are so ..." Edith couldn't finish.

She went over to Jenny and put her arms around her daughter. "I know how difficult this all is, but soon the baby will be born and you can get on with your life. You haven't heard from Henry in months. Perhaps he has moved on already."

Edith paused so Jenny could absorb what she had said. Jenny was so much like her father, easily swayed by a little subtle reasoning.

"Jenny," her mother continued, looking into her daughter's eyes, "It's best to just leave it be. Please don't phone Henry again. Don't complicate his life or yours any more than it already is."

Tears rolled silently down Jenny's cheeks. She couldn't speak so she just nodded.

"And let's just keep this between us girls, okay? It bothers your father so much that you're pregnant. He blames himself for all the disruption in your life. This would only add to his grief."

Jenny nodded again.

CHAPTER THIRTY-SIX

I N THE EIGHT DAYS that followed his father's departure, Aunt Darlene came over every night after supper as she had promised. At the beginning, Henry was skeptical that the novena would have any results, but as each day passed, he saw such faith in his mother's eyes that he too began to believe that their prayers would be answered.

On the following Saturday, Henry was about to leave for work when the phone rang. His mom rushed to answer it.

"Hello? Yes, this is Mary. Oh hi, George."

Henry's hand had been on the front doorknob, but he stood there, unable to move as he eavesdropped. *George?* It must be his Uncle George who lived in Vancouver.

"I see," his mom's voice quavered. "And you're certain he wants to come home? We can't afford a plane ticket. Are you sure? We'll pay you back. Oh, no, we couldn't accept that. So, where is he now? I see. And you're sure he wants to come home? Yes, yes, I'll write it down. He leaves Vancouver at seven, or is that when he arrives in Regina? All right. Yes, someone will be there to meet him. Yes, thank you very much, George, for all your help—and we'll pay you back. Oh, no, we definitely will. Okay,

I'll let Darlene know. Henry's fine. Yes, it's very cold here, around minus twenty-eight today. Oh my, that must be nice, just a light rain. Well, okay, George, thank you, again. Yes, we'll be in touch. 'Bye, George."

Henry's hand slid off the doorknob as his mom hung up. It was the ninth day of the novena, and their prayer had been answered. He was stunned, unable to move. Although he had hoped, deep down he'd had his doubts. From the hallway, Henry heard his mom crying.

Henry had met Uncle George and his family once, about three years earlier when they'd passed through Regina on their way to the East Coast. It had been fall, and he remembered Uncle George saying how beautiful it was in Eastern Canada in autumn and that they just had to see it. He also remembered his cousin Jimmy and what a brat he had been.

How on earth had Uncle George gotten involved, and how had he found his dad in such a big city?

Henry kicked off his boots and walked towards the kitchen, but his mom was no longer there. On his way back to the front door he saw her on her knees in front of the sofa, her hands cupped together under her chin. She looked like a saint. He wanted so much to ask her the details, and put his arms around her and comfort her and share in her joy and grief, but then decided to just let her be. She was already being comforted by a far greater power than he.

He thought about his parents as he walked to work. He was glad his dad was coming home and yet he dreaded it. How would Mom treat him after what he'd done? How should *he* treat him? What would they talk about? What should he say? It seemed far too awkward to discuss and yet how could he just ignore it?

Then there was Jenny—not so much that he had yet to receive a letter from her—which he'd all but given up on—but his worry that she might be pregnant. Ever since Eddy told him that Pete might have raped her, Henry had an unexplainable uneasiness in the pit of his stomach. Even though Eddy and

John didn't think anything had happened, he just couldn't shake his bad feeling.

He'd dreamed of Jenny the previous night, of her having sex with Pete, getting pregnant and soon giving birth. It sent shivers down his spine. Henry knew he didn't have any facts to support any of it, knew Jenny hadn't even *known* Pete, let alone liked him enough to do that, yet he was helpless to dispel those thoughts. He hoped he could talk to Mr. Engelmann about it all.

It was almost nine when Henry got to work. and Mr. Engelmann was already on the phone, taking orders. There was a customer in the store and the delivery boys would arrive any minute.

Mr. Engelmann nodded at him when he came in, keeping his attention on the phone order. Henry was anxious to tell him what had happened. When they'd talked the other day, Henry hadn't told him about the novena. It had felt a little silly and uncomfortable at the time. Still, Mr. Engelmann believed in prayer and Henry wanted to get his reaction. But it would have to wait. Saturdays were just too busy. He and the other delivery boys were run off their feet.

Around four-thirty, Eddy popped into the store.

"Hey, Hank, how's it going?"

"Hi, Eddy. It's been busy. What brings you here?"

"I was just visiting my cousin Ned on Reynolds Street. I ran out of smokes though and ..." he trailed off as he realized Mr. Engelmann had come in from the storeroom and had heard every word.

Mr. Engelmann knew Eddy, had sold him groceries on the odd occasion. When Eddy bought cigarettes, Mr. Engelmann assumed they were for his dad; he didn't approve of teenagers smoking and drinking. Now it was clear he'd heard who the cigarettes were really for. He raised an eyebrow and Eddy jumped into the silence.

"Hey, look, Mr. Engelmann, with all due respect, I gotta tell you the smokes are for me. But I'm going to be straight with you. I've been smoking since Grade 7 and I'm not about to quit. My parents know I smoke, and I smoke right in front of them. In fact, my dad bums more smokes off me than my friends do.

"If you're worried about my height being stunted or whatever, forget it. I had polio when I was two and the docs told my parents it would probably affect my growth. Well it did, but not my brains, and it sure hasn't stunted my personality! So, there it is. If you don't sell me the weeds, I'll just get them somewhere else. So, what's it gonna be?"

Without showing any expression, Mr. Engelmann looked Eddy straight in the eyes. When Henry detected an almost imperceptible nod, he knew Eddy would get his cigarettes. That was Mr. Engelmann's way. If something touched his heart, it was clearly the direction he would follow.

"What brand, Eddy?"

"Black Cat," said Eddy, eyes glued to Mr. Engelmann's every move.

Mr. Engelmann took a pack of Black Cat cigarettes off the shelf and laid it on the counter. "That's thirty-five cents, Eddy."

Eddy reached into his pocket and laid down forty.

"Thanks, Mr. Engelmann."

Henry held his breath as he watched, hoping Eddy wouldn't tell Mr. Engelmann to keep the change—his boss might interpret that as a bribe and be offended. But Eddy, for once, kept his mouth shut. He was smart enough to know how Mr. Engelmann operated, too.

Mr. Engelmann rang in the amount and gave Eddy five pennies.

Eddy turned to Henry. "So, Hank, you going to the basketball game next week?"

"Yeah, I think so."

"Good, should be a good game." Then, true to his nature, Eddy peeled off the cellophane, removed the aluminum cover, crumpled the wrapper up along with the plastic and this time tossed it into the garbage beside the door rather than on the floor. He shook out a smoke, lit it and took a deep drag, tossing the match into the garbage as he opened the door to leave.

"I'll see you there, Hank." Eddy flipped up the collar of his jacket and went out, a trail of smoke wafting behind.

Mr. Engelmann didn't look at Henry or mention Eddy. He simply went back to the orders to be filled, putting on his white apron and taking out a roll of fresh salami.

By five, Henry was wiped out even more than usual. He'd trouble keeping his mind on his work. He kept thinking about his dad's homecoming that night. He was excited and nervous and worried. And Jenny. Always Jenny. He wasn't living in the present, that was for sure.

Henry made two rush deliveries while both delivery boys were out. The store had been swamped all day and he still hadn't had a chance to tell Mr. Engelmann about his dad. He hadn't even had a chance to take a break with the other delivery boys, something he looked forward to every time he worked with them on Saturdays.

By five-thirty, both delivery boys had returned and Mr. Engelmann paid them. They thanked Mr. Engelmann and said good-bye to Henry on their way out. Finally, he and Mr. Engelmann were alone. He went to the storeroom and got his coat. When he came back, Mr. Engelmann was already doing up the sales for the day.

"You must be tired, Mr. Engelmann. Today was unbelievable."

"Yes, yes, Henry, I am a bit tired. This was one of our busiest days. All the promotions we are doing along with the delivery service is paying off, thanks to you."

Henry acknowledged the compliment even though he wasn't really looking for one. He only wanted to find a way to start the conversation.

"So, how are you, Henry? Tired, too?"

"Yeah, I am. How is Mrs. Engelmann today?"

"She seems a bit better, Henry, thank you for asking. At lunchtime when I went upstairs, she was up and reading in the chair in the living room.. She loves the sun and likes reading by the window with a blanket on her lap."

"Can I tell you something before I go, Mr. Engelmann?"

Mr. Engelmann stopped what he was doing and looked at him. "What is it, Henry?"

"They found my dad. He was in Vancouver, and I think he's coming home tonight on the plane at seven."

When Mr. Engelmann didn't answer, Henry continued. "I didn't tell you the other day, but we decided to say a novena for nine days to pray that my dad would come back. Today is the ninth day, and first thing this morning, my Uncle George phoned and told us he'd found my dad and that he wants to come home."

"That is very good, Henry. The Lord answers prayers, and now we need to pray even more that God heals your family and makes it stronger and better than was before."

"That's just the thing, Mr. Engelmann. How should we be when he comes home? I'm kinda worried about it."

"Yes, yes, I understand, Henry. And I'm sure he is very nervous, too. He will feel ashamed and sorry for what he did. I hope you find it in your heart to forgive him and welcome him home."

"Yeah, I want my dad home, and I think after our talk the other day, I can forgive him—although I'm still mad at him."

"Yes, yes, that is natural, Henry, but keep trying, and pray for God to help you accept your dad and the mistake he made. We are all human, and as you go through life, you too will err many times and seek forgiveness from others and from God."

"Yeah, I know, Mr. Engelmann. I just have to keep reminding myself of that. Well, I just wanted you to know."

"Yes, yes, thank you for sharing that with me. It makes me very happy. I will pray for you all."

Henry looked down and took a breath, but didn't say anything. He wasn't sure if he should tell Mr. Engelmann his worries about Jenny. Mr. Engelmann looked so tired and, after all, he didn't even know if it was true. It was just that he couldn't shake this feeling ...

"Is there something else you want to tell me?" his boss asked, demonstrating his uncanny knack for reading Henry's mind.

"Well, there is," Henry hesitated, "but we're both tired. You know, it'll keep until next week."

"Are you certain, Henry?"

"Yeah, it's okay. Thanks again, Mr. Engelmann. Good night."

It was almost seven by the time Henry stepped out of the store and into the cold, clear night. Stars sparkled in a sky hosted by a full moon. Henry walked slowly, thinking about all that Mr. Engelmann had said. He was still amazed how quickly their prayers had been answered, and on the very day they had requested, too.

Would it work to get Jenny back? He had prayed about it many times, but never a novena. And he recalled Aunt Darlene saying, "Where two or three are gathered in His name, He is there in their midst." Perhaps if his mom and aunt said the novena with him, his prayer would be answered too. Henry felt a flutter of renewed hope thinking about it.

He wondered if his dad was home yet, and what he would say. He was still worried about how to act. Well, maybe he would try to be natural, as if his dad had just come from work. In a few days things would be back to normal, wouldn't they?

Henry thought he could forgive his dad, but he wondered if his mom could. What would his parents' relationship be like? He wished he could have talked to Mr. Engelmann for a while longer. Everything would have been so much clearer then.

As Henry reached the front door of their house, nervousness made his guts clench. He didn't want to go in. He didn't know what to expect. If things were normal, his mom would be in the kitchen making supper, and his dad in the living room, reading the paper, but things were decidedly abnormal. Well, there was no help for it.

He opened the door and went in.

"Mom? I'm home!"

Henry waited for an answer, but there was none. He walked to the kitchen and found the oven set to warm and his supper inside.

There was a note on the table.

Hi Henry,

I put some supper in the oven for you. I'm going to the airport with Darlene and Ron to pick up your dad. We left early, just in case the plane comes in sooner than expected. We should be home between eight and nine o'clock.

Love, Mom

The note gave Henry goosebumps and his gut clenched again. His dad was coming home. He really wanted everything to turn out okay. Henry opened the oven door and pulled out the tinfoil-covered plate. He sat down to a meal of roast beef, mashed potatoes and creamed corn. Appetite sated, he sat there, waiting. He looked at the kitchen clock, and watched the second hand tick its way around. It was five minutes to eight. He tapped his fingertips on the tabletop in time with the silent tick of the clock.

Shortly after the clock chimed eight, a car door slammed, and then another and another. Henry felt like bolting to his room, but didn't. His heart hammered against his ribs as footsteps climbed the front stairs and the handle of the front door turned.

Suddenly Henry's mom, Aunt Darlene and Uncle Ron were in the kitchen, and Henry thought for moment his dad had not come, but then he appeared. Henry's heart raced faster. He got up, but his legs felt all rubbery. His dad stood there with his coat on, like a stranger in his own home.

"Hi, Henry," he said, his voice tight with emotion.

Mr. Engelmann was right. His dad was nervous too.

"Hi, Dad."

That seemed to galvanize his dad and he came to Henry and hugged him lightly. "It's good to be home, son."

Henry stood there, arms hanging motionless. Finally he said, "I'm glad you're home, too."

"Well, let's get the coffee on," Aunt Darlene said, with as

much cheer as she could muster. "I'm still so cold." She wrapped her arms around herself, shivered and shook, trying to make fun of it all, cutting through the tension. With that, everyone took off their coats and pulled up a chair around the kitchen table.

Henry was grateful Aunt Darlene and Uncle Ron were there. He thought he would have died if he'd had to be there alone with his mom and dad. Soon the smell of fresh coffee filled the air and that was one small step in the direction of normal. Ron started to talk about work and the stunts the boys had played on one of his coworkers on his birthday. Everyone laughed when Ron talked. He was a storyteller, and the way he said things and the expressions on his face made people laugh even when the story wasn't really all that funny.

While his Uncle Ron was talking, Henry studied his mom. She seemed happy and content, but he wondered what she was really thinking and feeling inside. Her eyes were still a little red and swollen. She looked tired. He bet she'd hardly slept the night before. His heart went out to her.

Every now and then, Henry cast cursory glances at his dad. His parents were sitting next to each other. Their hands rested on the table side by side, almost touching. Henry wished they were. His dad was staring at Ron, but Henry sensed he wasn't really listening to him as occasionally he glanced at Henry as well. When that happened, they both turned away, shifting in their chairs.

In spite of Ron's efforts and Darlene's cheery disposition, Henry felt the undercurrent of pain and sorrow tug at them all. His dad would be feeling so ashamed and guilty. Henry's knees bounced up and down as he thought about it. He was glad his legs were under the table.

Henry wondered when his Uncle Ron and Aunt Darlene were leaving; he didn't want to be around his mom and dad when they did. When the conversation petered out, Henry said good night to everyone. As he passed his mom and Aunt Darlene, he gave each a kiss on the cheek. He felt compelled to put a hand on his dad's shoulder to let him know he was glad he was home. "Good night, Dad."

"G'night, son."

Ron cracked another joke that Henry didn't really hear, he was so anxious to get out of there. He went to the bathroom and then to his room. He quickly changed into his pajamas and crawled into bed. He wanted to be asleep before his aunt and uncle left and his parents were alone. He turned off the lights and lay there, wide-eyed. He couldn't sleep. He tossed and turned and stared at the ceiling, frustrated, tense and worried. Would this ever get better?

About an hour later, Henry heard his Aunt Darlene and Uncle Ron leave. There was a long silence, but then he heard his parents' voices. They started out soft then grew louder and he knew they were arguing. It was only the fourth or fifth time he had heard them quarrel.

Henry could make out some of the words but didn't want to hear them. He grabbed his pillow, put it over his head and pressed the ends over his ears, trying to shut it out. He wanted to hear voices of love, not anger and betrayal. He wondered if everything would ever be the same.

God, please make us a family again.

He squeezed his eyes tightly together, trying with all his might to convey to God the earnestness of his prayer, trying to influence His decision. Henry stayed like that for the longest time, and finally his brow relaxed as sleep overtook him and provided temporary relief for his troubled mind.

IN THE DAYS THAT FOLLOWED, things began to revert to normal, yet tension hovered between his mom and dad. His dad had gotten his job back, with only a reprimand. By eavesdropping, Henry had found out that the woman his dad had gone off with had stayed in Vancouver with her cousin. She was married, too, and had wanted to get away from her husband, who beat her. Henry wondered how people could treat each other that way.

Once, when Henry and his mom were alone, he asked her

for the novena prayer book, explaining he wanted to say the novena also, in the hopes that Jenny would write.

Mary opened her mouth as if about to say it wouldn't work for him, but then, after a long pause, she merely said, "Yes, I'll ask Aunt Darlene for it, and maybe we can say it together."

"That would be great, Mom," Henry's relief was palpable.

Two days later, he had the novena booklet in his hands. His mother encouraged him to embrace the scriptural passage of Mark 11:24: "'What things so ever ye desire, when ye pray, believe that ye receive them, and ye shall have them.' Faith is important, you must believe God's word."

She promised to come to his room each night and they would say it together before he went to sleep. She did not want his dad to know about it for reasons Henry didn't want to pry into. The nine days came and went, and still no Jenny. Somehow it wasn't the same. Their prayers seemed to lack the anticipation that they would be answered. It was almost anticlimactic compared to what had happened in his parents' case. Yet deep down, Henry still believed God heard their prayers, and in His own time and way, He would answer them.

About three weeks after his dad returned home, things seemed to be mostly back on track. Grateful, Henry had almost forgotten what his dad had done, and his parents seemed to be getting along okay. All that changed, however, when he arrived home on a Thursday afternoon after school. Two trucks were parked in front of their house. The first truck was just leaving. Brown's Auction was written on the side. The second truck was from Simpsons-Sears. Two delivery men in blue coveralls emerged from the house as Henry walked up the front stairs. Inside, he asked his mom what they had brought.

"Oh, it's nothing, Henry, just some furniture for our bedroom."

"What kind of furniture?"

"Oh, it's nothing." It was clear his mom didn't want to talk about it. "Don't you have to go to work?"

"Yeah, I do. I have to shovel the snow off the walk. It's too hard for Mr. Engelmann to do it. Do you want me to do ours before

I go?"

"Oh, that would be great, Henry. Then your dad doesn't have to be out in the cold when he comes home."

Henry was curious about the mysterious new furniture, but was hesitant to open his parents' bedroom door. Two days later, he knew. The bedroom door was ajar and his mom was in the kitchen. He peeked in. His parents' double bed was gone, and in its place were twin beds, at least three feet apart. His mom had not yet forgiven his dad and was punishing him for his unfaithfulness.

It all made sense now. Since his dad had come home, he was always the last to go to bed and the first to rise. That had not been the case before. Usually he went to bed before Henry or shortly afterwards. And one morning when Henry went to the bathroom, he had seen his dad sleeping in his clothes on the living room couch. His parents were no longer sleeping together and he guessed that's what they had been arguing about, at least in part, the night his dad had returned home from Vancouver. The twin beds told the unspoken story of the status of their relationship.

Henry wanted to talk to Mr. Engelmann about it, but it was just too private. It was his mom and dad's problem and if they wanted to talk to someone, they would have to do it themselves.

They never did.

Chapter Thirty-Seven

Towards the end of April, Jenny's water broke. Edith confined her to bed, with minimal walking. A few hours later, labour started.

Fortunately the hospital wasn't far from where they lived. Each time Jenny cried out with a contraction, Ted stomped on the accelerator. Edith had phoned the doctor to alert the hospital to be ready for them. Two interns were waiting with a stretcher when they arrived.

All Jenny could think about in the delivery room was how she wished Henry were by her side. Her mother stayed with her, while her father paced the floor in the waiting room. As Jenny's pain increased, she was given gas through a mask to ease it. She was slow in dilating, and the two doctors on hand considered a cesarean section. These teen births were never easy. A month ago the baby had been in a breach position, and Jenny had worried about having to be cut open. Thankfully, the doctor had managed to turn the baby and the baby had stayed head down.

As soon as Henry woke that morning, the nervous feelings he'd had for months intensified. Usually the walk to school settled him down, but not today. In fact, by second period, the feelings of uneasiness strengthened into pain and nausea and he had to excuse himself from history class. At the very hour and moment that Jenny gave birth, Henry's stomach pain became so excruciating, he threw up. The school nurse attributed it to indigestion—there was no sign of fever. But Henry knew differently; he was sure it had something to do with Jenny.

FOR THE NEXT TEN MINUTES, Jenny laboured in a sort of giddy stupor thanks to the laughing gas, and requested that it be stopped. She didn't want to sleep or be distracted in any way when the baby was born. She knew she had only one chance to see her baby. All she could see right now was the white sheet covering her knees. She wished they would take it away. Her heart rate jumped when she heard someone say, "The head's out."

"Push, Jenny," one of the doctors commanded. Jenny complied, and the baby was born.

Edith squeezed Jenny's hand and rose in her chair to peek at the baby. Jenny felt an overwhelming rush of love for her child. She just had to see it. With all her might Jenny struggled up on her elbows. She saw the doctor holding the baby by its feet. The baby let out a loud cry.

"What is it?" Jenny asked.

The doctor turned to her. "It's a girl."

"Oh, Mom," Jenny pleaded, "I want to hold her, give her a kiss ... just for a minute."

Edith looked at her daughter. Tears welled up in her eyes, and she was unable to speak. A nurse approached the doctor, wrapped the baby in a white blanket, and scurried out of the delivery room.

Jenny heard the baby crying for her and lay there, helpless.

"Goodbye, Camilla," she murmured, collapsing back on the bed.

Jenny was immediately moved out of the maternity ward to another floor. The sight and sound of babies were the last things she needed. In her private room all she could think about was the memory of giving birth, the image of her baby dangling there and the sound of her cry for her mother, a mother who would never hold her, feed her, care for her, love her. Jenny would never see Camilla grow, take her first steps or say her first words. Jenny could only imagine those things happening to a faceless baby and envy other mothers who enjoyed those simple moments with their children.

Jenny rolled over and buried her head in the pillow, but the thoughts kept coming. Jenny could picture the nurse carrying her baby from the delivery room to the waiting arms of the adoptive parents, their hearts filled with joy. Would Camilla be feeding now? Would her adoptive mother be holding her, cuddling her … loving her?

"Oh, it's not fair," cried Jenny. "It's just not fair … I want my baby."

Jenny remained in the hospital for another day. They all thought the sooner she got on with her life, the better—and that included returning to school as soon as possible.

AFTER HE THREW UP AT SCHOOL, Henry no longer had stomach pains or that pervasive gut-wrenching feeling. He wondered how Jenny was, and if she ever thought of him. He still longed for her and wished there was a way to investigate all his thoughts and intuitions, but he was helpless to do anything. He had no address, no phone number, nothing but a business address for Mr. Sarsky, who had so far ignored or blocked all Henry's attempts to communicate with Jenny. All Henry could do was pray and hope that someday they would be together again.

It was that latter thought that set a plan into motion, a plan that might take years to carry out, but Henry was determined to make it happen. The following Saturday after Mr. Engelmann paid Henry his wages, he went straight home and placed the money, together with the delivery tips he had made that day, into an envelope, hiding it in the bottom of his desk drawer.

IN THE WEEKS THAT FOLLOWED, Jenny fell into a serious state of depression. No amount of counselling seemed to help, neither from the social worker assigned to her by the hospital, nor from the psychologist Dr. Breck referred her to.

For days, Jenny locked herself in her room. She lay in bed most of the time, and her appetite had not returned. Somehow in the months leading up to Camilla's birth, Jenny had been able to ward off the full impact of the pregnancy, but the turmoil of giving her child away, Henry's ongoing rejection and the acknowledgement of having been raped bombarded her full force.

She tried to shut her feelings out, but the pain of motherhood wouldn't let her forget. Despite the medication they'd given her, Jenny's breasts nearly doubled in size, filling with milk, and reminding her of her loss. Jenny longed to hold and feed her baby. Body, mind and spirit screamed to carry out what nature intended. She felt trapped but accepted the pain as punishment for giving up her child. Eventually the milk would dry up and the physical pain subside, but would the agony of losing both her loves ever go away?

CHAPTER THIRTY-EIGHT

SPRING ARRIVED IN OTTAWA early that year. By mid-April, all the snow was gone and the fury of the spring runoff was done. By the third week of May, green grass had replaced the brown leftovers from the fall, slowly replenishing the landscape. The gardeners, laid off last fall, returned to the Sarsky estate, planning the flowerbeds to be planted, clearing out all the dead leaves and trimming the hedges.

On his way to work that morning, Ted felt the need to say good-bye to his daughter. He hadn't seen her for days. He rapped lightly on her door, but there was no answer. When he opened it, the room was dark, a sharp contrast to the morning sun pouring into his and Edith's bedroom. Ted felt an overwhelming urge to let the sun into Jenny's room, too. His little girl had always loved nature and the sun. Her bright smile had often reminded him of a ray of sunshine. Come to think of it, when was the last time he'd seen Jenny smile? Without thought or permission, he went over to the window, pushed aside the curtains and raised the blinds.

Jenny stirred in her bed and opened one eye. "Oh, it's you. Please close the blinds. I'm so tired ..."

"Good morning, Jenny, it's a beautiful morning." As Ted peered out the window, he added, "Look. The gardeners are starting to put the flowers in. Come on, Jenny. Get up and enjoy the day. I know how much you love being outside."

"Please go, Dad. I'd like to sleep some more." Jenny turned abruptly onto her side and tossed the blankets over her head.

"See you tonight, dear," he said softly as he walked out of the room.

At breakfast, Ted and Edith discussed their daughter's condition once again. Edith had finally accepted the fact that Jenny might have been telling the truth about being raped and was going to make an appointment with another psychiatrist who specialized in those sorts of cases.

"Well, I'll leave it for another week," Edith said, "then perhaps see if the psychiatrist would come to the house."

"That might be a good idea," said Ted, kissing his wife on the cheek.

LATER THAT MORNING Jenny got up to go to the bathroom. When she returned to her room, she stood in front of her window. After a few minutes she sat down on the built-in bench seat of the dormer and looked out over the bare garden. She opened the window and a soft, warm, spring breeze wafted in along with the sounds of nature. The sights and sounds soothed her, and for the rest of the day Jenny sat transfixed at the window, gazing at the beauty she had somehow forgotten existed.

Jenny watched the landscapers work and the unfolding transformation of the grounds. It reminded her of Henry. How he loved to restore things and make them look more beautiful. How excited and motivated he'd been to transform Mr. Engelmann's store and his business. Jenny just loved that about him. Watching the gardeners' efficient work result in emerging beauty, Jenny could understand what motivated Henry. She found his desire to make the world a better place uplifting.

For the next two days, Jenny sat by the window. For the first time in a very long time, she lost herself in moments of nature.

Her past dissolved and her future faded into the morning sun. She lived only in the present, the here and now of life. It was then that she reconnected with her true self.

At once she felt the joy and peace that had always been within her. She realized she had covered her happiness with layer upon layer of heartache and only she held the key to her well-being. Quietly she thanked her guardian angel for this knowledge.

Accompanying this quiescence, a thought emerged that gave Jenny further comfort. She was certain there was a reason, a purpose for her having given birth to Camilla. Her protector had spared her from the memory of a rape but had not spared her the pregnancy itself. Why? It may have been an answer to the prayers of Camilla's adoptive parents, but Jenny sensed there was some special design yet to unfold.

The thought sustained her and added to her present peace as well as hope for the future. It allowed clarity to enter her mind. If she persisted in drowning in despair, she would be lost forever in depression over the past and the bleakness of the future, and would likely only attract more of the same. She must carry the memory of her child and Henry forward as cherished possessions that made her free and strong. They were expressions of love in her life. The memories would always be a part of her life, and she was richer for them.

The following morning when Ted opened her bedroom door to say good-bye to his daughter, she wasn't there. Her bed was made, the blinds drawn and the window open. A gentle breeze freshened the room. At the window, he held the fluttering curtains still. Unbidden tears welled up in Ted's eyes. There, with the other gardeners, was Jenny, kneeling down, planting marigolds and petunias. Jenny, like the flowers, exuded the beauty and joy intended from the beginning of all time.

JENNY NEVER DID MAKE IT back to school in the late spring. She continued to grow and heal at home, spending most of her days outside, either working in the garden or reading in the gazebo.

She loved being surrounded by flowers and the fragrance they gave off. Seeing life and growth around her helped her move past the difficult areas of her life. She began to accept Camilla's adoption. Her daughter would be loved. Jenny knew she was too young to properly care and provide for her, and her daughter would know a mother and father, would be secure in a home filled with much love.

Rather than dwell on regret, Jenny focused on the joy she had given Camilla's adoptive parents. With each positive thought, Jenny released her pain and encompassed more good energy. She still missed Henry terribly—yet there, too, she thought it better to have known such a love than not at all. She had been blessed by a relationship she would treasure all her life. Although the possibility of Henry returning in her future looked bleak, there was still a glimmer of hope in the deep recesses of her heart. Perhaps some day their guardian angels would bring them back together.

And perhaps, someday, she would meet her Camilla.

It was this kind of trust in herself and in life that helped Jenny recover. Spending so much time surrounded by nature's example had renewed Jenny's faith in the healing power of time and the natural unfolding of life. She knew when the sun went down, it would come up again in the morning. Fall would follow summer, spring would return after winter. And when a seed was planted in mother earth, a new flower, full of beauty and glory, would be born. Nature supplied the assurance and security Jenny needed. It was not so fickle and heartless as relationships could be.

Perhaps more than anything else on the estate, the wild flower patch renewed Jenny's spirit. Her father had asked the head gardener to prepare a garden patch for her. She had no idea what flowers were in the mix the gardener had given her to sow, but she loved the excitement, anticipation and unpredictability of what would flower so freely. No matter what flower appeared, it complimented the garden. Every day, the garden patch grew more lovely.

It was only natural that Jenny should find her greatest healing there. She could easily reconnect with her inner spirit, for it, too, was wild and needed freedom. She could easily recapture her spontaneity, gaiety and inner beauty. But perhaps more than anything, the wild flower garden helped Jenny connect with Camilla. Each flower reminded Jenny of her little baby. In the same way the earth gave life to a seed, she had given life to a little girl who would blossom. She could visualize Camilla growing, unfolding and budding into a wildflower, the most beautifully free of them all.

CHAPTER THIRTY-NINE

I T'S AMAZING HOW AN ENTIRE MOVIE can be made about a guy just looking out of his rear apartment window at the neighbourhood."

"Yeah, and it sure was suspenseful. Alfred Hitchcock movies are usually pretty good, Gary."

"I wasn't sure if a murder had happened or not. It looked like Jimmy Stewart was just trying to pass the time by letting his imagination run wild while his broken leg mended."

"I had my eye more on Grace Kelly; she sure is something else. I could watch her all day long. Jenny and I saw her and Bing Crosby in *High Society* last summer. I even bought the 45 of the song she and Bing sang: "True Love." I hum it all the time."

"That's because you can't sing, Hank."

The two boys chuckled as they walked home down 11th Avenue. It reminded Henry of his walk home with Jenny almost a year ago. Gary must have read his thoughts.

"Jenny sure looks a lot like Grace Kelly, come to think of it. They both have blond hair, are fair-skinned, and kinda have a classy look about them. How is she doing, anyway?"

"Well, you remember shortly before you left for Notre Dame,

Jenny and her parents moved to Ottawa."

"Yeah I remember, you were pretty shook up about that."

"I hated to see her go. I was going to tell you what happened in the letters I sent you, but I didn't want to concern you with it."

"So what did happen, Hank?"

"After she left I wrote a ton of letters and waited for her to write me with her address, but to this day I've never gotten a single letter from her."

"You're kidding. That doesn't seem like Jenny. Not one letter?"

"No, not one. And we promised to write to each other … I think it was her parents who stopped her from writing. I know Jenny's mom was concerned about how close Jenny and I got last summer."

"That's too bad, Hank. She was really a nice girl and I know you liked her a lot."

"Maybe sometime down the road I'll see her again. I sure hope so, anyway. I still think about her a lot."

At Winnipeg Street the boys turned and headed to Victoria Avenue. Henry got goosebumps as they passed Eddy Zeigler's place. Henry was tempted to tell Gary what Eddy and his friends had done to him and Jenny, but decided not to. Eddy was becoming his friend and he wanted to forgive and forget. Instead, Henry followed up on what they had been talking about earlier.

"And how about you, Gary, are you looking forward to going back to Notre Dame? Any girl you're interested in there yet?"

"Actually, I am, Hank." Gary said, taking one question at a time. "There's something special about Notre Dame. It's strict, that's for sure, and yet there's a strong spiritual aspect and feeling of belonging that I like. My dad calls it camaraderie, a sort of friendship with people you spend a lot of time with. And I did meet a girl there at the first dance last fall. Her name is Jane. But they're pretty strict; Father Murray doesn't allow much dating and curfews have to be followed or else."

"Well, I'm sure gonna miss you. It was great having you back this summer and working at the store."

"I can't believe how busy the store has become, Hank, and

how much it's improved. It all looks so nice and everything is always so well stocked … it was pretty rundown before. Someone must have helped Mr. Engelmann fix everything up."

Not wanting to brag, Henry hadn't written Gary everything that he'd help the Engelmanns accomplish, but in the next breath, Gary came to the conclusion on his own.

"You probably helped him a lot, Henry. I see how you always get right to it and stock the shelves. And I see how much Mr. Engelmann likes you."

"We *have* become pretty good friends. He sure is wise, Gary."

"And so is Mrs. Engelmann. She talks to so many ladies. She seems like such a holy person, so peaceful."

"Yeah, she's something else, almost like some kind of a psychologist or something. She always heads to the back storage room when some woman wants to confide in her; it's used more than the front when she's around. I'm glad she's getting better, I sure like it when she's in the store." And turning to Gary, Henry continued, "I saw her give you a hug at closing time today. I think she really likes you, Gary."

"Well, I shared something with her that I never told anyone else and she was real happy about it. So was I." He glanced at Henry, then seemed to think his friend would understand. "It made her cry and I was so relieved to speak to someone, I got a bit teary myself."

Henry didn't want to pry, yet he was sure curious now. He really admired Gary's honesty and liked that about their friendship; they could tell each other stuff without worrying about being teased or ridiculed. Henry remained silent, hoping Gary would share what had happened. A moment later, he did.

"What I told her Hank, was that I feel called to the priesthood."

Henry wasn't sure he'd heard Gary right. "What did you say?"

"Yeah, I know it's hard to believe—Gary Franklin wants to become a priest." Gary sort of chuckled.

Henry stopped and turned to his friend. "Geez, Gary, that's really something. How do you know?"

"Well, since attending Notre Dame and going to mass every morning, I ... I just feel something that's hard to explain. And when I go into the chapel in the evening when no one's around, it's so peaceful and I seem to be drawn to Him."

Henry looked at his buddy with a kind of awed astonishment. Never would he have expected to hear someone his age say something like that. "Geez, Gary, that's ... that's wonderful."

"I haven't even told my parents yet. I don't know how my dad will take it. I know he wants me to join the army and work my way up the ranks but I don't really care about that. I just want to be of some service to others ... like Mrs. Engelmann! That's why I think she gave me a hug, I told her I want to do what she does, and help people."

"Geez, Gary, and *I* want to be like Mr. Engelmann. He's been such a big part of my life this past year and I love talking to him."

The two boys just gazed at one another. Who'd have thought that a part-time job would have had such influence on both of them?

"So, would you still go to military college like you planned?"

"I think so," Gary answered. "I want to check into being a chaplain or something like that. Maybe the two can work together somehow. Father Murray says that God has a plan for each of us and that we should pray and ask Him what His plan for us is. I'm sure by the time I finish Grade 12, I'll know for sure what I should do."

Henry was still sort of shocked to be having this kind of a conversation with even as good a friend as Gary. And what about Gary's girlfriend? He knew how much he had wanted to marry Jenny. "So if priests don't marry, where would that leave the girl you mentioned. Jane, wasn't it?"

"Yeah, she's really great, Hank, and I like her a lot—but that's the thing, our friendship is based on what we have in common. We both want to devote our lives to Jesus. You see, she wants to be a nun and enter a convent after Grade 12. Actually," he glanced at Henry, "we spend a lot of time praying together."

It was almost too much for Henry. He couldn't believe his

friend that he had known since Grade 2 was talking like this.

"I don't know what to say Gary, it's all so incredible."

"Yeah, I'm pretty excited about it all. I told my sister about it already and plan to talk to Mom and Dad in the next day or so."

When they came to the corner of Broder and Victoria Avenue they stopped and looked at Engelmann's Grocery.

"It's quite the store, isn't it?" Henry said. "If people only knew what goes on in there beside selling groceries."

"I think people know, Hank, the neighbourhood is pretty devoted to the Engelmanns and appreciates the way they serve the people here. Sometimes I feel it's like a church."

"You're right, Gary! I never thought of it like that. I've learned so much from them, especially Mr. Engelmann. I just have two more days, tomorrow and Saturday and then I'm back at school Monday. I hate to see the summer come to an end."

The boys turned and headed down Broder Street to their homes, trailing a hint of sadness. They probably wouldn't see each other until Christmas holidays.

"I hope you'll still write. I've always considered you my best friend and I'm sure going to miss you."

Gary started to extend his hand but instead stepped forward and the two boys gave each other a hug.

"You're my best friend too, Hank, and you always will be. And now that I know how much you miss Jenny, I'm going to start praying for you and her."

"Thanks, Gary, that's really nice of you." And then Henry said something he never thought he would say to anyone. "I'll pray for you too, Gary, that things work out between you and your dad and what you want to do. It's something real special."

There was a soft sheen in both their eyes as they each raised a hand and slapped them together in mid-air.

"See ya, buddy."

"Yeah, see ya, Hank."

WHEN HENRY TURNED INTO HIS YARD, he was surprised to see his dad sitting on the steps. His dad had changed a lot since coming home. He seemed to be trying to pay more attention to Mom and him. But it seemed to Henry that his dad was still hurting inside from it all.

"Hi, son. How was the movie?"

"It was real good, Dad." Henry sat next to his father. "You and Mom should see it. It's actually quite a thriller. It all takes place in a neighbourhood with a guy looking out his window into the backyard, taking in how everyone lives their lives."

"I saw it advertised in the paper, *Rear Window*. Hitchcock, right?"

"Yeah. This is the second time I've seen it. I get more out of it each time. It's supposed to be one of his best."

"Perhaps Mom and I will take it in. So, how's Gary doing?"

"Fine. He's heading back to Wilcox on Sunday. I'm going to miss him. It was sure good to have someone to chum around with after work this summer."

"You two have been close pals for a long time."

Henry nodded. "He told me something tonight that really surprised me. I'm still trying to let it sink in. He said he wants to become a priest."

Bill didn't answer for a moment. "That's quite a commitment for someone his age." And, after a long pause, "That's real good. Gary's a fine young man. Mom and I have always been glad that he is your friend."

"Yeah, I have always considered him my best friend. I hope we stay in touch."

"You will if you work on it, Henry."

"Is Mom still up?"

"No, she went to bed about a half-hour ago and I guess I better head off, too."

"Thanks for staying with me awhile, Dad."

Bill got up and patted Henry on the shoulder. "'Night son."

"See ya in the morning, Dad.

It was good to sit with his dad and talk a bit. Henry wished he had more to say to keep the conversation going. He wanted to get to know his dad better.

Henry looked over at Jenny's old house. A dim light was coming through the closed drapes. If only Jenny was still living there. *Man, this summer sure wasn't anything like last year.* It was good sitting out back with Mr. Engelmann at the store, but it just wasn't the same without seeing Jenny every day.

What a summer that had been!

Loneliness washed over Henry as he gazed into the darkness. Only a sliver of a moon adorned the sky. Henry looked to see if the star of the east was out, but with so many stars ablaze in the heavens he could no longer tell which one it was. He longed for Jenny and wondered what had happened to her. He was glad school was starting again; it would keep his mind preoccupied on other things. It was at times like this he thought his heart would break. A tear fell on his hand as he got up. He wiped both eyes at the same time with his fingers. "Yeah," he murmured, trying to shake off thoughts about Jenny, "It'll be good to get back at it. And basketball season will soon be here. I think we can win the provincials this year for sure."

Henry turned and gazed towards Gary's place, still trying to take it all in. It was amazing how easily Gary talked about his vocation and how he'd been influenced by Mrs. Engelmann and the college he was going to. People could affect each other so greatly. For the first time he felt an inkling of the tremendous influence one can have on another, often without even knowing it. Henry thought about what Mr. Engelmann had said to him that day they had talked about sex and marriage, out back of the store: *"Henry, this world so desperately needs people who have thought things through and don't go through life like a leaf tossed by the wind. We need, more than ever, strong people whom others will want to emulate because of the wholesome way they live."*

Mr. Engelmann led by example. He walked the talk and Henry was definitely influenced by him. And as he thought about it, he realized Gary had really influenced him tonight as well—how boldly he had talked about God and what he wanted to do with his life. If Gary had said he wanted to be an electrician or teacher or any other professional that would have seemed normal. But to talk about serving Jesus and working for God was something that people shied away from talking about.

Why?

Henry visualized Gary and his friend Jane holding hands and praying and wondered if he would ever be able to do that with a girl. And yet, every now and then he saw Mr. and Mrs. Engelmann in the back storage room, holding hands with their heads bowed, praying and offering up their day to God. Maybe if his mom and dad had prayed like that, his dad would never have done what he did. Henry knew his mom prayed a lot and had strong faith, but he never saw them hold hands and pray together. Henry now wished they did, or at least would start.

Maybe then, things wouldn't have …

"WELL, IT SURE WAS GOOD working for you again this summer, Mr. Engelmann. I'm sorry it'll only be part-time again next week."

"You were a big help to us, Henry. It does concern Anna and I that you didn't take a few days off to enjoy your summer holidays."

"But Mr. Engelmann, working here is like a holiday. I enjoy it so much; it doesn't even seem like work!"

"My, my, Henry, it's good of you to feel that way."

"We're really going to miss Gary's help making deliveries, Mr. Engelmann. I noticed it today already—the other two delivery boys had trouble keeping up."

"Yes, Mr. Peters phoned me yesterday and wanted to know if his son could work here on Saturdays. I told him to send George along after school this week sometime and I would talk to him about it. I'm also going to hire Mr. Fellinger to deliver the groceries during the week. He is retired and has a car, which makes deliveries easier to do during the wintertime."

"Good idea, Mr. Engelmann. I can still help after school and I'm glad Mrs. Schmidt can work every day now."

"Yes, yes, she's a big help, especially when Anna isn't feeling well enough to come down."

"That reminds me, Mr. Engelmann. Gary told me last night

that he's going into the priesthood and said he'd told Mrs. Engelmann too."

"Anna mentioned it to me. Gary is a fine young man and if he is truly called, he will make a good servant for the Lord. Anna was impressed by how Gary listens to God in the silence of the chapel. He has learned the secret of communicating with his Maker."

"Yeah, isn't that something. I was sure surprised to hear Gary talk like that … it seemed more grown-up, more serious, more to do with what he wanted to do with his life rather than the games we used to play. Things are changing between me and Gary. Even things with Timmy seem to be changing. We don't seem to talk as much about when we were kids … it's more serious somehow, more to do with the future."

"Yes, Henry, you and your friends are growing up into fine young men and making new beginnings; you're changing. Life is like that, we are always moving ahead. First it's elementary school and then high school and soon university or perhaps employment. With each new beginning we leave the old behind. What you are feeling, Henry, is the uneasiness of the separation between what was and the uncertainty of the future. But slowly you will know what God's plan is for you."

"Yeah. Gary's kinda getting a handle on it."

"And so will you. The Lord has blessed you with many talents and gifts. Your job is to use them to the fullest in ways that best serve others and God."

Henry smiled. "That's some responsibility, Mr. Engelmann."

"Yes it is. Many people don't even realize that they are here to work for the Lord and make the world a better place. But if you pray, meditate and listen in silence like your friend Gary does, the Lord will reveal to you exactly where and how and in what capacity you can do your best to serve Him." And after just a momentary pause, Mr. Engelmann added, "Actually, Henry, it's a wonderful journey of discovering how you can best live out God's will for you."

CHAPTER FORTY

B Y THE END OF THE SUMMER, Jenny was ready for Grade 10 and was looking forward to it. By her second week back to school, her friends and some of her teachers had encouraged her to run for the student representative council, and she decided to do that. She also joined the English club and spent a lot of time in the library, putting away books and talking to the librarian. She loved reading. To be surrounded by books was like being surrounded by flowers; both were filled with beauty, wonder and mystery.

The most daring thing she considered doing was in late September; Jenny decided to try out for cheerleading and was thrilled when Miss Lake put her on the squad. When Jenny put on the cheerleading outfit with its short skirt and tight white sweater, her long, slender legs, small waist and shapely figure were the envy of every girl in the locker room. She was lucky not to have any stretch marks and had lost all the baby weight—in fact, she bore no outward sign of having been pregnant at all.

Jenny had always been pretty, but her eyes now sparkled with an inner glow; she had matured and she was stunning.

Yet Jenny didn't think of herself as being any different from the other girls. She began to join in the teasing laughter of her friends and relax into her naturally exuberant self, goofing around with them in the locker room, pulling faces and making jokes. In the seclusion of the girls'- only change room, she could be herself.

But when she left the locker room, it was a different story. Jenny couldn't help but be aware of her looks when the cheerleading squad ran out onto the field. Unlike some of the other girls, Jenny had no need to pad her bra with tissues. And her heart-shaped face, surrounded by glimmering wheat-gold hair, featured in many boys' fantasies.

When the boys headed for football tryouts burst through the back door on their way to the practice field and saw Jenny, pandemonium broke loose.

"There she is," they howled. "Hey, blondie! Hey, gorgeous! Hey, sexy! Come and be my baby doll." Some hooted and whistled. A couple even dared to run right up to her and ask for a date. Miss Lake and Mr. Murray, the football coach, had trouble controlling the boys, but after much hollering and threats of detention, they finally moved on.

Red-faced and hot with embarrassment, Jenny held her pom-poms protectively in front of herself and looked straight ahead at Miss Lake.

"Well, have you decided on our first routine, Miss Lake?" Jenny asked, trying to draw the attention back to cheerleading instruction. What more could she do? She couldn't help how she looked. All she could do was try to handle it as humbly as possible. And it was her grace and sincerity that saved her from the malice of the other girls. Jenny never thought herself better than other girls, and her peers recognized that and accepted her because of it.

But no matter how much Jenny tried to ignore the attention she drew, she couldn't stop it from happening. There was always some sort of scene whenever she went onto the field or the basketball court. Some guys only came to see Jenny and had no interest in football or basketball whatsoever.

Jenny could have had any guy she wanted. She was chased by almost every male athlete in the school. And word had gotten out. Guys from other schools would even drive to Springview High over the noon hour with hopes of seeing Jenny and asking her out. But she demurred at their advances and declined their invitations.

There was only one boy who had caught her eye.

Arriving late for lunch at the school cafeteria one day, Jenny scanned the area for a seat, ignoring offers from guys to sit on their laps. She eventually found a place to sit.

"Hi, is this chair saved for anyone?"

James only needed a quick glance—he was already half standing when he quickly replied, "I bought and paid for that chair just for you."

Jenny smiled and pink tinged her cheeks. "Well, does that mean I have to pay rent?" she responded coyly.

Before waiting for a reply, Jenny sat down and began unwrapping the wax paper from her sandwich. James Hamilton, duly impressed by both her beauty and her witty retort, was, for once, speechless. He dropped back onto his seat, leaned back and crossed his arms while he took Jenny in.

Meanwhile, Jenny shot a furtive glance at the boy sitting across from her. She knew of him—he was different from the other students. She didn't know his name, only what other students called him: "Slick James," "Mr. Big Business" and "the Prez." Going by the first nickname she assumed his name might be James.

"I'm Jenny. And you are...?" Jenny dared to ask, trying to break the ice and his stare.

While every other boy in school had taken notice of Jenny, James was usually too busy with ideas of how to take over the world to bother with girls. He had never laid eyes on Jenny before and although he was not one to ever be at a loss for words, he was nevertheless finding it difficult to believe that such a gorgeous (and clever and bold) girl was sitting across from him.

Jenny looked at him, wondering why he wasn't answering.

Before James could think of something clever to say, Jenny repeated, "Excuse me, perhaps you didn't hear me in all this chattering and noise. I'm Jenny, do you have a name?"

"Yes, of course, it's just that I am so taken by you that ..." A bit thrown off his game, James stammered.

Jenny glanced down, her face reddening ... he wasn't flirting or flattering her. He seemed sincere, yet perhaps a bit nervous. She didn't know how to respond. She took a bite of her sandwich hoping he would say something before she swallowed her food.

Finally, clearing his throat and suddenly readjusting himself so that he leaned not away, but towards Jenny, James looked her in the eye and replied with his customary confidence and straightforwardness. "Look, I'm sorry for staring and not answering, but you're really very pretty, and I have to be honest, I *am* taken by you ... sorry, my name is James. James Hamilton."

And the moment James stuck out his hand, it reminded Jenny of what Henry had done when she'd first met him, too. She liked it then and she liked that now. She slowly reached out and wondered if he would grab it like Henry had. Instead, James half stood up and took hold of her hand ever so gently.

"I'm very pleased to meet you Jenny. And I suppose you have a last name too?"

"It's Sarsky. Jenny Sarsky. I'm pleased to meet you too, James."

James was different, that was obvious. He seemed mature and sort of refined. Jenny liked his jet black hair and the way he combed it straight back. It had a sheen to it just like Henry's. *Brylcreem for sure.* He looked athletic, ruddy complexioned with a square jaw, and yet his dress didn't match that of the typical jock—or the typical student for that matter.

"Can I get you a drink? I see you don't have one and I was just going to get one myself."

"That's okay, thanks. I usually have a drink of water from the fountain after I eat."

"Please, let me buy you an orange juice or something, you must be pretty thirsty... it's no trouble."

Jenny looked up at him. He was standing and his dark eyes

almost pleaded for her to say yes. He reminded her so much of Henry she couldn't turn him down.

"Sure, okay. That would be nice."

"Great, I'll be right back."

James walked quickly over to the counter with the drinks. As Jenny watched him walk away, she couldn't get over his attire: a heavily starched white shirt with two buttons open below his collar, black dress slacks, and what looked like Italian shoes similar to what her dad wore. He looked like a businessman or one of those suave Italian lovers she read about in romance novels. He was definitely interesting.

"Well, here you are, Jenny. I brought you a glass as well."

"Thank you, James," Jenny said, as he handed her a bottle of orange juice. "Actually I prefer to drink it from the bottle, but thanks anyway."

Jenny took a sip of juice while James returned to his place across the table from her. When he sat down, Jenny asked, "So what grade are you in?"

"Eleven, just one more year after this and I'm out of here. My dad wants me to go to college and take business administration, but I would sooner join my father's executive staff and learn about it on the job. It's all I think about. I see so many ways I could improve what's going on there."

James dark eyes darted and flashed as he spoke about his business plans. Once again, she saw a bit of Henry and the way his eyes lit up when thinking of ways to improve Mr. Engelmann's store.

"Oh my gosh, James, you remind me so much of someone I knew. He was so excited about improving a business as well."

Jenny was amazed and delighted to have met someone with interests similar to Henry's. By the time the noon hour was over, Jenny had agreed to go out with him to a movie on Saturday night. She'd thought he was joking when he said he would pick her up in a limo, but she would later learn that he was dead serious.

As they walked back to their respective classrooms after

lunch, Jenny heard many teasing remarks directed towards her new friend.

"Hey, look who's coming: it's the Prez."

"What business deal are you making today, man? He's probably selling something to the blond ..."

The comments didn't faze James in the least. In fact, Jenny thought that he rather enjoyed the teasing.

"Someday, Jenny, these guys are all gonna work for me," he said, looking straight ahead.

"Boy, you sure are confident, James."

"You have to be, Jen. I always know exactly what I want and I always get exactly what I want. I'm telling you now, I'm going to be a successful executive by the time I'm twenty-five. It's all I think about. I even dream about it. My dad gets a kick out of the way I think, but he has to agree—if you live your dream, you're sure to realize it."

Jenny had never heard anyone talk that way before. Henry was ambitious too, but in a different sort of way, it seemed to her. While Henry was driven by a desire to help out, more bent on serving others and making the world a better place, James' seemed motivated by a desire to get to the top, take over his dad's business and build an empire. Over time, Jenny would learn that there were far more differences between James and Henry despite her initial impressions.

Within that first hour of meeting, Jenny saw that James' crisp appearance reflected a razor sharp mind. She had to admit, James definitely made an impression on her.

IN THE WEEKS THAT FOLLOWED, James and Jenny quickly became an item. They were the talk of the school. When they walked down the hall, students would stop and stare, they made such a dazzling couple. It was almost as if cameras should flash or people should ask for their autographs while a black limousine waited outside the school to pick them up at the end of the day. In fact, if Jenny let James have his way, he would have arranged for a limo to pick them up from school on occasion; it would have felt just right to James, the Prez himself, but Jenny was far too modest to draw so much attention to herself.

Although James had definitely caught Jenny's eye and tugged at her heart, he still was no match for Henry. There had been a special connection—a spiritual connection—she and Henry had shared. Jenny still felt it, through and through to the core of her being, even though she couldn't explain it. But, unlike Henry, James was someone here, in the flesh, she could actually talk to—not some far-off memory. James was a start, and she was thankful he had come along to fill the void and help heal her broken heart.

ON THE TWENTY-FOURTH of every month, Jenny held a private celebration in her mind for her little girl. She read books on child development in the library so she would know what Camilla would be up to. At nearly five months old, Jenny was certain Camilla could now roll over and was perhaps even crawling. Jenny imagined what it would be like to be called Mommy or tickle Camilla's tummy and hear her laugh.

With Christmas coming in a couple of months, thoughts and memories flooded Jenny's mind more than they usually did. She would love to see her baby and give her a Christmas gift. She wished the rules weren't so stringent and she could know who had adopted Camilla, and visit them and her daughter. Sometimes the loss was too great to bear, and she cried herself soundlessly to sleep. She had asked the social worker about it, but she had made it clear that the identity of the adoptive parents could not be revealed.

Just thinking about Christmas reminded her of the special gift she had sent to Henry almost a year ago. That he hadn't responded still pulsed like a dull ache within her. Her guardian angel had let her down. Neither the angel she had sent nor the one she prayed to each night had resulted in an answer that would appease her longing heart.

She wondered how Henry was doing and if he still cared for her as much as she cared for him, or if he ever even thought of her at all. Sometimes Jenny was certain that Henry should be told she had given birth to Camilla. He'd been so concerned that night at the park. And, oh, how often she wished Camilla was Henry's child.

Jenny's only consolation was reading and re-reading the fencepost notes she had received from Henry. She smiled as she thought about the game they had played, each trying to outdo the other with loving thoughts. *"If I had a flower for every time I thought of you, I could walk in my garden forever,"* was a thought she wished she could send to Henry now. If only she were back in Regina she would attach a note with that sentiment to her fencepost with an elastic like they used to. The wish lifted her spirits. She was very glad she hadn't destroyed the notes the previous January—they were such a comfort now.

As she read one of the notes over again, her father peeked into her room.

"'Morning sweetheart, up early I see."

"Just reading some notes, Dad."

Ted walked into her room and to her desk. He looked at the scattering of small squares. "Writing notes to your friends?"

Jenny didn't know if she should tell her dad who the notes were from. She didn't want to upset him, yet she felt so lonely for Henry she had to talk to someone about him.

"Actually, Dad, these are notes Henry wrote to me when we lived in Regina. We played this game, writing notes to each other and then putting them on our fencepost with an elastic." Tears rolled down Jenny's cheeks as she spoke and she wiped them away with the back of her hand.

"Ah, Jenny …" was all that Ted could manage before he too got all choked up. Gazing at the tattered and worn notes tore away at his heart. They were all the poor thing had to cling to. By the looks of it, she must have read them a thousand times over. She could very well be reading one the letters Henry sent to her if they hadn't …

"Oh Dad, I don't want to upset you, but I miss him so much! I sent him *so* many letters and he hasn't written back even one.

We had such a wonderful time together that summer and now it seems it was all a dream."

Ted still couldn't speak, he thought his heart would explode. The guilt, the lies, the deception crushed down on him. He put an arm around his little girl and drew her in so hard Jenny squirmed and had to nudge him slightly away.

"I thought for sure Henry would respond to the last letter I sent him just before last Christmas—I even put a gift inside for him."

Finally gaining his composure and something to respond to Ted blurted out something he immediately wanted to take back.

"Yes, I remember ..."

Jenny looked up at her father, her eyes widening. "You remember? I never told anyone ..."

Ted was momentarily tongue-tied. "But you did tell me, Jenny, I—I ... think it was at the front door, the morning you gave it to me to mail."

"But Dad, I'm certain ..." Jenny gazed into her father's eyes, confused and wary.

"Good morning, you two," Edith said as she walked by Jenny's room. "I'm making a special breakfast. Don't be long—it will be ready soon."

"We'll be down in a minute, Edith." Ted felt a wave of relief at his wife's timely interruption.

"Look, sweetheart, I know how much those notes from Henry mean to you, but they are just keeping alive a painful memory. I can see how it's hurting you, Jenny. You have to let go and get on with your life. What about this James—how do you feel about him?"

"He's nice, Dad, but it's just not the same as it was with Henry and me."

"Well, you have to give it a chance, Jenny. New relationships take time sometimes. Especially for you now ... you will be comparing him to Henry for awhile but soon you may get to like him just as much. Give it a chance, honey."

"I suppose you're right, Dad."

"And why not put those notes in a large envelope, seal it and put it away? Pretend you're putting it in a hope chest along with other things you want to keep memories of. Don't tell your mom, but I still have a letter an old girlfriend wrote me when I was in college tucked away in a box downstairs, along with pins, rings report cards … you know, stuff that still has a memory or two of times past."

Jenny shrugged and started gathering up the notes, stacking them into a neat pile. Slowly she reached into the bottom drawer of her desk and pulled out an envelope. It broke Ted's heart to watch his little girl place her notes into the brown envelope and seal it.

"Perhaps you're right, Dad. The notes *are* just memories."

Jenny placed the envelope in the bottom drawer of her desk, stood up and gave her dad a hug. Unwanted tears spilled over on his cheeks. Jenny could see how much it pained her father to see her suffer over a lost love. She would have to get over it somehow, not just for her sake but her parents as well.

"Come on, let's go see what your mother's made." Ted put his arm around his daughter's shoulder and together they walked out of the room and downstairs. The aroma of a salmon quiche baking in the oven wafted up to greet them.

AND ALL AT ONCE, it seemed that Jenny's heartache stopped. She neither spoke of writing Henry nor asked her parents if any letters had come for her. She began spending more and more time with James Hamilton. The immensity of the relief Ted felt slowly made itself known and he actually began to look forward to coming home. The baby—he couldn't bear to think of her as his granddaughter—had been born and adopted. It was finally over. Maybe they could finally reconnect as a family. Although he still felt guilt over keeping Jenny and Henry apart, at least the constant reminder of the hurt he and Edith had inflicted on their daughter wasn't evident any longer.

He'd thought that his need for what he still thought of as the occasional relaxing drink would have waned too, but it hadn't.

And guilty as he'd felt about everything else, he wasn't about to deny himself the one thing that made it all fade away. Besides, every man had stresses; he was simply coping with his. It wasn't a problem—it was actually a kind of help. Wasn't it?

Ted dreaded the upcoming winter. He hated driving on icy roads and was a nervous wreck by the time he got to his downtown office. Added to that was the worry of being pulled over by the police and caught for drinking too much.

And things might be better at home but they weren't going well at work. He was under growing pressure to produce bigger results and worried the board of directors would soon be asking for his resignation if he didn't deliver. He had received more and more calls from the board chairman, Mr. Peakan, asking about monthly sales stats and improvement strategies. A couple of quick ones helped him feel he could get back on track.

ON THE SURFACE it seemed as if Jenny was finally getting on with her life yet, Ted was still worried about her. She was cheerleading and had joined several clubs, including the school drama club— she'd been given the lead in *The Wizard of Oz*—and was busy with rehearsals and dates with the Hamilton boy.

Still, though he wanted more than anything to take her smiles at face value, Ted grew suspicious of the change in his daughter. Was she really getting on with her life or was it just an attempt on her part to be so involved in other things that it would shut out her memories of Henry? She seemed to have accepted the adoption of her daughter. She'd found some closure there, but Ted suspected the boy still lingered in her thoughts. Just the other day, when she was talking about James, he was sure she was about to say that the Hamilton boy reminded her of Henry, but she'd stopped herself before saying the name. It seemed his daughter could not erase Henry from her life, try as she might to forget him.

His suspicions were only confirmed and reinforced when Jenny approached him one day at the beginning of November.

"Dad, are you going to make a trip to Regina to check on

things there before winter sets in?"

Ted looked at his daughter. The reason she asked was written all over her pretty face.

"No, honey, I have other people looking after that for me."

"But you used to make trips like that all the time."

"That was before I became president, Jenny. I simply don't have time for those kinds of trips anymore and there's no reason to go."

I sure have a reason to go!

If looks could reveal a heart's desire, Jenny's face displayed it all. It pained Ted to see his little girl so dejected and downhearted. He watched as her eyes lost their sparkle, her spirit its hope. The last glimmer of any chance for her to see her beloved was all but completely snatched away.

Slowly, Ted understood that Jenny's exuberance and apparent interest in life was, at least in part, feigned, a façade meant to keep herself busy and forget what might have been. For awhile, Ted had thought she'd gotten over Henry. Slowly, however, her longing for that boy crept back—he noticed that though she never asked about letters anymore, she still looked to see if he'd brought any—evidence that her longing had probably never left her for even a moment.

Jenny was full of tears that did not fall, held in by months of sorrow with no closure … or release.

IN THE SAME WAY his daughter couldn't seem to let go of Henry, Ted could not let go of the guilt and shame he felt for being the cause of it all. His life at home and at work became a living hell. Nightmarish dreams filled his sleep and his office provided no escape: there were too many memories of his wrongdoing. Each time he sat at his desk he saw the box filled with Henry's letters he'd had Elaine destroy, or the letters Jenny had written that he himself had consigned to the incinerator's flames.

As Ted was mulling over these troubling thoughts, there was a light tap on the door. He knew it would be Elaine; he was to get some papers for her from the wall safe. Ted rushed over to the painting, swung it back and dialed in the numbers before she was fully in the room.

"'Morning, Mr. Sarsky, sorry to disturb you."

But her boss didn't seem to hear her or note that she had entered his office. Elaine stood there, waiting, stunned by what she was witnessing.

Her boss opened the safe and pulled out two letters, a white one and pink one, held together by elastics. He stopped and stared at the letters with a look of consternation.

"How the hell did you get to the front of the safe?" Ted asked aloud. His face reddened and his voice rose as he went on, "If you do this one more time you're gonna burn for sure."

He reached inside of the safe and shoved the letters to the very back. Almost three-quarters of his arm disappeared.

"Now stay there!"

He slammed the safe door shut, spun the dial and swung the painting back against the wall, concealing the safe and its contents.

Elaine was about to remind him of the papers he'd obviously forgotten she needed when Ted's unusual behaviour continued.

He was studying the painting intently and drew near to it again, his nose almost touching the artwork. He raised a hand to the clouds and began to swat away as if a fly had rested on the white fluffy clouds.

Elaine cautiously stepped closer to see what it was, but nothing was there.

"How did you get out?!" Ted demanded furiously. He shook his head and stared again, and now his voice was menacing. "You'd better get back there."

He turned on his heel and headed for the liquor cabinet. He opened the doors and quickly fixed himself a drink, downing the entire glass in one long swallow. And then he poured another.

Elaine watched the troubled man slowly begin to relax.

How could a man as smart and as stable as Mr. Sarsky go over the edge like this? She'd been so impressed by his high standards, and his integrity preceded him wherever he went. Clearly, a wrongdoing would bother him immensely. She knew too, that people with addictions try to suppress those things in their lives they are ashamed of or feel blamed for.

What did he do? she wondered.

Without any doubt, those letters were at least part of the problem. What was in them that was causing Mr. Sarsky to behave so erratically and feel so guilty about?

Elaine wished now more than ever that she had kept one of the letters when she'd had the chance. Perhaps she would now understand what this was all about and be able to help her boss somehow.

Suddenly words came to his lips. "Why don't we take a walk to the gazebo, Jenny—I have something I want to tell you ..."

Ted finished his drink, closed the doors to the cabinet and had turned to go to his desk when he noticed Elaine.

"Elaine! I didn't realize you'd come in! Is there something you need?"

"Yes, Mr. Sarsky. I need those contracts you signed with Forbes Company. I have to—"

"Oh. Yes, certainly. They're in the safe."

"You were about to get them for—"

But Ted was staring at the painting again. "I have something I need to do, Elaine. I'll bring the contracts out to you later."

"I need them before noon."

"Of course. I'll have them to you momentarily ... and by the way, Elaine, would you cancel my appointments for next week? Edith and I are going to the cottage for a few days before winter sets in."

"Certainly, Mr. Sarsky—you have been working very hard lately, a few relaxing days at the lake sounds wonderful."

Ted gazed at his secretary and wondered vaguely how long she'd been there. What had she seen? Or heard?

As soon as she left, Ted walked over to his chair and sat down. He again began to compose his conversation with Jenny. A walk to the gazebo would be the perfect way to begin his confession. The thought gave him some peace. But maybe it was too late? Jenny was always so at peace around nature, the sunshine, even the now-dormant plants around the gazebo had a kind of comfort in them, a promise that spring would return. There, he too could draw on nature's solace and find the courage to sit with his daughter and tell her what he and Edith had done.

But the sky out his window was grey and the serenity of that scene in Ted's mind was quickly clouded by the turmoil his confession would cause rather than the freedom that lay just beyond. The valley in which he now lived was too low, too far in the shadows of his misgivings to catch even a glimmer of light and hope.

He glanced again at the painting. He had to get those papers for Elaine. *There they are again.* He was sure the angels had streaked across the brush-stroked sky. And the way they'd perched on the clouds earlier with that awful look of condemnation still sent shivers down his back. He should have taken the letters down to the incinerator right then.

Ted shook his head. The visions of those angels were more torment than the dreams that accompanied his restless sleep at night. He needed another drink in the worst way.

And so he sought the aid of his only friend—at the liquor cabinet Ted reached once again for his confidant and consoler. He poured himself a good stiff drink, and tossed one and then another back, until he could no longer remember why he'd needed a drink in the first place.

But just before he crossed into the safe haven of delusion, Ted felt a flutter inside, the gift his Maker had instilled in all of mankind. Sinful deeds can never remain secret, held captive in the darkness of the heart. In the same way the body works to heal a wound, Ted's soul desired to heal the unclean wounds of his sins. It was this ever-present cry and yearning for forgiveness, which only the truth of light can bring, that Ted could neither suppress nor drown, even if he drank a river of vodka.

Perhaps tomorrow his friend would betray him and he would find himself on the harsh loneliness of the valley floor, wrapped in a fog of iniquity and delirium. Or perhaps the wings of the angels would lift him up into the light and lead him to the peace his troubled mind and heart so deeply longed for.

Or perhaps, someday, the pewter angels would once more rekindle the sparkle of life in his daughter's eyes.

CHAPTER FORTY-ONE

T HE MILD AUTUMN WEATHER continued right into the first
week of November. Henry was glad he was still able to ride
his bike to work on Saturday and use it to make deliveries rather
than waddle around all bundled up as he had in previous years.

As soon as he parked his bike in the usual spot, he noticed
something that instantly shot his spirits up like a rocket. He
quickly ran up the front steps, opened the front door to the store
and stuck his head inside.

"Mr. Engelmann," he said excitedly, "Come quick, you gotta
see this!"

Mr. Engelmann rushed to the door and came outside. Henry
was on the front lawn staring at the lot next door, face beaming
as if struck by the sun.

"Yes, yes, what is it, Henry?"

"See for yourself," Henry said, pointing to the west side of the
store.

A tentative smile grew stronger on Mr. Engelmann's face as
he made his way down the steps, anticipating what it was Henry
was so pleased about. He came to Henry's side and put his arm
around his young assistant's shoulder.

"It was just over a year ago that I saw them put up a for sale sign on that lot. It's finally gone, Mr. Engelmann! Man, is it good to just see weeds there! That sign bothered me every time I came to work."

"The city must have removed it in the last day or so. This is a surprise to me as well." Mr. Engelmann's grip on Henry tightened. "Yes, it makes my heart happy to see this ... Henry, you have been such a huge help to Anna and me. As young as you are, you were the answer to our prayers. You still are. Without you we could very well be looking at a closed store and a for sale sign on the storefront instead."

Henry glanced away, then looked Mr. Engelmann in the eye. "I love working here, Mr. Engelmann, and helping the business get better. Christmas holidays can't come soon enough for me so I can work full time again."

Mr. Engelmann laughed outright and clapped Henry on the shoulder. "You are an entrepreneur at heart, Henry, and a very talented one at that! Come, let us celebrate, I know how much you like hot chocolate."

A horn honked and a blue 1949 Ford sedan rolled to a stop at the curb. Mr. Mahoney got out and put on his black Stetson. He came around to greet them. For once he had a smile on his face.

"I see you've noticed the sign was taken down. I was in the neighbourhood and wanted to tell you it had been removed in case you hadn't noticed yet."

"That is kind of you, Mr. Mahoney. Henry brought it to my attention when he arrived at work this morning."

"You can thank the director. Yesterday morning he called me into his office and instructed me to get rid of the sign. He didn't think you needed to be reminded of that anymore and besides he, and I too, of course, have full confidence in your store's future. It's quite incredible what you've achieved in such a short time."

Mr. Mahoney looked at Henry and then at the old store owner. "I've got to admit, this young man of yours has turned out to be quite the employee."

"Yes, we were just discussing it. He has truly been a blessing to us."

Henry's face reddened a bit and grew even redder as both men stared at him. Not knowing what to say, Henry just nodded.

"It is good of you to have the sign taken down, though we still have two more payments to make. I'm happy no one was interested enough to purchase the property."

"Well, we did receive several offers, but I told the potential buyers it was already sold—which, of course, was true." Mr. Mahoney winked at Mr. Engelmann. "Like I said, the director and I—"

With a start, Henry realized he probably shouldn't be listening to this business talk and excused himself. "I'll restock the shelves and get the hot water started, Mr. Engelmann."

"That's a good idea, Henry. I'll be along in a moment."

"See ya, Mr. Mahoney," Henry said as he turned to go.

"You've done a fine job for Mr. Engelmann, young man. You should be very proud of yourself. If you're looking for a job after Grade 12, you be sure to come see me."

Henry nodded and went into the store.

HENRY HAD TWO STEAMING CUPS of hot chocolate on the counter when Mr. Engelmann came back inside.

"Ah, the air is crisp in the morning. This will drive the chill out of my bones," Mr. Engelmann said as he picked up the hot chocolate, blew on it and took a careful sip.

Henry put down the can he was about to set on the shelf and came to the counter. He picked up his mug of chocolate and tipped it towards the one in Mr. Engelmann's hand, a wide smile lighting his face.

Mr. Engelmann grinned in response. "Yes, here's to our success, Henry! And Anna will be so happy to hear the news."

"How is Mrs. Engelmann today?"

"Well," Mr. Engelmann's smile faded a bit. "She is not doing as well as I'd like. The doctor wants to admit her into the hospital, but I always tell him no. Anna loves it here at home and especially enjoys sitting by the window in the afternoon and reading the Bible. She enjoys watching the comings and goings, and the visits from the people in the neighbourhood."

"Yeah, she sure knows a lot of ladies."

"Yes, in spite of her illness, she still continues to help many people. And that reminds me. She does ask about you all the time and the thought came to me this morning when I was praying that you may want to visit her as well."

"I would like that, Mr. Engelmann. When she's in the store it makes the whole place seem different somehow ... she brings something to the store that's kind of hard to explain—and I like talking to her."

"I've heard that many times before, Henry. She brings charm and grace and makes the store a home to our customers. She communicates from the heart."

"Yes, that's it, Mr. Engelmann! I feel such a peace in her presence, and so did Gary." And after a bit of thought Henry blurted, "If I go upstairs to talk with Mrs. Engelmann, it would mean I would be away from working in the store. Is that okay with you?"

"It's fine with me, Henry. I know she will receive so much joy from your presence ... that is something that money cannot buy."

That last comment pierced Henry's heart. Mr. Engelmann had it the wrong way around.

Suddenly the door burst open and Eddy rushed in. "How ya doing, Hank? Hey, Mr. Engelmann. Geez, I ran out of smokes last night! The drugstore's still closed so I decided to see if you were open—I need a weed like right now."

Henry smiled and held back a chuckle at Eddy's brashness.

"You sure you need to smoke?" Mr. Engelmann gazed hard into Eddy's eyes.

Eddy stepped up to the counter and laid down a dollar and stared back at Mr. Engelmann with a questioning look. "Well..."

"Well, what?"

"Did you forget my brand already?"

Mr. Engelmann cracked a slight smile, turned around and took a pack of Black Cat off the shelf and laid it on the counter.

"Very good, Mr. Engelmann."

Eddy removed the cellophane, opened the packet and had pulled off the aluminum foil even before Mr. Engelmann rang in the purchase. Smoke was trailing on the counter as Eddy picked up his change.

"Hey, Hank, there's a re-run of the Harlem Globetrotters movie at the Roxy on Friday, wanna go?"

"Yeah, sure, maybe you'll finally pick something up about the game," ribbed Henry.

"Not a chance, Hank, you taught me more than I'll never learn from those amateurs."

"Should I come to your place and we'll take the trolley?"

"Nah, my ol' man'll take us."

"Eddy, that's not the way to refer to your father."

Eddy looked at Mr. Engelmann, "Yeah, you're right … so, okay, Hank, me and pop will pick you up. Thanks for the weeds, Mr. Engelmann. See ya, Hank."

"Yeah, see you, Eddy."

Mr. Engelmann waved his hand, trying to dissipate the smoke Eddy left behind. "That's some young man," Mr. Engelmann said, shaking his head.

"Yeah, he's that all right. You know, as bad a thing Eddy and his friends did, there's a part of Eddy that's appealing."

"Yes, Henry, there is good in all of us. Unfortunately there is a tendency to focus on the bad. Still, it seems you have become friends."

"Yeah, but I still can't seem to forget what he did. Just when I think I've forgiven him, angry feelings begin to stir in the pit of my stomach."

"What did the Lord say? We must forgive seventy times seven. Forgiveness starts in the head and eventually it gets to the heart. It's the journey we must take each time someone harms us."

"I know, Mr. Engelmann. I've forgiven Eddy from my head …

but if I had really forgiven him I wouldn't still be harbouring this anger every now and then. Now that I think of it ... it's sort of like the sun is shining while at the same time a silent storm is brewing just beyond the horizon."

Mr. Engelmann smiled at Henry's analogy. "We've been through this before, Henry, but it doesn't hurt to go over it again. Unforgiveness is one of the main obstacles to peace of mind. It's the culprit that steals from the enjoyment of our present moments time and time again. I've been guilty of playing the tape over in my mind in the past too.

"What you're feeling, Henry, is that part of you that doesn't want to let go. That part of you that wants to get even, wants to pay back for the hurt the other has caused. Most of its pride, Henry ... like 'I'm going to make you pay for what you've done to me.'"

Henry nodded and remained silent. He knew Mr. Engelmann would reinforce what he'd just said and he was right.

"You're still trapped in the bondage of unforgiveness. Even if Eddy were to say he was sorry, you would still not be free of what you're feeling until you forgive from the heart and let go. The joy and freedom that comes with forgiveness can come in a split second or it can be painfully long. Some people will hold onto hurts all their lives, not even able to remember what the initial injury was on their dying day! No. You have to choose constantly, Henry, seventy times seven. Even though the other caused the injury, it's up to you to forgive and love them ... and do so quickly."

Henry stared hard at his mentor, taking it all in again—and then Mr. Engelmann said something that was a warning, something he realized he had better listen to.

"Remember what Jesus said after He was scourged and nailed to the cross: 'Forgive them, Father.' Imagine! He loved us even in our sins, our rejection of Him, and our cruelty to Him. We are called to forgive too, Henry, and unless you do so, Jesus cannot forgive you ... how can He come into your heart if a spirit of anger, resentment and revenge resides there? Oh, how He wants to forgive you of your sin, but it is you that keeps Him out!"

"Geez, Mr. Engelmann, you sure know how to plaster a guy to the wall!"

After a silent moment, Henry continued in a subdued voice that carried wisdom, insight and sorrow. "You know, Mr. Engelmann, I feel that same undercurrent of not letting go exists in our family. I think Mom is stuck like I am. On the surface it looks like Mom has forgiven Dad for what he did, but I know she really hasn't .... Will they ever love each again like before ... well, you know."

Mr. Engelmann reached across the counter and patted Henry's hand. "Pray, Henry, and trust in the Lord. That is the best thing you can do. Forgiveness must come freely from the person harmed. Just as you have difficulty forgiving Eddy, your mother may still have difficulty forgiving your father.

"Prayer is what is needed now. Pray that we receive the grace and strength from God to do what is best for all. As I said earlier, Henry, you will find as you go through life—as I'm sure others will too—the biggest and most important hurdle you must overcome is the spirit of unforgiveness."

Mr. Engelmann paused for a moment and Henry was willing to wager that his teacher was trying to recall a scripture that would apply to the matter at hand. He would have won the bet.

"There is a passage I often quote to remind myself of the power of prayer ... yes, Mark 11:24: "What things so ever you desire when you pray, believe that you receive them and you shall have them."

"Geez, Mr. Engelmann, that's the same one my mom asked me to read a few weeks ago when we started a novena for Jenny to write a letter to me. Mom said she quoted that scriptural passage every day when she prayed for Dad to come back."

"And what were the results? She believed with all her heart and trusted and had faith in her Lord that He would help her. She has given you that same gift to use in your life ... the power of prayer, the power of God's Word."

Henry gazed at his wise mentor and tears came to his eyes.

He wanted so much for his parents to make up and for them to be a family again. He could clearly see what Mr. Engelmann meant about how unforgiveness could hold one in bondage, hold a family in bondage.

But there's nothing I can do. It has to come from them.

Yeah, prayer and trusting in its power to heal was all that could really help, and he knew deep in his heart that his prayers to God for Jenny and him would someday be answered too.

A soothing quietness settled over the store and Henry was glad. He enjoyed these moments with his mentor. Henry took a sip of hot chocolate and then asked Mr. Engelmann something that had been burning in his heart for some time.

"Do you think I'll ever see Jenny again, Mr. Engelmann?" The sparkle in Henry's eyes that had reflected the success of the store had been replaced by a more forlorn look when he spoke of his parents troubles, and now suddenly deepened with pain, loss and heartache.

Mr. Engelmann was so startled by the question his spectacles almost slid off the end of his nose. He adjusted his glasses and after a thoughtful moment said, "Yes, Henry, if it's meant to be, you will see Jenny again …. You have not mentioned her for some time."

"Well, I promised you after we sent that box of letters to Mr. Sarsky that if I didn't hear from Jenny I would get on with my life. But even though I've tried really hard to forget her I just can't. When Jenny left, you told me that time would heal our separation, but it hasn't! I ache for her as much now as the day she left … even more, maybe. Shouldn't I be getting over her?"

"It *is* unusual to still have such strong feelings—"

Henry interrupted, "I have a confession to make, Mr. Engelmann. I never told you but I sent another letter to Mr. Sarsky to give to Jenny last Christmas. I—I copied his business address off the box of letters."

Henry studied his mentor for a moment to see if he was angry with him for doing so and for breaking his promise. Mr. Engelmann held his gaze, but his expression was neutral. He nodded for Henry to continue.

Henry took a deep breath and rushed to explain.

"I missed her so much last Christmas I just had to do it and besides, I'd found a gift to send her. It was a pewter angel. It was perfect because I know how much Jenny loves her guardian angel. I thought for sure Mr. Sarsky would give it to Jenny, being Christmas and all. But not even the pewter angel got a response."

Henry lowered his head and stared at a spot on the marble counter. If he blinked tears would roll. He rubbed at the spot with his finger, struggling to keep his emotions in check.

"That must have been very disappointing for you."

Henry raised his chin, "Yeah, and it still is .... Do you believe in angels, Mr. Engelmann?"

"Yes, of course, Henry. From the moment we are conceived, God sends an angel to our side to watch over and protect us."

"Do you remember that day Jenny almost got hit by the car and at the last moment she was suddenly out of harm's way? I still dream about it. It was a miracle she wasn't hurt! Jenny told me she believed her guardian angel had saved her. And you told me the same thing too. Do you remember?"

"I remember only too well. I am still bewildered by what happened—"

"What do you mean, Mr. Engelmann? How Jenny was saved?"

"Yes, that and also how I was at your side so quickly. One moment I was behind the counter, watching you stare out of the front window—and the next I was by your side, supporting you. When you went outside, I followed and felt compelled to tell you Jenny's guardian angel was protecting her, even though I hadn't seen what you did."

"Geez, Mr. Engelmann, I remember that clearly. You were just suddenly right there!"

"Yes. When I told Anna what had happened that day—that it seemed to me I was transported to your side somehow—she told me I was getting absentminded, that I'd probably followed you without realizing. But I'm certain I stayed behind the counter; I was working on an invoice ..." Mr. Engelmann scratched his head, brow wrinkling in concentration. Then his forehead cleared. "Ach, well. Perhaps Anna's right … it all happened so quickly and I have no memory of it other than one moment here and the next there." Mr. Engelmann shrugged.

"You know, Mr. Engelmann, before that happened, I hadn't thought about guardian angels since I was little. It was only after you mentioned it to me that day that I remembered I have this unseen helper. Now I feel so many times that he is there watching over me—and so did Jenny. That's why I was so happy to find that pewter angel for her."

Mr. Engelmann leaned forward and rested his elbows on the counter.

"When I was five or six years of age, it was then that my mother in earnest explained to me about angels—that they are always beside us, guiding us and that we should always be on our best behaviour.

"From that time on she always reminded me of the importance of living in a manner that glorifies God—because your guardian angel is very hurt and disappointed when you don't. And she explained the meaning of our family name."

"Your name? What do you mean?" Henry was puzzled.

"Ah, Henry. *Auf Deutsch*, in German, the name Engelmann means 'angel man.' And my first name, David, means 'beloved.' So my mother always told me that I was a man beloved of the angels and must forever be worthy of my name."

Mr. Engelmann smiled gently and pushed his glasses back up his nose. "I don't know whether it has to do with the name or not but I have always felt a responsibility to help guide those who come into my life, to be a good example to others, and to serve them as well."

"Angel man," Henry whispered. "That's beautiful, Mr. Engelmann. I've always considered you to be a kind of guardian …" A quiet joy lit within Henry. "And now I know why."

Mr. Engelmann chuckled. "I see a guardian angel in you as well, Henry. As I explained to you outside, you have been a huge help to Anna and me … an answer to our prayers." The rims of

Mr. Engelmann's eyes reddened.

Henry was a little embarrassed by all the praise lavished on him this morning. And besides, he couldn't take all the credit. There were lots of times Henry was as surprised as Mr. Engelmann by all the ideas he had for the store.

After a brief silence, Henry said, "I sure wish Mr. Sarsky's angel would prompt him to give my letters to Jenny. I just know he and Jenny's mom are keeping the letters from her."

"That may be true, but Henry, you must keep in mind … perhaps Jenny has found new friends and has gone on with her life."

Mr. Engelmann looked at the young man he cared about, hoping his remarks were not too hard to accept.

But Henry's answer was firm. "No, I know Jenny, Mr. Engelmann. If she had received any of my letters she would have written back. I'm afraid Mr. and Mrs. Sarsky aren't letting her write to me either. I don't think they want me to have their home address."

Mr. Engelmann remained silent though he almost imperceptively shrugged his shoulders and tilted his head. Henry hoped it was a sign of agreement and he pressed on.

"I still can't believe the pewter angel didn't get to Jenny. I know she would have loved it. Jenny's dad must have a cold, cold heart not to have given it to her. It was Christmas and contained a gift I know Jenny would have loved to receive and—"

"Yes, Henry, that is your perspective. We have talked about this many times over the past year. Everybody sees things from their own point of view. What you consider to be wrong, another may very well see it as the right thing to do. Our only hope is that Mr. Sarsky changes his mind on the matter."

"Yeah, I suppose so. But someday, Mr. Engelmann, regardless of whether or not Mr. Sarsky changes his mind, I'll find out what happened. Our guardian angels are going to bring us back together again, I just know it."

Henry pushed himself away from the counter and straightened his shoulders. Unbidden tears sat on the edge of his eyelids. "I have a plan, Mr. Engelmann. Soon, I will know the truth …"

Mr. Engelmann straightened too. Resting his hands on the edge of the counter, he looked hard into Henry's eyes and nodded. And Henry saw his own determination to seek out his first love clearly reflected in his teacher's face.

COMING SOON

THE ANGELIC LETTERS SERIES

Book Two

——— ✷ ———

ANOTHER
ANGEL OF LOVE

1959-1964

HENRY K. RIPPLINGER

The following is a preview of Chapter One

CHAPTER ONE

ON JULY 6TH, 1959, two days after his eighteenth birthday, Henry awoke thinking about Jenny for the second year in a row. It was three years to the day since he'd first laid eyes on her. He remembered it vividly. Jenny Sarsky had walked past his house on her way to Mr. Engelmann's store; they had met there, and the moment he gazed into her eyes he'd been completely smitten. It had been love at first sight; the yearning in his heart for Jenny as strong now as it had been back then.

When they'd walked home together, she'd said, "Quickly, hold my hand!" as they rushed across the busy avenue, the touch of her warm palm sending an electrifying surge through his body. He would never forget the wonderful phrase Jenny had said so often that summer. *Quickly, hold my hand*, Henry softly repeated to himself as he lay in bed, recalling it all: their summer together, walks, dates, secret notes, a bike ride at the park, then her sudden departure.

That day at the park ... they had almost made love. In a way, he still regretted that they hadn't, although he knew stopping had been the right thing to do. And then there were those guys who'd dragged her off one night ... he still hoped to find out what had really happened.

He knew if he stayed in bed dwelling on it any longer, he'd just grow despondent and self-pitying. It had happened to him a year ago. Memories had flooded his mind and heart so intensely that for days after he could think of nothing except Jenny. He'd started meditating and praying every morning to help him get through it. Mr. Engelmann suggested it and Henry had seen how it helped him deal with and accept his wife's illness.

He was glad for summer holidays. It had been a good year! He'd finished Grade 11 with excellent grades and had loved his art class. He had been elected president of the student council and gotten along well with most of his classmates.

As much as he liked school, he also loved working for Mr. Engelmann and would be working full-time for the next two months. They'd had incredible success over the past two years. Business had more than tripled and was flourishing in all aspects. Henry loved the challenge of the business and the opportunity to make it a success, but even more so, he loved the talks he and Mr. Engelmann had out back behind the store, sitting on the old weathered crates in the warmth of the sun.

Mr. Engelmann was one of the wisest people Henry had ever met. Mr. Engelmann must have been a great teacher back in Austria and influenced the lives of many young people. Although Mr. and Mrs. Engelmann had every reason to be bitter about what had happened to them and their families during the Second World War, they weren't. Mr. Engelmann always said, "Regardless of where we find ourselves in life, regardless of our circumstances, it's what we do with life, how we live it—and ultimately how we serve—that is the important thing."

And serve is what they did. David and Anna Engelmann dedicated their lives to the service of others. It was evident every day in the store. For Mr. and Mrs. Engelmann, selling groceries was simply a way to reach out to others. They lived modest, humble lives. They never talked about or boasted of their educational background. No one even suspected they were both university graduates and had probably forgotten more about worldly affairs than most people in the neighbourhood ever learned in a lifetime.

Indeed, Henry was privileged to know Mr. Engelmann. If it hadn't been for his mentor's help in dealing with Jenny's sudden departure, Henry was almost certain he wouldn't have been able to cope. The loss he'd felt, compounded by not hearing from her again, would have been too much to bear without Mr. Engelmann's support, care, empathy and advice.

He stretched and scratched his head, tugging the sheet up. Summer holidays would mean that they had more time to talk. On schooldays, they had to wait until they closed the store for the day, but then they talked over the counter for however long it took. "You can't share your heart in a hurry," was something Mr. Engelmann often said.

During the summer, either Mrs. Engelmann or Mrs. Schmidt tended to the store so he and Mr. Engelmann could go out back, have a soda pop and talk about life. At times Mr. Engelmann used big words and referenced famous psychologists or psychiatrists: Eric Fromm, Abraham Maslow, Ivan Pavlov, B.F. Skinner, Victor Frankl, Sigmund Freud, Carl Jung and Carl Rogers. He and Henry would compare the different schools of thought, regarding conditioning, Gestalt psychology, existentialism, rational emotive therapy and behaviour modification.

Mr. Engelmann would say, "It's not the person's name or who said it or the school of thought that is important, but rather the lesson on life that they taught."

Henry clung to Mr. Engelmann's every word as if they were the last ones he ever expected to hear. Mr. Engelmann had a way of explaining the most complex thoughts and topics in a simple and straightforward way that somehow always applied to whatever difficulty Henry was facing. In the end, it usually had to do with making choices based on values, and those in turn, seemed always to relate to the values and principles of the Bible.

"It's all there, Henry. It's very important to read the Bible every day, so you stay focused on what is really important in life. All the psychologists, philosophers and psychiatrists in the world have not really discovered anything new. They are simply relating what was already taught from the beginning when our good Lord walked the earth and showed us the way, the truth and the light."

Who passing by, seeing a young man and an old man sitting on an old crate behind an old grocery store, would have thought that such knowledge was being discussed and passed down?

Henry stretched again. It was only six in the morning and the thin cotton curtains on the window couldn't keep the bright sun from flooding his bedroom with a soft light. Time to get up and pray. It always started his day off right. Mornings were so peaceful, and because it was summer and he didn't have to worry about school, Henry actually looked forward to getting up early.

He rolled out of bed, dressed and sat at his desk. He read a few chapters in the Bible and then sat quietly with his eyes closed. He was getting better at emptying his mind of all thought and found it very relaxing. The first step in the process was to focus on his breathing. It brought him into the present moment.

Mr. Engelmann would say, "We need to think about the past at times, and also of the future, but to fret and worry about it constantly is a waste of life. Living in the now is living a focused life, an undivided life and a full life. The more we can live in the present, the more aware we are of our true selves and our ability to serve others."

Presently, the stillness was broken by the sound of his mother in the kitchen, getting ready for the day and planning her meals. He decided to get some breakfast.

Henry passed his father in the hallway. "Have a nice day, Dad."

"Yeah, you, too, Henry. You're up early."

"Yeah, I couldn't sleep any longer and I'm anxious to get to the store."

"Well, I'm glad you like your work."

Henry didn't respond because he knew his dad didn't really care for his own job. He wished his dad could find something else. It must be awful to go to work every day and not enjoy it. How trapped and unfulfilling that must feel.

"What would you like for breakfast, Henry?" his mother asked when he appeared in the kitchen.

"Oh, corn flakes and toast will be fine."

He looked forward to sitting and chatting with his mom for awhile. The sun beamed through the east window of the kitchen, filling the room with peace and warmth. It complimented the love he and his mom felt for each other.

They chatted about the day ahead, her gardening and her desire to find some part-time work. He sensed a loneliness in his mom as they talked. He knew it had something to do with his dad. His parents' relationship hadn't been the same since his father returned home after running off. Henry wanted to talk about it at some point but felt he had already thought too much about life for one day.

When he stepped outside he realized it was going to be another warm day. The sky was clear, not a cloud in sight. A lone jet climbed high above him and left a long double trail of white vapour that converged into one wide streak and dissipated into the cerulean blue sky. He took in a long breath of fresh morning air. Many of their neighbours had already turned on their sprinklers before the water demand got too high, reducing the pressure to a trickle. It hadn't rained in days, and homeowners were putting a heavy strain on the city's tenuous water supply. Henry reminded himself to put the hose on Mr. Engelmann's front lawn as he walked between the houses to get his bike.

Henry waved to Mr. Weichel, who was always up and out working in the yard if the weather was nice. Mr. Weichel's garden and the flower bed in his front yard were the nicest on the block.

And there was Mrs. Kartush, watering her petunias.

"'Morning, Mrs. Kartush," Henry yelled as he sped past her. He didn't know if she had heard him; her hearing was starting to go. Henry loved the people in the neighbourhood, and because of his job he knew almost everyone. They were mainly

European in origin, hard-working and God-fearing. They helped each other out whenever they could. Henry felt a strong sense of belonging.

Mr. Engelmann was always up and downstairs in the store by seven-thirty and usually had the front door unlocked by eight in anticipation of Henry's arrival. When he entered the store that morning, however, the front door was unlocked, but the lights were still off and Mr. Engelmann was not downstairs.

Henry went to the back storage room and flipped the light switches to both the back and front parts of the store, bringing a bit of life to the old building. It was unusual for Mr. Engelmann not to be down yet. He hoped the old man wasn't sick. Perhaps Anna needed his attention; she hadn't been well again lately.

In tenth grade, Henry had started visiting Anna in her bedroom on occasion. On his first visit, he'd found her resting in an ornate antique canopy bed, her face as pale as the lacy white sheets. Anna's parents had owned such a bed, and when she'd seen one like it in an antique store, she'd told her husband she just had to have it. So they had purchased the bed, along with two end tables to go on either side, a dresser, chest of drawers and two lamps. The end tables didn't match the other furniture but they seemed to fit because they were antiques and elegant in their own right.

Since that first visit, Henry had visited Anna many times. He liked talking to her. She was as wise as Mr. Engelmann but softer spoken, preferring to listen. Henry often worried about her health, and hoped his visits cheered her and weren't too strenuous. Mr. Engelmann was very protective of Anna's need to rest and she didn't often come down into the store anymore.

Over the months, Anna had conveyed to Henry how much she and her husband enjoyed having him around and what a blessing he was to them. One morning, she had told him they thought of him as their son. Henry sensed such love when she'd said that, he couldn't help but lean over and kiss her on the cheek before he left. And after that, each time Henry visited her, he did that as naturally as if she *were* his mother.

When nine o'clock came and went and Mr. Engelmann didn't appear downstairs, Henry knew something was wrong. Obviously, Mr. Engelmann had been down at some point because the front door was open, but for some reason, he hadn't stayed downstairs or turned on any of the lights. Yet he didn't want to intrude on the Engelmanns' privacy, especially if Anna was having one of her bad days.

The phone rang, startling Henry.

"Engelmann's Grocery, how may I help you? And good morning to you, Mrs. Neaster. Yes, it is a beautiful day. Sure, we can deliver that. Two pounds of salami, a loaf of fresh French bread and a pound of butter. Is there anything else, Mrs. Neaster? Do you need it before lunch? Okay then, we'll deliver it sometime today. Good-bye."

Henry replaced the receiver and left the order for Mr. Engelmann. Mr. Engelmann always knew how each customer preferred their meat cut. The sun streamed in, making the dust motes dance and Henry remembered the front lawn. He went to water it, hoping Mr. Engelmann would be down by the time he finished.

A half hour later, Henry was back inside. But Mr. Engelmann was still nowhere to be seen. There was no choice but to go upstairs and find out what was wrong.

The staircase was dimly lit by the south-facing window. It was usually brighter up here, especially by this hour of the morning. The blinds must still be closed. Not a good sign.

Henry always worried that he would be intruding or might startle Anna by going up there. But at that moment he was more afraid than nervous.

"Mr. Engelmann," he called out in a low whisper. After a moment, he repeated the call again, a little louder this time. There was no answer. Henry climbed up a few steps and peered into the dim light, trying to see. He wondered if he should call the police.

But then it might be nothing. Maybe Mr. Engelmann had just gone back to bed after opening the store for him. He'd never done that before but he'd been awfully tired lately.

Henry summoned up more courage and climbed a few more stairs. Once again he called out for Mr. Engelmann, but didn't receive a response. At the top of the stairs, he looked around. All the lights were off, and as he had assumed, the blinds on the window beneath which Mr. Engelmann and Anna usually sat and read were closed, the only light seeping in around the edges.

He gazed down the hall and saw a soft glow in the bedroom doorway. Henry didn't know if he should go in. He was sure the Engelmanns were just sleeping. But he had to wake up Mr. Engelmann, didn't he? He'd be mortified if he slept the morning away while Henry worked alone downstairs. Henry imagined Mr. Engelmann's ruddy face next to Anna's pale one. What a contrast. The image only added to his growing nervousness.

Henry tiptoed down the hall, not really knowing why since he had every intention of waking Mr. Engelmann anyway. He neared the doorway, hearing nothing but the pounding of his heart. Perspiration rolled down his back. Finally, he reached the doorway and dared to peek in—and the image in front of him was forever imprinted in his mind and heart.

Mr. Engelmann sat in a chair beside the bed, holding Anna's still hand in both of his. His head was bowed. Anna's eyes were closed. Mr. Engelmann's curved back heaved slightly. He was sobbing, the tears silent. Henry knew then that Anna was gone. He stood there, half in and half out of the doorway, frozen, unsure what to do.

A chill trickled down Henry's back as if all the warmth had left the room with Anna's spirit. Slowly, he drew close to Mr. Engelmann and put his hand on his shoulder. As he did, Mr. Engelmann's sobbing increased. Mr. Engelmann took one hand away from Anna's and placed it on top of Henry's. In the peace and stillness of the moment, they mourned their loss.

Henry's heart went out to Mr. Engelmann. He had loved his wife and would miss her so much. Henry knew he would really miss their visits; he'd loved her like a second mom. Actually, now that he thought of it, he was surprised he wasn't crying, too.

Maybe he was in shock. He couldn't keep his eyes off Anna. He'd never seen someone who'd just died.

Mrs. Engelmann looked perfectly peaceful, a soft smile on her face and a gentle glow on her skin. She finally looked at rest. She had been ill for so long. She should have been in the hospital, but Mr. Engelmann had refused, insisting on carrying the burden of looking after her day after day himself. He had never complained, only loved his wife and served her until the end. Mr. Engelmann had told him it was an honour to look after Anna, and often commented on how she cheered him up when everyone thought it was the other way around.

Suddenly Henry remembered the store was open and unattended. He had no idea how long he'd been upstairs.

"Mr. Engelmann," he said in a low voice, "I better go back downstairs."

"Yes, yes, go ahead," Mr. Engelmann whispered back. He patted Henry's hand then took Anna's again. "Thank you, Henry."

Henry backed out of the room, a picture seared in his mind's eye: Anna Engelmann still under the sheets, the warm glow of the lamp caressing her face; Mr. Engelmann behind the light as if in the shadows, weeping and holding her hand, giving it his warmth, and the wooden cross on the wall above them with the bronze sculpture of the Lord reflecting the light. It was He who was at the centre of their lives, at the heart of their marriage. It was He who helped them carry their burdens, and it was He who united them now.

Henry was deeply moved by the beauty of that moment, by love that was shared even in death. He felt the urge to draw what he'd seen, paint it, freeze it on canvas. Why would he think such a thing at a time like this? He bumped into the doorway, startling Mr. Engelmann and himself. He slowly turned and made his way into the light coming up the stairs from the storage room below.

Downstairs, the phone jangled. He ran towards it, but it stopped ringing as he got there. He was glad. He wasn't ready to talk to a customer just yet. He looked around the store and was grateful no one had come in. He decided to sweep the floor and restock the shelves. He'd wait for Mr. Engelmann to tell him what more he should do.

He was concerned about Mrs. Engelmann, though. Surely she couldn't stay in the bedroom? How was Mr. Engelmann going to get her out of there? Henry thought about the funeral. His mind buzzed with questions. Who would Mr. Engelmann want as pallbearers? Would Mr. Engelmann have to go buy a coffin? Where would the funeral be held?

It's so complicated to die.

Then Mr. Engelmann appeared in the storeroom doorway. He looked tired and sad. His eyes were swollen and his shoulders slouched a little more than usual. His glasses were so smudged they looked frosted over, as he'd just come in from the cold. He wore the same sweater vest he usually did. He could afford a new one and maybe a nicer one, but he was satisfied with what he had. He was comfortable, liked things simple and saw no need to change his appearance.

Mr. Engelmann walked towards Henry, patting his shoulder as he passed. When he got to the front door, he turned the deadbolt above the doorknob to the right until it clicked and locked, then flipped the sign, which Henry had turned to OPEN when he'd come in, back to CLOSED. Mr. Engelmann slowly walked back to Henry and put his arm around his young partner's shoulder. "Come, Henry. Let us go sit on the old crate out back and feel the morning sun on our faces for awhile."

As they emerged from the back of the store, they squinted against the bright sun. They sat down side by side as they had done so many times before.

Fully expecting a conversation about loss and death, Henry was surprised when Mr. Engelmann began talking about how he had first met Anna, how he'd known from the first day she would be his wife. He talked about her qualities, charm, mannerisms and looks, all the things that had attracted him to her. He talked about their life, marriage, honeymoon, first apartment and first home. He talked about their trials and sorrows, including the fact that they could not have children. He talked about their love of theatre and music. He talked about how they'd gotten out of Germany during the war and come to Canada. Mr. Engelmann told Henry his life story, passing on the legacy to the only son they had.

Mr. Engelmann finished shortly after noon, ending with how they'd bought the store and the plans they'd had, some of which had not turned out. In a sense he was reliving his life with his chosen mate, not regretting one minute of it. If there were any regrets, it would be that his time with Anna hadn't been long enough. Mr. Engelmann was deeply in love with Anna.

Henry could relate; it was how he felt about Jenny.

They sat in silence, each in his own thoughts. Henry thought of Jenny and how he had wanted her for his wife. He envied Mr. Engelmann for having married his true love .

"Well, Henry, you can sit for awhile longer if you wish. I have things that need to be done."

When Henry came back into the store, Mr. Engelmann was on the phone to the funeral home. When he hung up, Henry asked if they should open the door to customers.

"No, today is a day for mourning, Henry. It is Anna's day. We respect her passing today. I am not interested in making money or carrying on any other business than what I have to do now. When the ambulance comes, let them in, Henry, and show them the way upstairs. I am going up now, to get Anna ready. You stay here, answer the phone, and tell people we are closed and why. Do the same for anyone who comes to the door. Tell them we will be open again tomorrow, but will be closed on the day of Anna's funeral."

As Mr. Engelmann turned to leave, he said, "Maybe phone Mrs. Schmidt and tell her to come in for awhile today, and for sure tomorrow because I won't be here for most of the day. I have many things to do and many preparations to make."

As Mr. Engelmann headed upstairs, Henry remembered Mrs. Neaster's phone call. "Mr. Engelmann, Mrs. Neaster phoned when I got in this morning and placed an order for salami, bread and butter. I told her I would deliver it today. Should I phone and tell her that we can't right now?"

"No, no, if you promised her it would be delivered today, then we must honour your word." He walked over to the meat counter, took out the salami and cut the meat the way he knew Mrs. Neaster liked it, then wrapped it first in clear wax paper and then coated brown paper. He wrote the weight and price on the outside of the package then laid it on top of the glass display case.

"Here, Henry, finish the order and take it to her this afternoon when you can."

So Henry phoned Mrs. Schmidt and explained to customers who called and knocked about Anna, telling them the store would re-open the following day. Many cried as soon as Henry told them. He'd never realized how much the community loved Mr. and Mrs. Engelmann.

Besides their visits, Henry's most vivid memories of Anna were of her kindness and sincerity, and how she never complained about her pain. She always wanted to help, despite Mr. Engelmann's insistence that she rest. Henry had always liked it when she was able to come down to the store. She brought with her a sense of peace and an aura of simple elegance and charm.

A tapping at the front door startled Henry from his recollections. The ambulance had arrived. He opened the door and held it while the men entered, carrying a cot between them. He led the men upstairs, calling up to Mr. Engelmann that the ambulance men were there. When they arrived at the bedroom door, a teary Mr. Engelmann greeted them and swept a hand towards the bed.

It was still hard for Henry to believe. Anna looked as if she was asleep. Her arms lay on top of the covers, her hands holding each other naturally.

"I thought I would leave her nightgown on," said Mr. Engelmann, breaking the silence.

"That's fine," said the first man who entered the room. "They will dress her at the funeral home, if you have clothes you want to send along. You can stay if you wish, or you can wait down-stairs while we get her ready."

"No, no, I will stay."

It was evident that it bothered Mr. Engelmann to have to share the sanctity and privacy of his bedroom with other men.

The first attendant walked to the other side of the bed and reached for the covers. He gently slid them from underneath Mrs. Engelmann's arms and slowly lowered the sheets, making certain that he wouldn't expose her unnecessarily. But Mr. Engelmann had anticipated this and had prepared her so that her modesty was preserved, her gown pulled down as far as it could go, wrapped snuggly around her ankles and tucked in underneath. All that showed were her tiny feet, tight together and pointing straight up.

The man removed a heavy vinyl plastic bag of olive green from the case he'd been carrying. He set the bag down on the white bedspread beside Mrs. Engelmann and unrolled it in the space where Mr. Engelmann normally slept. The bag had a long zipper in the middle, running its entire length. He opened it wide and then motioned to the second man. They leaned over to the far side of the bed and slid their hands underneath Mrs. Engelmann. They appeared off-balance, but Mrs. Engelmann was so frail and light they had no trouble lifting her and placing her into the open bag.

Mr. Engelmann gasped as the first man took hold of the zip-per and slowly pulled it up over Anna's face, closing out the last image that Henry and Mr. Engelmann would ever have of Anna in her bedroom. It seemed a cruel thing to do, and yet it was necessary. Henry went over to Mr. Engelmann and put his hand on his shoulder.

They both stared at the cold plastic bag. It seemed so wrong for such a warm, loving person to be sealed inside it.

The ambulance attendants slid their arms underneath the plastic bag and shifted it towards the other side of the bed, making room to set down the stretcher. It was evident they had done this many times before. They laid the stretcher on the edge of the bed beside Mrs. Engelmann and shifted her onto it. The men then buckled up the straps, pulling very hard to make them tight so they wouldn't lose her going down the stairs. The first man then nodded to the second and they lifted the stretcher.

Under Henry's hand, Mr. Engelmann tensed as his wife's body left the bedroom.

MR. ENGELMANN STOOD MOTIONLESS in the bedroom as Henry and the ambulance men left with Anna's body. He had almost touched the bag as it went by, but seeing the bag had been bad enough without adding the memory of the feel of her body through its cold plastic.

He stared at the empty bed for a long time, then walked over to the bed and sat down where his wife had lain. He put his hand on the white sheet, hoping to feel the warmth of her body, but felt only cold emptiness.

He missed her already. How would he survive without her?

He leaned back and tried to position his body so that it covered the spot where Anna had been. He placed his head on her pillow, trying to fit it into the slight depression left by her head. He looked as still as Anna had a half-hour before. He closed his eyes, thinking to dream of her, but found himself praying instead ... that the Lord might take him this day, too.

ABOUT THE AUTHOR

HENRY RIPPLINGER is one of Canada's foremost prairie artists. His work is on display in private and corporate collections across Canada, most notably in his home province of Saskatchewan, and can be seen in the critically acclaimed book *If You're Not from the Prairie*, which he illustrated.

Henry came to writing late in life and has been led by his passion to complete a five-part, inspirational Christian romance series, "The Angelic Letters." Henry's lifelong experience and eclectic career as a high school teacher, guidance counsellor, professional artist and businessman extraordinaire have prepared him to craft this epic love story and indirectly realize his aspirations to write a self-development book.

Henry resides with his wife in a panoramic valley setting in Lumsden, Saskatchewan, Canada.

For more information, visit: www. henryripplinger.com

If You're Not from the Prairie written by David Bouchard and illustrated by Henry Ripplinger is a poetic and visual journey depicting the prairies and the people who have made this diverse land their own ... a treasure for the mind and soul.

For further information about this book as well as other artwork, limited editions prints and ancillary products, please visit: www.henryripplinger.com